TRue THiNGS
(ADULTS DON'T WANT KIDS TO KNOW)

SEE WHAT PEOPLE ARE SAYING ABOUT Jimmy Gownley's AMELIA RULES!™

"Haven't read comics before? This is where you'll want to start."
—*Girls' Life*

"Perfectly captures the heartbreak, humor, and high drama of the middle school experience."
—Gene Yang, author of *American Born Chinese*

"Comic genius."
—GraphicNovelReporter.com

"I wish I could go back to middle school and make a friend like Amelia. I wish I could go back and *be* a friend like Amelia."
—the-trades.com

"So clever, smart, funny, and true. . . . This is one of the best graphic novel series out there for kids—and for adults with vivid, funny memories of childhood."
—Elizabeth Bluemle, the Flying Pig Bookstore

"One of the best cartoonists I know of, [Gownley] has never written a story that hasn't left me grinning madly."
—The Geeky Librarian

"Amelia Rules! remains my favorite graphic novel series for kids!"
—Tweendom.blogspot.com

"A Peanuts for the twenty-first century."
—*Comics Buyer's Guide*

"Simply one of the best all-ages comics I've ever seen."
—Mark Crilley, author/illustrator of the Akiko books

"Delightfully drawn and cleverly written."
—Orson Scott Card

"Side-splittingly hilarious. . . . Highly recommended for all ages and all libraries."
—*Library Journal*

"Full of wise-cracking jokes and quips, ingenious gags, screamingly funny dialogue, and the best of classic comic book antics."
—Megan McDonald, author of the Judy Moody series

"Amelia Rules! is . . . absolutely essential. Not only is it one of the finest comics of all time, it is one of the best examples of children's literature I have ever read."
—Kidz Corner Comic Reviews

"Smart and genuine."
—David Fury, writer/producer for *Lost,* and *Buffy the Vampire Slayer*

"Inspiring and uplifting in ways that will make you want to stand up and cheer. . . . Here's hoping the series continues for a good long time."
—the-trades.com

"Amelia's family and friends will take up permanent residence in your heart."
—Bob Schooley and Mark McCorkle, creators of Kim Possible

"Wonderful all-ages comic."
—*New York* magazine

"Gownley excels at putting a powerful message inside of a kid-friendly story."
—BSCKids.com

"Amelia Rules! . . . is a delightful entry for lovers of comics and realistic fiction. . . . She is a character to rival Ramona and Judy Moody."
—*School Library Journal*

"These kids are real . . . Gownley is a genius at capturing their perspective."
—ComicsWorthReading.com

MEET THE GANG

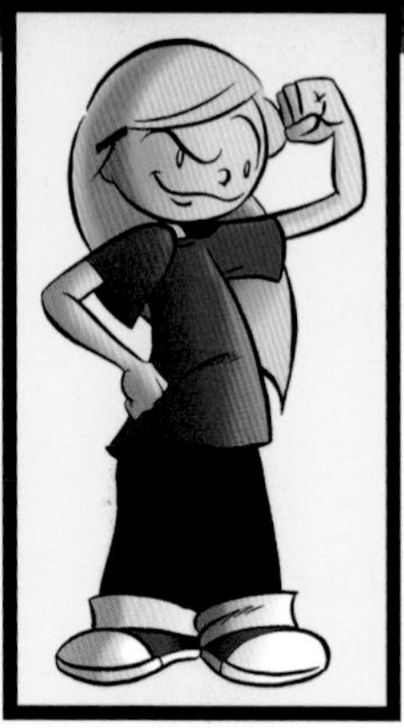

Amelia Louise McBride:
Our heroine. Wise cracking, yet sweet. She spends her time hanging out with friends and her aunt Tanner.

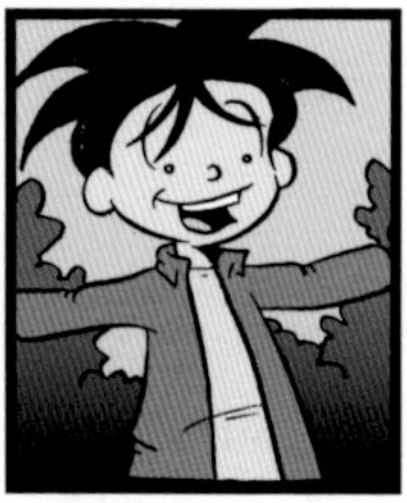

Reggie Grabinsky:
A.k.a. Captain Amazing. Founder of G.A.S.P., which he forces . . . er, encourages, his friends to join.

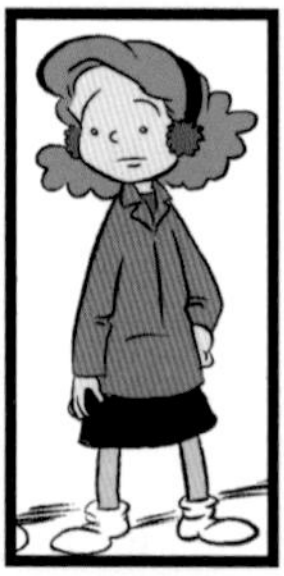

Rhonda Bleenie:
Smart, stubborn, and loud. She wears her heart on her sleeve and it's filled with love for Reggie.

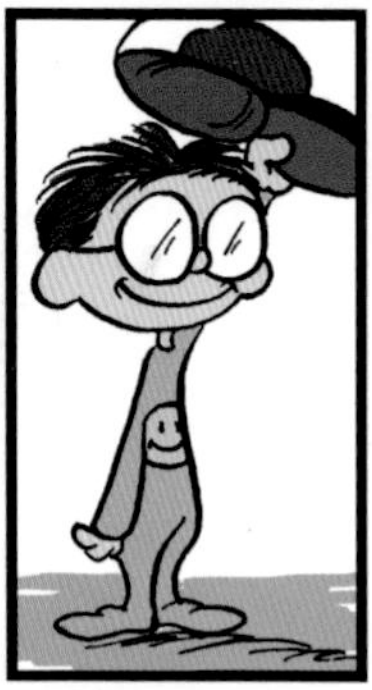

Pajamaman:
Never speaks. Always cool. His feetie jammies tell you what's on his mind.

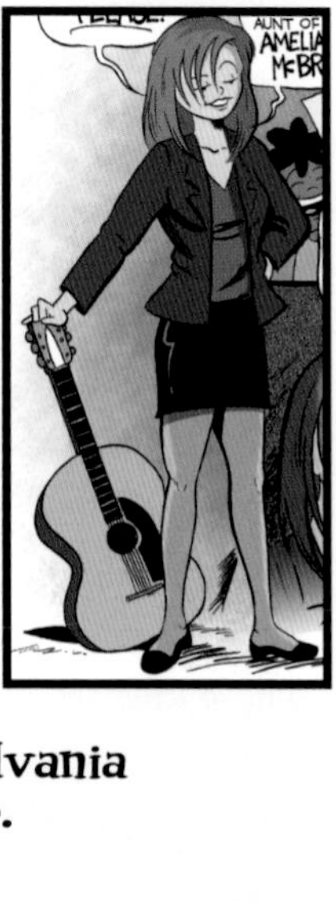
AUNT OF
AMELIA

Tanner:
Amelia's aunt and a former rock 'n' roll superstar.

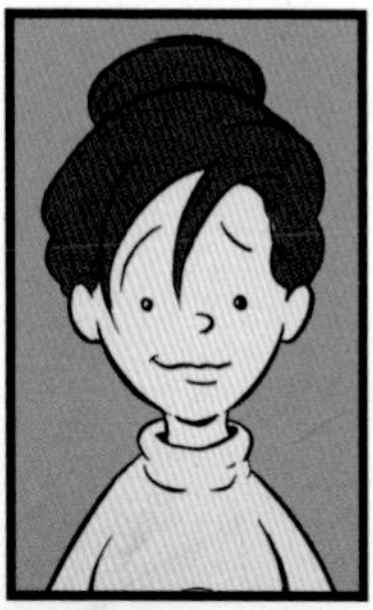

Amelia's Mom (Mary):
Starting a new life in Pennsylvania with Amelia after the divorce.

Amelia's Dad:
Still lives in New York, and
misses Amelia terribly.

G.A.S.P.
Gathering Of Awesome Super Pals.
The superhero club Reggie founded.

Park View Terrace Ninjas:
Club across town and nemesis
to G.A.S.P.

Kyle:
The main ninja. Kind of a jerk
but not without charm.

Joan:
Former Park View Terrace Ninja
(nemesis of G.A.S.P.), now friends
with Amelia and company.

Tweenie Zeenie:
A local kid-run magazine and Web site.

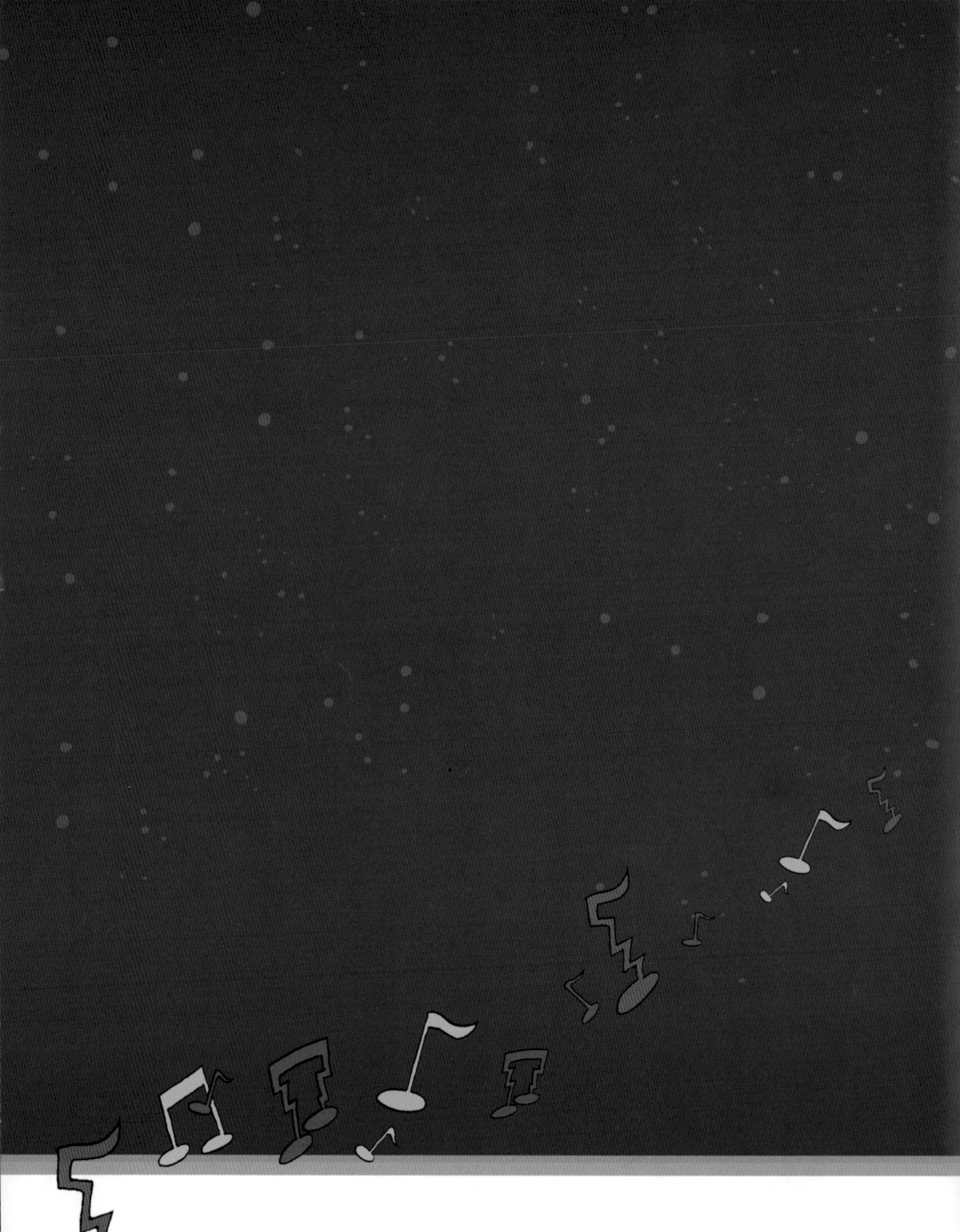

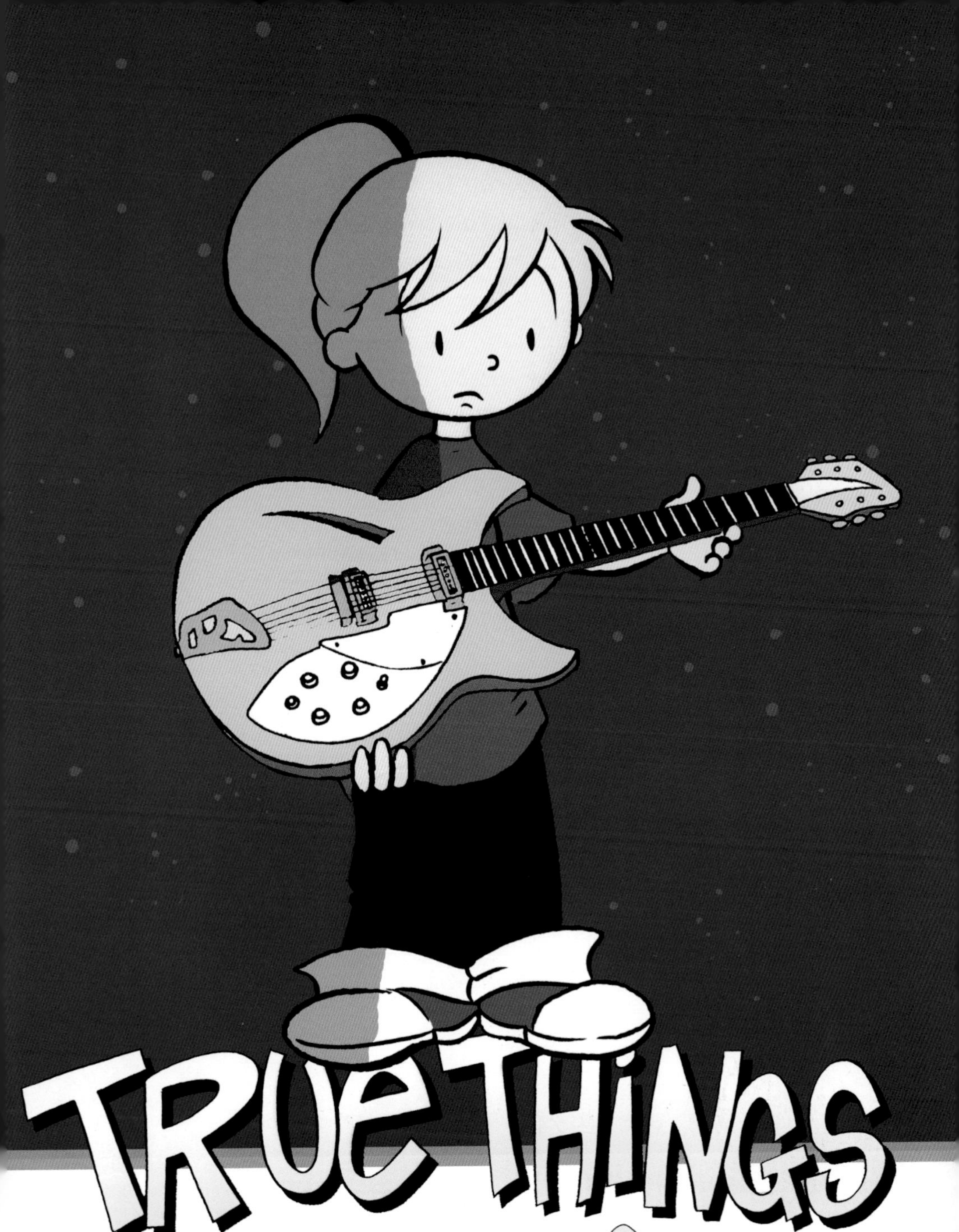

TRUE THINGS

(ADULTS DON'T WANT KIDS TO KNOW)

Atheneum Books for Young Readers
New York London Toronto Sydney

For Karen Gownley,
who made the completion
of this book possible,
and for Ed Fox, Dan Almoney,
and Adam Wisniewski,
who never heard a crazy idea
they didn't like.

ATHENEUM BOOKS FOR YOUNG READERS
An imprint of Simon & Schuster Children's Publishing Division
1230 Avenue of the Americas, New York, New York 10020
For information about special discounts for bulk purchases, please contact Simon & Schuster
Special Sales at 1-866-506-1949 or business@simonandschuster.com.
The Simon & Schuster Speakers Bureau can bring authors to your live event.
For more information or to book an event, contact the Simon & Schuster Speakers Bureau
at 1-866-248-3049 or visit our website at www.simonspeakers.com.
Also available in an Atheneum Books for Young Readers paperback edition
Book design by Sonia Chaghatzbanian
The text for this book is hand-lettered.
The illustrations for this book are digitally rendered.
Manufactured in China
0810 WGL
First Edition
2 4 6 8 10 9 7 5 3 1
Library of Congress Cataloging-in-Publication Data
Gownley, Jimmy.
True things : (adults don't want kids to know) / [by Jimmy Gownley]. — 1st ed.
p. cm. — (Jimmy Gownley's Amelia rules!)
Summary: Amelia Louise McBride's eleventh birthday party is fabulous, but soon her friends are
fighting all the time, she gets a terrible report card, and when she summons the courage to tell a
boy how she feels about him, she learns why it is called a "crush."
ISBN 978-1-4169-8611-9 (simultaneous hardcover) – ISBN 978-1-4169-8609-6 (simultaneous pbk.)
1. Graphic novels. [1. Graphic novels. 2. Schools—Fiction. 3. Popularity—Fiction. 4. Peer pressure—
Fiction. 5. Family life—Fiction.] I. Title.
PZ7.7.G69Tru 2010
741.5'973—dc22 2010007291

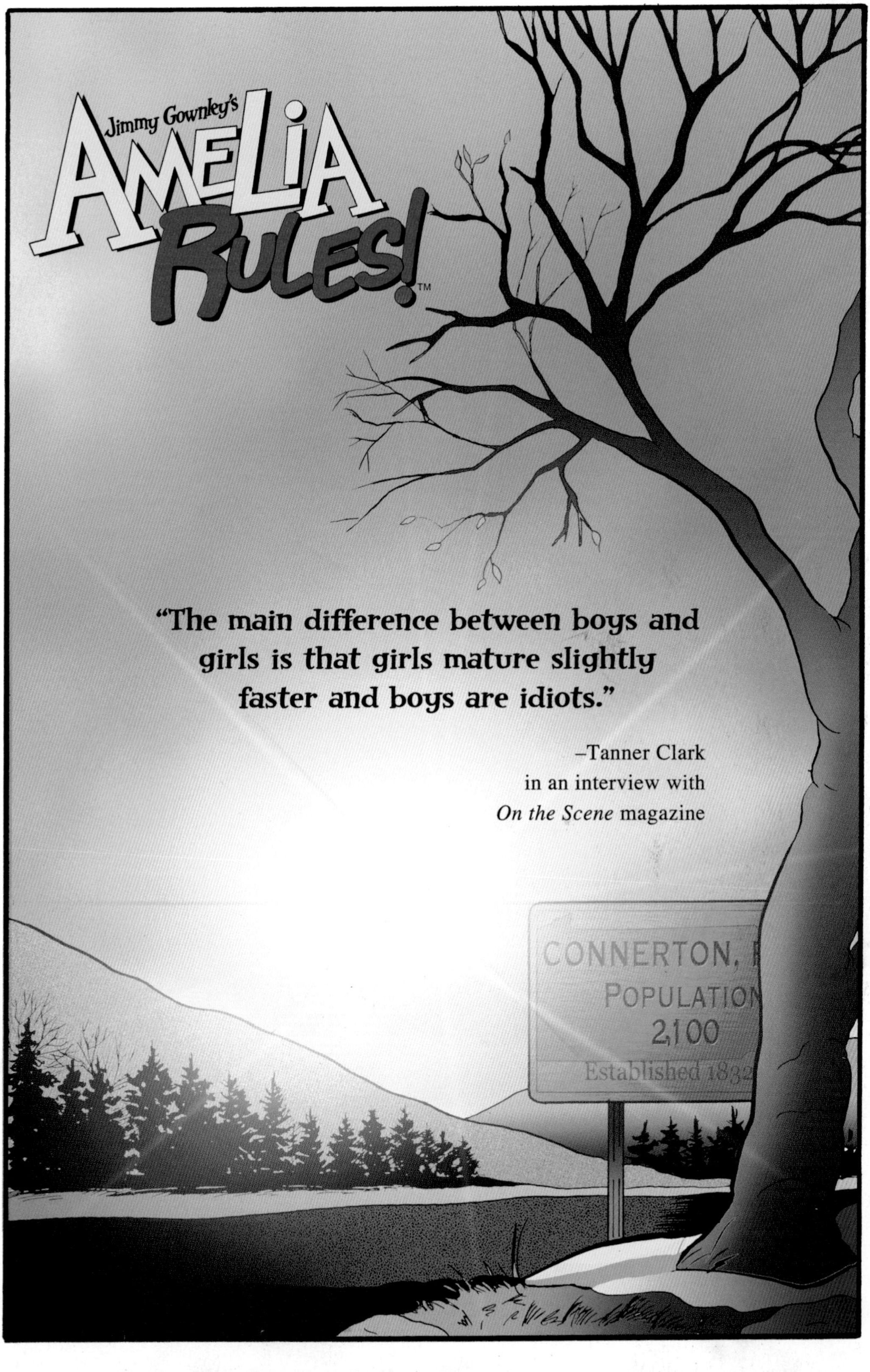
Jimmy Gownley's
AMELIA RULES!™
"The main difference between boys and girls is that girls mature slightly faster and boys are idiots."
–Tanner Clark
in an interview with
On the Scene magazine
CONNERTON,
2,100

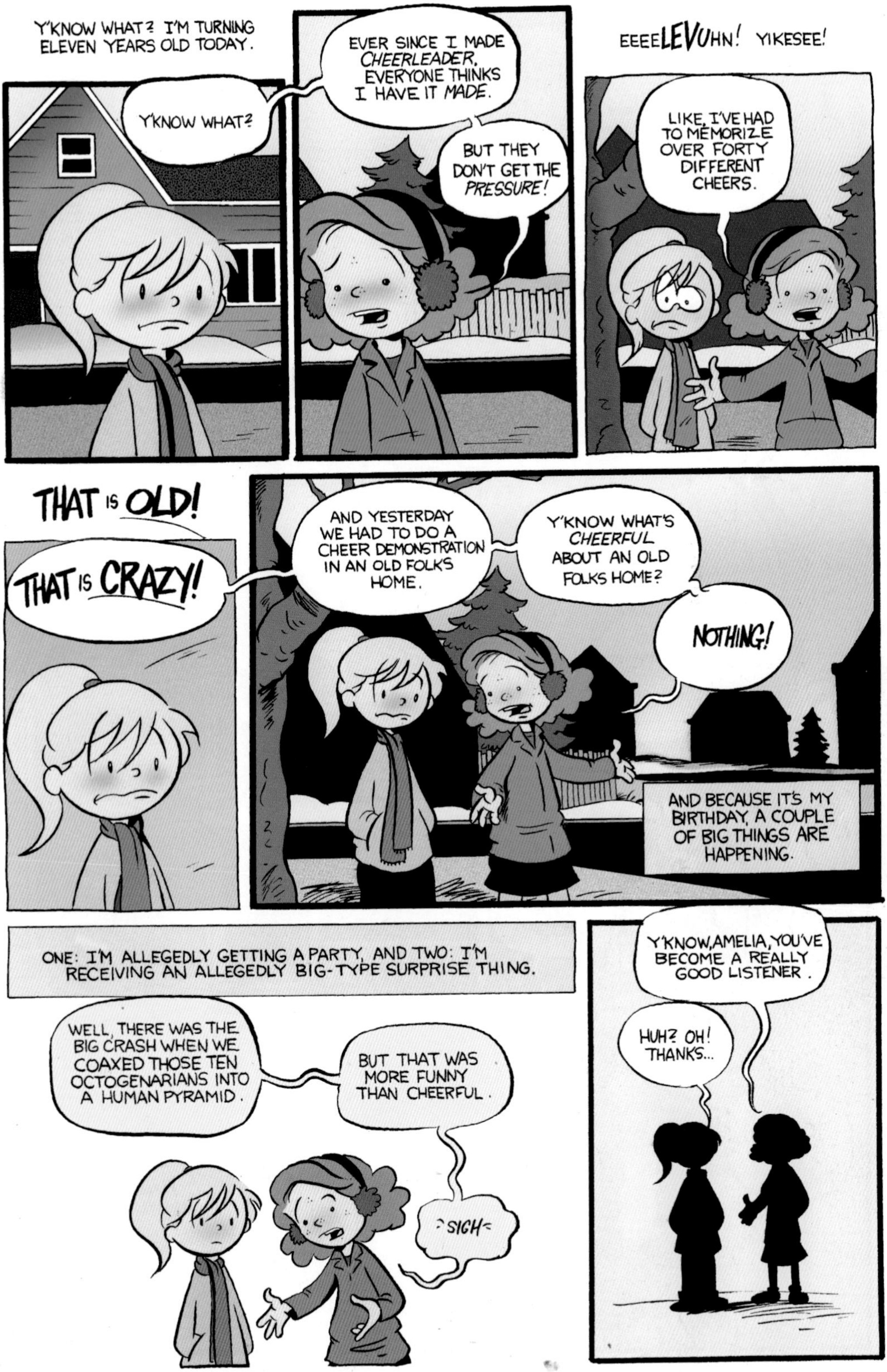
Y'KNOW WHAT? I'M TURNING ELEVEN YEARS OLD TODAY.
Y'KNOW WHAT?
EVER SINCE I MADE CHEERLEADER, EVERYONE THINKS I HAVE IT MADE.
BUT THEY DON'T GET THE PRESSURE!
EEEELEVUHN! YIKESEE!
LIKE, I'VE HAD TO MEMORIZE OVER FORTY DIFFERENT CHEERS.
THAT IS OLD!
THAT IS CRAZY!
AND YESTERDAY WE HAD TO DO A CHEER DEMONSTRATION IN AN OLD FOLKS HOME.
Y'KNOW WHAT'S CHEERFUL ABOUT AN OLD FOLKS HOME?
NOTHING!
AND BECAUSE IT'S MY BIRTHDAY, A COUPLE OF BIG THINGS ARE HAPPENING.
ONE: I'M ALLEGEDLY GETTING A PARTY, AND TWO: I'M RECEIVING AN ALLEGEDLY BIG-TYPE SURPRISE THING.
WELL, THERE WAS THE BIG CRASH WHEN WE COAXED THOSE TEN OCTOGENARIANS INTO A HUMAN PYRAMID.
BUT THAT WAS MORE FUNNY THAN CHEERFUL.
SIGH
Y'KNOW, AMELIA, YOU'VE BECOME A REALLY GOOD LISTENER.
HUH? OH! THANKS...

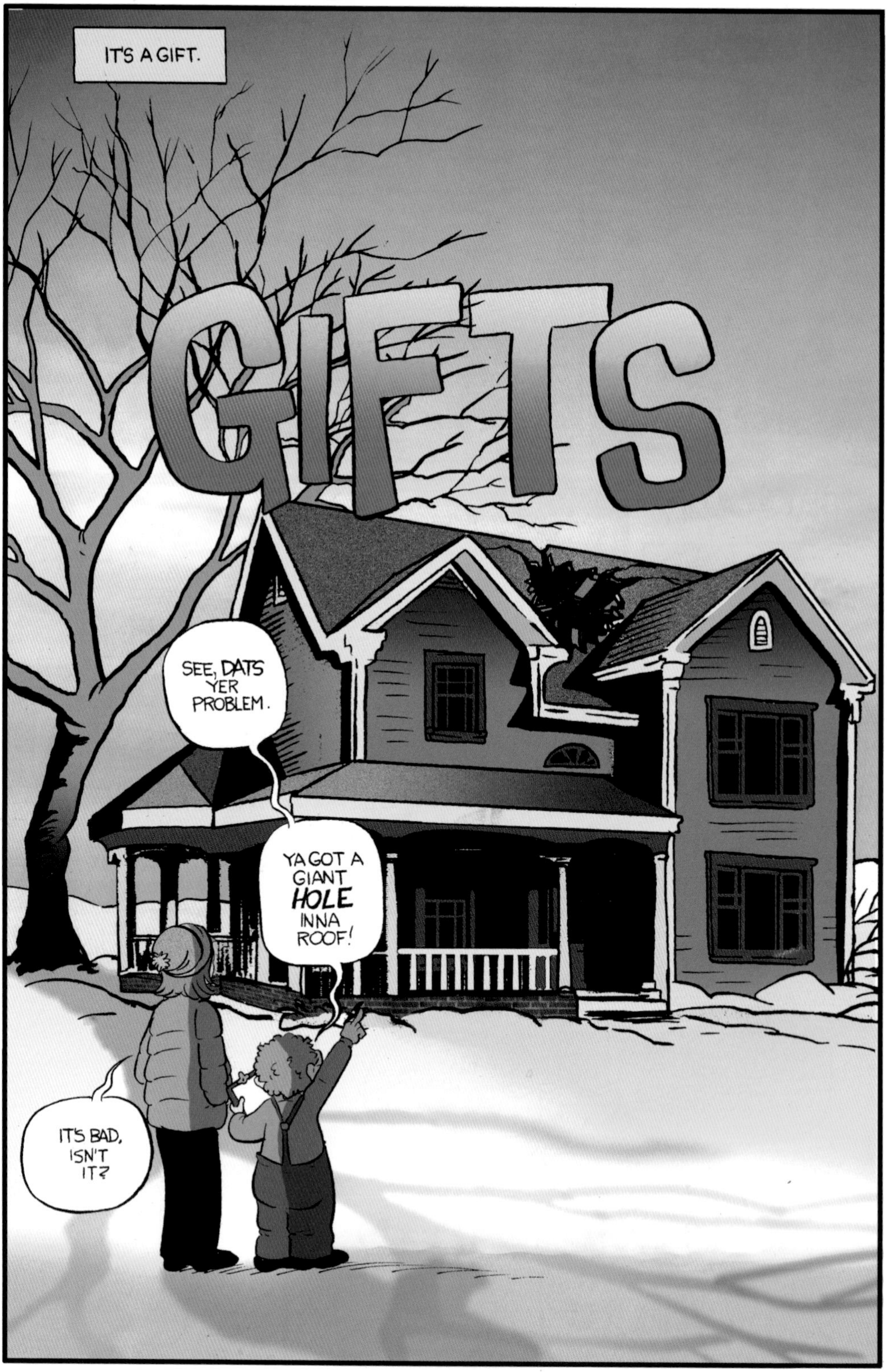
IT'S A GIFT.
GIFTS
SEE, DATS YER PROBLEM.
YA GOT A GIANT HOLE INNA ROOF!
IT'S BAD, ISN'T IT?

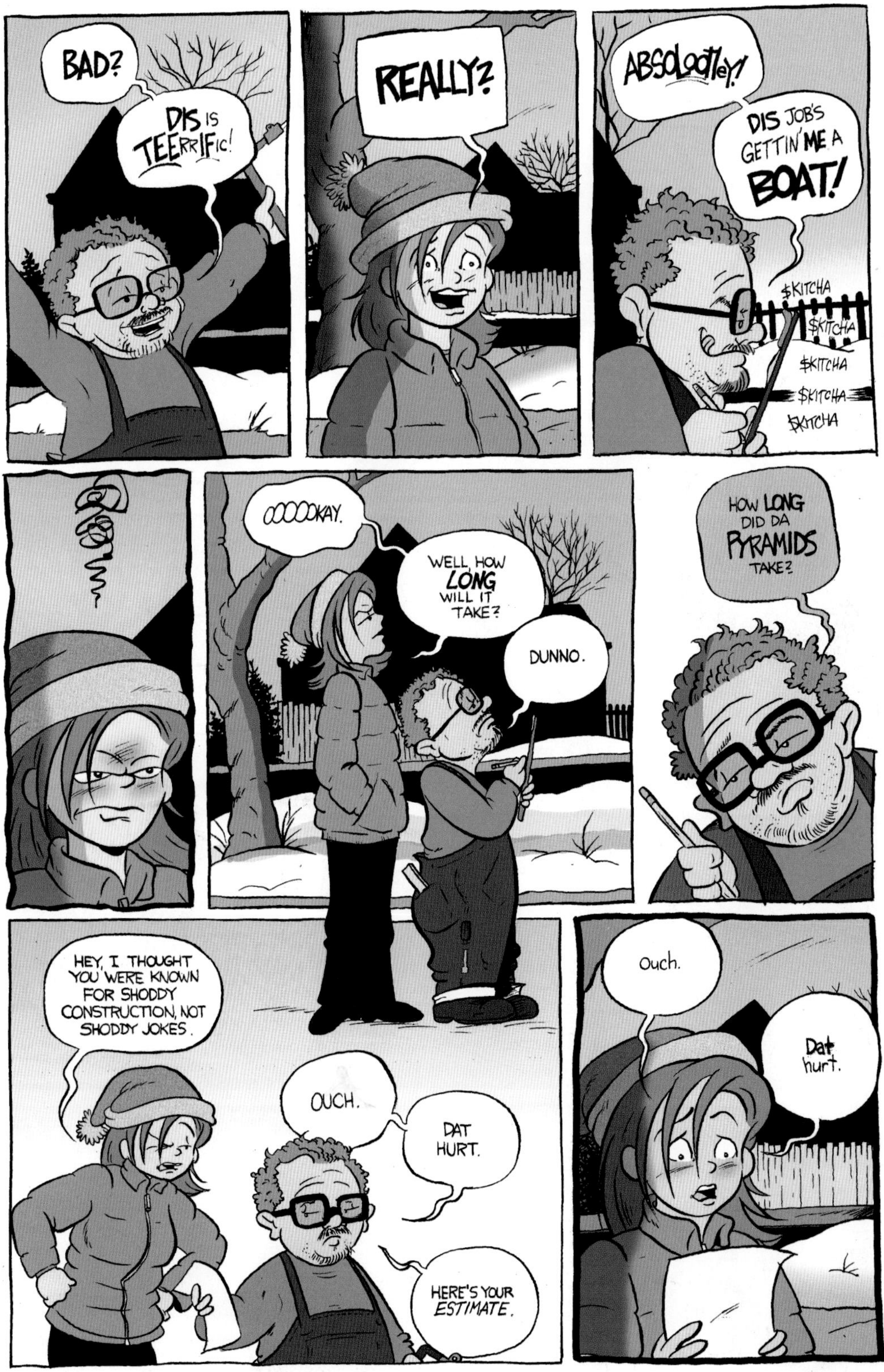
BAD?
DIS IS TEERRIFIC!
REALLY?
ABSOLOOTLEY!
DIS JOB'S GETTIN' ME A BOAT!
$KITCHA
$KITCHA
$KITCHA
$KITCHA
$KITCHA
OOOOOKAY.
WELL, HOW LONG WILL IT TAKE?
DUNNO.
HOW LONG DID DA PYRAMIDS TAKE?
HEY, I THOUGHT YOU WERE KNOWN FOR SHODDY CONSTRUCTION, NOT SHODDY JOKES.
OUCH.
DAT HURT.
HERE'S YOUR ESTIMATE.
Ouch.
Dat hurt.

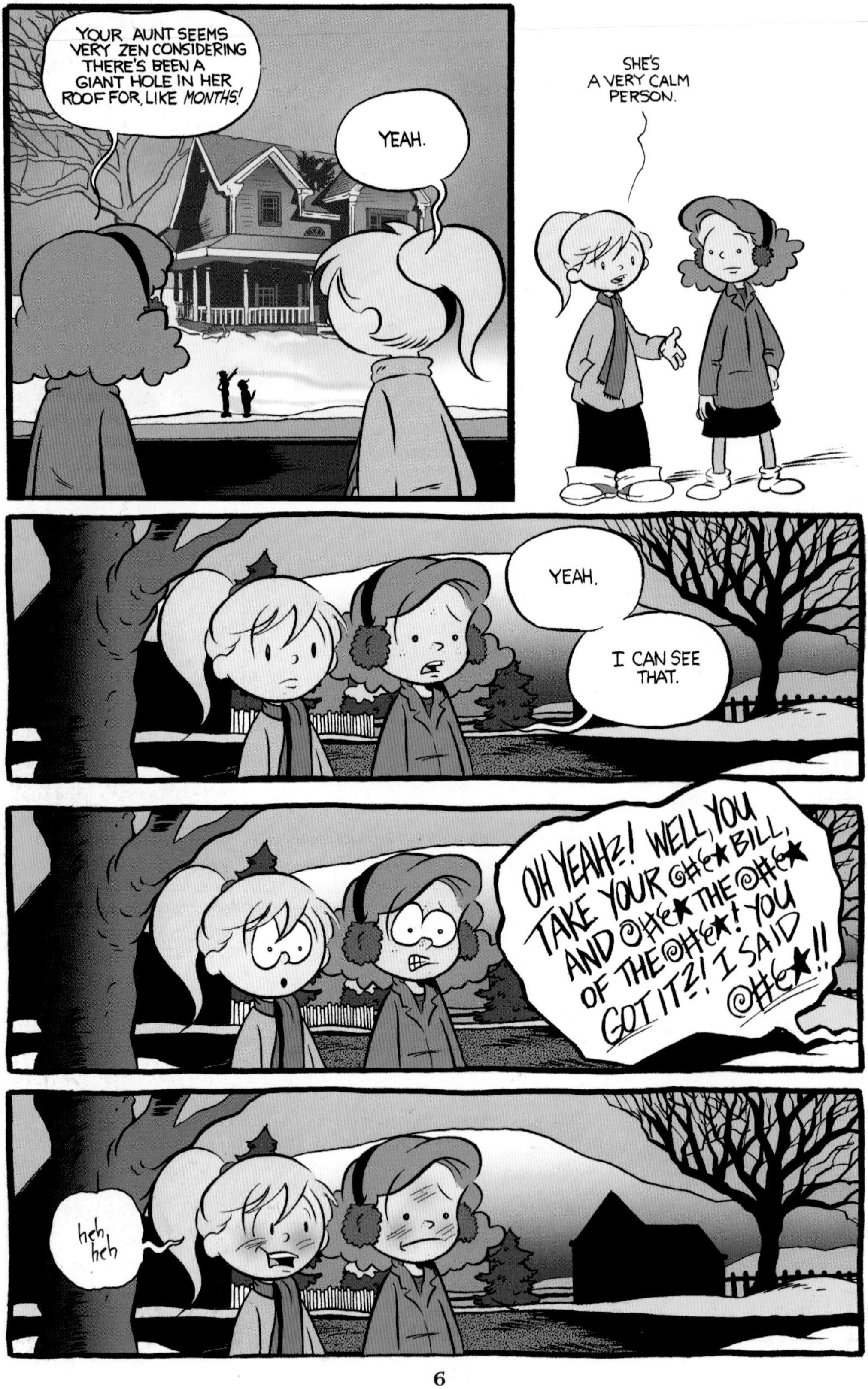
YOUR AUNT SEEMS VERY ZEN CONSIDERING THERE'S BEEN A GIANT HOLE IN HER ROOF FOR, LIKE *MONTHS*!
YEAH.
SHE'S A VERY CALM PERSON.
YEAH.
I CAN SEE THAT.
OH YEAH?! WELL YOU TAKE YOUR @#€★ BILL, AND @#€★ THE @#€★ OF THE @#€★! YOU GOT IT?! I SAID @#€★!!
heh heh

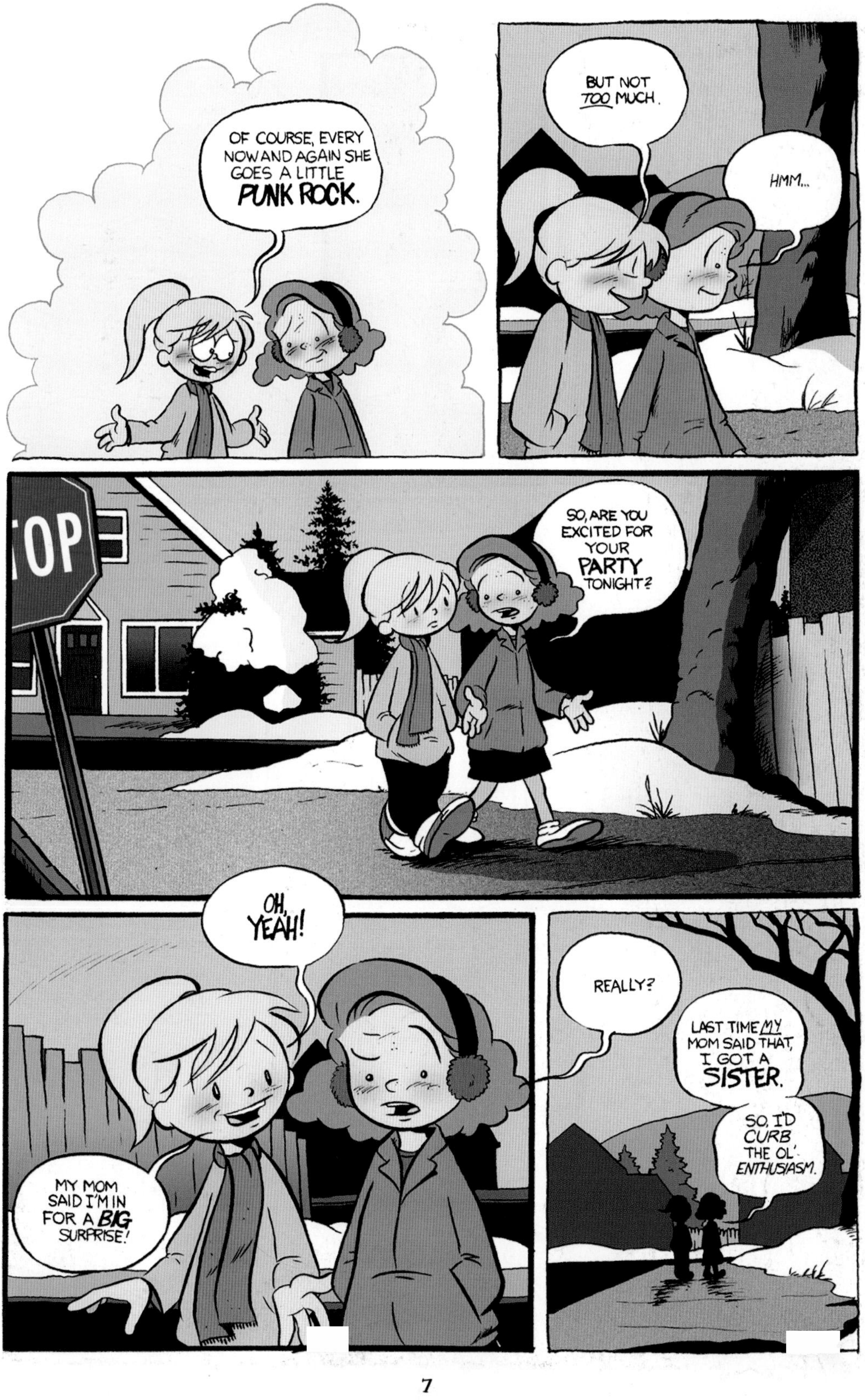
OF COURSE, EVERY NOW AND AGAIN SHE GOES A LITTLE PUNK ROCK.
BUT NOT TOO MUCH.
HMM...
STOP
SO, ARE YOU EXCITED FOR YOUR PARTY TONIGHT?
OH, YEAH!
MY MOM SAID I'M IN FOR A BIG SURPRISE!
REALLY?
LAST TIME MY MOM SAID THAT, I GOT A SISTER.
SO, I'D CURB THE OL' ENTHUSIASM.

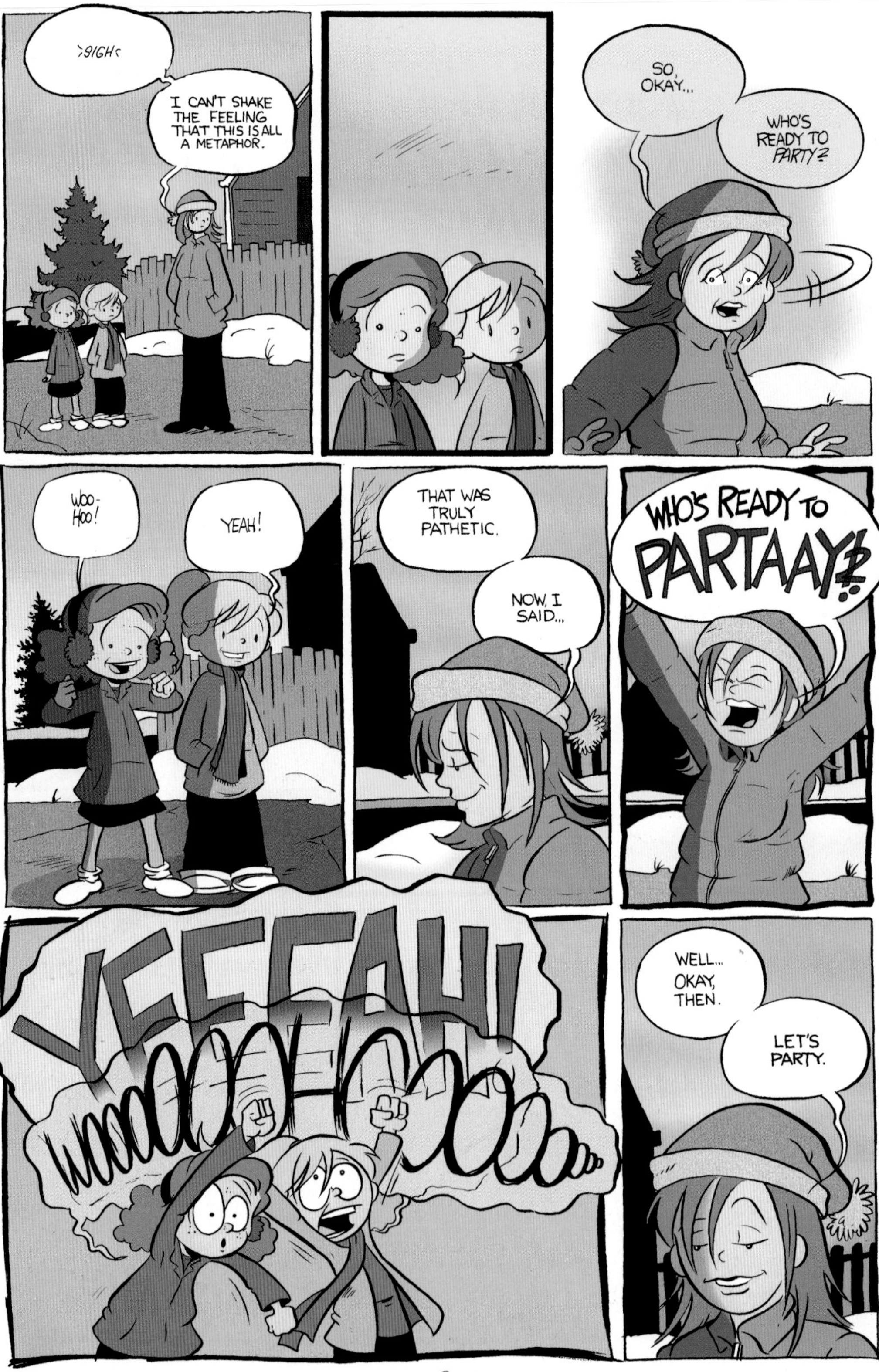

>SIGH<
I CAN'T SHAKE THE FEELING THAT THIS IS ALL A METAPHOR.
SO, OKAY...
WHO'S READY TO PARTY?
WOO-HOO!
YEAH!
THAT WAS TRULY PATHETIC.
NOW, I SAID...
WHO'S READY TO PARTAAY?!
YEEEAH!
WOOOOOOO...
WELL... OKAY, THEN.
LET'S PARTY.

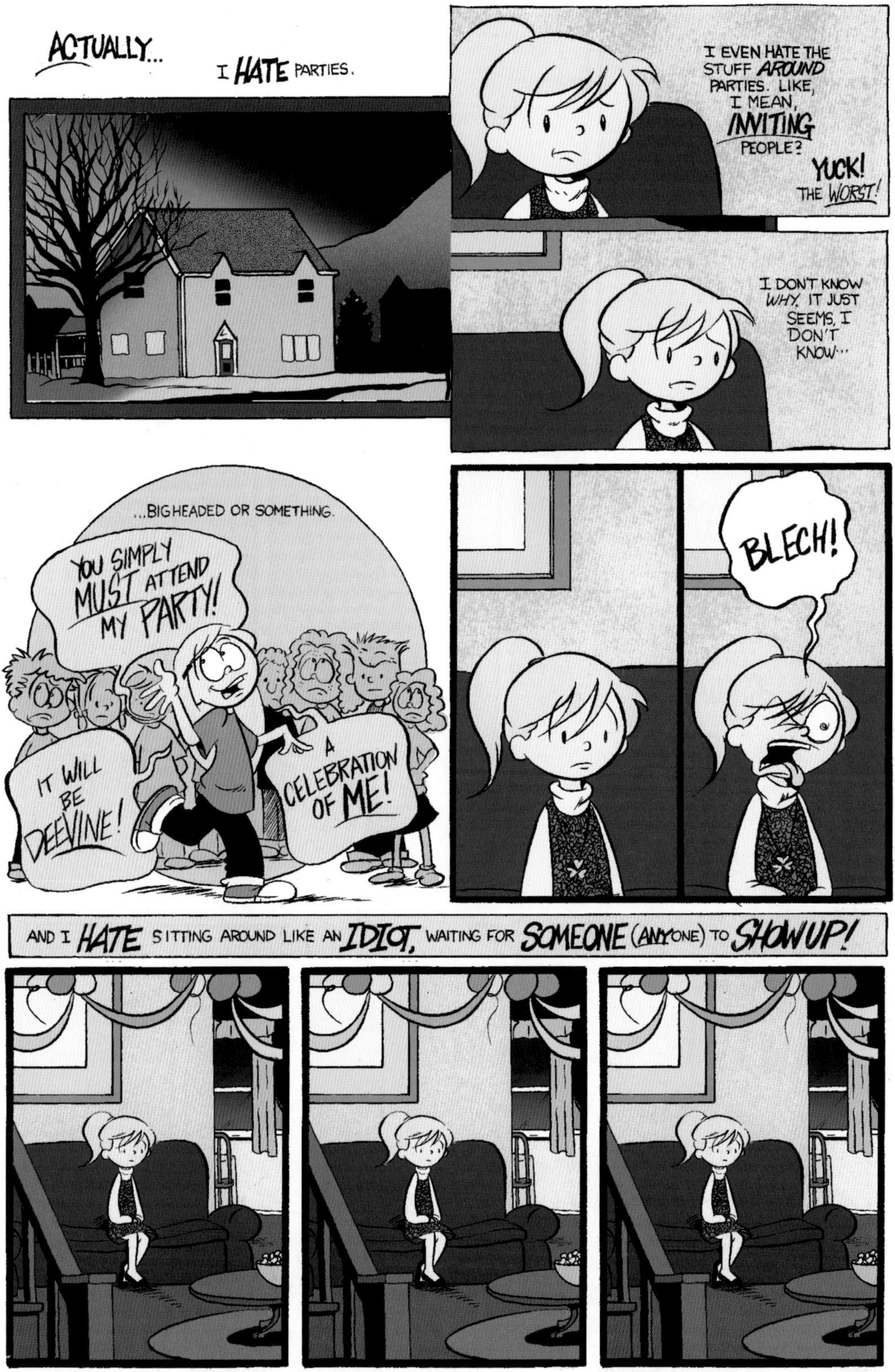
ACTUALLY...
I HATE PARTIES.
I EVEN HATE THE STUFF AROUND PARTIES. LIKE, I MEAN, INVITING PEOPLE?
YUCK! THE WORST!
I DON'T KNOW WHY, IT JUST SEEMS, I DON'T KNOW...
...BIGHEADED OR SOMETHING.
YOU SIMPLY MUST ATTEND MY PARTY!
IT WILL BE DEEVINE!
A CELEBRATION OF ME!
BLECH!
AND I HATE SITTING AROUND LIKE AN IDIOT, WAITING FOR SOMEONE (ANYONE) TO SHOW UP!

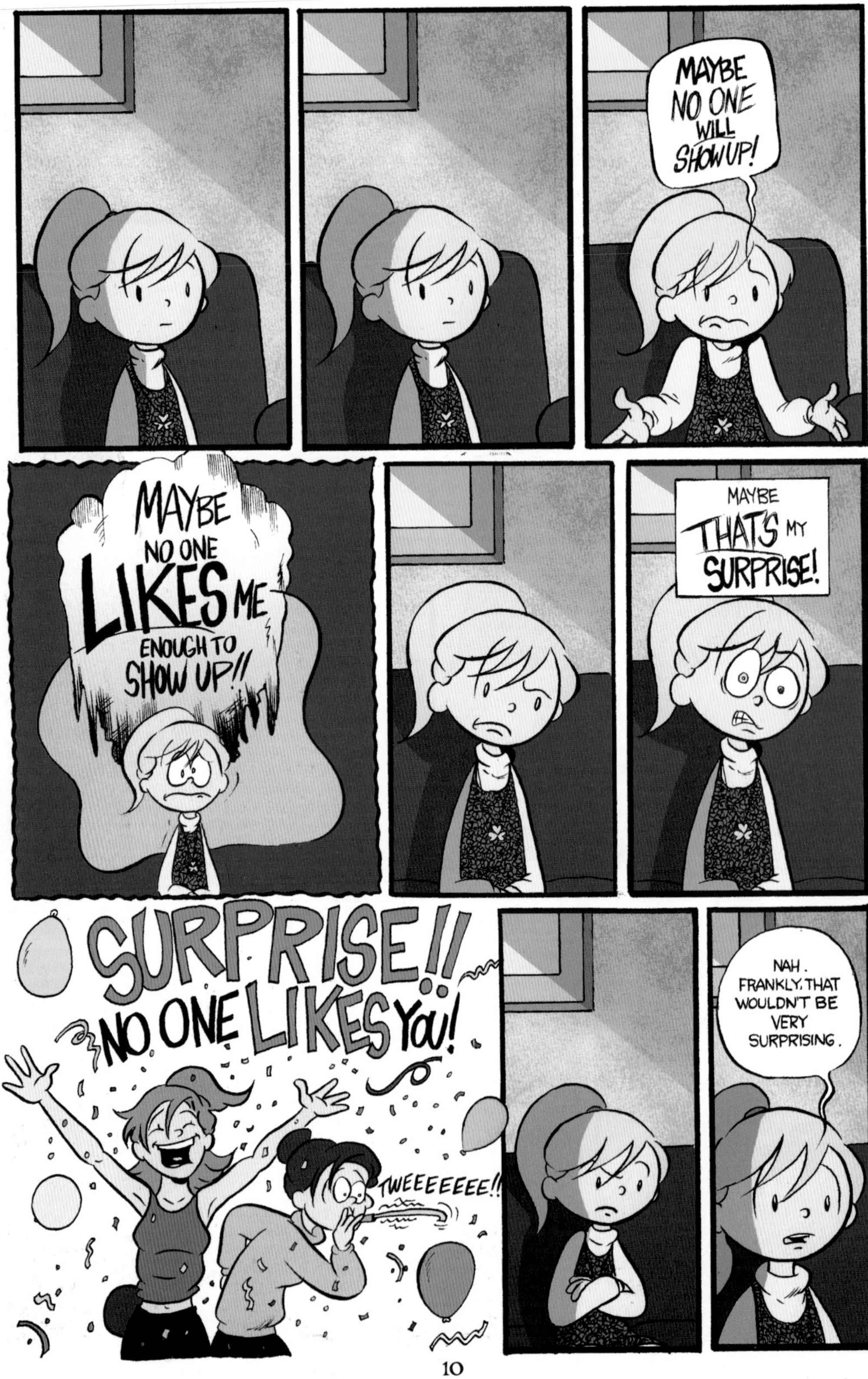
MAYBE NO ONE WILL SHOW UP!
MAYBE NO ONE LIKES ME ENOUGH TO SHOW UP!!
MAYBE THAT'S MY SURPRISE!
SURPRISE!! NO ONE LIKES YOU!
TWEEEEEEE!!
NAH. FRANKLY, THAT WOULDN'T BE VERY SURPRISING.

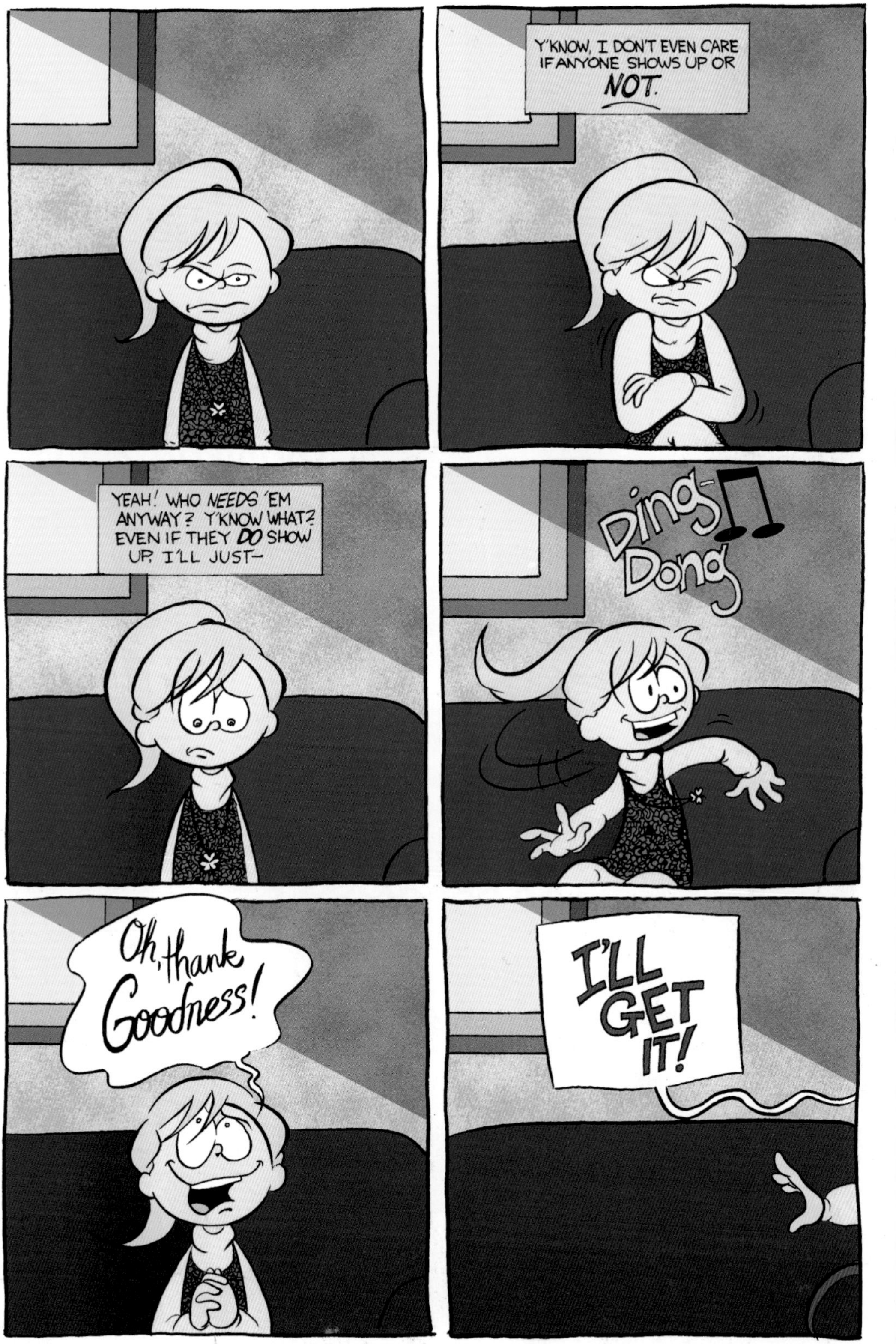
Y'KNOW, I DON'T EVEN CARE IF ANYONE SHOWS UP OR NOT.
YEAH! WHO NEEDS 'EM ANYWAY? Y'KNOW WHAT? EVEN IF THEY DO SHOW UP, I'LL JUST—
Ding-Dong
Oh, thank Goodness!
I'LL GET IT!

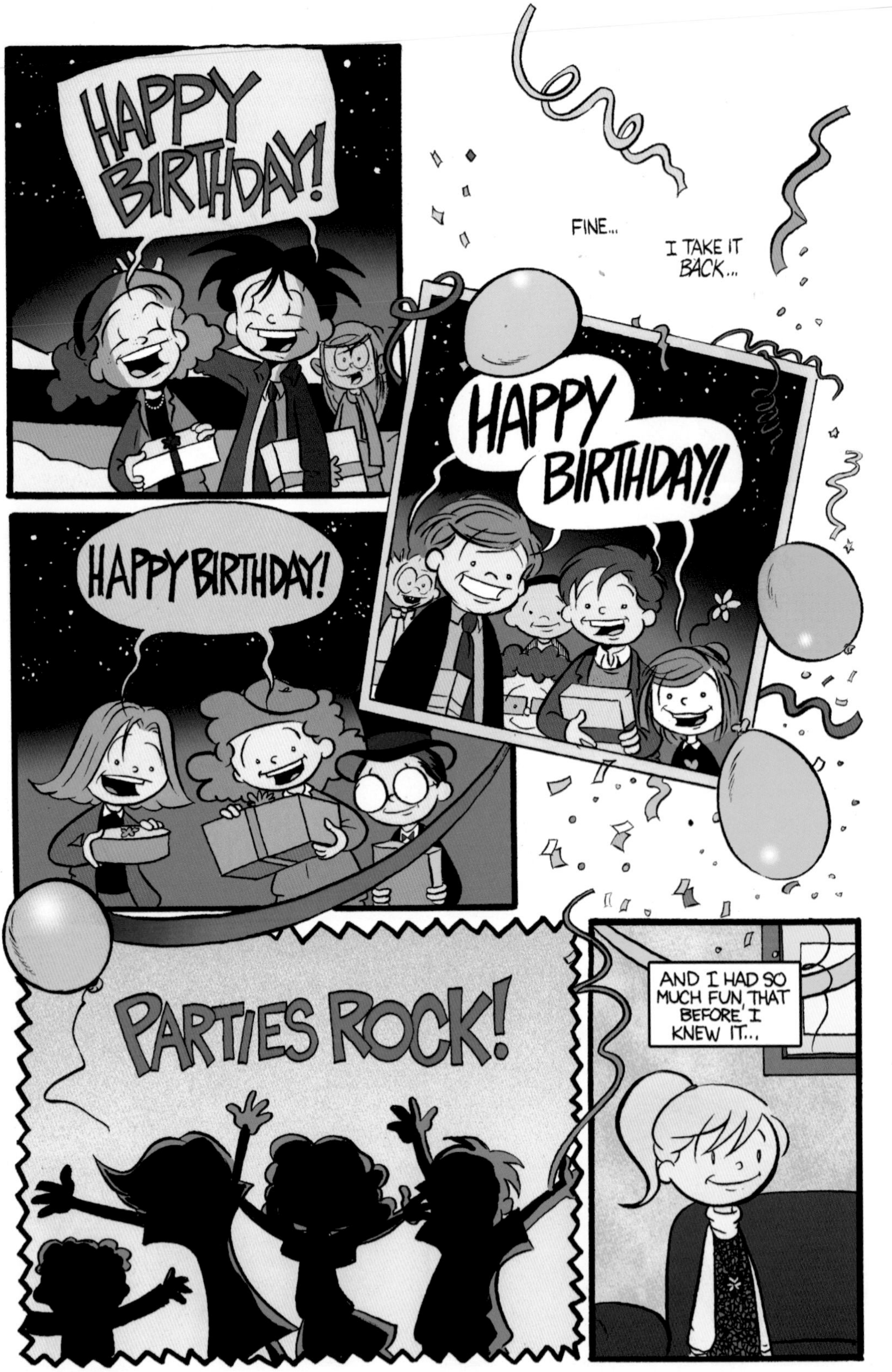

HAPPY BIRTHDAY!
FINE...
I TAKE IT BACK...
HAPPY BIRTHDAY!
HAPPY BIRTHDAY!
PARTIES ROCK!
AND I HAD SO MUCH FUN, THAT BEFORE I KNEW IT...

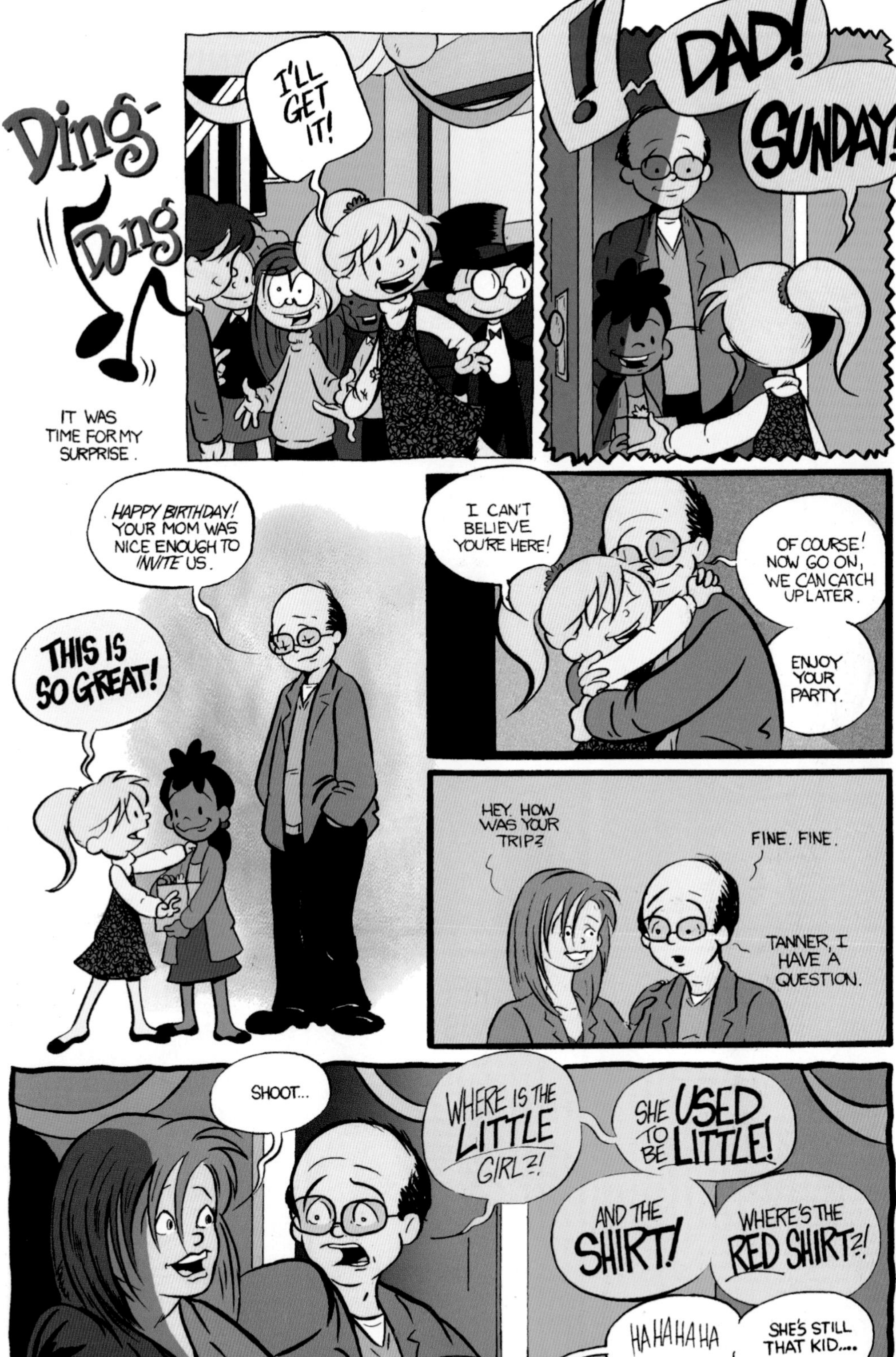
Ding-Dong
IT WAS TIME FOR MY SURPRISE.
I'LL GET IT!
!
DAD!
SUNDAY!
HAPPY BIRTHDAY! YOUR MOM WAS NICE ENOUGH TO INVITE US.
THIS IS SO GREAT!
I CAN'T BELIEVE YOU'RE HERE!
OF COURSE! NOW GO ON, WE CAN CATCH UP LATER.
ENJOY YOUR PARTY.
HEY. HOW WAS YOUR TRIP?
FINE. FINE.
TANNER, I HAVE A QUESTION.
SHOOT...
WHERE IS THE LITTLE GIRL?!
SHE USED TO BE LITTLE!
AND THE SHIRT!
WHERE'S THE RED SHIRT?!
HA HA HA HA HA
SHE'S STILL THAT KID....

SHE'S JUST WRAPPED IN A DIFFERENT PACKAGE.

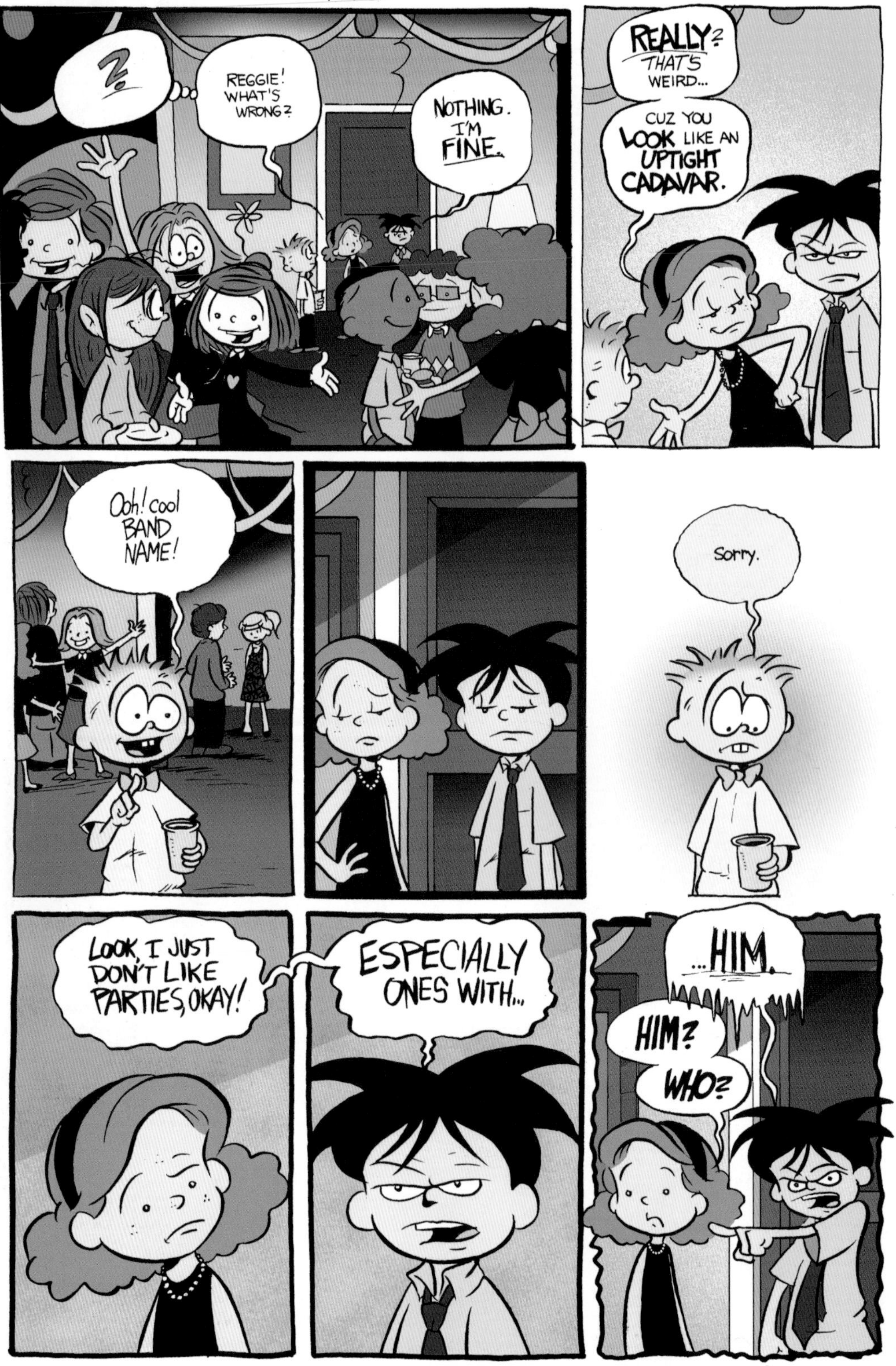
?
REGGIE! WHAT'S WRONG?
NOTHING. I'M FINE.
REALLY? THAT'S WEIRD...
CUZ YOU LOOK LIKE AN UPTIGHT CADAVAR.
Ooh! cool BAND NAME!
Sorry.
LOOK, I JUST DON'T LIKE PARTIES, OKAY!
ESPECIALLY ONES WITH...
...HIM.
HIM?
WHO?

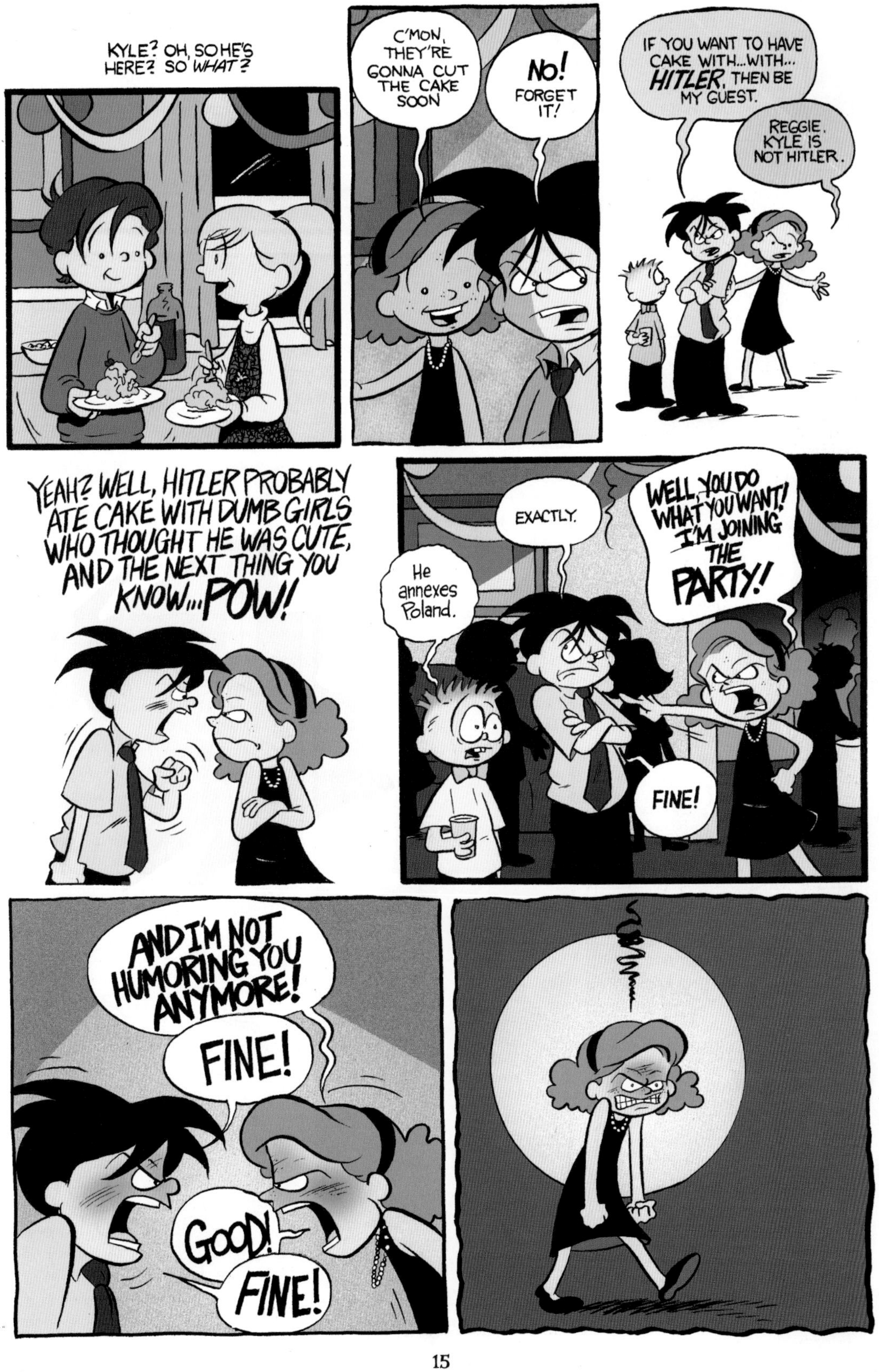
KYLE? OH, SO HE'S HERE? SO WHAT?
C'MON, THEY'RE GONNA CUT THE CAKE SOON
NO! FORGET IT!
IF YOU WANT TO HAVE CAKE WITH...WITH... HITLER, THEN BE MY GUEST.
REGGIE. KYLE IS NOT HITLER.
YEAH? WELL, HITLER PROBABLY ATE CAKE WITH DUMB GIRLS WHO THOUGHT HE WAS CUTE, AND THE NEXT THING YOU KNOW...POW!
He annexes Poland.
EXACTLY.
WELL, YOU DO WHAT YOU WANT! I'M JOINING THE PARTY!
FINE!
AND I'M NOT HUMORING YOU ANYMORE!
FINE!
GOOD!
FINE!

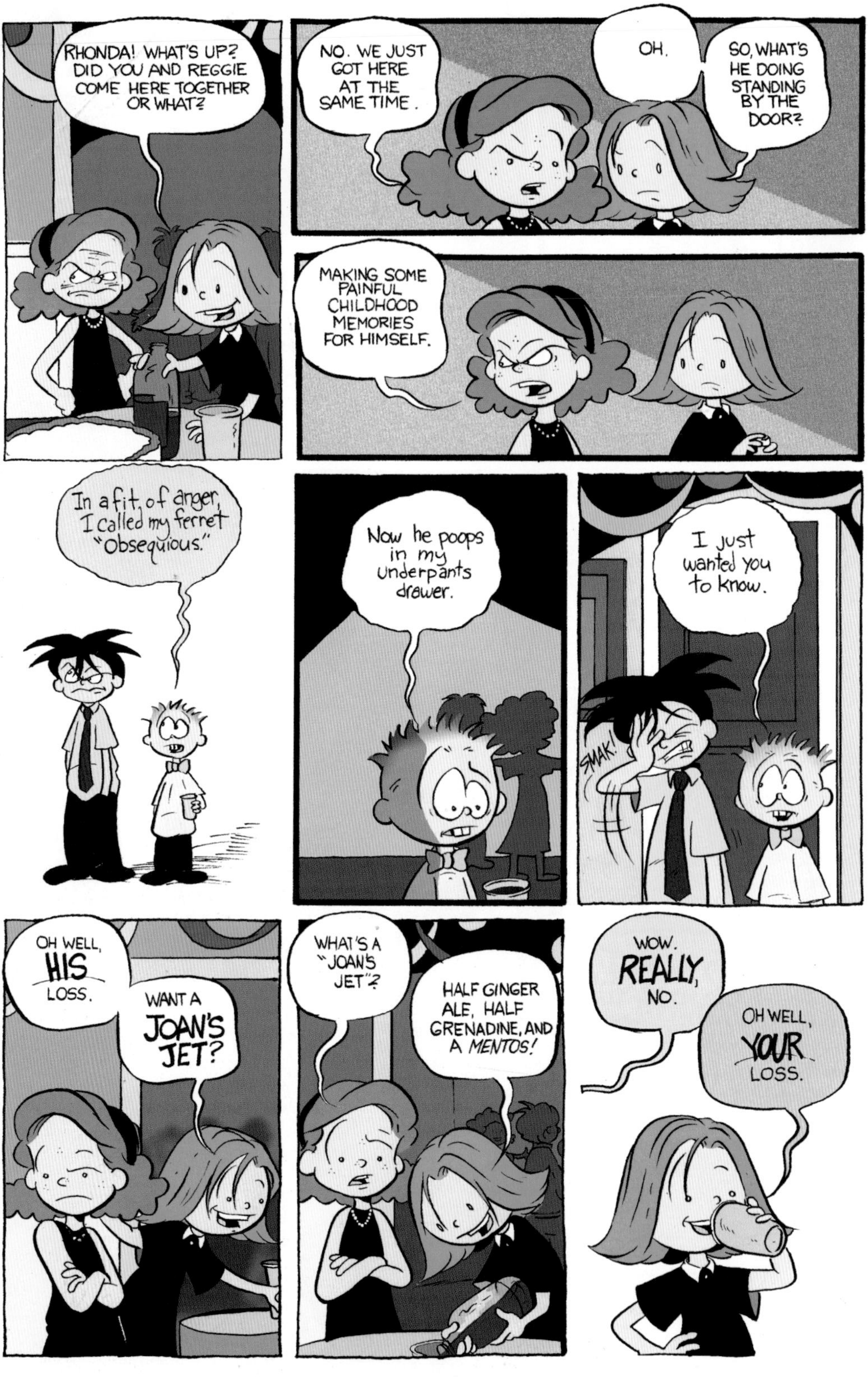
RHONDA! WHAT'S UP? DID YOU AND REGGIE COME HERE TOGETHER OR WHAT?
NO. WE JUST GOT HERE AT THE SAME TIME.
OH.
SO, WHAT'S HE DOING STANDING BY THE DOOR?
MAKING SOME PAINFUL CHILDHOOD MEMORIES FOR HIMSELF.
In a fit of anger, I called my ferret "obsequious."
Now he poops in my underpants drawer.
I just wanted you to know.
SMAK!
OH WELL, HIS LOSS.
WANT A JOAN'S JET?
WHAT'S A "JOAN'S JET"?
HALF GINGER ALE, HALF GRENADINE, AND A MENTOS!
WOW. REALLY, NO.
OH WELL, YOUR LOSS.

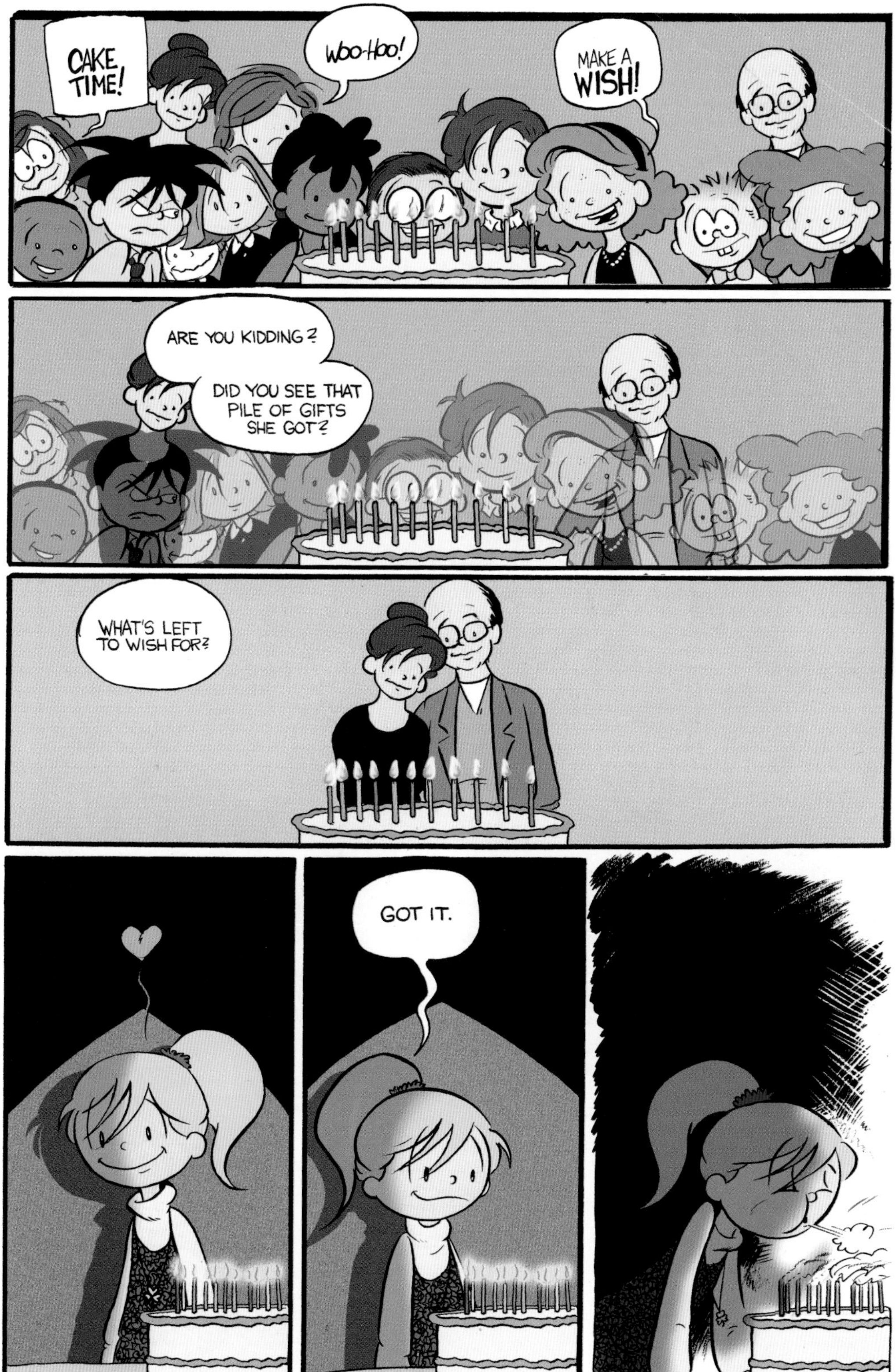
CAKE TIME!
WOO-HOO!
MAKE A WISH!
ARE YOU KIDDING?
DID YOU SEE THAT PILE OF GIFTS SHE GOT?
WHAT'S LEFT TO WISH FOR?
GOT IT.

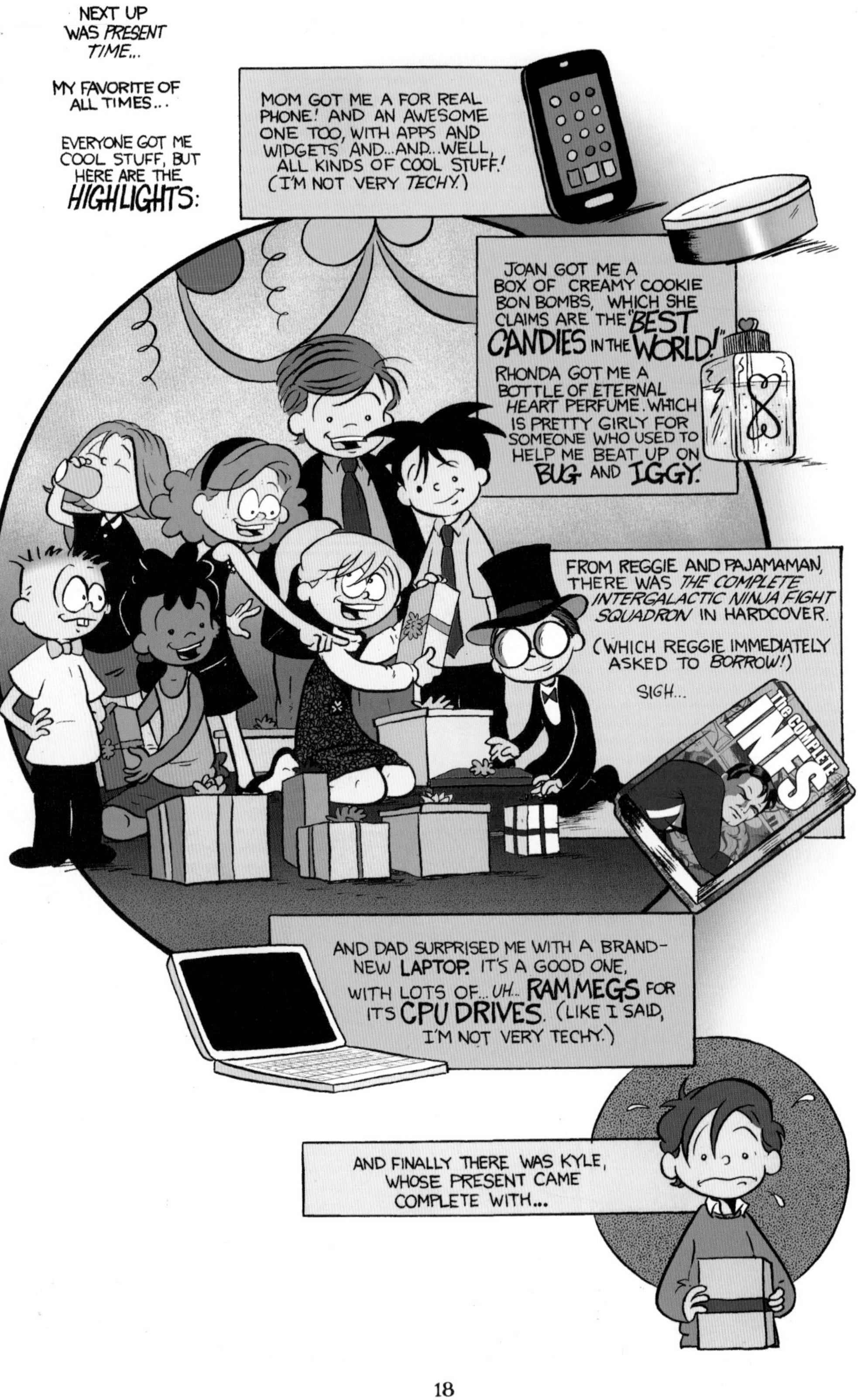
NEXT UP WAS PRESENT TIME...
MY FAVORITE OF ALL TIMES...
EVERYONE GOT ME COOL STUFF, BUT HERE ARE THE HIGHLIGHTS:
MOM GOT ME A FOR REAL PHONE! AND AN AWESOME ONE TOO, WITH APPS AND WIDGETS AND...AND...WELL, ALL KINDS OF COOL STUFF! (I'M NOT VERY TECHY.)
JOAN GOT ME A BOX OF CREAMY COOKIE BON BOMBS, WHICH SHE CLAIMS ARE THE "BEST CANDIES IN THE WORLD!"
RHONDA GOT ME A BOTTLE OF ETERNAL HEART PERFUME. WHICH IS PRETTY GIRLY FOR SOMEONE WHO USED TO HELP ME BEAT UP ON BUG AND IGGY.
FROM REGGIE AND PAJAMAMAN, THERE WAS THE COMPLETE INTERGALACTIC NINJA FIGHT SQUADRON IN HARDCOVER.
(WHICH REGGIE IMMEDIATELY ASKED TO BORROW!)
SIGH...
The COMPLETE INFS
AND DAD SURPRISED ME WITH A BRAND-NEW LAPTOP. IT'S A GOOD ONE, WITH LOTS OF... UH... RAM MEGS FOR ITS CPU DRIVES. (LIKE I SAID, I'M NOT VERY TECHY.)
AND FINALLY THERE WAS KYLE, WHOSE PRESENT CAME COMPLETE WITH...

... A SIDE OF DRAMA.

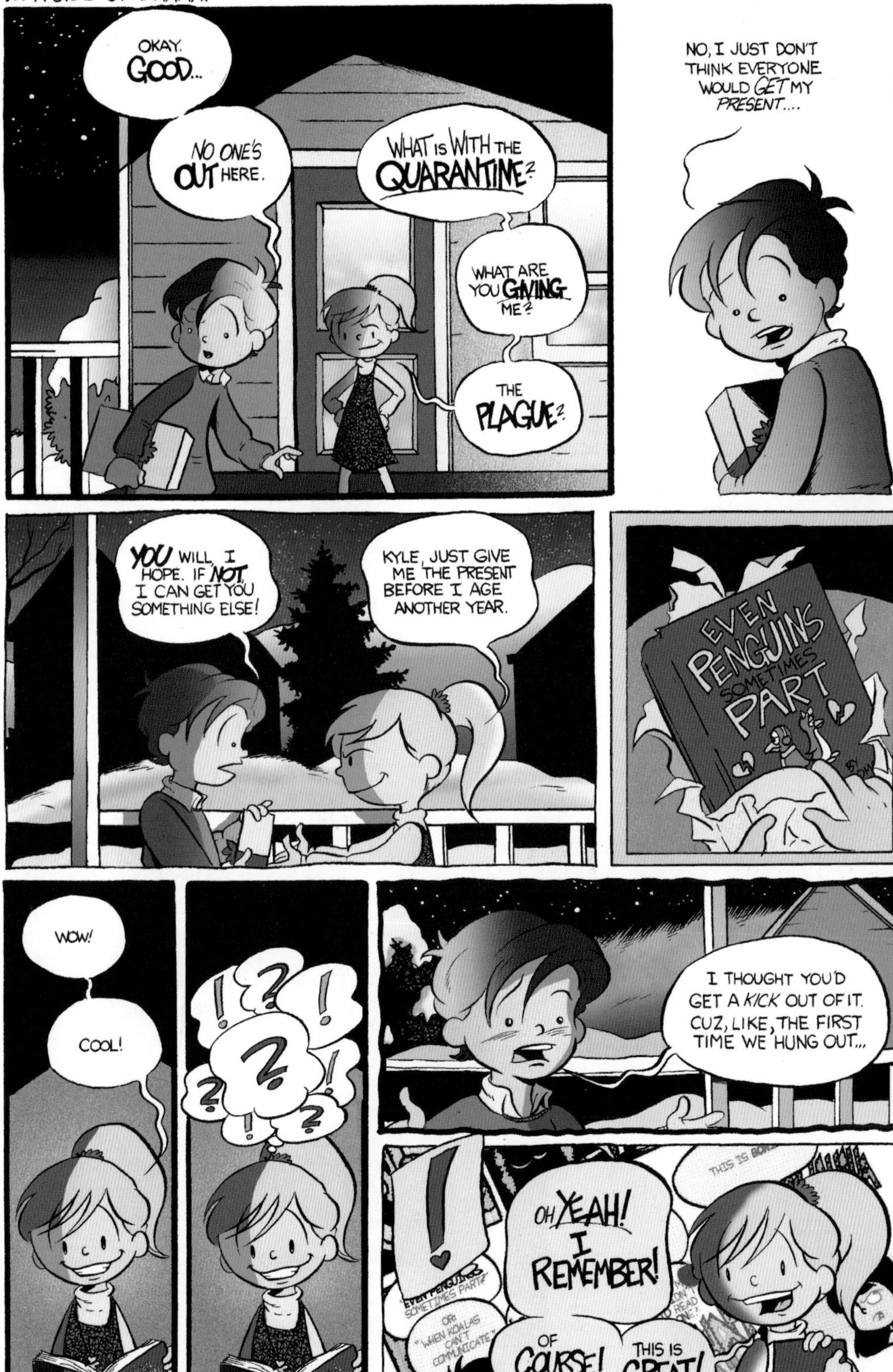

OKAY. GOOD...
NO ONE'S OUT HERE.
WHAT is WITH THE QUARANTINE?
WHAT ARE YOU GIVING ME?
THE PLAGUE?
NO, I JUST DON'T THINK EVERYONE WOULD GET MY PRESENT....
YOU WILL, I HOPE. IF NOT, I CAN GET YOU SOMETHING ELSE!
KYLE, JUST GIVE ME THE PRESENT BEFORE I AGE ANOTHER YEAR.
EVEN PENGUINS SOMETIMES PART
WOW!
COOL!
I THOUGHT YOU'D GET A KICK OUT OF IT. CUZ, LIKE, THE FIRST TIME WE HUNG OUT...
"EVEN PENGUINS SOMETIMES PART?"
OR: "WHEN KOALAS CAN'T COMMUNICATE"
OH YEAH! I REMEMBER!
OF COURSE!
THIS IS GREAT!

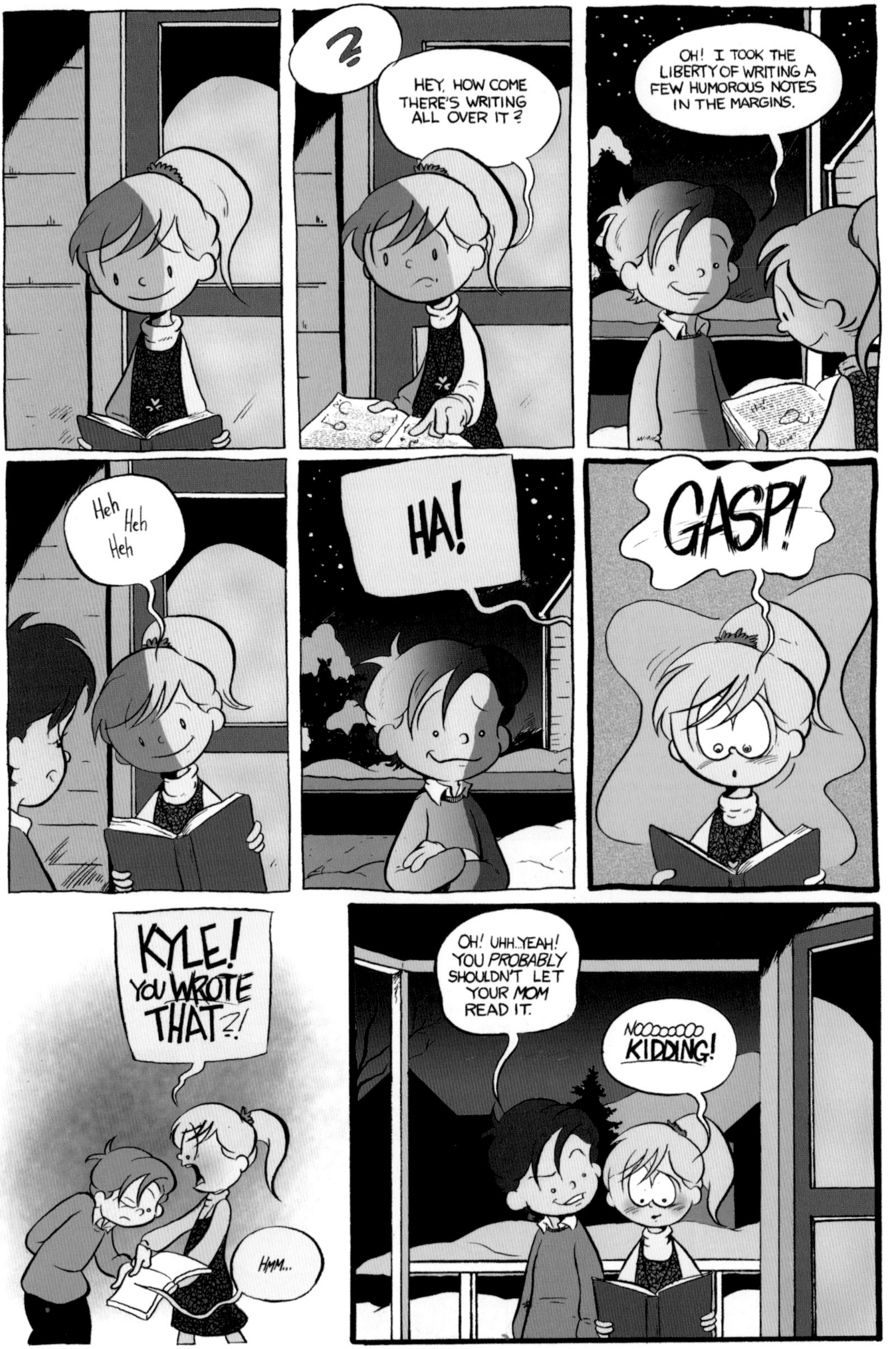
?
HEY, HOW COME THERE'S WRITING ALL OVER IT?
OH! I TOOK THE LIBERTY OF WRITING A FEW HUMOROUS NOTES IN THE MARGINS.
Heh Heh Heh
HA!
GASP!
KYLE! YOU WROTE THAT?!
HMM...
OH! UHH...YEAH! YOU PROBABLY SHOULDN'T LET YOUR MOM READ IT.
NOOoooOOO KIDDING!

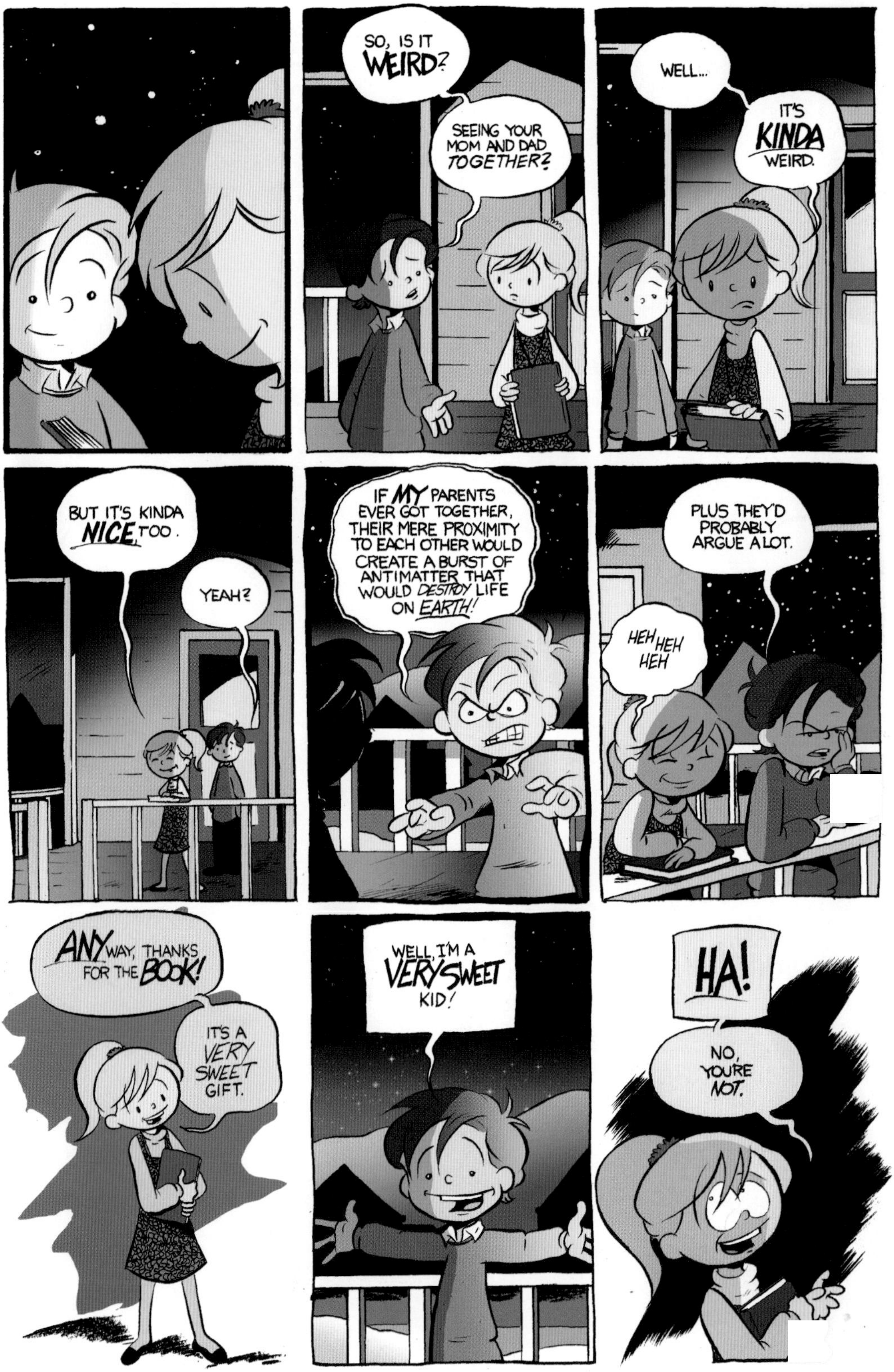

SO, IS IT WEIRD?
SEEING YOUR MOM AND DAD TOGETHER?
WELL...
IT'S KINDA WEIRD.
BUT IT'S KINDA NICE, TOO.
YEAH?
IF MY PARENTS EVER GOT TOGETHER, THEIR MERE PROXIMITY TO EACH OTHER WOULD CREATE A BURST OF ANTIMATTER THAT WOULD DESTROY LIFE ON EARTH!
PLUS THEY'D PROBABLY ARGUE A LOT.
HEH HEH HEH
ANYWAY, THANKS FOR THE BOOK!
IT'S A VERY SWEET GIFT.
WELL, I'M A VERY SWEET KID!
HA!
NO, YOU'RE NOT.

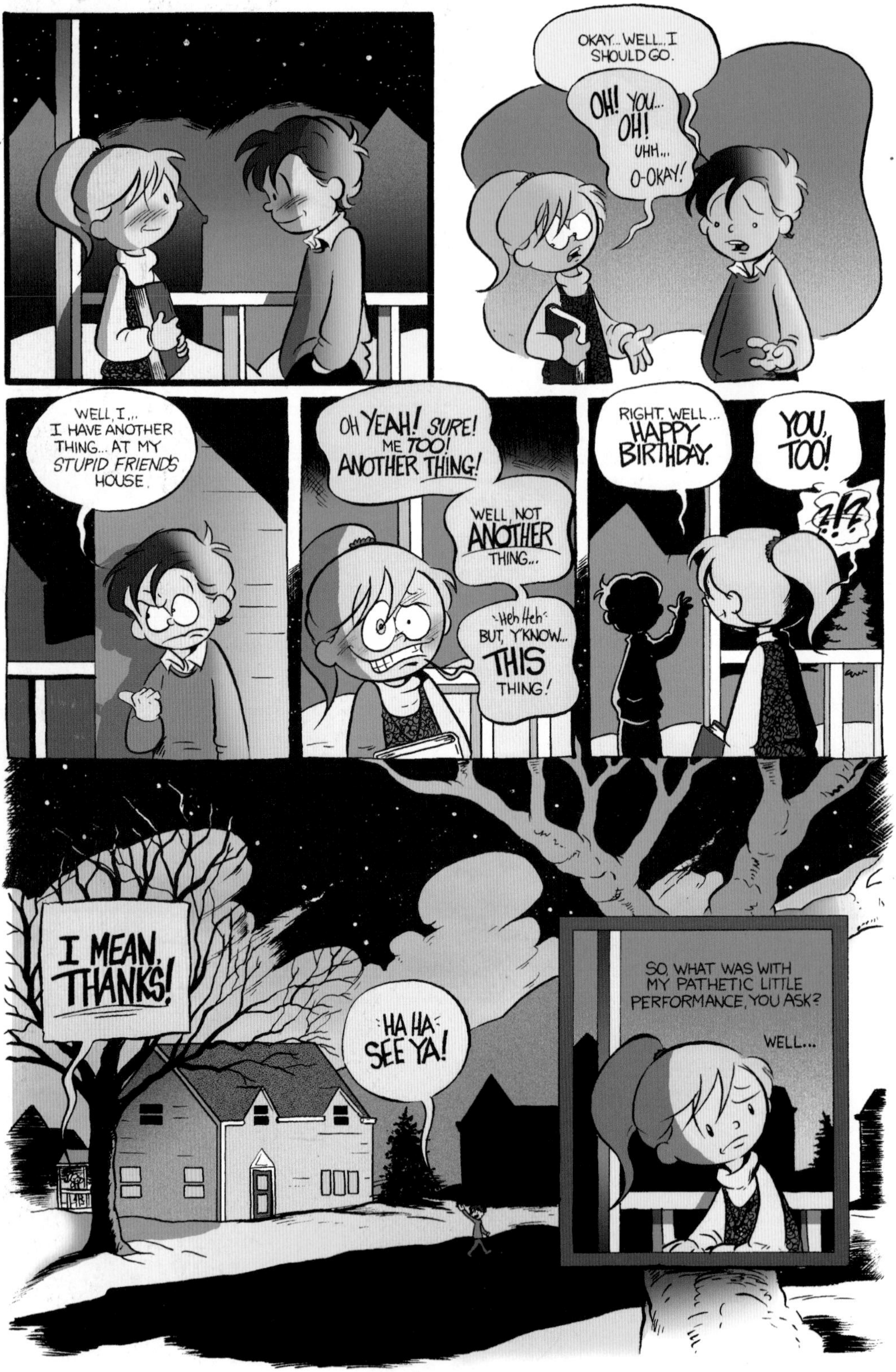

OKAY... WELL... I SHOULD GO.
OH! YOU... OH! UHH... O-OKAY!
WELL, I... I HAVE ANOTHER THING... AT MY STUPID FRIEND'S HOUSE.
OH YEAH! SURE! ME TOO! ANOTHER THING!
WELL, NOT ANOTHER THING...
Heh Heh BUT, Y'KNOW... THIS THING!
RIGHT. WELL... HAPPY BIRTHDAY.
YOU, TOO!
?!?
I MEAN, THANKS!
HA HA SEE YA!
SO, WHAT WAS WITH MY PATHETIC LITTLE PERFORMANCE, YOU ASK?
WELL...

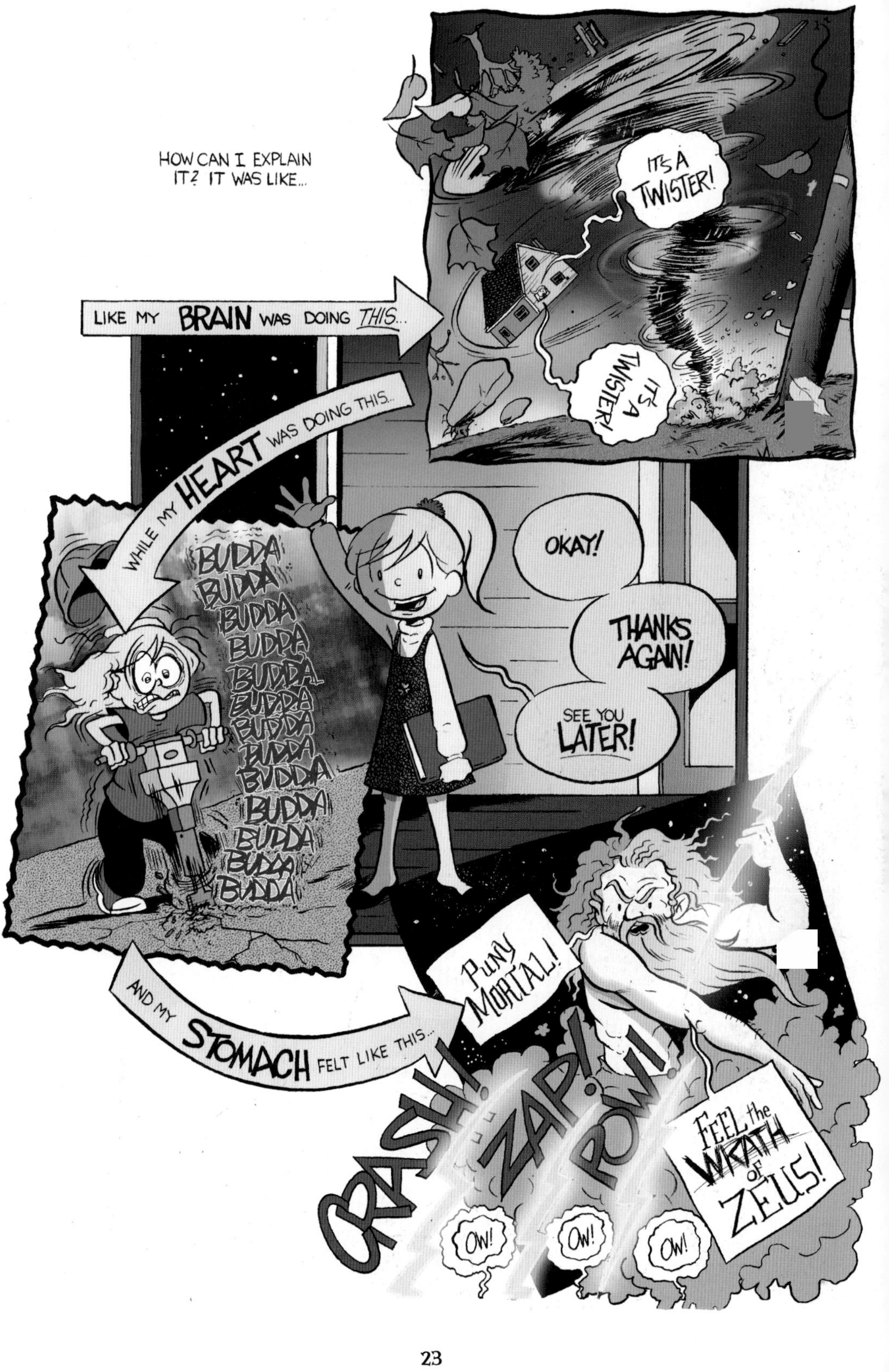
HOW CAN I EXPLAIN IT? IT WAS LIKE...
LIKE MY BRAIN WAS DOING THIS...
IT'S A TWISTER!
IT'S A TWISTER!
WHILE MY HEART WAS DOING THIS...
BUDDA BUDDA BUDDA BUDDA BUDDA BUDDA BUDDA BUDDA BUDDA BUDDA BUDDA BUDDA BUDDA BUDDA
OKAY!
THANKS AGAIN!
SEE YOU LATER!
AND MY STOMACH FELT LIKE THIS...
PUNY MORTAL!
CRASH! ZAP! POW!
OW!
OW!
OW!
FEEL the WRATH of ZEUS!

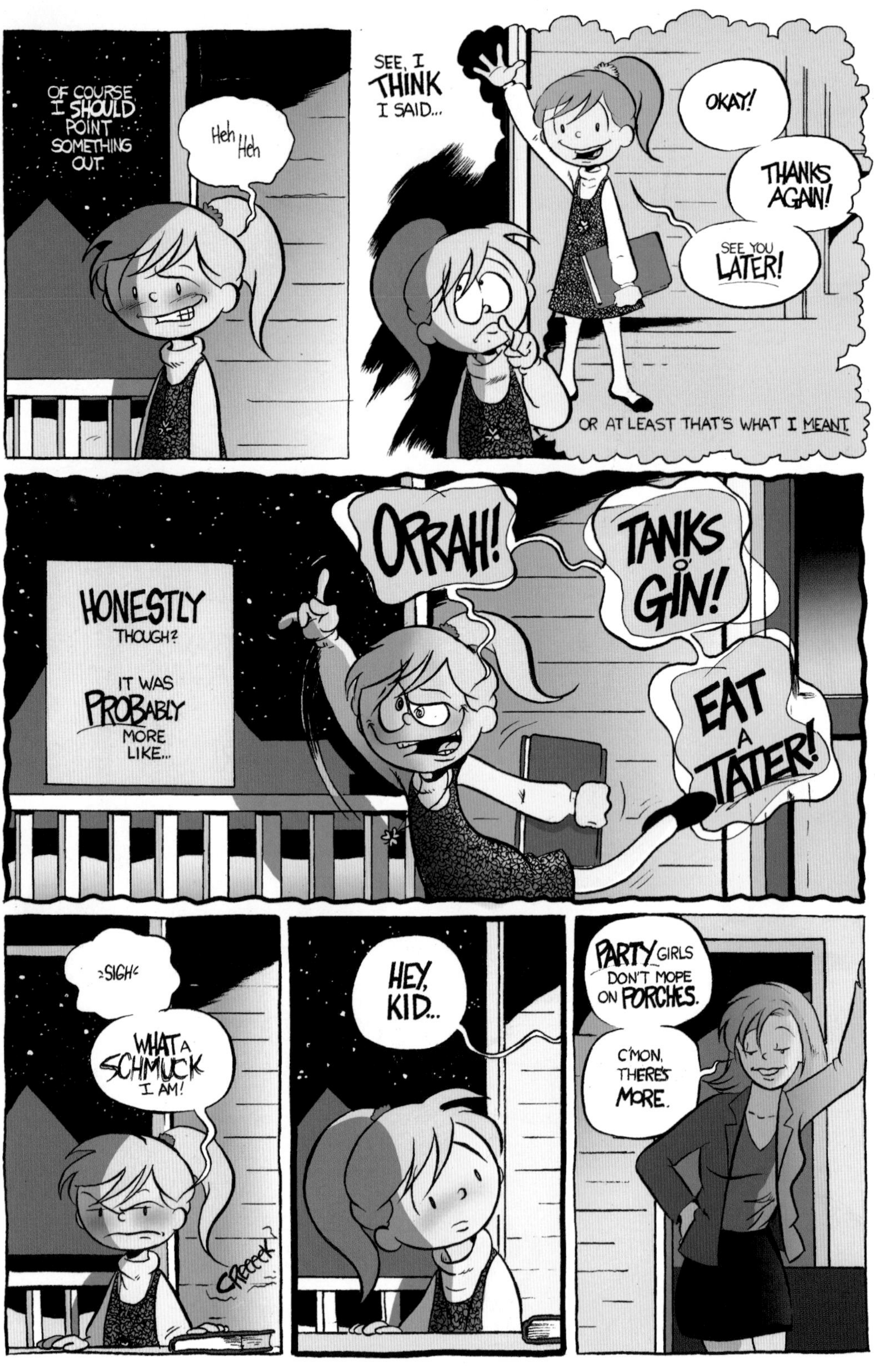
OF COURSE I SHOULD POINT SOMETHING OUT.
Heh Heh
SEE, I THINK I SAID...
OKAY!
THANKS AGAIN!
SEE YOU LATER!
OR AT LEAST THAT'S WHAT I MEANT.
HONESTLY THOUGH?
IT WAS PROBABLY MORE LIKE...
OPRAH!
TANKS O' GIN!
EAT A TATER!
SIGH
WHAT A SCHMUCK I AM!
CREEEEK
HEY, KID...
PARTY GIRLS DON'T MOPE ON PORCHES.
C'MON, THERE'S MORE.

AND AS IT TURNS OUT, THERE WAS ONE GIFT LEFT.

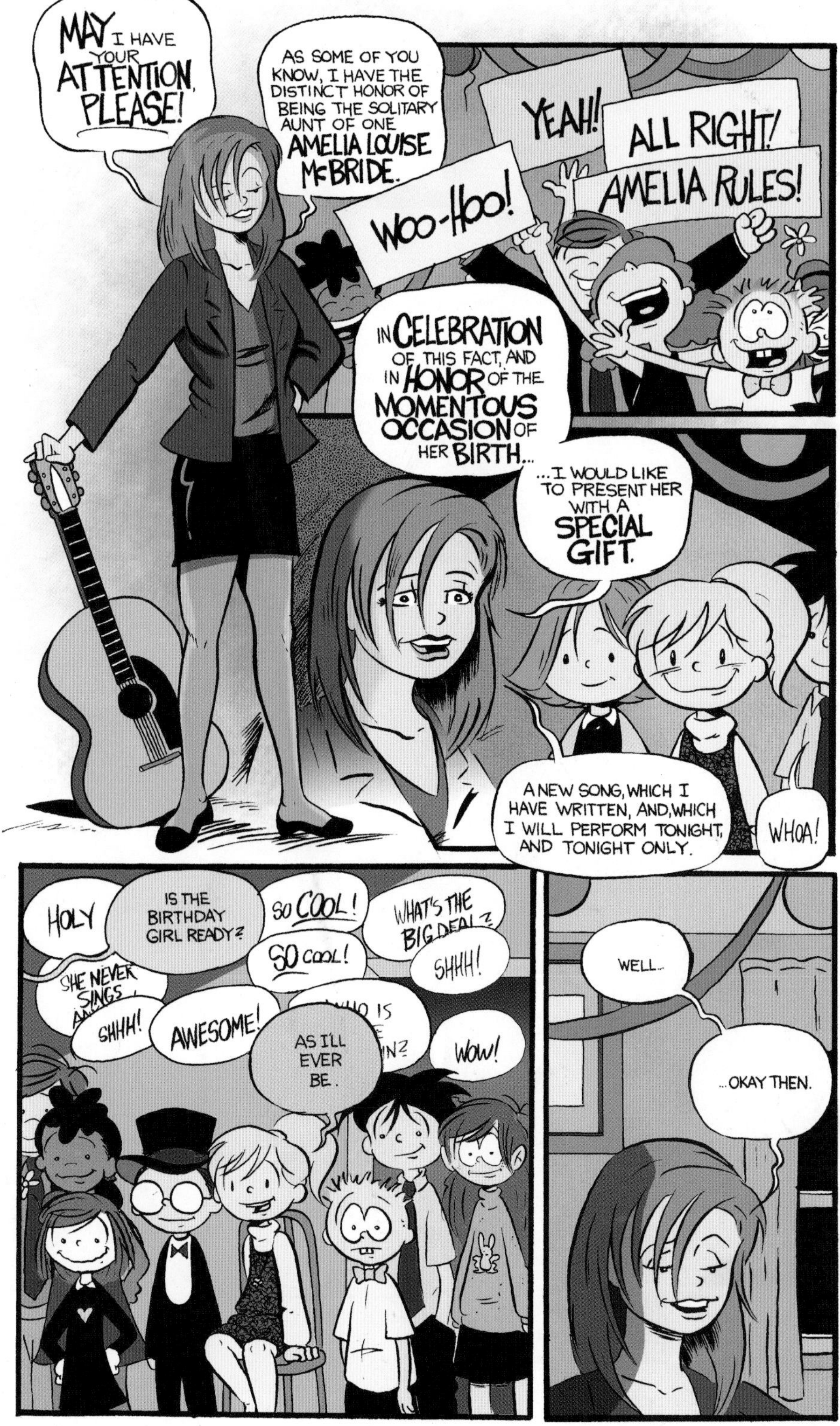
MAY I HAVE YOUR ATTENTION, PLEASE!
AS SOME OF YOU KNOW, I HAVE THE DISTINCT HONOR OF BEING THE SOLITARY AUNT OF ONE AMELIA LOUISE McBRIDE.
YEAH!
ALL RIGHT!
AMELIA RULES!
WOO-HOO!
IN CELEBRATION OF THIS FACT, AND IN HONOR OF THE MOMENTOUS OCCASION OF HER BIRTH...
...I WOULD LIKE TO PRESENT HER WITH A SPECIAL GIFT.
A NEW SONG, WHICH I HAVE WRITTEN, AND, WHICH I WILL PERFORM TONIGHT, AND TONIGHT ONLY.
WHOA!
HOLY
IS THE BIRTHDAY GIRL READY?
SO COOL!
SO COOL!
SHHH!
SHE NEVER SINGS
SHHH!
AWESOME!
AS I'LL EVER BE.
WOW!
WELL...
...OKAY THEN.

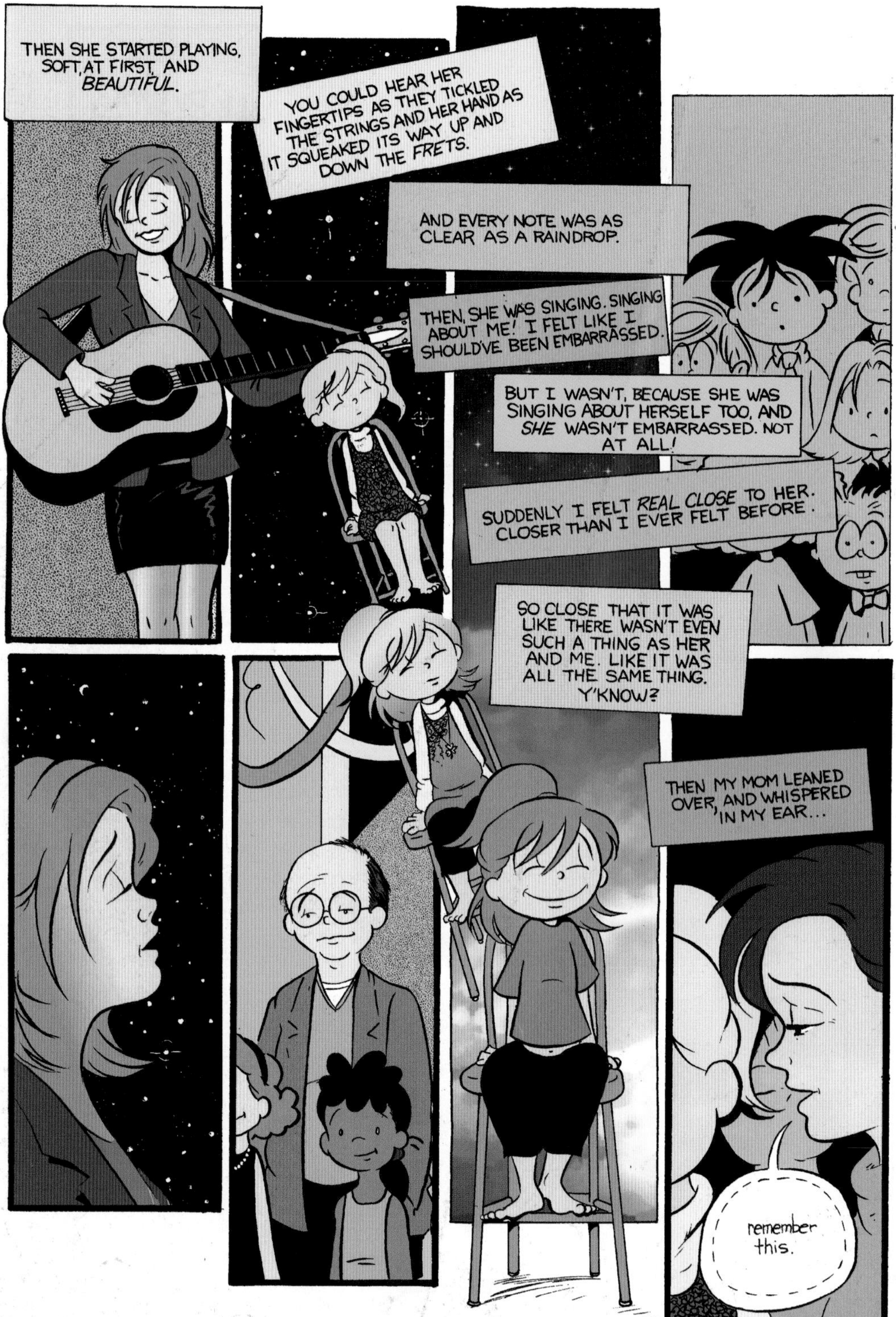
THEN SHE STARTED PLAYING, SOFT, AT FIRST, AND BEAUTIFUL.
YOU COULD HEAR HER FINGERTIPS AS THEY TICKLED THE STRINGS AND HER HAND AS IT SQUEAKED ITS WAY UP AND DOWN THE FRETS.
AND EVERY NOTE WAS AS CLEAR AS A RAINDROP.
THEN, SHE WAS SINGING. SINGING ABOUT ME! I FELT LIKE I SHOULD'VE BEEN EMBARRASSED.
BUT I WASN'T, BECAUSE SHE WAS SINGING ABOUT HERSELF TOO, AND SHE WASN'T EMBARRASSED. NOT AT ALL!
SUDDENLY I FELT REAL CLOSE TO HER. CLOSER THAN I EVER FELT BEFORE.
SO CLOSE THAT IT WAS LIKE THERE WASN'T EVEN SUCH A THING AS HER AND ME. LIKE IT WAS ALL THE SAME THING. Y'KNOW?
THEN MY MOM LEANED OVER, AND WHISPERED IN MY EAR...
remember this.

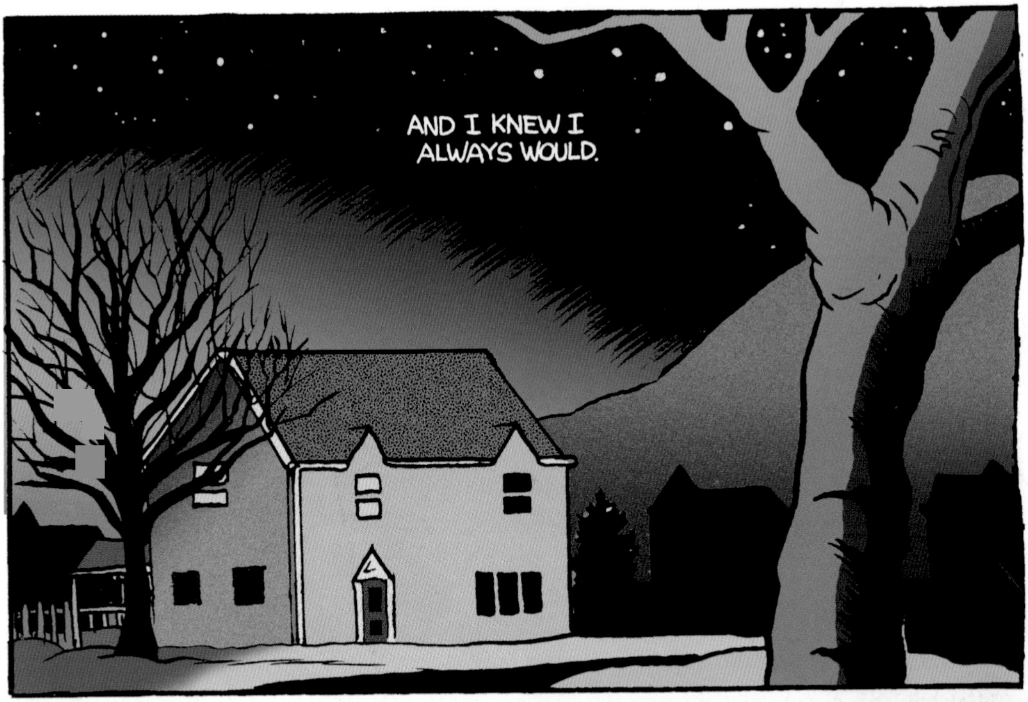
AND I KNEW I ALWAYS WOULD.

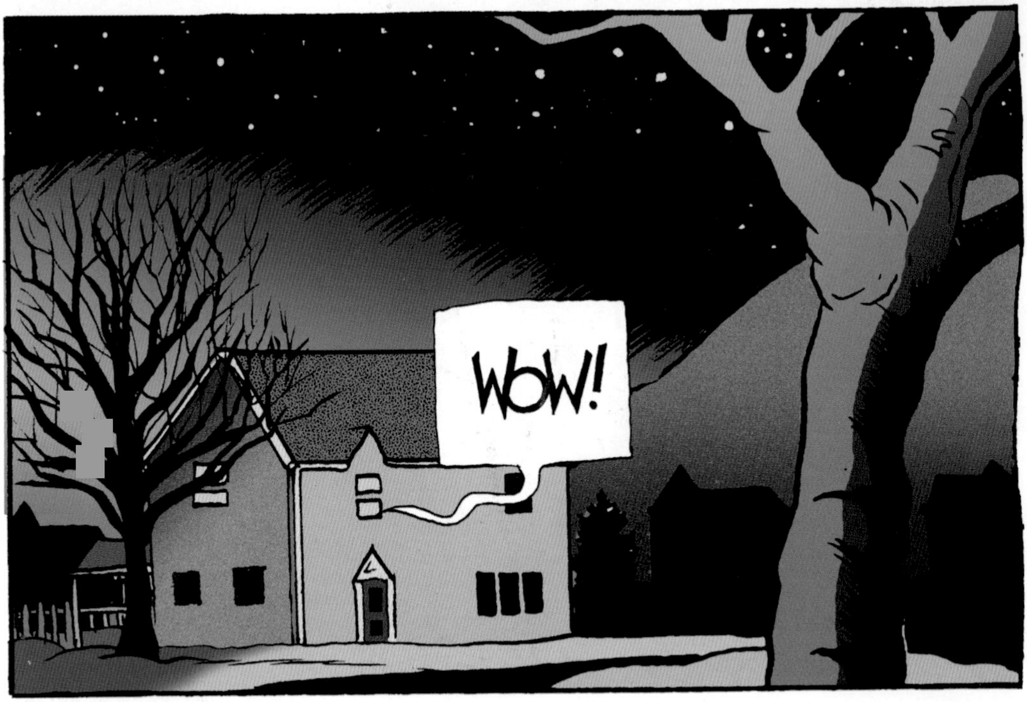
WOW!

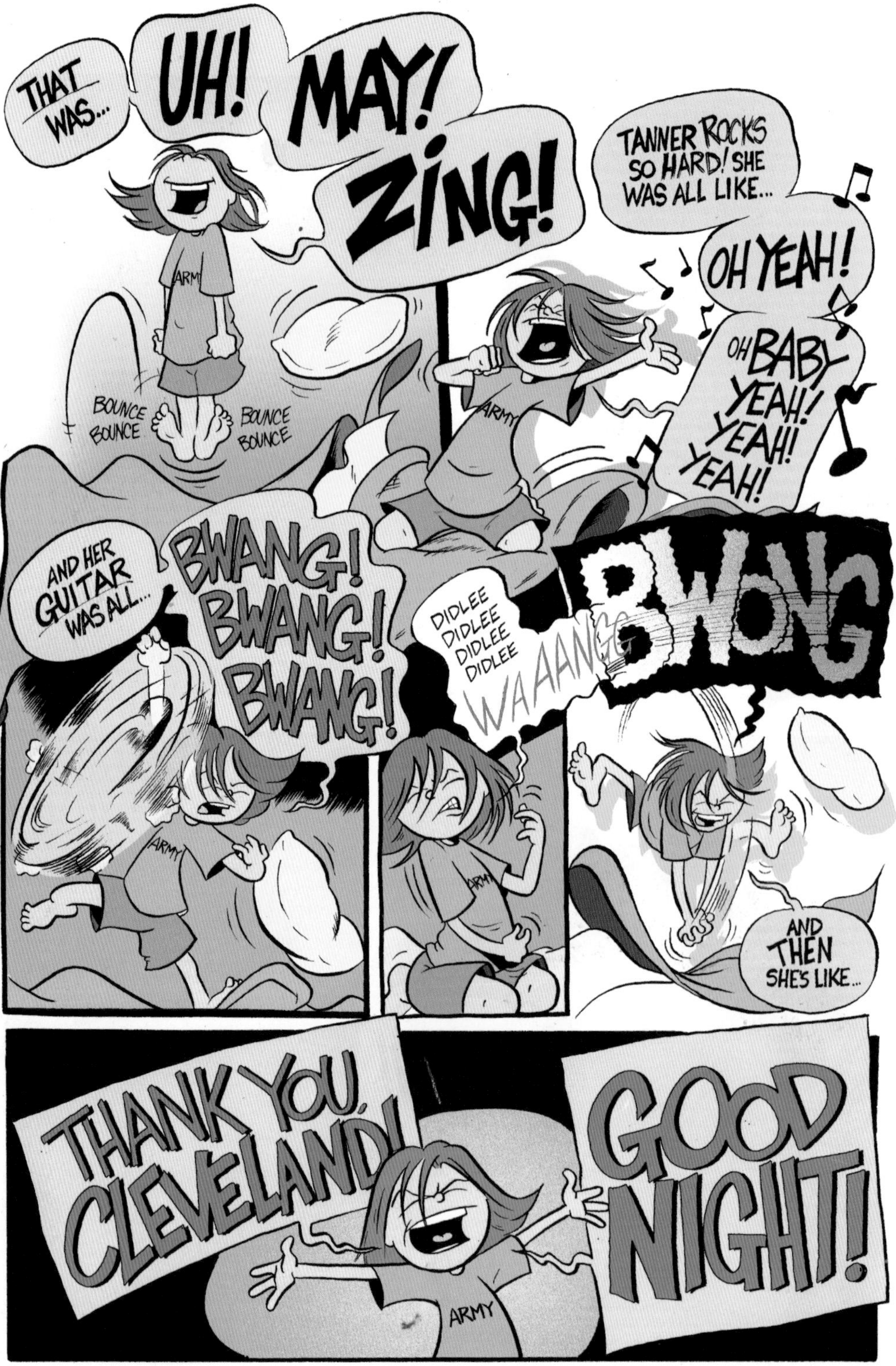
THAT WAS...
UH!
MAY!
ZING!
BOUNCE BOUNCE
BOUNCE BOUNCE
ARMY
TANNER ROCKS SO HARD! SHE WAS ALL LIKE...
OH YEAH!
OH BABY YEAH! YEAH! YEAH!
ARMY
AND HER GUITAR WAS ALL...
BWANG! BWANG! BWANG!
ARMY
DIDLEE DIDLEE DIDLEE DIDLEE
WAAANG
BWONG
ARMY
AND THEN SHE'S LIKE...
THANK YOU, CLEVELAND!
GOOD NIGHT!
ARMY

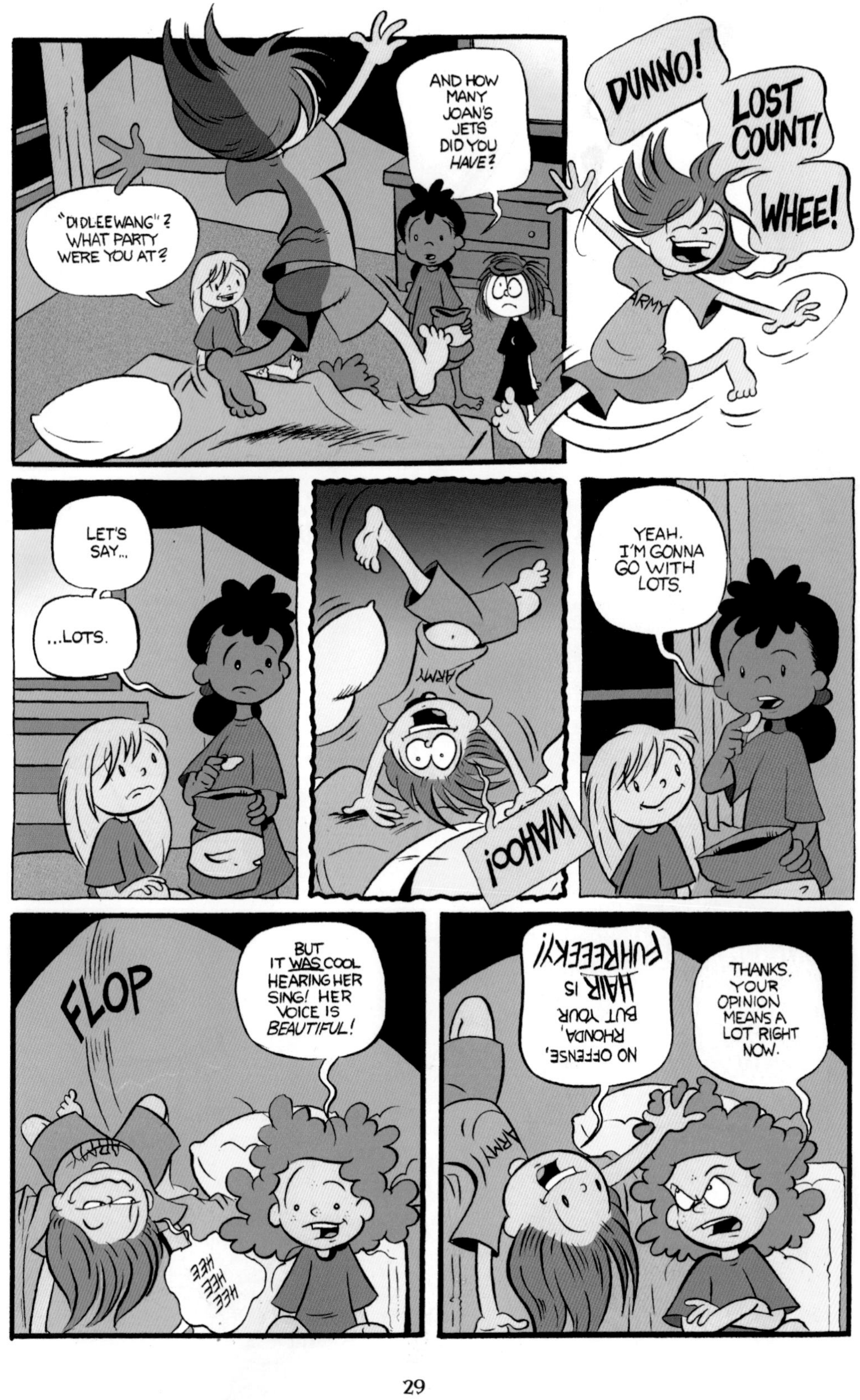
"DIDLEEWANG"? WHAT PARTY WERE YOU AT?
AND HOW MANY JOAN'S JETS DID YOU *HAVE*?
DUNNO!
LOST COUNT!
WHEE!
ARMY
LET'S SAY...
...LOTS.
WAHOO!
YEAH. I'M GONNA GO WITH LOTS.
FLOP
BUT IT WAS COOL HEARING HER SING! HER VOICE IS *BEAUTIFUL*!
HEE HEE HEE
NO OFFENSE, RHONDA, BUT YOUR HAIR IS FUHREEKY!
THANKS. YOUR OPINION MEANS A LOT RIGHT NOW.

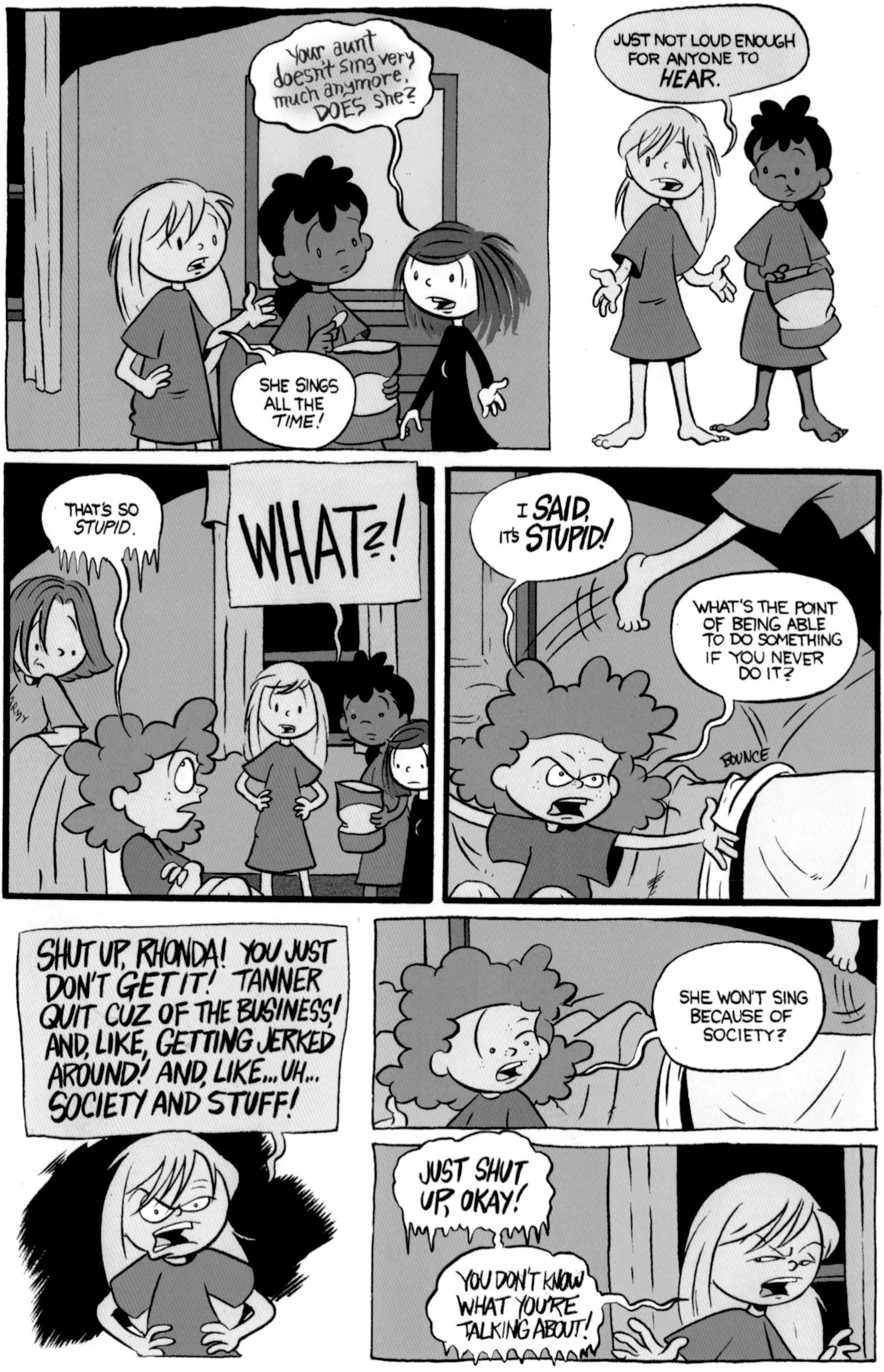
Your aunt doesn't sing very much anymore, DOES she?
SHE SINGS ALL THE TIME!
JUST NOT LOUD ENOUGH FOR ANYONE TO HEAR.
THAT'S SO STUPID.
WHAT?!
I SAID, IT'S STUPID!
WHAT'S THE POINT OF BEING ABLE TO DO SOMETHING IF YOU NEVER DO IT?
BOUNCE
SHUT UP, RHONDA! YOU JUST DON'T GET IT! TANNER QUIT CUZ OF THE BUSINESS! AND, LIKE, GETTING JERKED AROUND! AND, LIKE... UH... SOCIETY AND STUFF!
SHE WON'T SING BECAUSE OF SOCIETY?
JUST SHUT UP, OKAY!
YOU DON'T KNOW WHAT YOU'RE TALKING ABOUT!

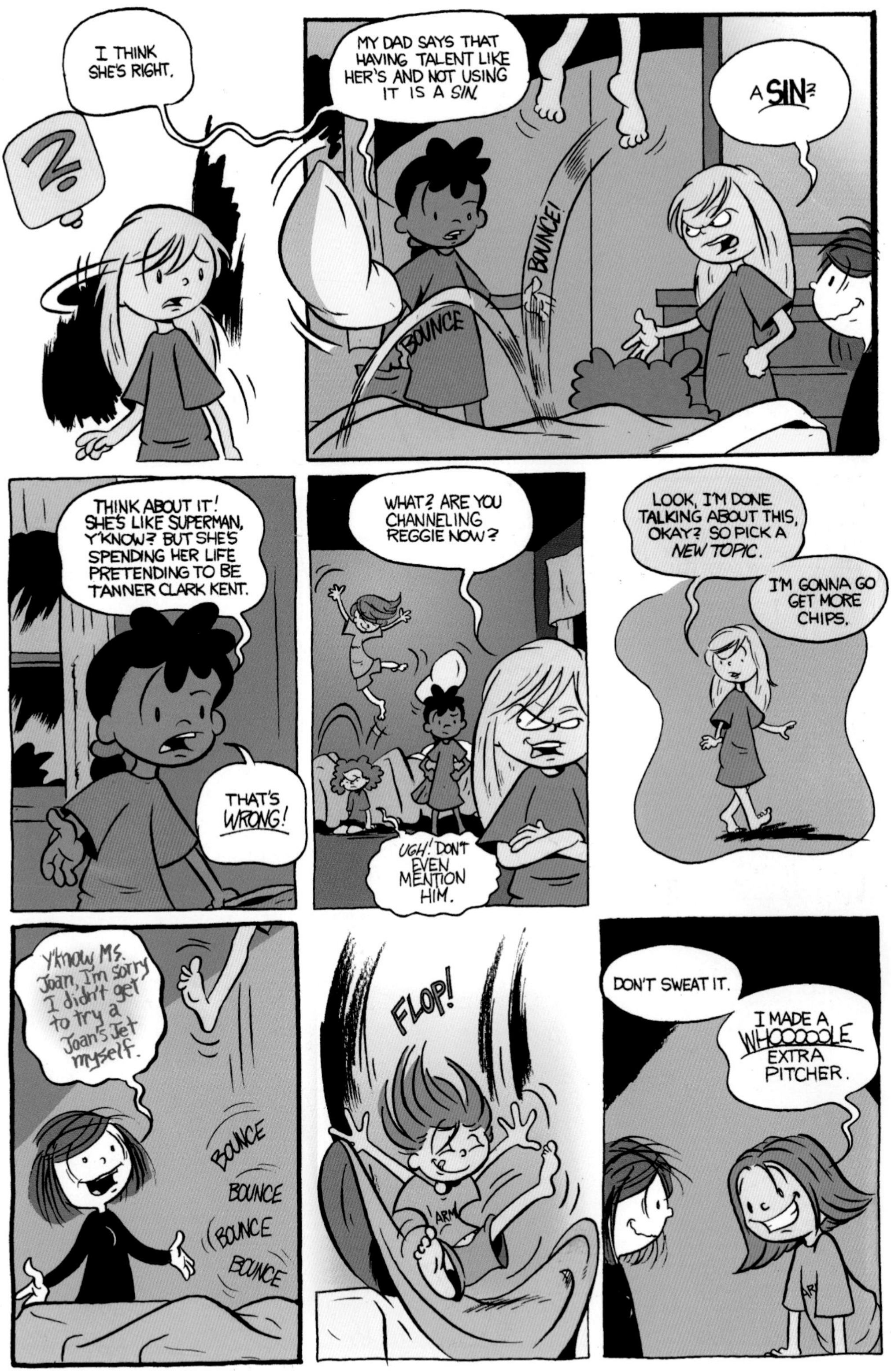
I THINK SHE'S RIGHT.
?
MY DAD SAYS THAT HAVING TALENT LIKE HER'S AND NOT USING IT IS A *SIN.*
A SIN?
BOUNCE
BOUNCE!
THINK ABOUT IT! SHE'S LIKE SUPERMAN, Y'KNOW? BUT SHE'S SPENDING HER LIFE PRETENDING TO BE TANNER CLARK KENT.
THAT'S WRONG!
WHAT? ARE YOU CHANNELING REGGIE NOW?
UGH! DON'T EVEN MENTION HIM.
LOOK, I'M DONE TALKING ABOUT THIS, OKAY? SO PICK A *NEW TOPIC.*
I'M GONNA GO GET MORE CHIPS.
Y'know, Ms. Joan, I'm sorry I didn't get to try a Joan's Jet myself.
BOUNCE
BOUNCE
BOUNCE
BOUNCE
FLOP!
ARM
DON'T SWEAT IT.
I MADE A WHOOOOOOLE EXTRA PITCHER.

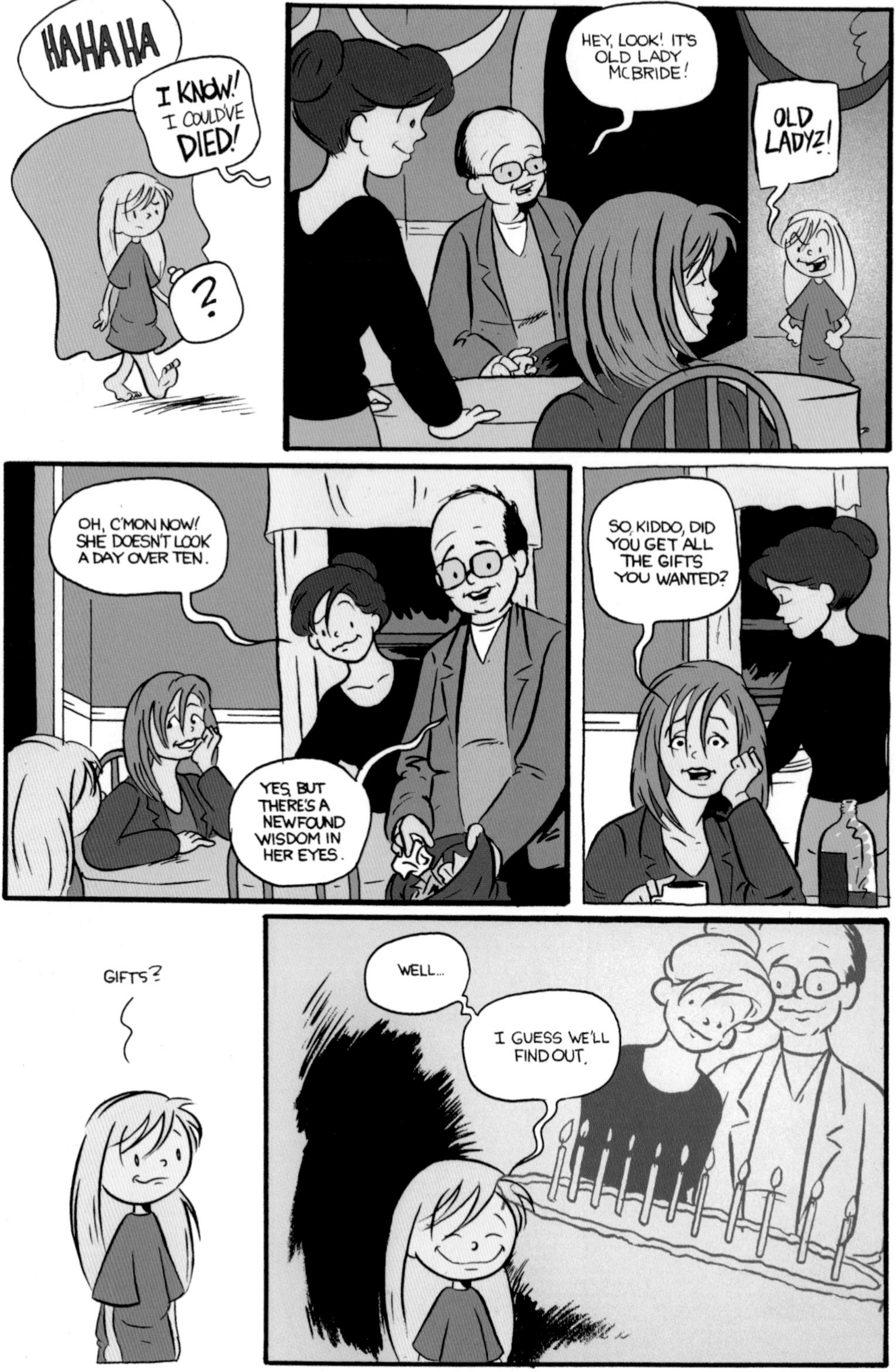
HAHAHA
I KNOW! I COULD'VE DIED!
?
HEY, LOOK! IT'S OLD LADY McBRIDE!
OLD LADYZ!
OH, C'MON NOW! SHE DOESN'T LOOK A DAY OVER TEN.
YES, BUT THERE'S A NEWFOUND WISDOM IN HER EYES.
SO, KIDDO, DID YOU GET ALL THE GIFTS YOU WANTED?
GIFTS?
WELL...
I GUESS WE'LL FIND OUT.

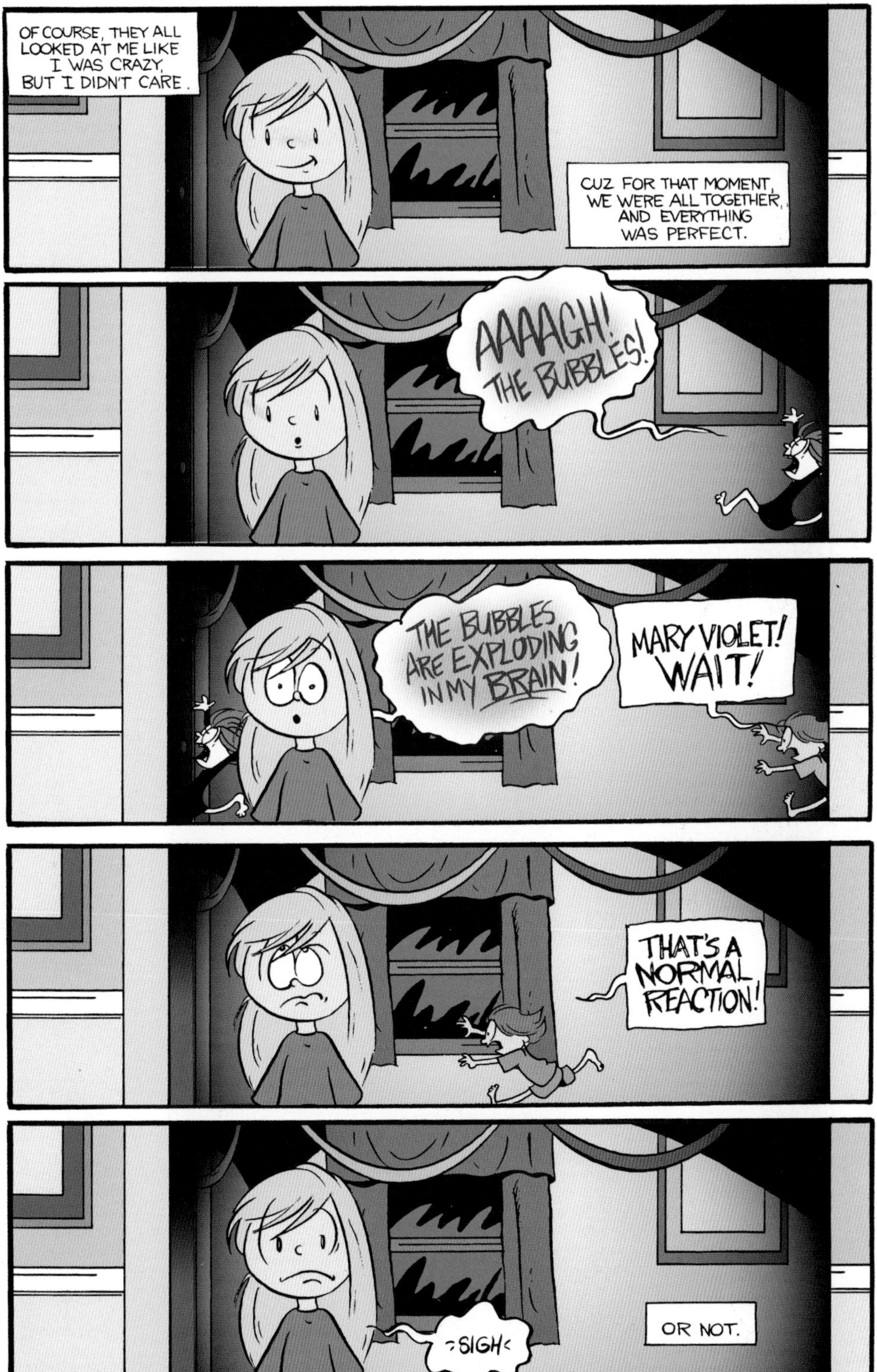

OF COURSE, THEY ALL LOOKED AT ME LIKE I WAS CRAZY, BUT I DIDN'T CARE.
CUZ FOR THAT MOMENT, WE WERE ALL TOGETHER, AND EVERYTHING WAS PERFECT.
AAAAGH! THE BUBBLES!
THE BUBBLES ARE EXPLODING IN MY BRAIN!
MARY VIOLET! WAIT!
THAT'S A NORMAL REACTION!
-SIGH-
OR NOT.

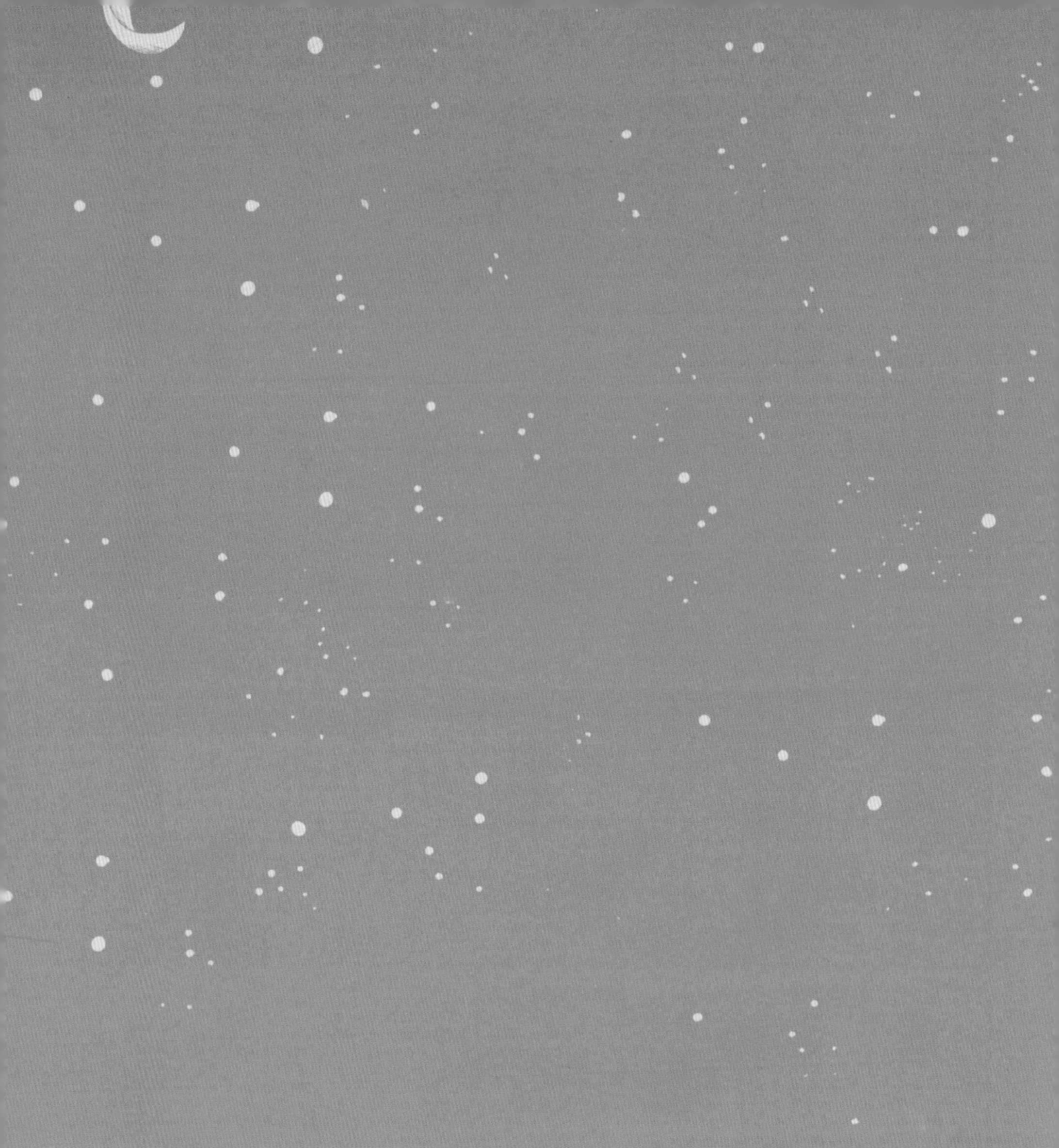

"I'm still waiting to use algebra."

–Tanner Clark

from a profile printed in her high school alumni newsletter

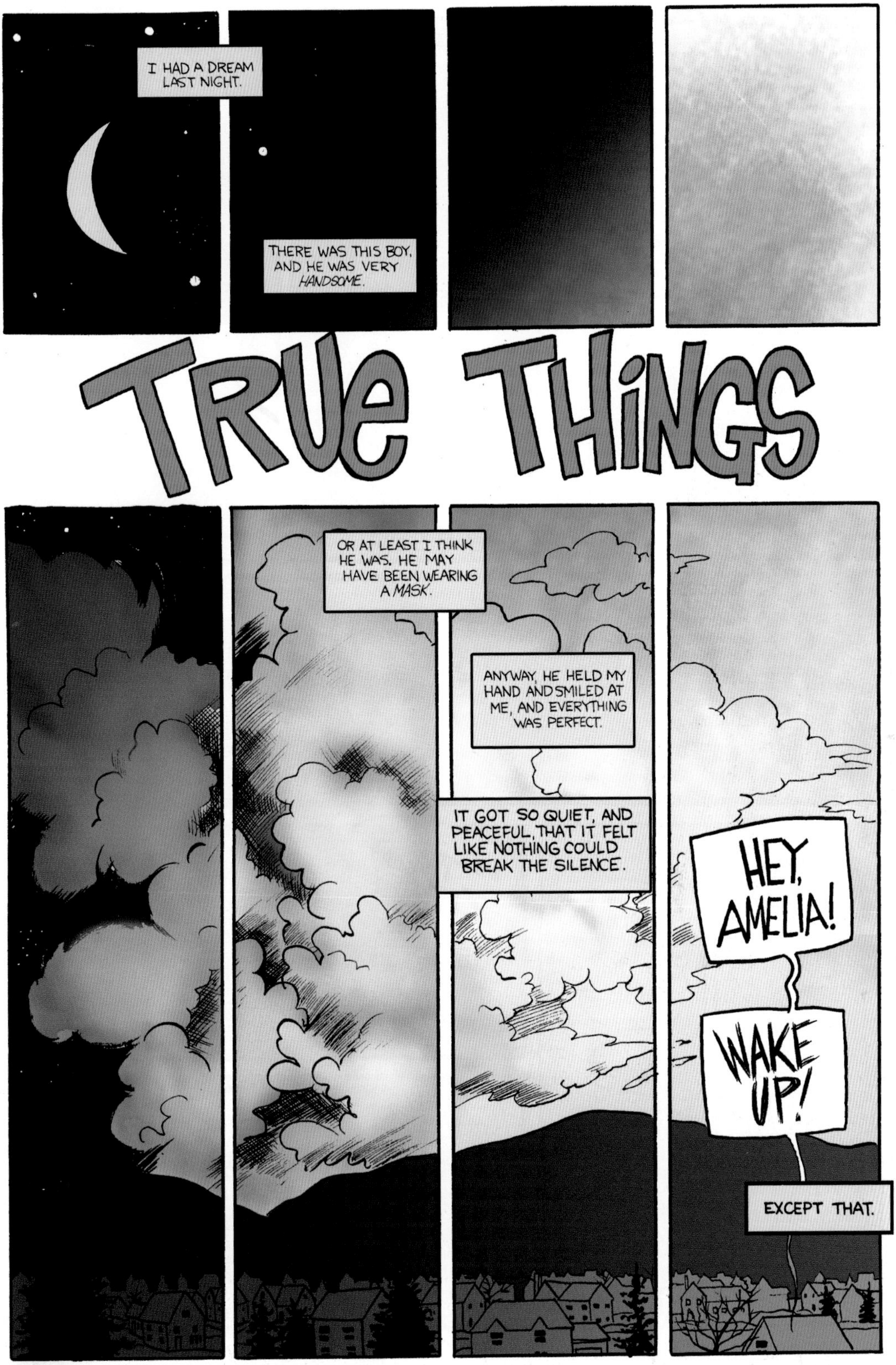
I HAD A DREAM LAST NIGHT.
THERE WAS THIS BOY, AND HE WAS VERY *HANDSOME*.
TRUE THINGS
OR AT LEAST I THINK HE WAS. HE MAY HAVE BEEN WEARING A *MASK*.
ANYWAY, HE HELD MY HAND AND SMILED AT ME, AND EVERYTHING WAS PERFECT.
IT GOT SO QUIET, AND PEACEFUL, THAT IT FELT LIKE NOTHING COULD BREAK THE SILENCE.
HEY, AMELIA!
WAKE UP!
EXCEPT THAT.

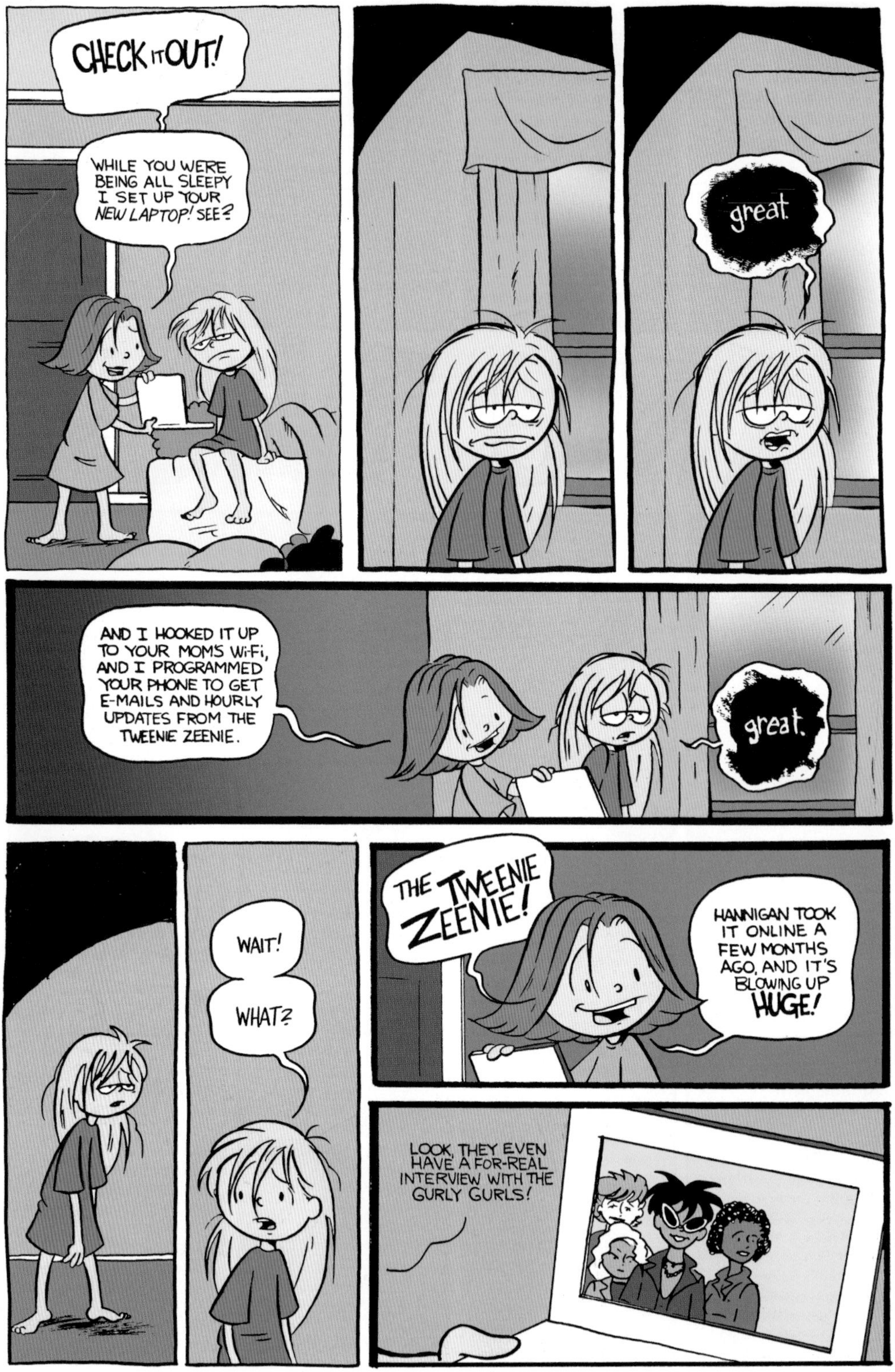
CHECK IT OUT!
WHILE YOU WERE BEING ALL SLEEPY I SET UP YOUR NEW LAPTOP! SEE?
great.
AND I HOOKED IT UP TO YOUR MOM'S Wi-Fi, AND I PROGRAMMED YOUR PHONE TO GET E-MAILS AND HOURLY UPDATES FROM THE TWEENIE ZEENIE.
great.
WAIT!
WHAT?
THE TWEENIE ZEENIE!
HANNIGAN TOOK IT ONLINE A FEW MONTHS AGO, AND IT'S BLOWING UP HUGE!
LOOK, THEY EVEN HAVE A FOR-REAL INTERVIEW WITH THE GURLY GURLS!

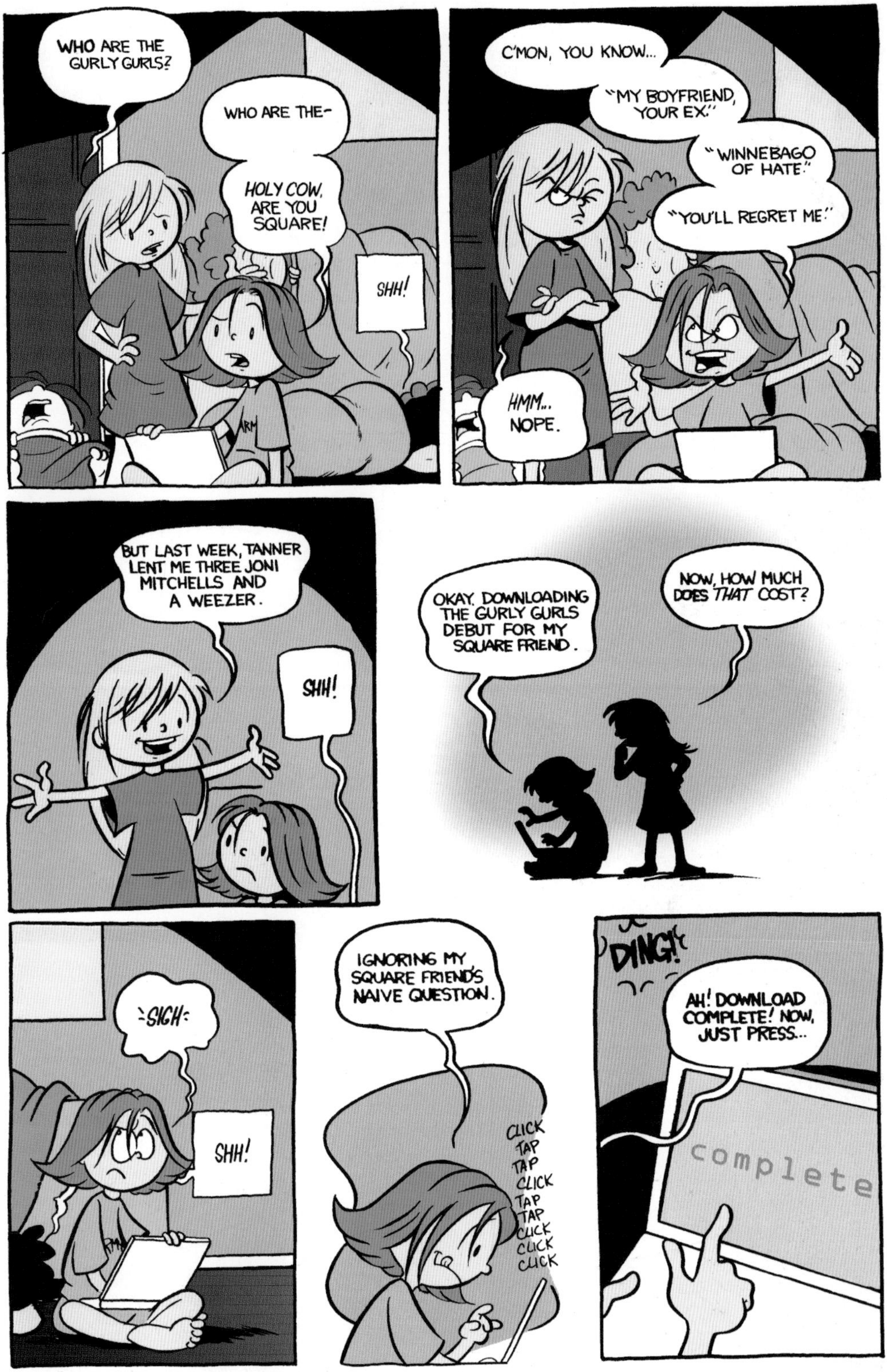
WHO ARE THE GURLY GURLS?
WHO ARE THE-
HOLY COW, ARE YOU SQUARE!
SHH!
C'MON, YOU KNOW...
"MY BOYFRIEND, YOUR EX."
"WINNEBAGO OF HATE."
"YOU'LL REGRET ME."
HMM... NOPE.
BUT LAST WEEK, TANNER LENT ME THREE JONI MITCHELLS AND A WEEZER.
SHH!
OKAY. DOWNLOADING THE GURLY GURLS DEBUT FOR MY SQUARE FRIEND.
NOW, HOW MUCH DOES THAT COST?
SIGH
SHH!
IGNORING MY SQUARE FRIEND'S NAIVE QUESTION.
CLICK TAP TAP CLICK TAP TAP CLICK CLICK CLICK
DING!
AH! DOWNLOAD COMPLETE! NOW, JUST PRESS...
complete

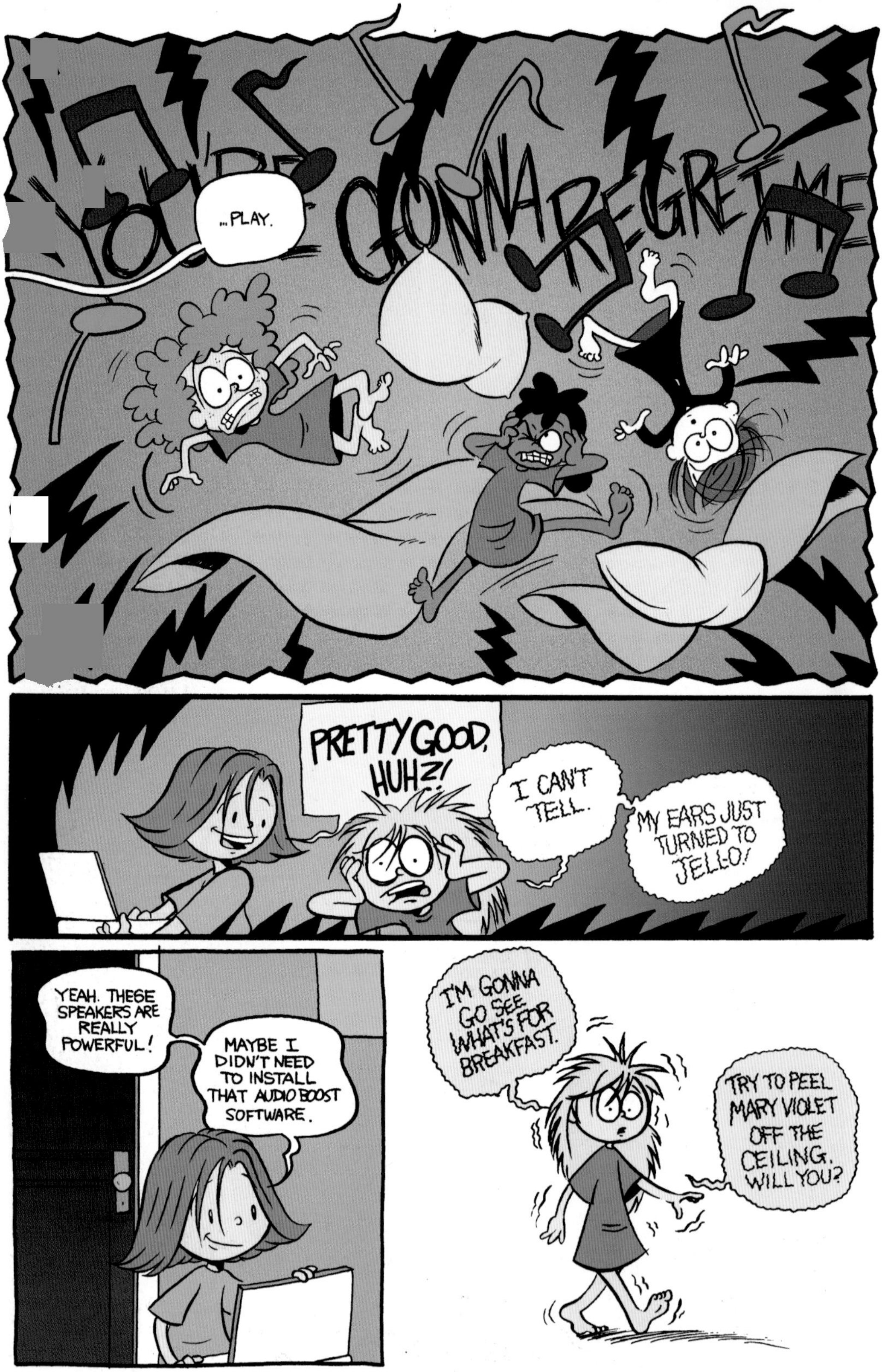

...PLAY.
YOU'RE GONNA REGRET ME
PRETTY GOOD, HUH?!
I CAN'T TELL.
MY EARS JUST TURNED TO JELLO!
YEAH. THESE SPEAKERS ARE REALLY POWERFUL!
MAYBE I DIDN'T NEED TO INSTALL THAT AUDIO BOOST SOFTWARE.
I'M GONNA GO SEE WHAT'S FOR BREAKFAST.
TRY TO PEEL MARY VIOLET OFF THE CEILING, WILL YOU?

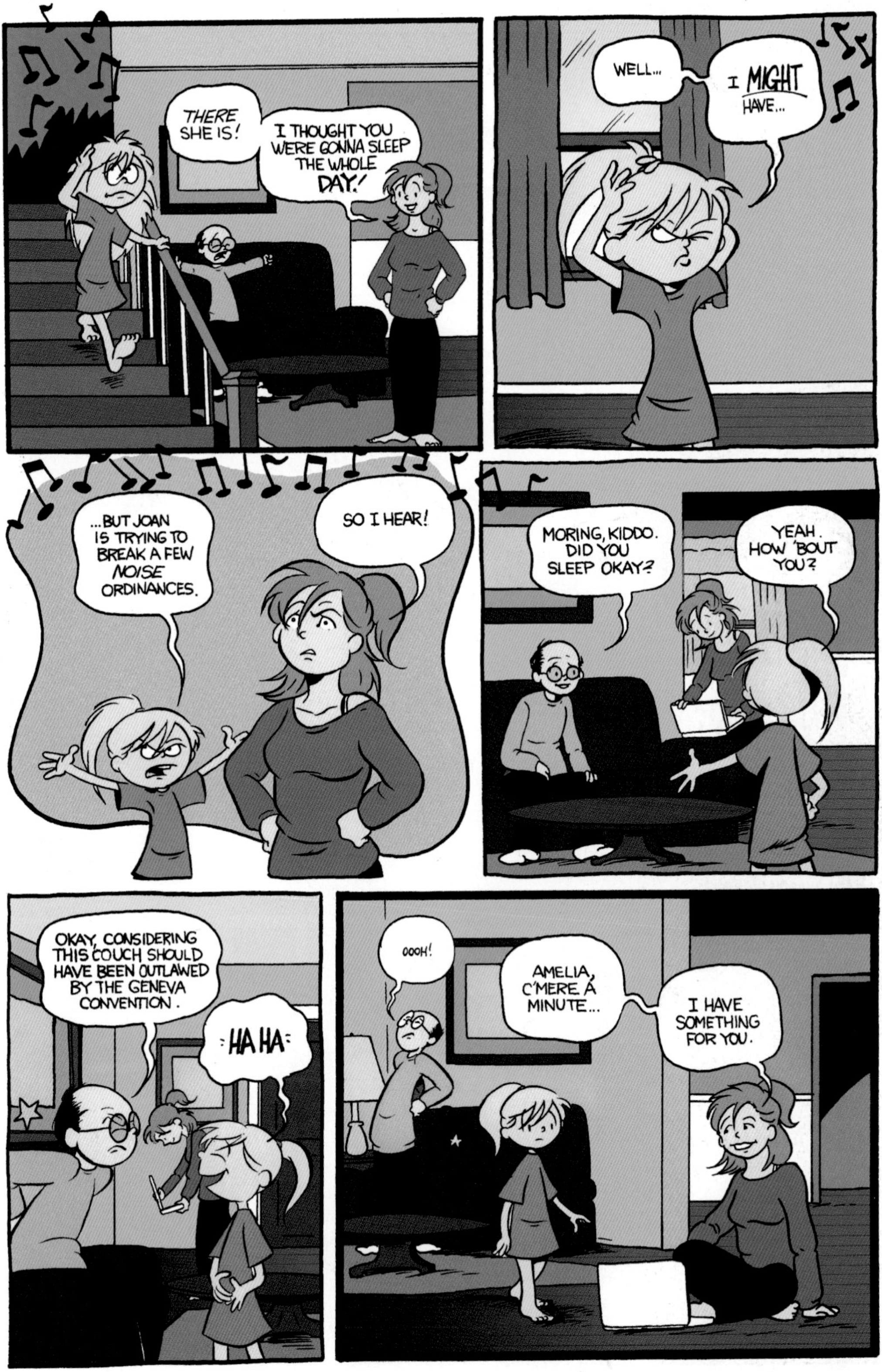
THERE SHE IS!
I THOUGHT YOU WERE GONNA SLEEP THE WHOLE DAY!
WELL...
I MIGHT HAVE...
...BUT JOAN IS TRYING TO BREAK A FEW NOISE ORDINANCES.
SO I HEAR!
MORING, KIDDO. DID YOU SLEEP OKAY?
YEAH. HOW 'BOUT YOU?
OKAY, CONSIDERING THIS COUCH SHOULD HAVE BEEN OUTLAWED BY THE GENEVA CONVENTION.
HA HA
OOOH!
AMELIA, C'MERE A MINUTE...
I HAVE SOMETHING FOR YOU.

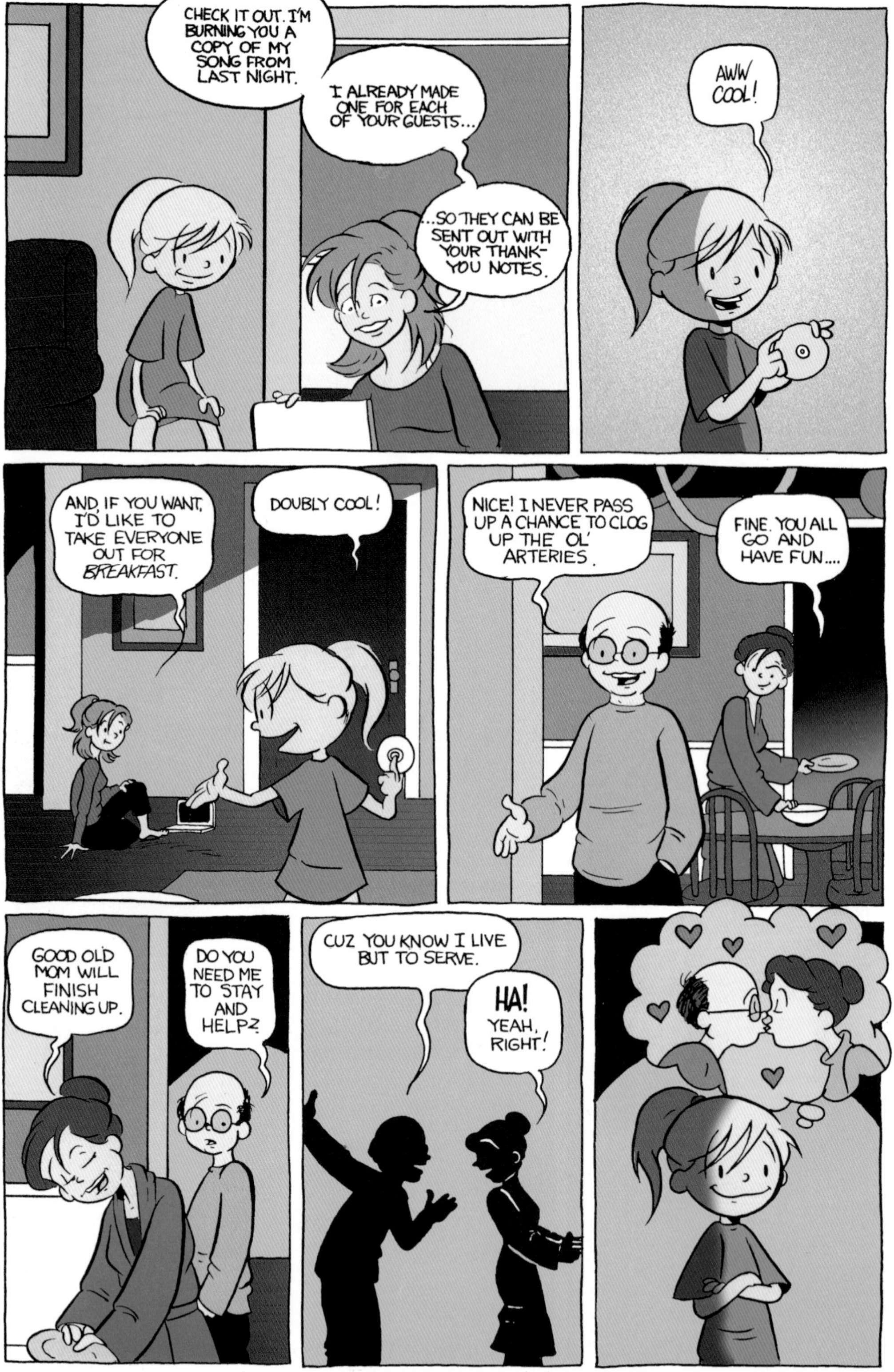
CHECK IT OUT. I'M BURNING YOU A COPY OF MY SONG FROM LAST NIGHT.
I ALREADY MADE ONE FOR EACH OF YOUR GUESTS...
...SO THEY CAN BE SENT OUT WITH YOUR THANK-YOU NOTES.
AWW COOL!
AND, IF YOU WANT, I'D LIKE TO TAKE EVERYONE OUT FOR BREAKFAST.
DOUBLY COOL!
NICE! I NEVER PASS UP A CHANCE TO CLOG UP THE OL' ARTERIES.
FINE. YOU ALL GO AND HAVE FUN....
GOOD OLD MOM WILL FINISH CLEANING UP.
DO YOU NEED ME TO STAY AND HELP?
CUZ YOU KNOW I LIVE BUT TO SERVE.
HA! YEAH, RIGHT!

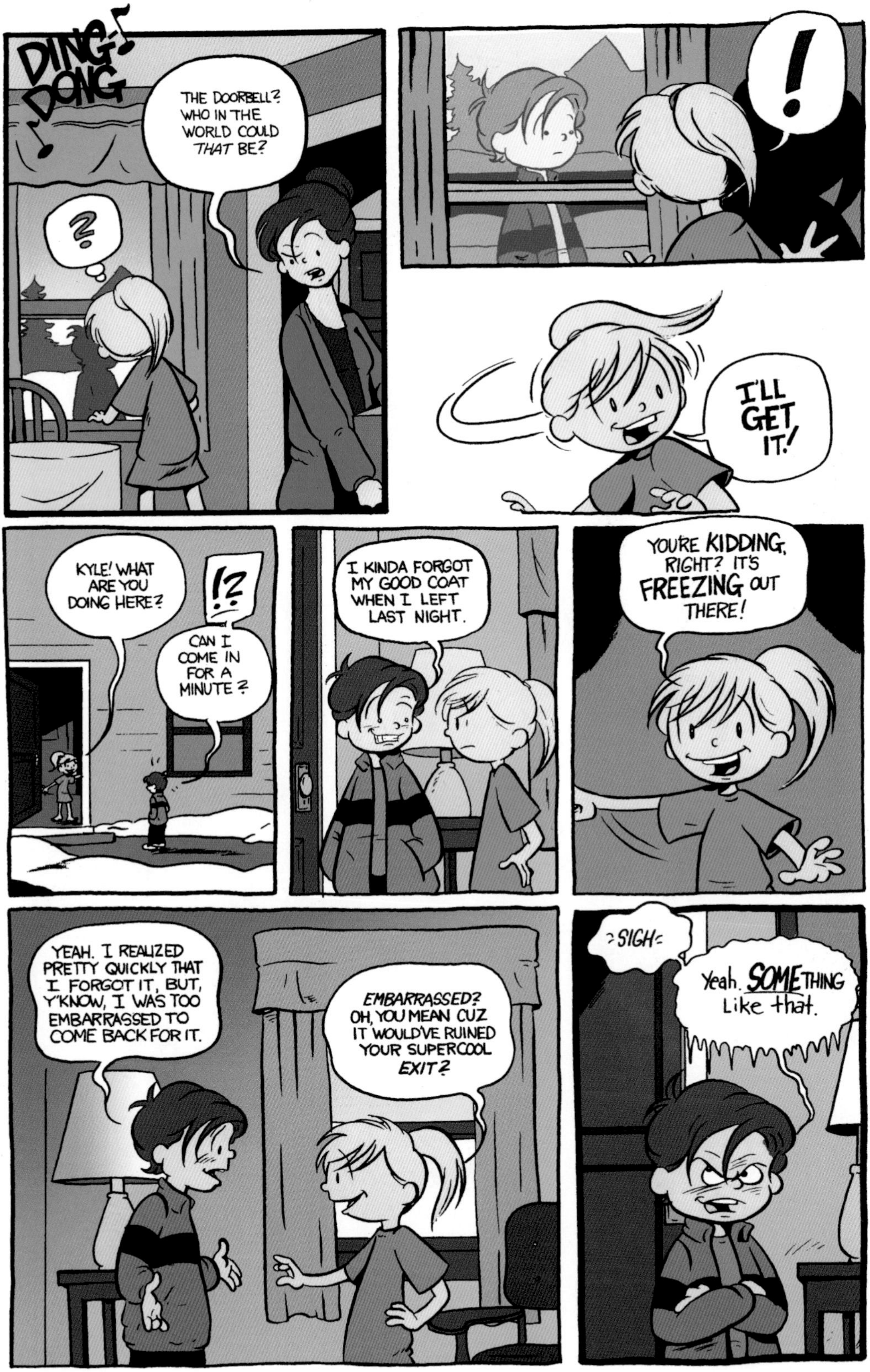
DING-DONG
THE DOORBELL? WHO IN THE WORLD COULD THAT BE?
?
!
I'LL GET IT!
KYLE! WHAT ARE YOU DOING HERE?
!?
CAN I COME IN FOR A MINUTE?
I KINDA FORGOT MY GOOD COAT WHEN I LEFT LAST NIGHT.
YOU'RE KIDDING, RIGHT? IT'S FREEZING OUT THERE!
YEAH. I REALIZED PRETTY QUICKLY THAT I FORGOT IT, BUT, Y'KNOW, I WAS TOO EMBARRASSED TO COME BACK FOR IT.
EMBARRASSED? OH, YOU MEAN CUZ IT WOULD'VE RUINED YOUR SUPERCOOL EXIT?
SIGH
Yeah. SOMETHING Like that.

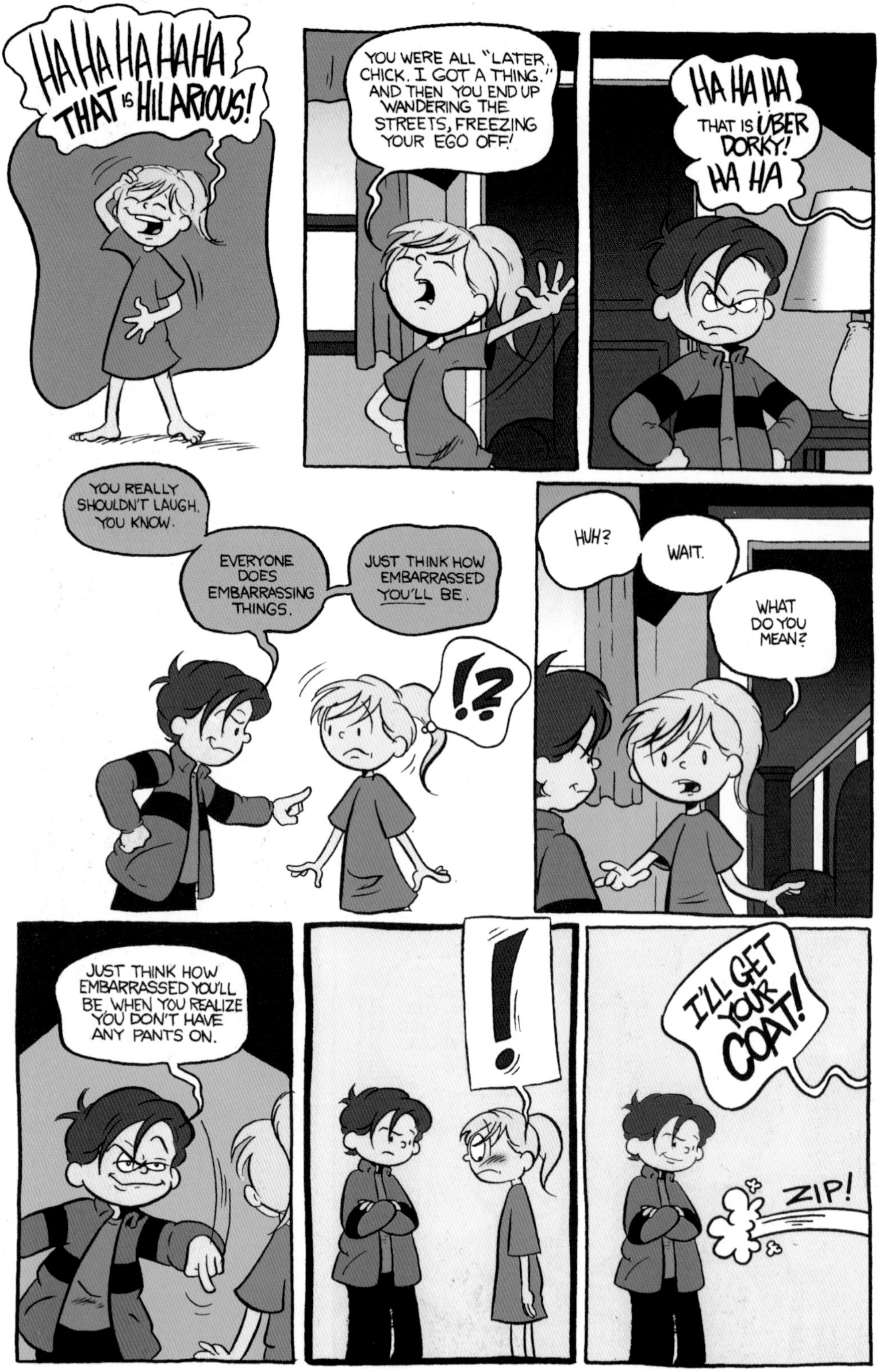
HA HA HA HA HA
THAT is HILARIOUS!
YOU WERE ALL "LATER, CHICK. I GOT A THING." AND THEN YOU END UP WANDERING THE STREETS, FREEZING YOUR EGO OFF!
HA HA HA
THAT IS ÜBER DORKY!
HA HA
YOU REALLY SHOULDN'T LAUGH, YOU KNOW.
EVERYONE DOES EMBARRASSING THINGS.
JUST THINK HOW EMBARRASSED YOU'LL BE.
!?
HUH?
WAIT.
WHAT DO YOU MEAN?
JUST THINK HOW EMBARRASSED YOU'LL BE, WHEN YOU REALIZE YOU DON'T HAVE ANY PANTS ON.
!
I'LL GET YOUR COAT!
ZIP!

PSST... TANNER...

WHO IS **THAT**?

HMM?

OH YEAH... THAT'S KYLE FISCHER. YOU REMEMBER JULIE REYNOLDS FROM INDIANA?

NO.

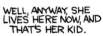
WELL, ANYWAY, SHE LIVES HERE NOW, AND THAT'S HER KID.

TEE HEE HEE

I **HATE** HIM.

!

OKAY. WELL, AS LONG AS YOU'RE NOT *OVERREACTING!*

HA HA

HEY, I HATE TO BREAK IT TO YOU, BUT THAT'S THE BOY WHO TOOK HER TO HER FIRST *DANCE.*

DEAR LORD! AND YOU HAD TO *WITNESS* IT?

WHAT WENT THROUGH YOUR *MIND?*

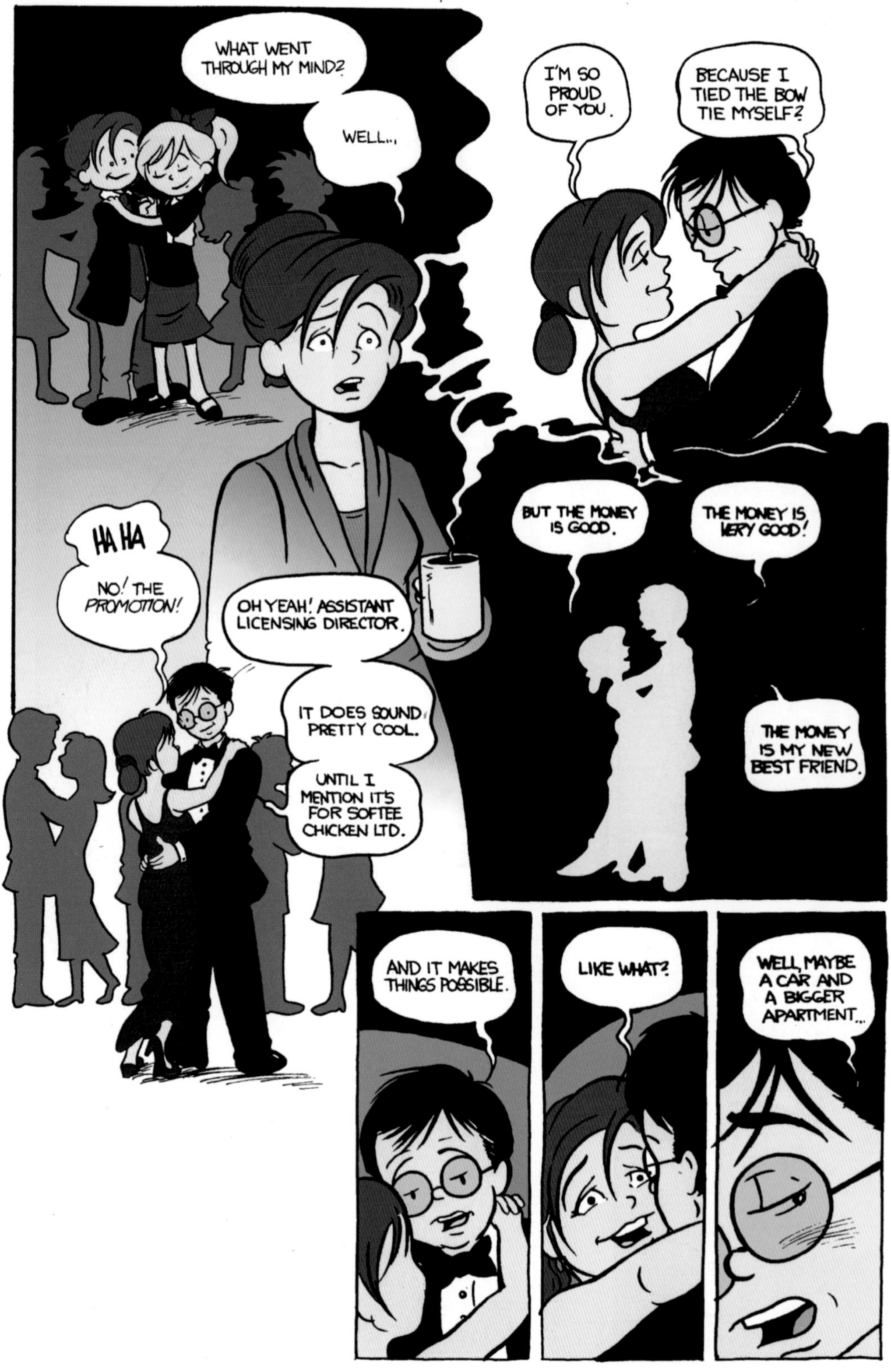

WHAT WENT THROUGH MY MIND?
WELL...
I'M SO PROUD OF YOU.
BECAUSE I TIED THE BOW TIE MYSELF?
HA HA
NO! THE *PROMOTION!*
OH YEAH! ASSISTANT LICENSING DIRECTOR.
IT DOES SOUND PRETTY COOL.
UNTIL I MENTION IT'S FOR SOFTEE CHICKEN LTD.
BUT THE MONEY IS GOOD.
THE MONEY IS *VERY* GOOD!
THE MONEY IS MY NEW BEST FRIEND.
AND IT MAKES THINGS POSSIBLE.
LIKE WHAT?
WELL, MAYBE A CAR AND A BIGGER APARTMENT...

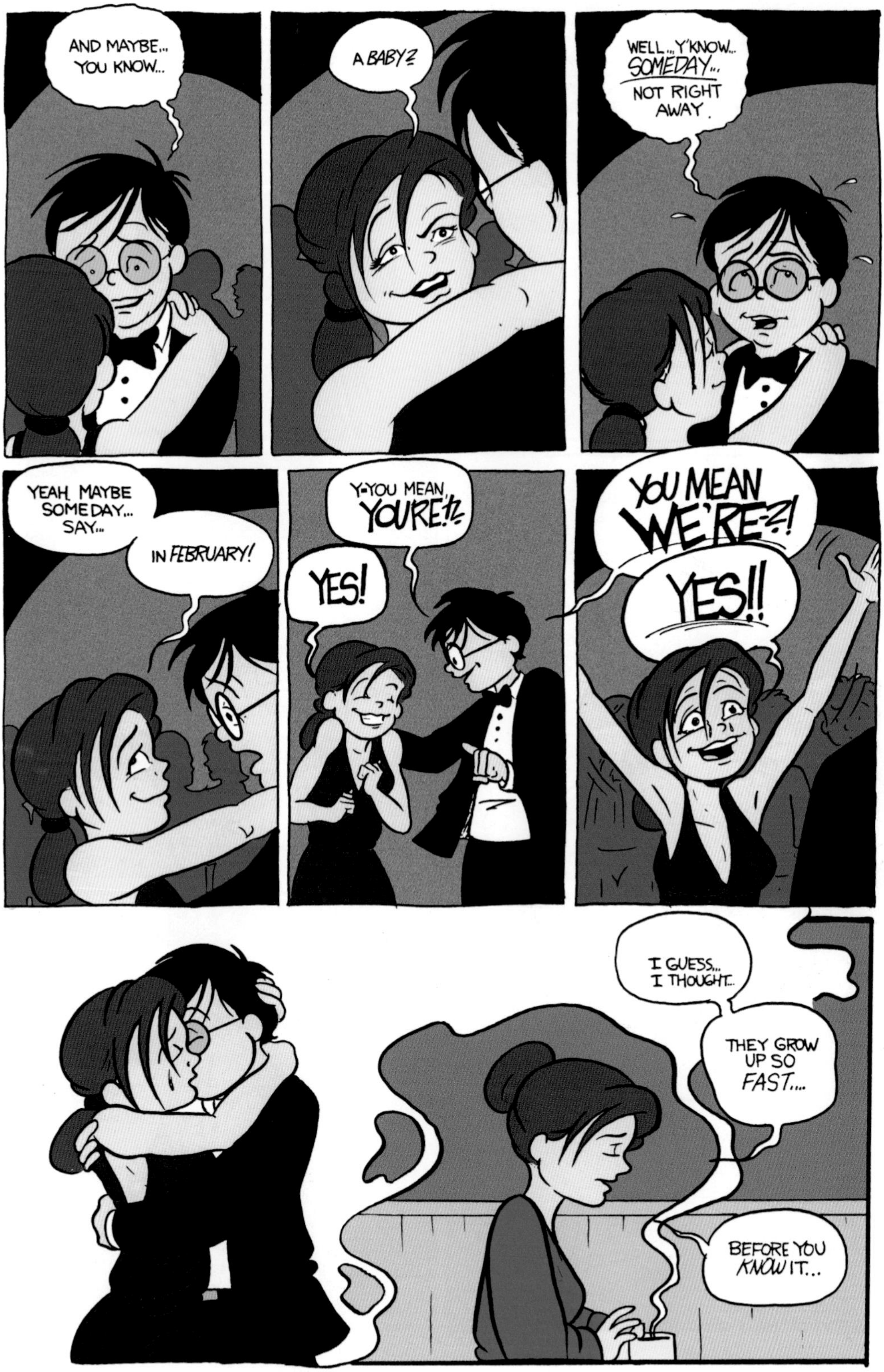
AND MAYBE... YOU KNOW...
A BABY?!
WELL... Y'KNOW... SOMEDAY... NOT RIGHT AWAY.
YEAH, MAYBE SOMEDAY... SAY...
IN FEBRUARY!
Y-YOU MEAN YOU'RE?!
YES!
YOU MEAN WE'RE?!
YES!!
I GUESS... I THOUGHT...
THEY GROW UP SO FAST....
BEFORE YOU KNOW IT...

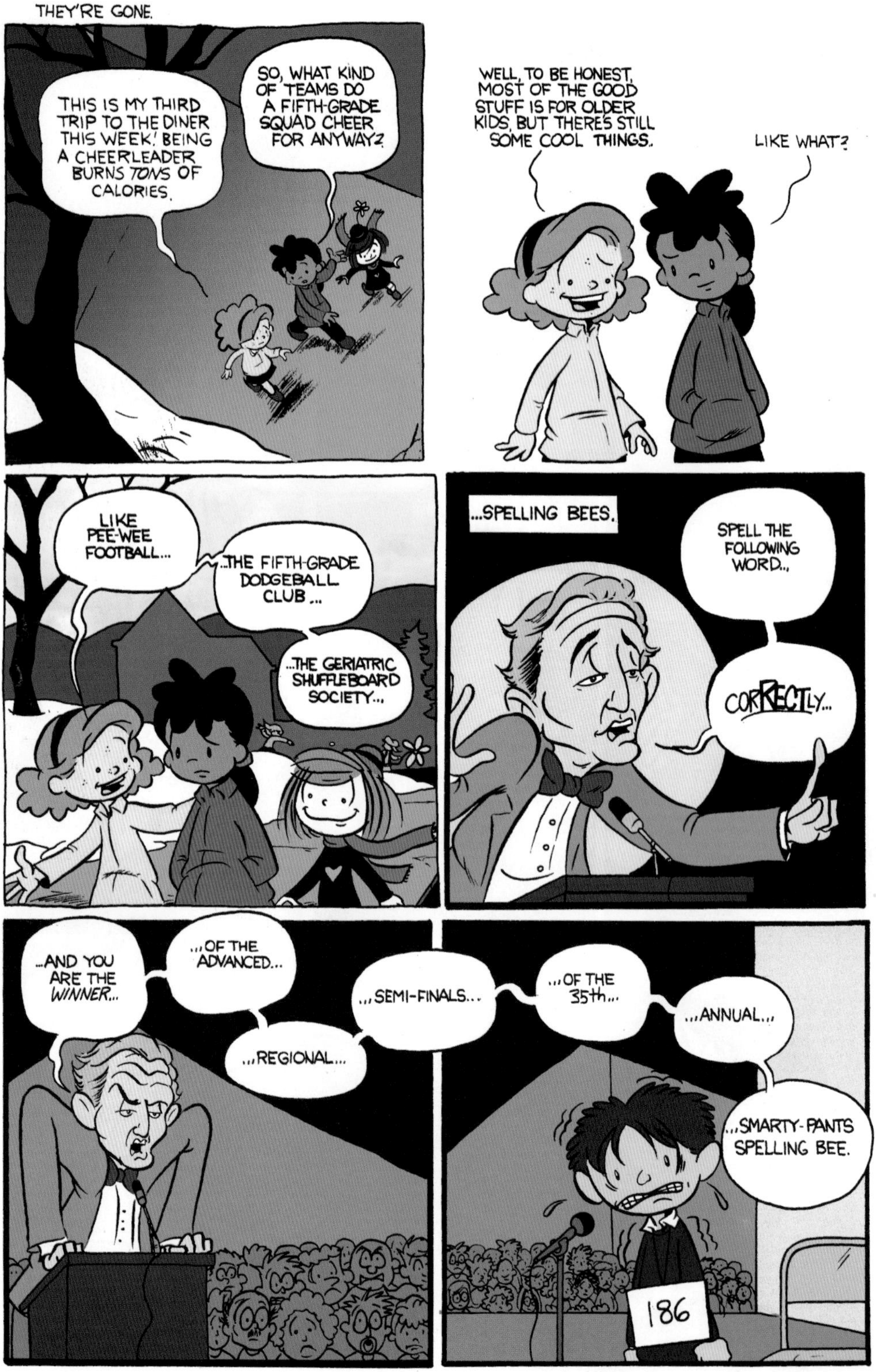
THEY'RE GONE.
THIS IS MY THIRD TRIP TO THE DINER THIS WEEK! BEING A CHEERLEADER BURNS TONS OF CALORIES.
SO, WHAT KIND OF TEAMS DO A FIFTH-GRADE SQUAD CHEER FOR ANYWAY?
WELL, TO BE HONEST, MOST OF THE GOOD STUFF IS FOR OLDER KIDS, BUT THERE'S STILL SOME COOL THINGS.
LIKE WHAT?
LIKE PEE-WEE FOOTBALL...
...THE FIFTH-GRADE DODGEBALL CLUB...
...THE GERIATRIC SHUFFLEBOARD SOCIETY...
...SPELLING BEES.
SPELL THE FOLLOWING WORD...
CORRECTLY...
...AND YOU ARE THE WINNER...
...OF THE ADVANCED...
...REGIONAL...
...SEMI-FINALS...
...OF THE 35th...
...ANNUAL...
...SMARTY-PANTS SPELLING BEE.
186

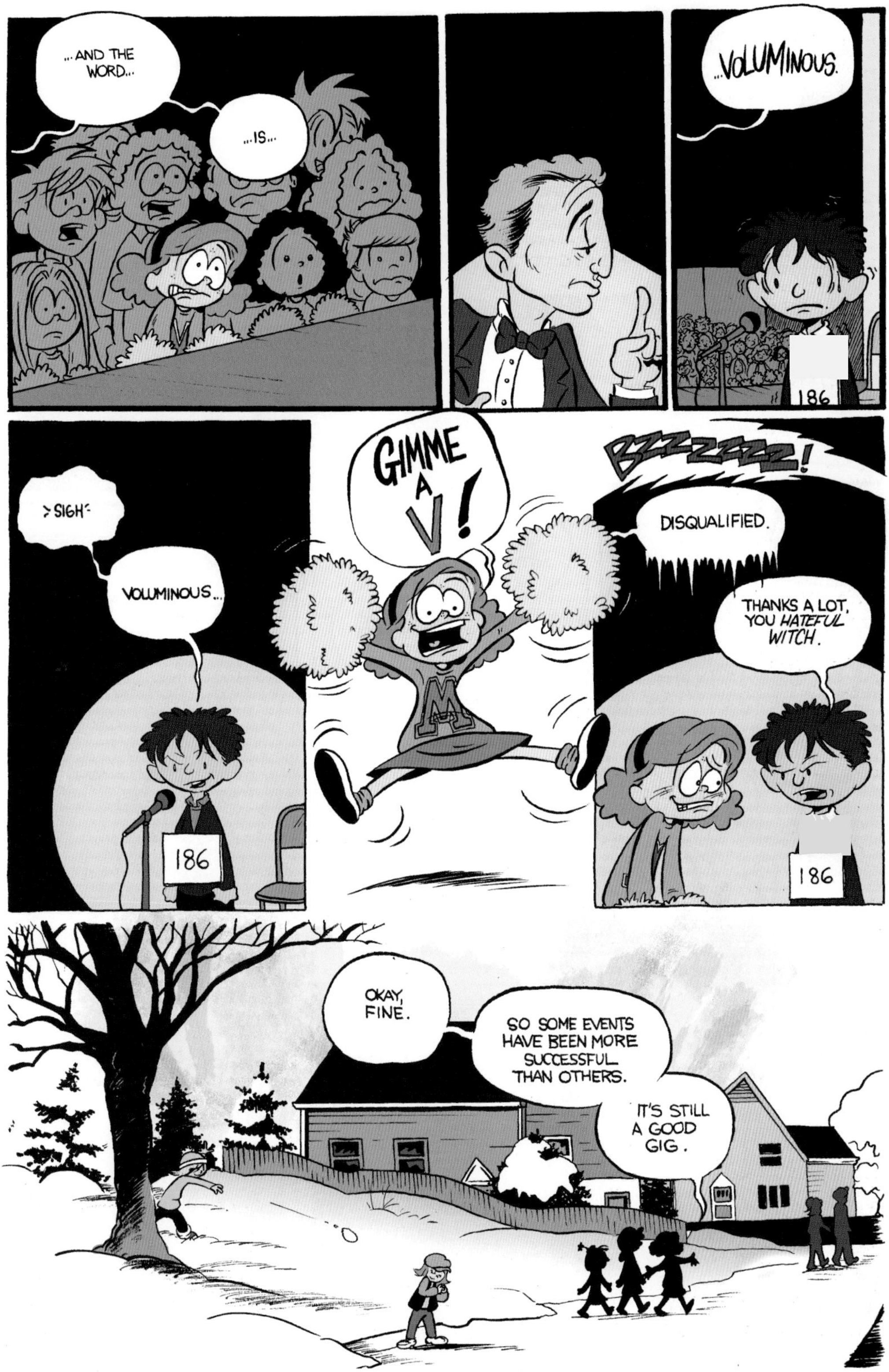
...AND THE WORD...
...IS...
...VOLUMINOUS.
186
GIMME A V!
BZZZZZZZZ!
DISQUALIFIED.
THANKS A LOT, YOU *HATEFUL* WITCH.
186
>SIGH<
VOLUMINOUS...
186
OKAY, FINE.
SO SOME EVENTS HAVE BEEN MORE SUCCESSFUL THAN OTHERS.
IT'S STILL A GOOD GIG.

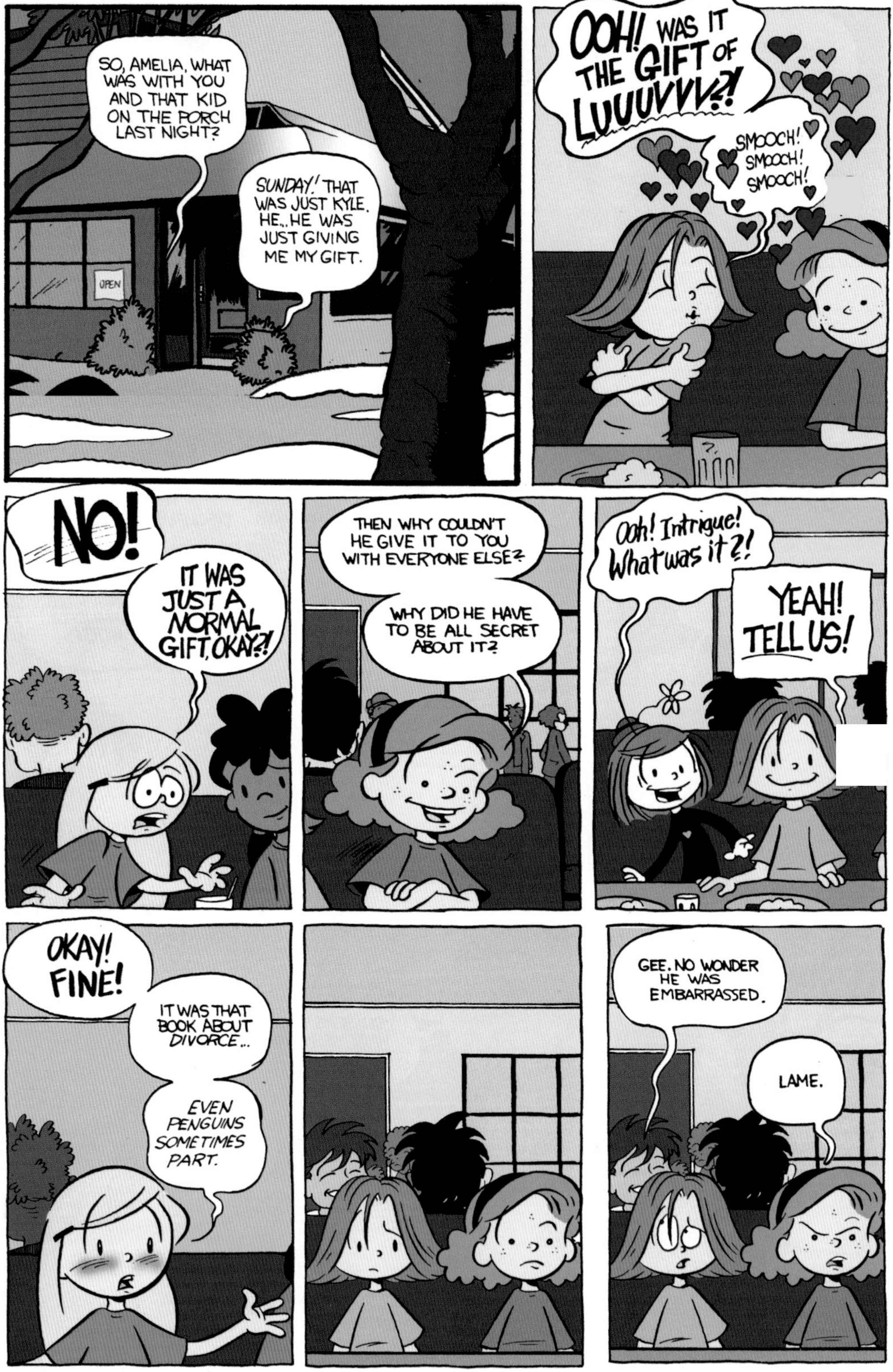
SO, AMELIA, WHAT WAS WITH YOU AND THAT KID ON THE PORCH LAST NIGHT?
SUNDAY! THAT WAS JUST KYLE. HE...HE WAS JUST GIVING ME MY GIFT.
OPEN
OOH! WAS IT THE GIFT OF LUUUVVV?!
SMOOCH! SMOOCH! SMOOCH!
NO!
IT WAS JUST A NORMAL GIFT, OKAY?!
THEN WHY COULDN'T HE GIVE IT TO YOU WITH EVERYONE ELSE?
WHY DID HE HAVE TO BE ALL SECRET ABOUT IT?
Ooh! Intrigue! What was it?!
YEAH! TELL US!
OKAY! FINE!
IT WAS THAT BOOK ABOUT DIVORCE...
EVEN PENGUINS SOMETIMES PART.
GEE. NO WONDER HE WAS EMBARRASSED.
LAME.

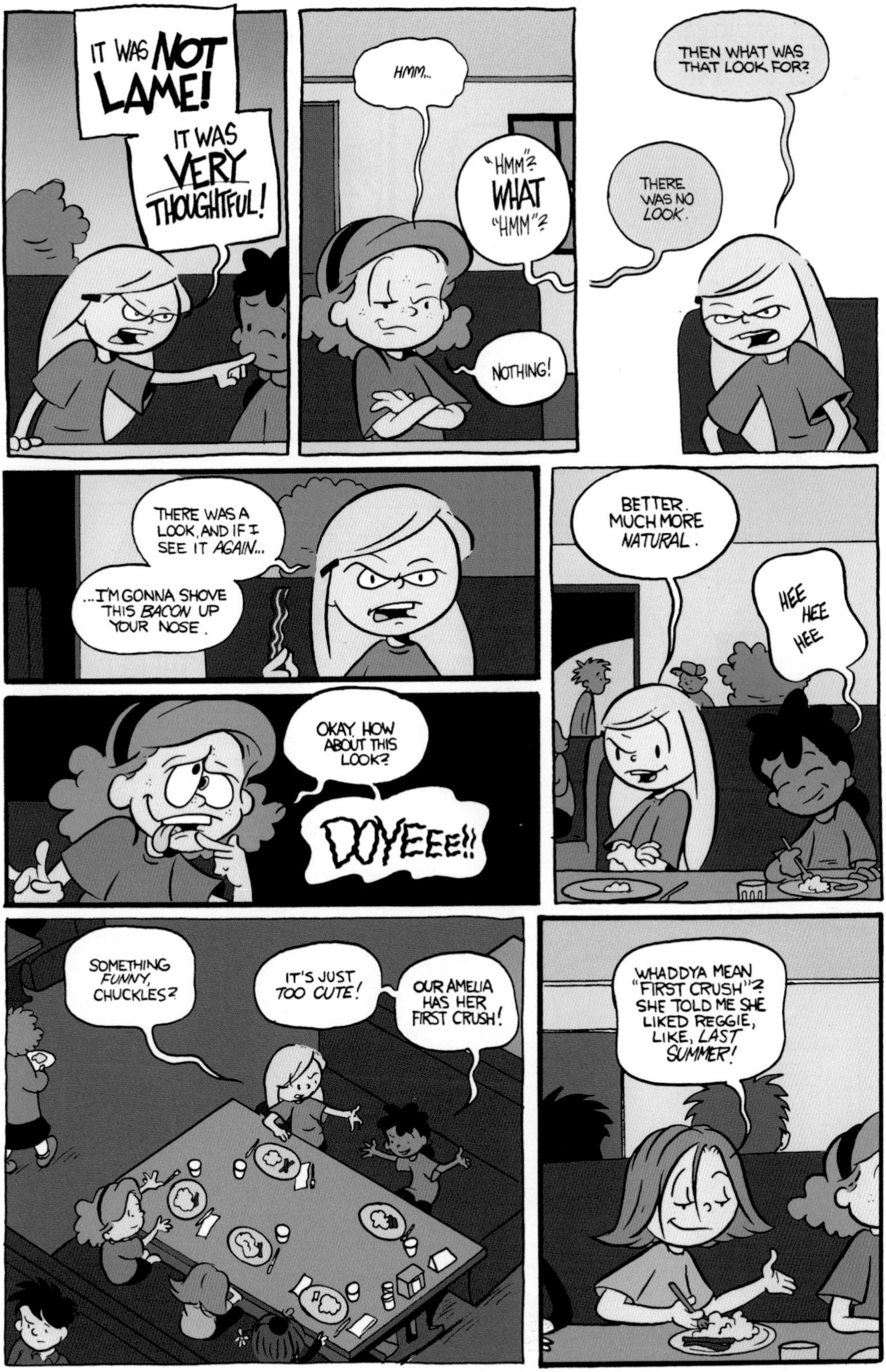
IT WAS NOT LAME!
IT WAS VERY THOUGHTFUL!
HMM...
"HMM"? WHAT "HMM"?
NOTHING!
THEN WHAT WAS THAT LOOK FOR?
THERE WAS NO LOOK.
THERE WAS A LOOK, AND IF I SEE IT AGAIN...
...I'M GONNA SHOVE THIS BACON UP YOUR NOSE.
BETTER. MUCH MORE NATURAL.
HEE HEE HEE
OKAY, HOW ABOUT THIS LOOK?
DOYEEE!!
SOMETHING FUNNY, CHUCKLES?
IT'S JUST TOO CUTE!
OUR AMELIA HAS HER FIRST CRUSH!
WHADDYA MEAN "FIRST CRUSH"? SHE TOLD ME SHE LIKED REGGIE, LIKE, LAST SUMMER!

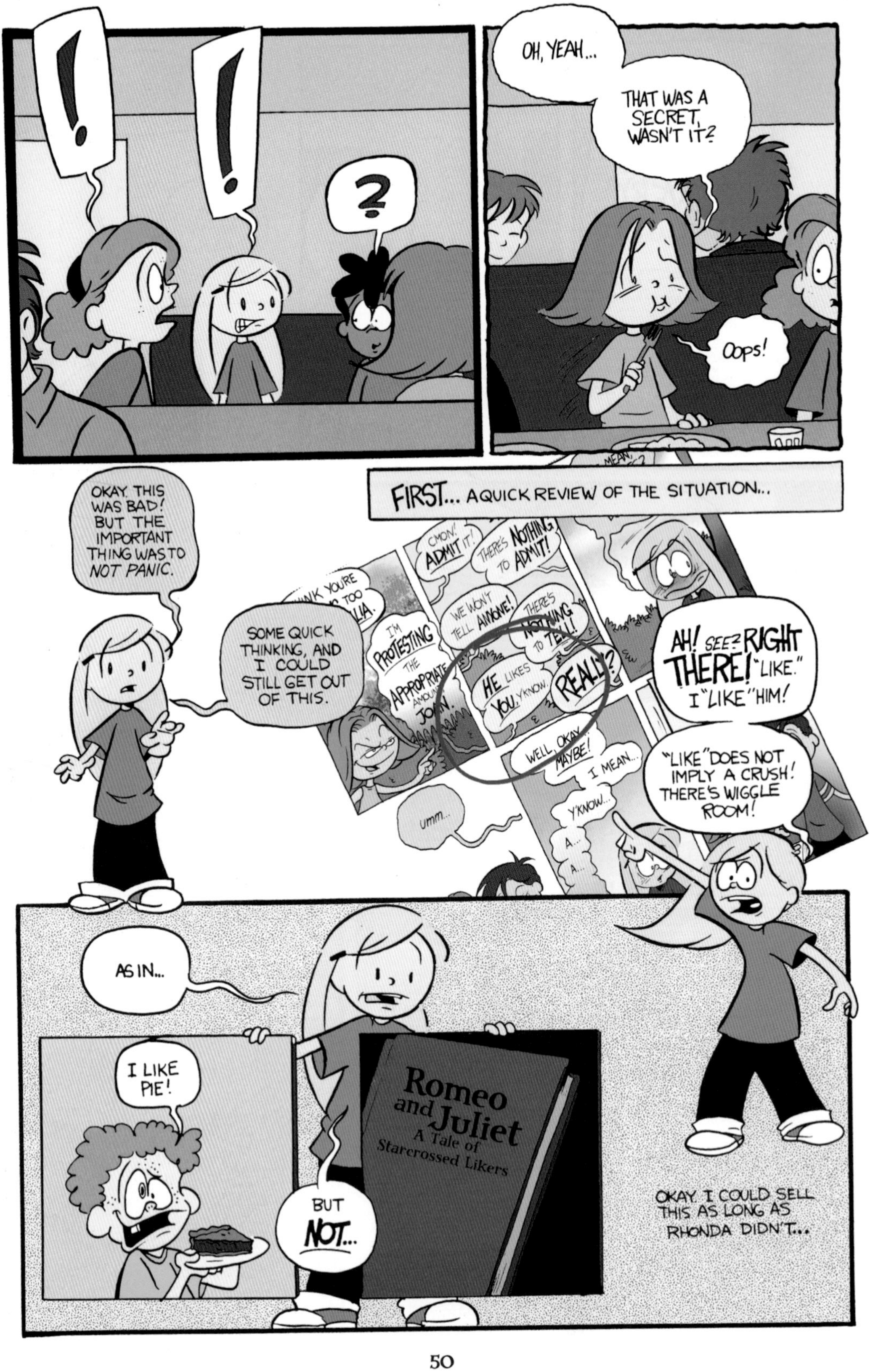
!
!
?
OH, YEAH...
THAT WAS A SECRET, WASN'T IT?
Oops!
FIRST... A QUICK REVIEW OF THE SITUATION...
OKAY. THIS WAS BAD! BUT THE IMPORTANT THING WAS TO NOT PANIC.
SOME QUICK THINKING, AND I COULD STILL GET OUT OF THIS.
C'MON! ADMIT IT!
THERE'S NOTHING TO ADMIT!
I'M PROTESTING THE APPROPRIATE
WE WON'T TELL ANYONE!
THERE'S NOTHING TO TELL!
HE LIKES YOU, Y'KNOW.
REALLY?
WELL, OKAY... MAYBE!
I MEAN...
Y'KNOW...
A...
A...
Umm...
AH! SEE? RIGHT THERE! "LIKE." I "LIKE" HIM!
"LIKE" DOES NOT IMPLY A CRUSH! THERE'S WIGGLE ROOM!
AS IN...
I LIKE PIE!
BUT NOT...
Romeo and Juliet
A Tale of Starcrossed Likers
OKAY. I COULD SELL THIS AS LONG AS RHONDA DIDN'T...

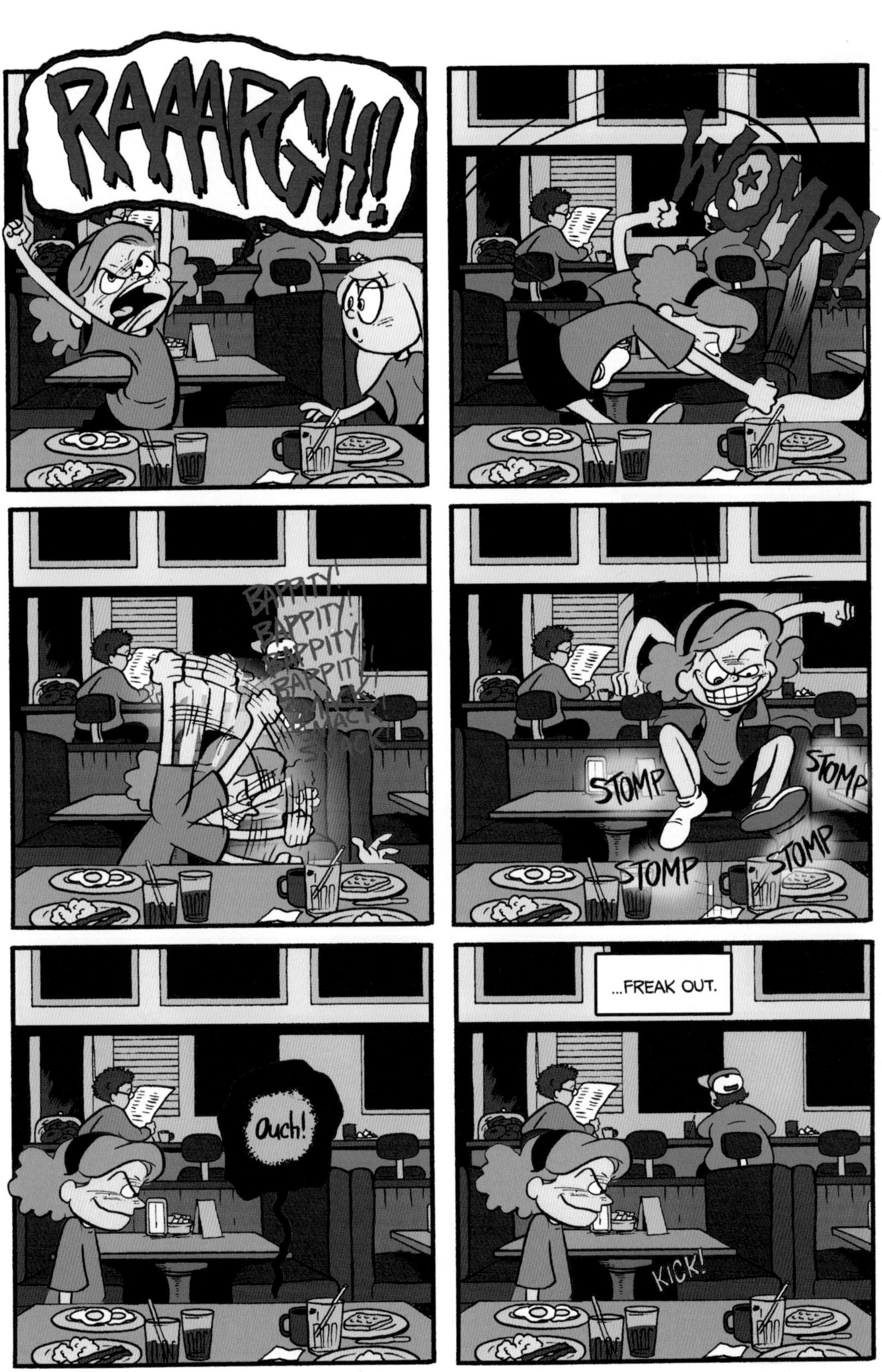
RAAARGH!
WOMP!
BAPPITY!
BAPPITY!
SMACK!
STOMP
STOMP
STOMP
STOMP
Ouch!
...FREAK OUT.
KICK!

BUT INSTEAD...

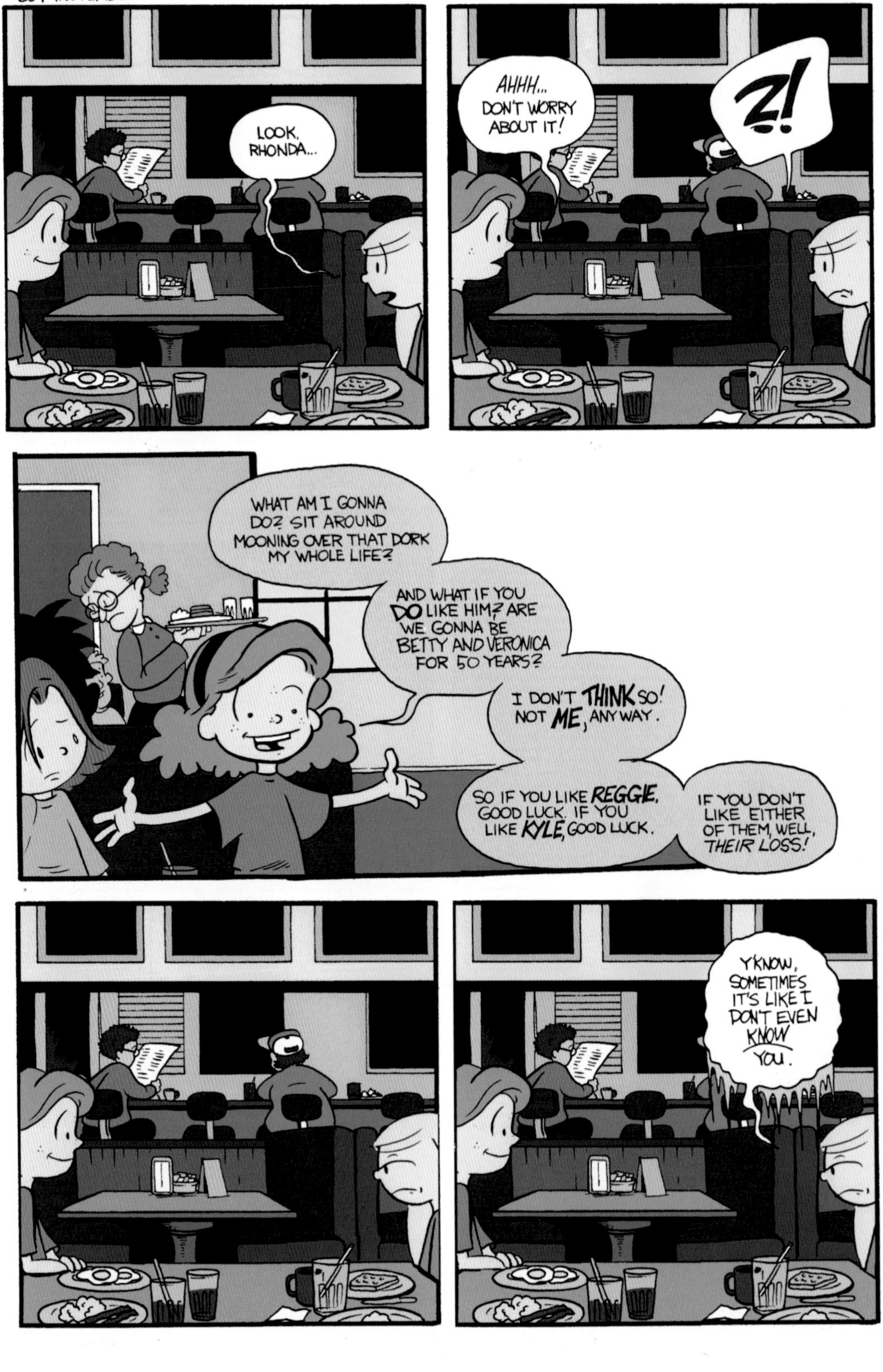
LOOK, RHONDA...
AHHH... DON'T WORRY ABOUT IT!
Z!
WHAT AM I GONNA DO? SIT AROUND MOONING OVER THAT DORK MY WHOLE LIFE?
AND WHAT IF YOU DO LIKE HIM? ARE WE GONNA BE BETTY AND VERONICA FOR 50 YEARS?
I DON'T THINK SO! NOT ME, ANYWAY.
SO IF YOU LIKE REGGIE, GOOD LUCK. IF YOU LIKE KYLE, GOOD LUCK.
IF YOU DON'T LIKE EITHER OF THEM, WELL, THEIR LOSS!
Y'KNOW, SOMETIMES IT'S LIKE I DON'T EVEN KNOW YOU.

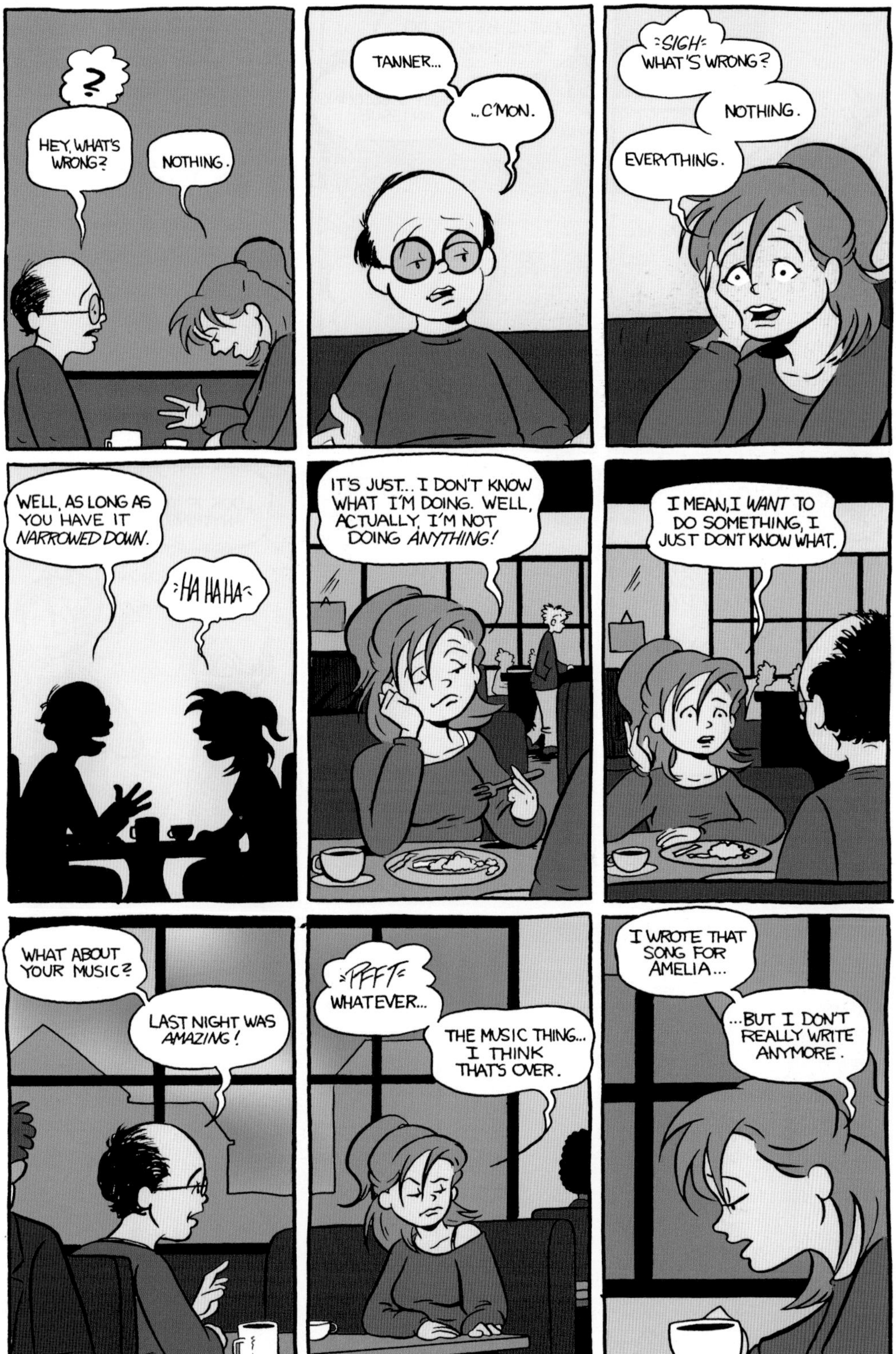
?
HEY, WHAT'S WRONG?
NOTHING.
TANNER...
...C'MON.
SIGH
WHAT'S WRONG?
NOTHING.
EVERYTHING.
WELL, AS LONG AS YOU HAVE IT NARROWED DOWN.
HA HA HA
IT'S JUST... I DON'T KNOW WHAT I'M DOING. WELL, ACTUALLY, I'M NOT DOING ANYTHING!
I MEAN, I WANT TO DO SOMETHING, I JUST DONT KNOW WHAT.
WHAT ABOUT YOUR MUSIC?
LAST NIGHT WAS AMAZING!
PFFT
WHATEVER...
THE MUSIC THING... I THINK THAT'S OVER.
I WROTE THAT SONG FOR AMELIA...
...BUT I DON'T REALLY WRITE ANYMORE.

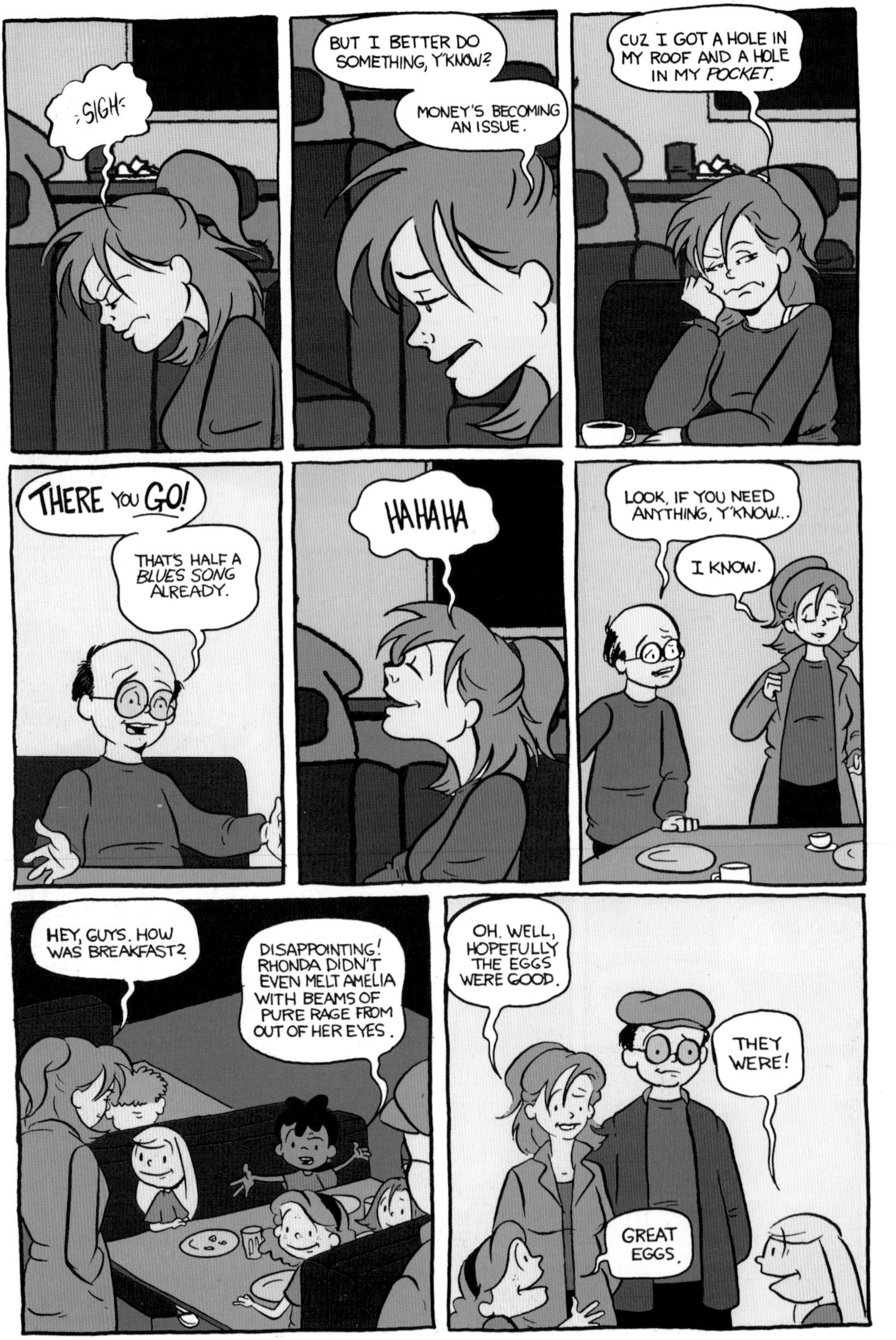
SIGH
BUT I BETTER DO SOMETHING, Y'KNOW?
MONEY'S BECOMING AN ISSUE.
CUZ I GOT A HOLE IN MY ROOF AND A HOLE IN MY *POCKET*.
THERE YOU GO!
THAT'S HALF A *BLUES* SONG ALREADY.
HAHAHA
LOOK, IF YOU NEED ANYTHING, Y'KNOW...
I KNOW.
HEY, GUYS. HOW WAS BREAKFAST?
DISAPPOINTING! RHONDA DIDN'T EVEN MELT AMELIA WITH BEAMS OF PURE RAGE FROM OUT OF HER EYES.
OH. WELL, HOPEFULLY THE EGGS WERE GOOD.
THEY WERE!
GREAT EGGS.

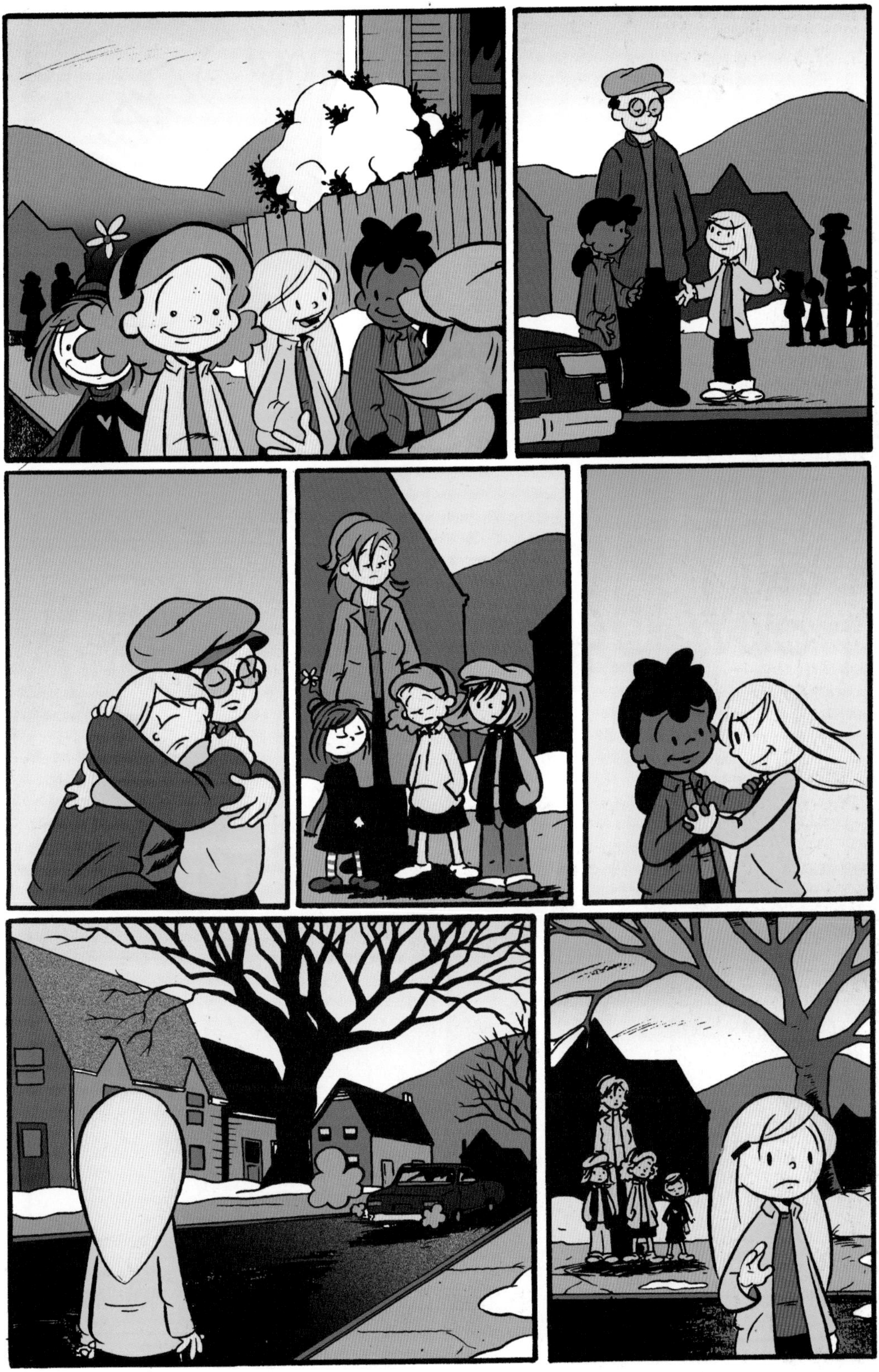

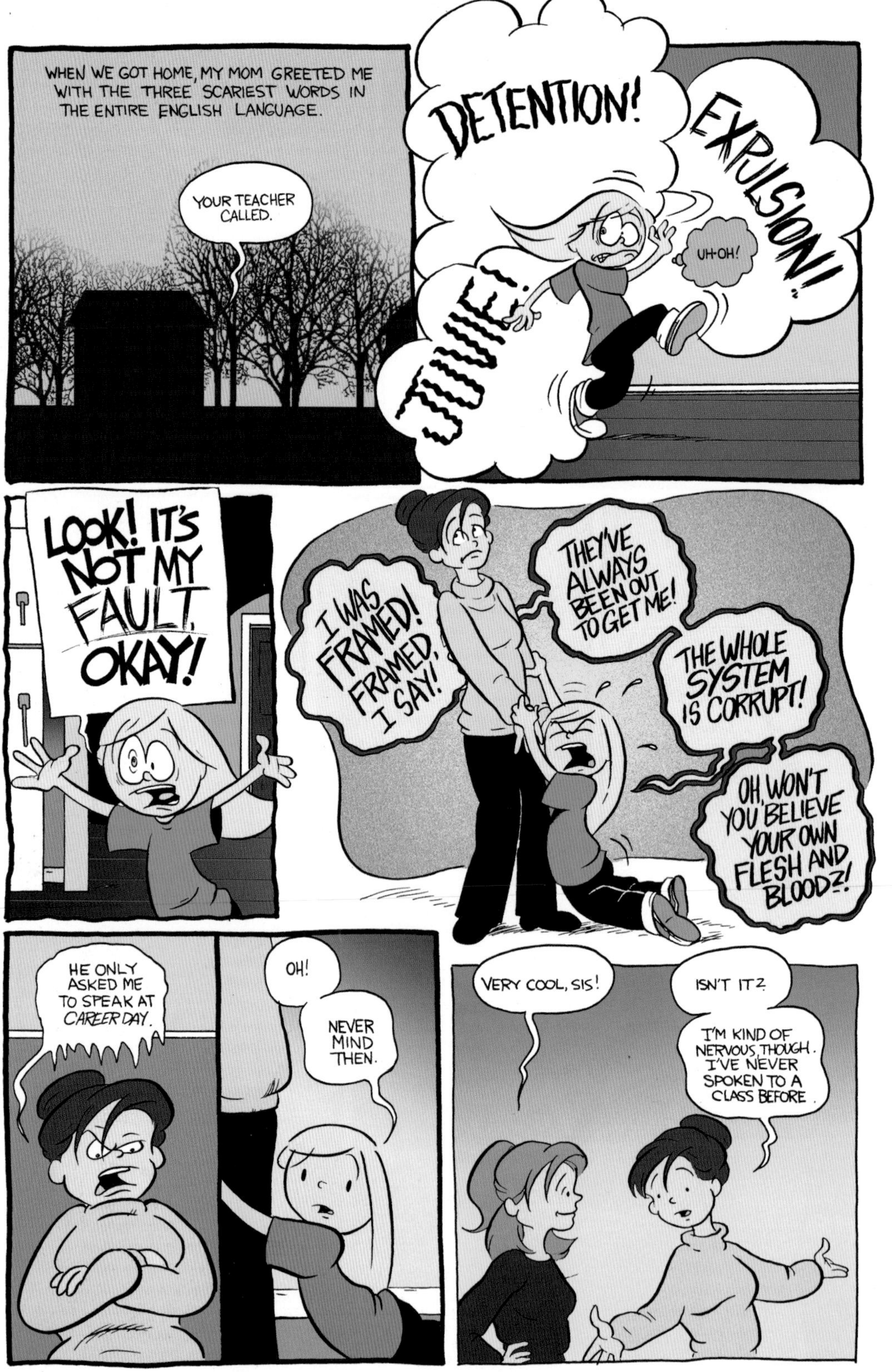

WHEN WE GOT HOME, MY MOM GREETED ME WITH THE THREE SCARIEST WORDS IN THE ENTIRE ENGLISH LANGUAGE.
YOUR TEACHER CALLED.
DETENTION!
EXPULSION!
JUVIE!
UH-OH!
LOOK! IT'S NOT MY FAULT, OKAY!
I WAS FRAMED! FRAMED, I SAY!
THEY'VE ALWAYS BEEN OUT TO GET ME!
THE WHOLE SYSTEM IS CORRUPT!
OH, WON'T YOU BELIEVE YOUR OWN FLESH AND BLOOD?!
HE ONLY ASKED ME TO SPEAK AT CAREER DAY.
OH!
NEVER MIND THEN.
VERY COOL, SIS!
ISN'T IT?
I'M KIND OF NERVOUS, THOUGH. I'VE NEVER SPOKEN TO A CLASS BEFORE.

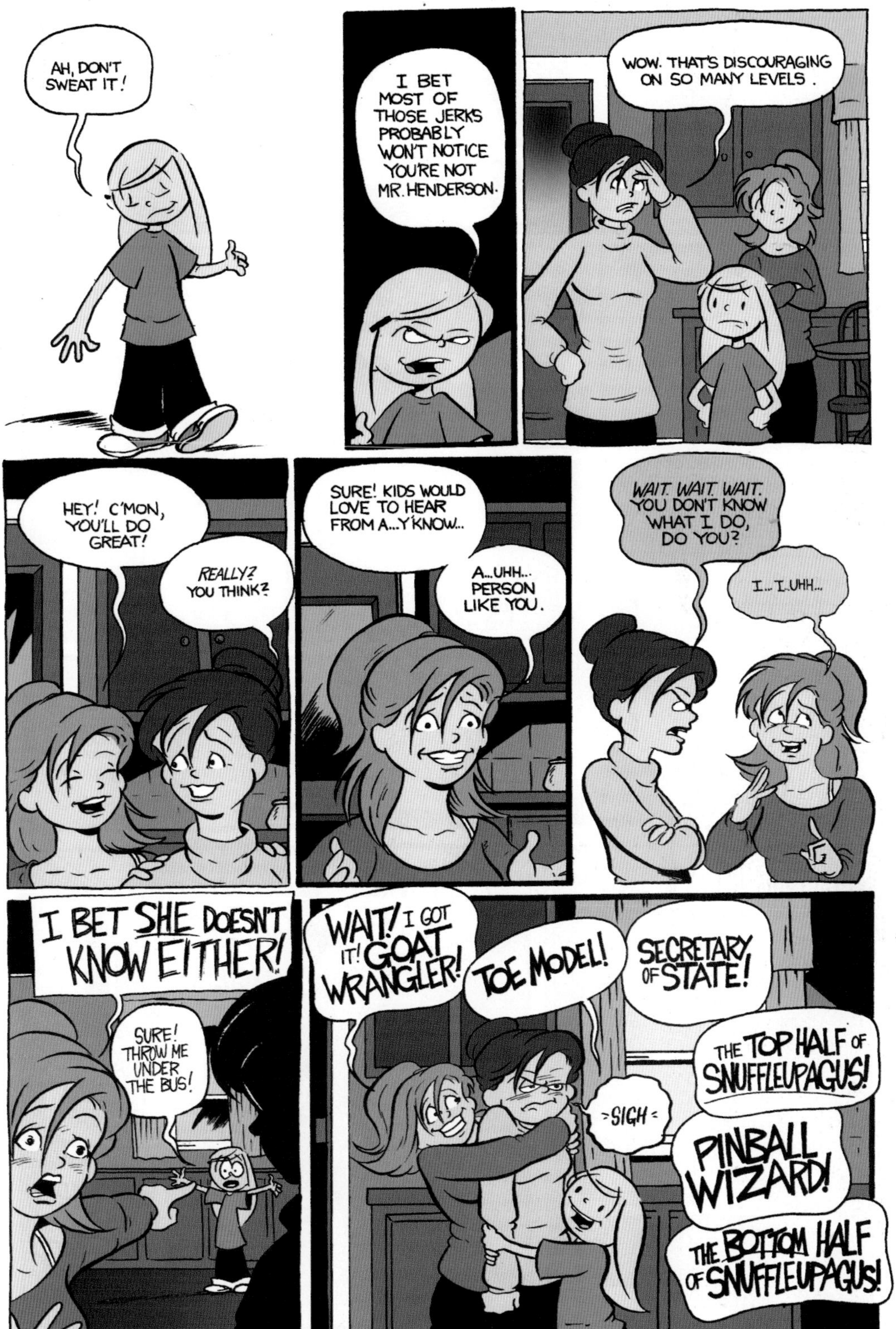
AH, DON'T SWEAT IT!
I BET MOST OF THOSE JERKS PROBABLY WON'T NOTICE YOU'RE NOT MR. HENDERSON.
WOW. THAT'S DISCOURAGING ON SO MANY LEVELS.
HEY! C'MON, YOU'LL DO GREAT!
REALLY? YOU THINK?
SURE! KIDS WOULD LOVE TO HEAR FROM A...Y'KNOW...
A...UHH... PERSON LIKE YOU.
WAIT. WAIT. WAIT. YOU DON'T KNOW WHAT I DO, DO YOU?
I... I...UHH...
I BET SHE DOESN'T KNOW EITHER!
SURE! THROW ME UNDER THE BUS!
WAIT! I GOT IT! GOAT WRANGLER!
TOE MODEL!
SECRETARY OF STATE!
THE TOP HALF OF SNUFFLEUPAGUS!
=SIGH=
PINBALL WIZARD!
THE BOTTOM HALF OF SNUFFLEUPAGUS!

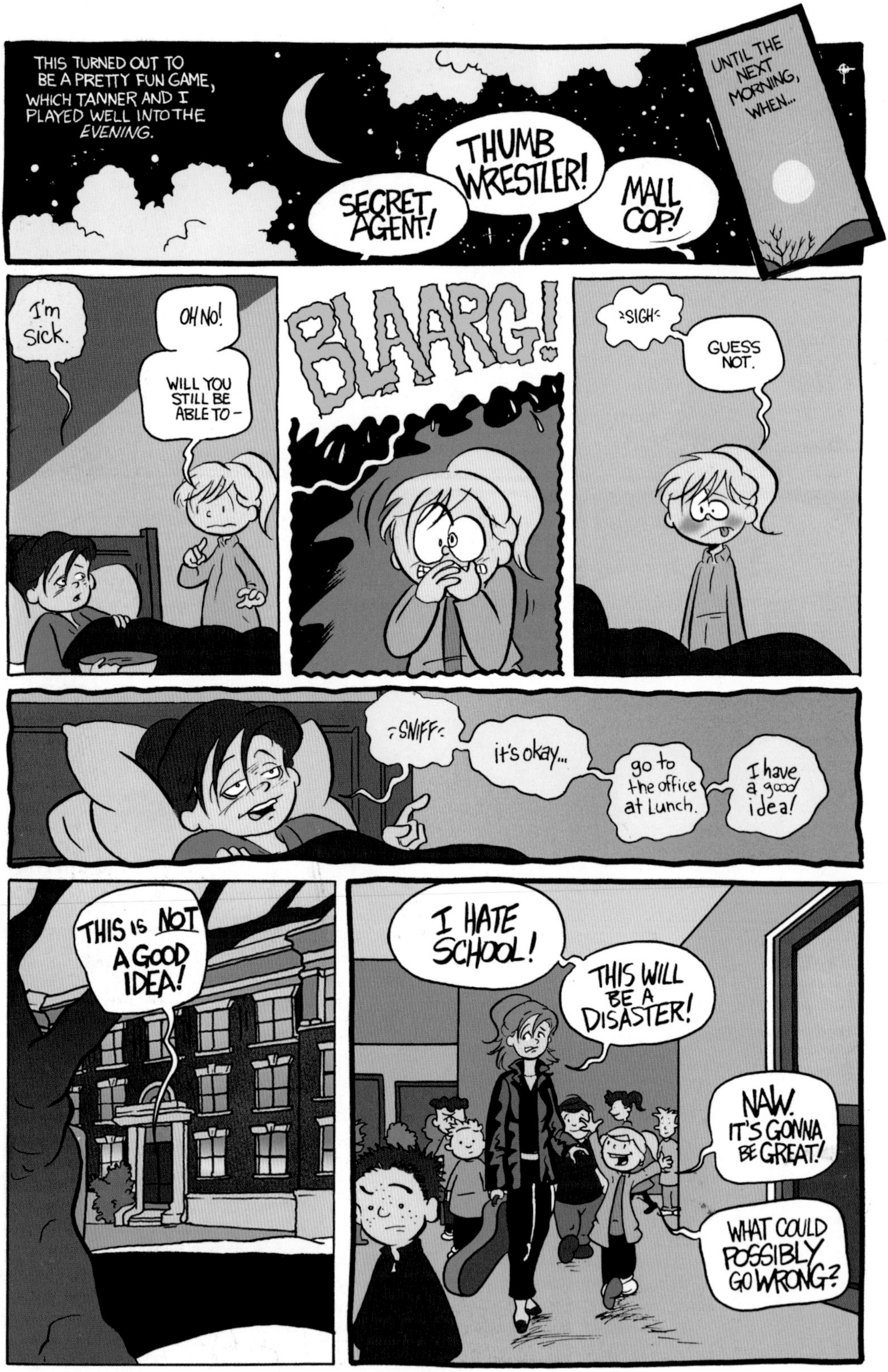
THIS TURNED OUT TO BE A PRETTY FUN GAME, WHICH TANNER AND I PLAYED WELL INTO THE EVENING.
SECRET AGENT!
THUMB WRESTLER!
MALL COP!
UNTIL THE NEXT MORNING, WHEN...
I'm sick.
OH NO!
WILL YOU STILL BE ABLE TO-
BLAARG!
SIGH
GUESS NOT.
SNIFF
it's okay...
go to the office at Lunch.
I have a good idea!
THIS IS NOT A GOOD IDEA!
I HATE SCHOOL!
THIS WILL BE A DISASTER!
NAW. IT'S GONNA BE GREAT!
WHAT COULD POSSIBLY GO WRONG?

ACTUALLY, I COULD THINK OF LIKE *FORTY-SIX* THINGS THAT COULD GO WRONG, AND, LIKE, SEVEN THAT WOULD END WITH US AS THE TOP STORY ON FOX NEWS. ANYWAY, THE DAY WAS SUPER BORING! TANNER WENT LAST, BEHIND A DENTIST, A POLICE MAN, AND TWO WEBMASTERS. BUT THEN, *FINALLY*...

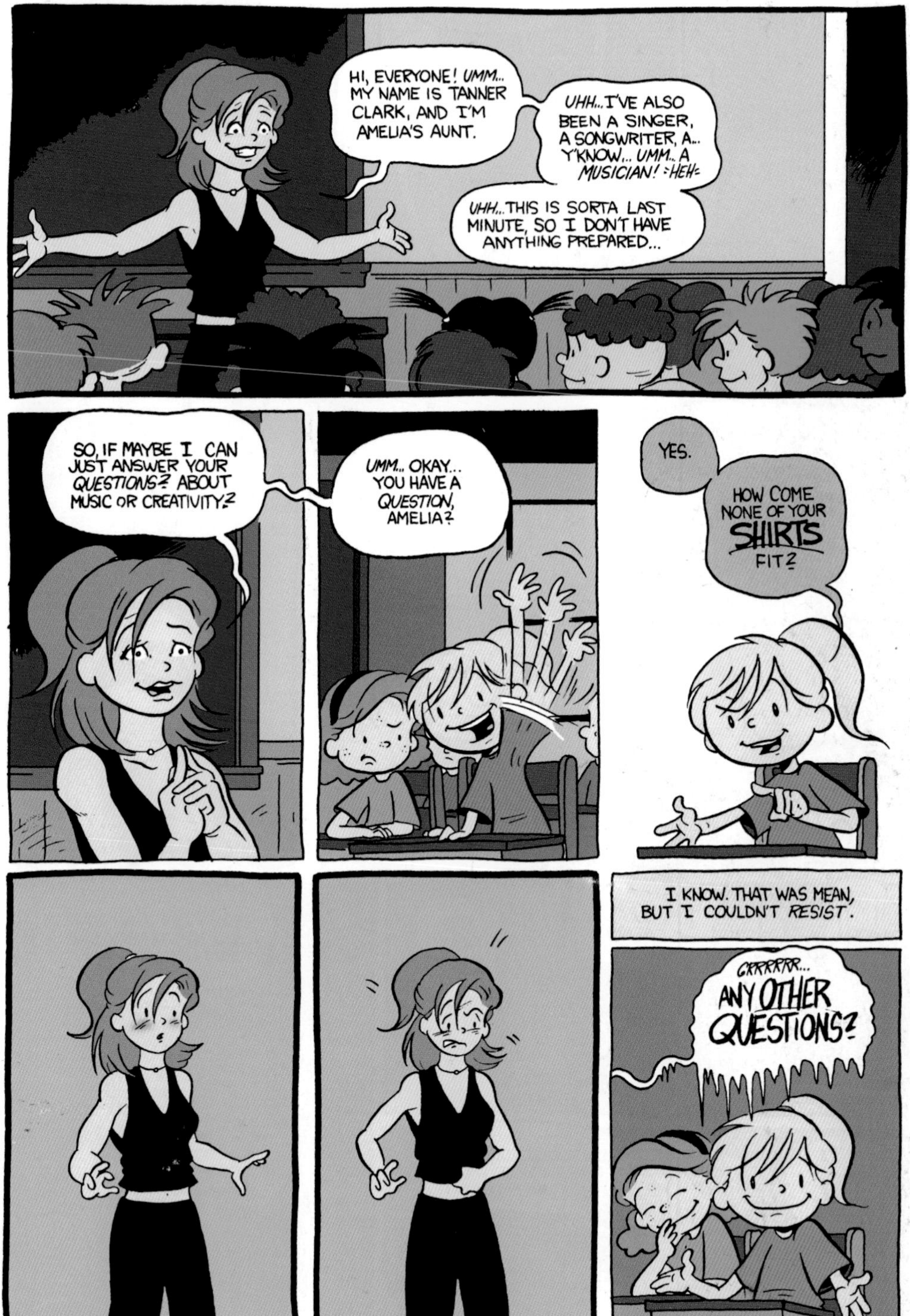

HI, EVERYONE! UMM... MY NAME IS TANNER CLARK, AND I'M AMELIA'S AUNT.
UHH... I'VE ALSO BEEN A SINGER, A SONGWRITER, A... Y'KNOW... UMM... A MUSICIAN! =HEH=
UHH... THIS IS SORTA LAST MINUTE, SO I DON'T HAVE ANYTHING PREPARED...
SO, IF MAYBE I CAN JUST ANSWER YOUR QUESTIONS? ABOUT MUSIC OR CREATIVITY?
UMM... OKAY... YOU HAVE A QUESTION, AMELIA?
YES.
HOW COME NONE OF YOUR SHIRTS FIT?
I KNOW. THAT WAS MEAN, BUT I COULDN'T RESIST.
GRRRRRR... ANY OTHER QUESTIONS?

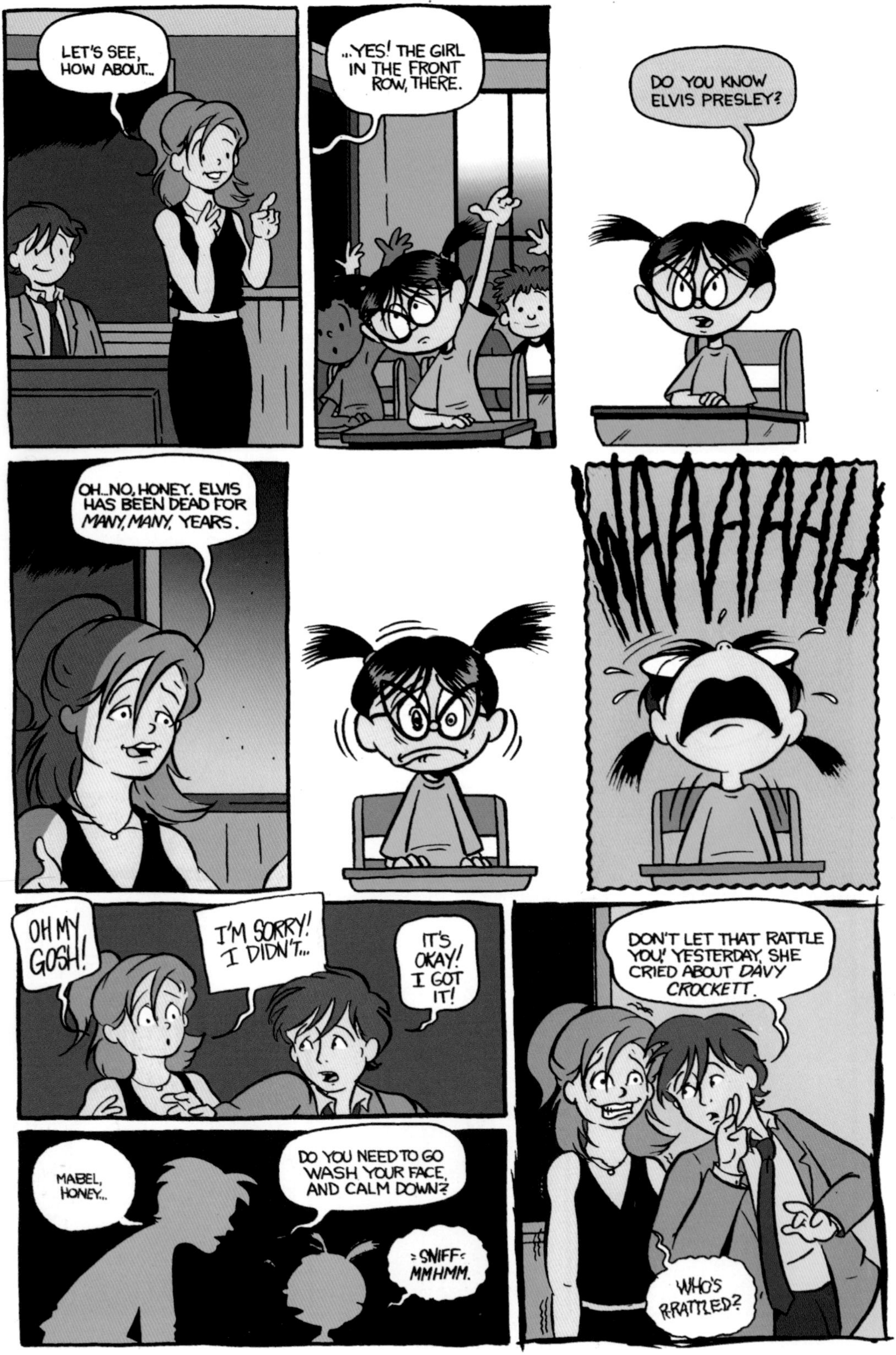
LET'S SEE, HOW ABOUT...
...YES! THE GIRL IN THE FRONT ROW, THERE.
DO YOU KNOW ELVIS PRESLEY?
OH...NO, HONEY. ELVIS HAS BEEN DEAD FOR MANY, MANY, YEARS.
WAAAAAH
OH MY GOSH!
I'M SORRY! I DIDN'T...
IT'S OKAY! I GOT IT!
MABEL, HONEY...
DO YOU NEED TO GO WASH YOUR FACE, AND CALM DOWN?
SNIFF MMHMM.
DON'T LET THAT RATTLE YOU! YESTERDAY, SHE CRIED ABOUT DAVY CROCKETT.
WHO'S R-RATTLED?

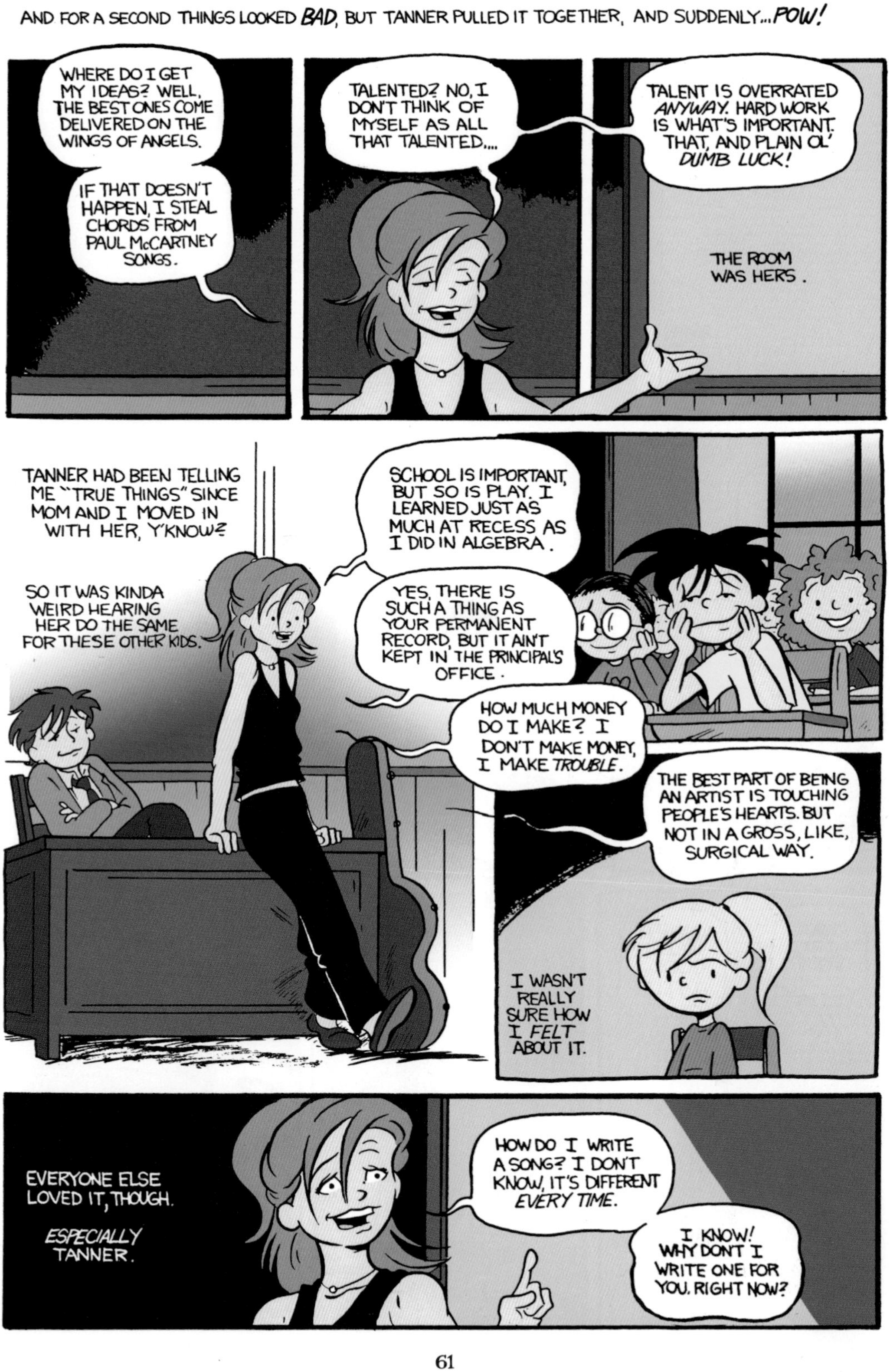

AND FOR A SECOND THINGS LOOKED *BAD*, BUT TANNER PULLED IT TOGETHER, AND SUDDENLY... *POW!*
WHERE DO I GET MY IDEAS? WELL, THE BEST ONES COME DELIVERED ON THE WINGS OF ANGELS.
IF THAT DOESN'T HAPPEN, I STEAL CHORDS FROM PAUL McCARTNEY SONGS.
TALENTED? NO, I DON'T THINK OF MYSELF AS ALL THAT TALENTED....
TALENT IS OVERRATED *ANYWAY*. HARD WORK IS WHAT'S IMPORTANT. THAT, AND PLAIN OL' *DUMB LUCK!*
THE ROOM WAS HERS.
TANNER HAD BEEN TELLING ME "TRUE THINGS" SINCE MOM AND I MOVED IN WITH HER, Y'KNOW?
SO IT WAS KINDA WEIRD HEARING HER DO THE SAME FOR THESE OTHER KIDS.
SCHOOL IS IMPORTANT, BUT SO IS PLAY. I LEARNED JUST AS MUCH AT RECESS AS I DID IN ALGEBRA.
YES, THERE IS SUCH A THING AS YOUR PERMANENT RECORD, BUT IT AIN'T KEPT IN THE PRINCIPAL'S OFFICE.
HOW MUCH MONEY DO I MAKE? I DON'T MAKE MONEY, I MAKE *TROUBLE*.
THE BEST PART OF BEING AN ARTIST IS TOUCHING PEOPLE'S HEARTS. BUT NOT IN A GROSS, LIKE, SURGICAL WAY.
I WASN'T REALLY SURE HOW I *FELT* ABOUT IT.
EVERYONE ELSE LOVED IT, THOUGH.
ESPECIALLY TANNER.
HOW DO I WRITE A SONG? I DON'T KNOW, IT'S DIFFERENT *EVERY TIME*.
I KNOW! WHY DON'T I WRITE ONE FOR YOU. RIGHT NOW?

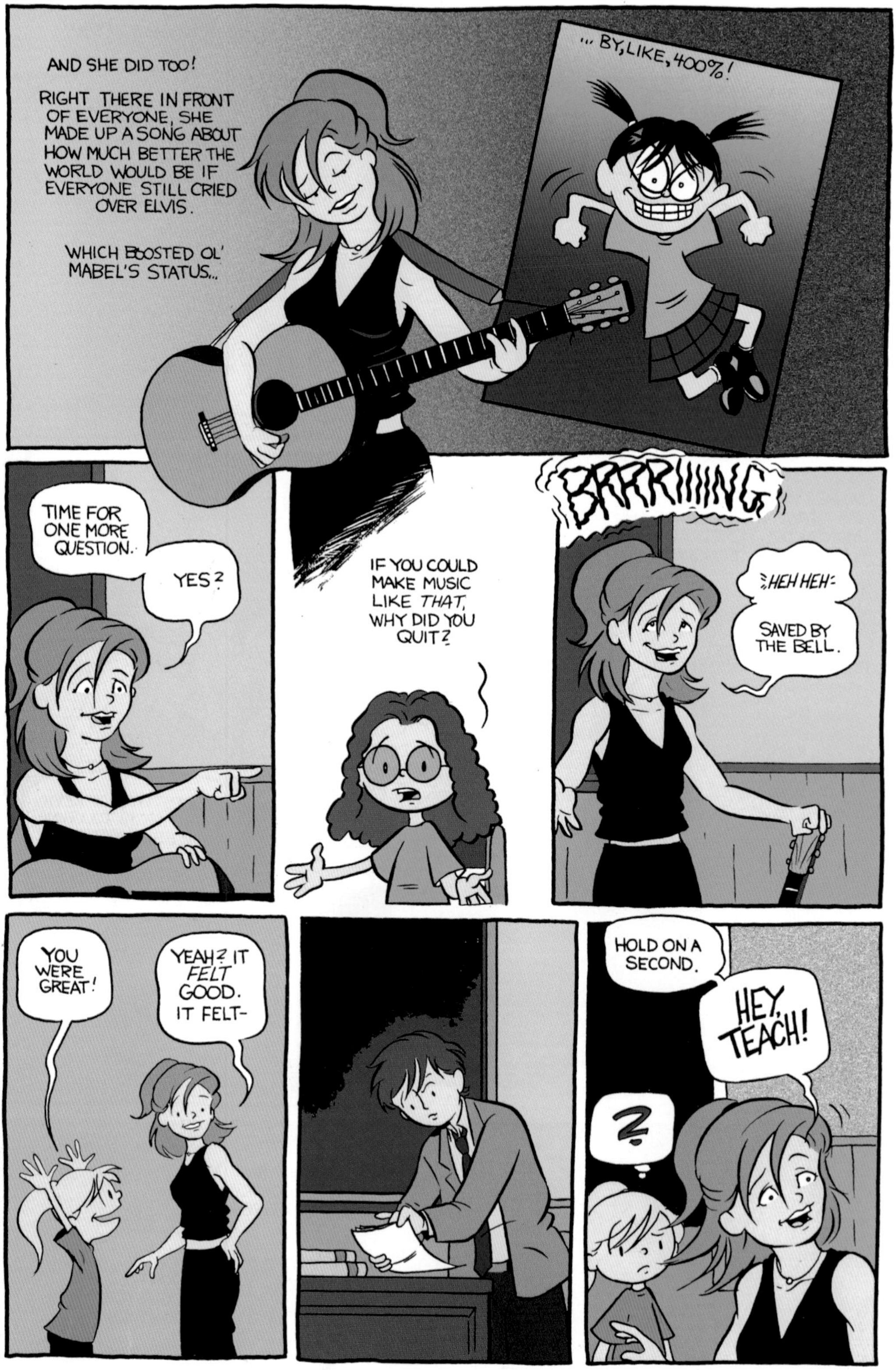
AND SHE DID TOO!
RIGHT THERE IN FRONT OF EVERYONE, SHE MADE UP A SONG ABOUT HOW MUCH BETTER THE WORLD WOULD BE IF EVERYONE STILL CRIED OVER ELVIS.
WHICH BOOSTED OL' MABEL'S STATUS...
... BY, LIKE, 400%!
TIME FOR ONE MORE QUESTION.
YES?
IF YOU COULD MAKE MUSIC LIKE *THAT*, WHY DID YOU QUIT?
BRRRIIIING
HEH HEH
SAVED BY THE BELL.
YOU WERE GREAT!
YEAH? IT *FELT* GOOD. IT FELT-
HOLD ON A SECOND.
HEY, TEACH!
?

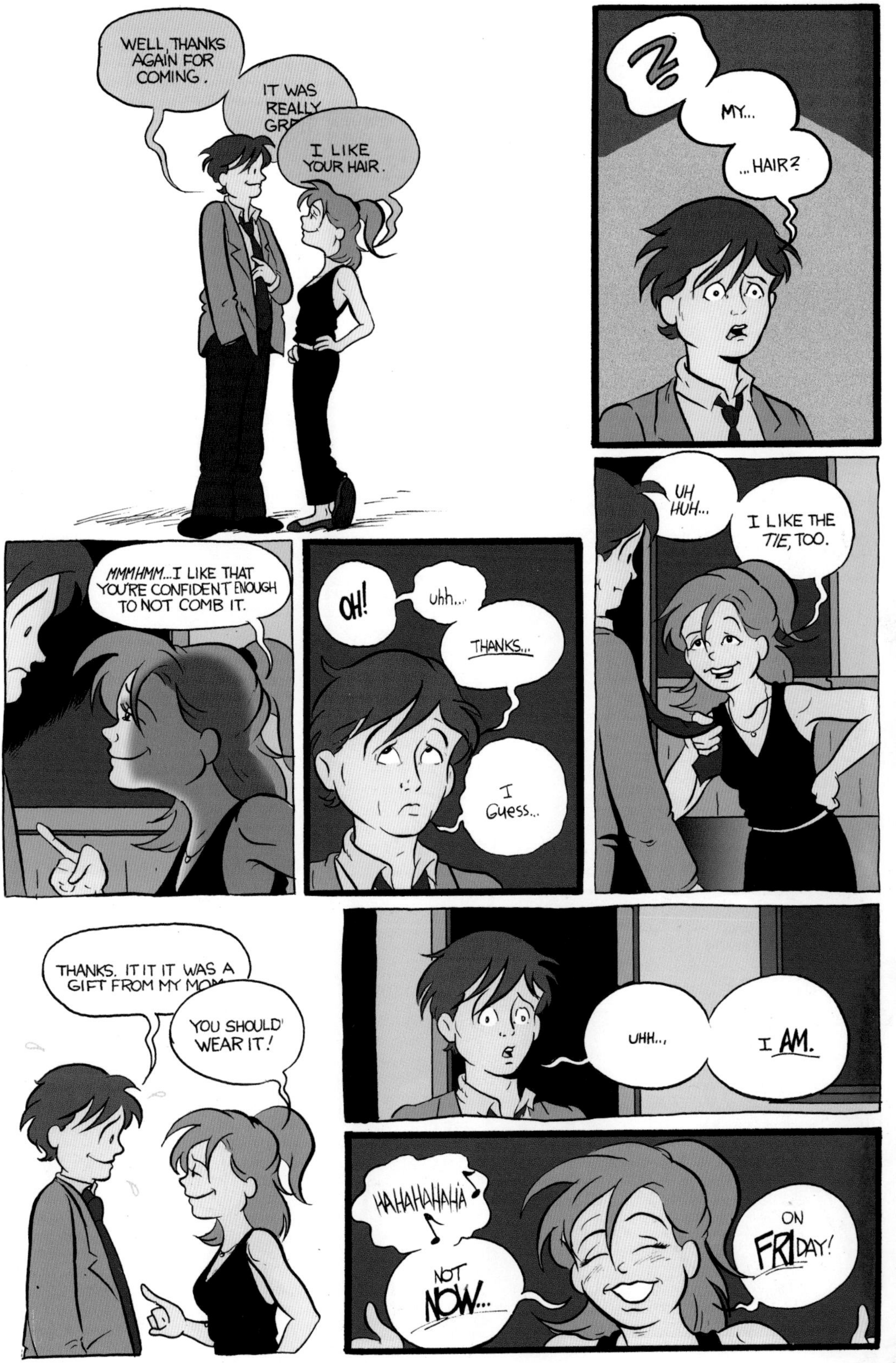

WELL, THANKS AGAIN FOR COMING.
IT WAS REALLY GR
I LIKE YOUR HAIR.
?
MY...
...HAIR?
MMMHMM...I LIKE THAT YOU'RE CONFIDENT ENOUGH TO NOT COMB IT.
OH!
Uhh...
THANKS...
I Guess...
UH HUH...
I LIKE THE TIE, TOO.
THANKS. IT IT IT WAS A GIFT FROM MY MOM
YOU SHOULD WEAR IT!
UHH...
I AM.
HAHAHAHAHA
NOT NOW...
ON FRIDAY!

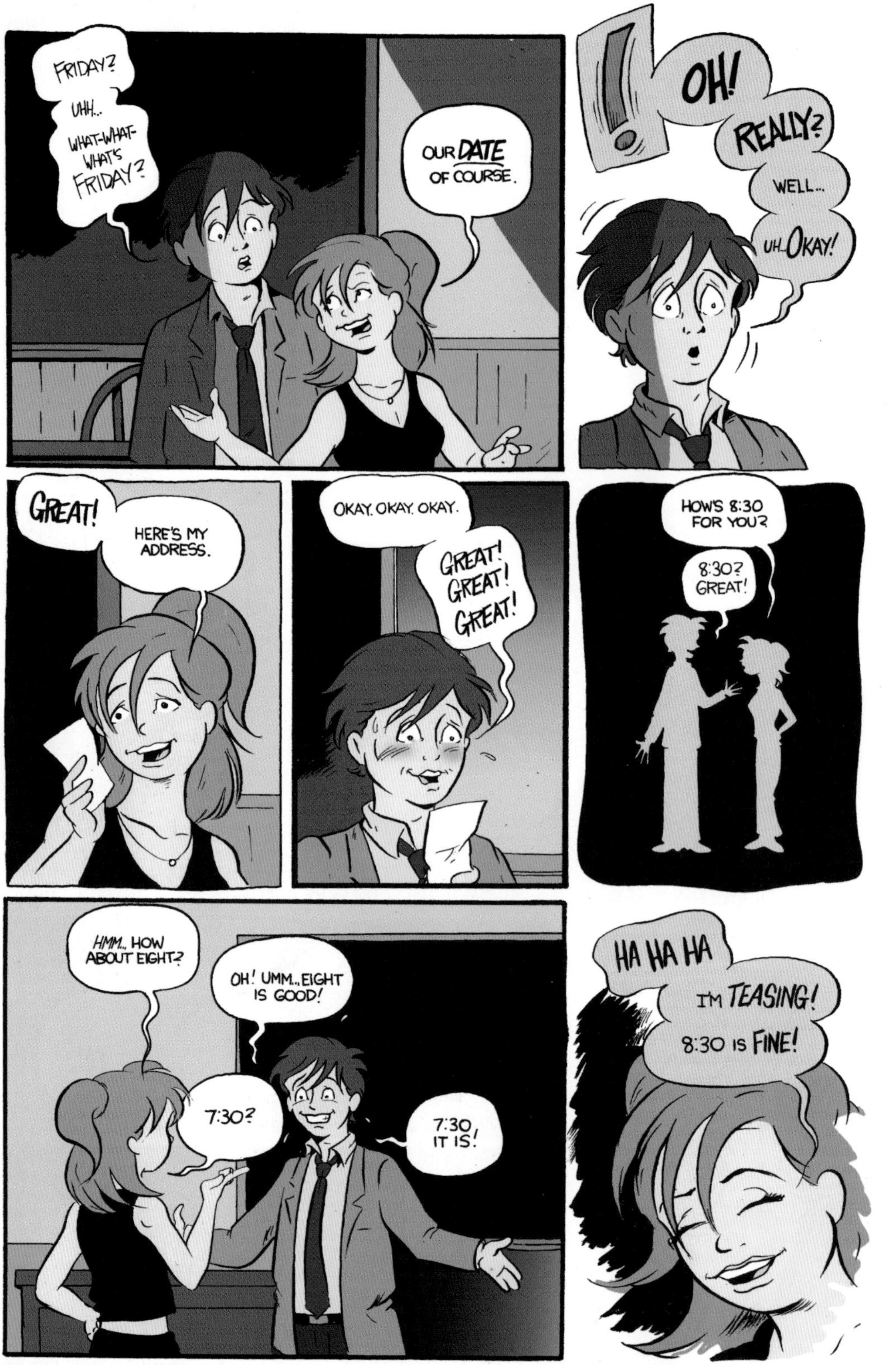
FRIDAY? UHH... WHAT-WHAT-WHAT'S FRIDAY?
OUR DATE OF COURSE.
OH! REALLY? WELL... UH...OKAY!
GREAT!
HERE'S MY ADDRESS.
OKAY. OKAY. OKAY.
GREAT! GREAT! GREAT!
HOW'S 8:30 FOR YOU?
8:30? GREAT!
HMM... HOW ABOUT EIGHT?
OH! UMM... EIGHT IS GOOD!
7:30?
7:30, IT IS!
HA HA HA
I'M TEASING!
8:30 IS FINE!

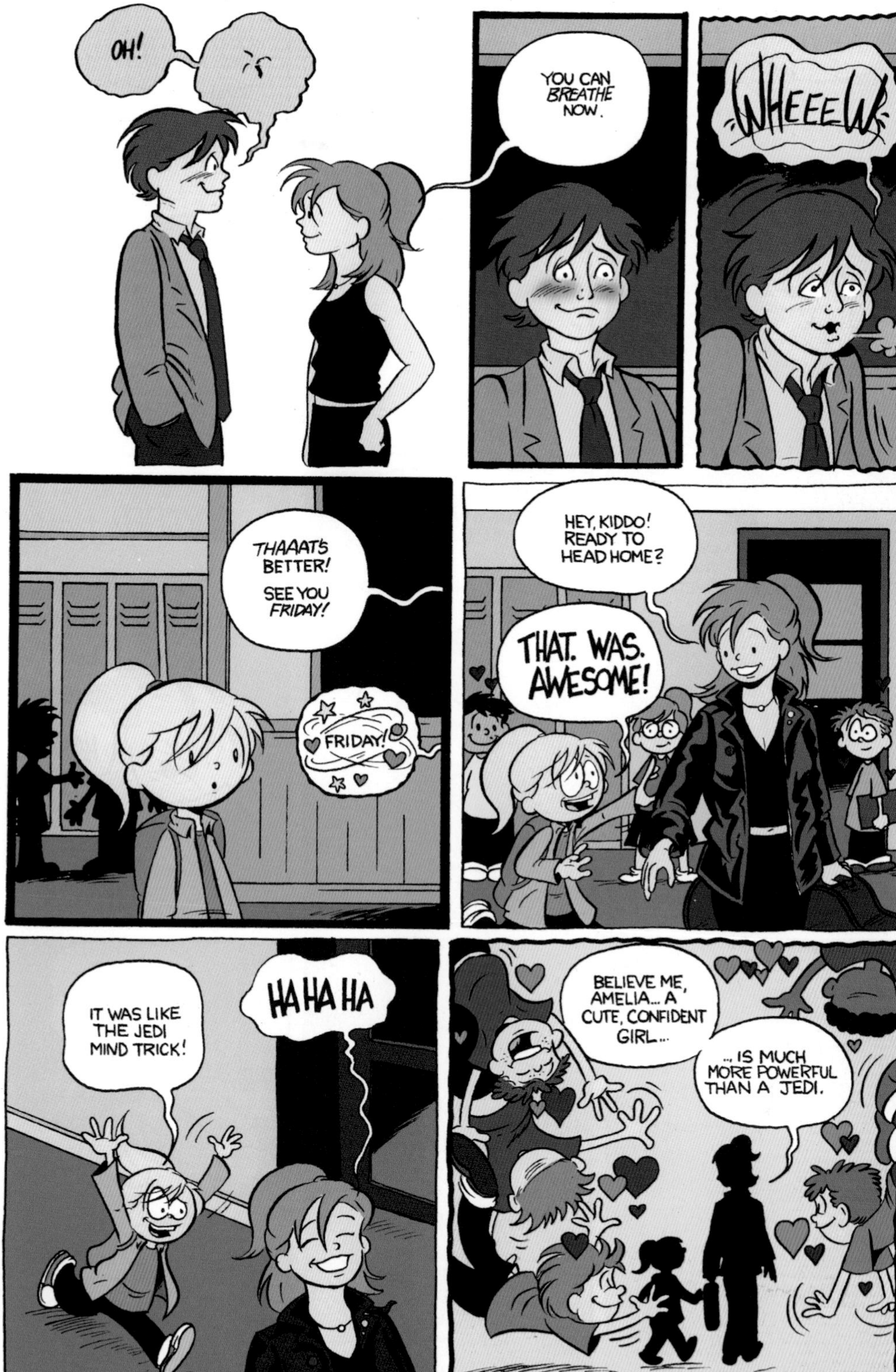
OH!
YOU CAN BREATHE NOW.
WHEEEW
THAAAT'S BETTER!
SEE YOU FRIDAY!
FRIDAY!
HEY, KIDDO! READY TO HEAD HOME?
THAT. WAS. AWESOME!
IT WAS LIKE THE JEDI MIND TRICK!
HA HA HA
BELIEVE ME, AMELIA... A CUTE, CONFIDENT GIRL...
... IS MUCH MORE POWERFUL THAN A JEDI.

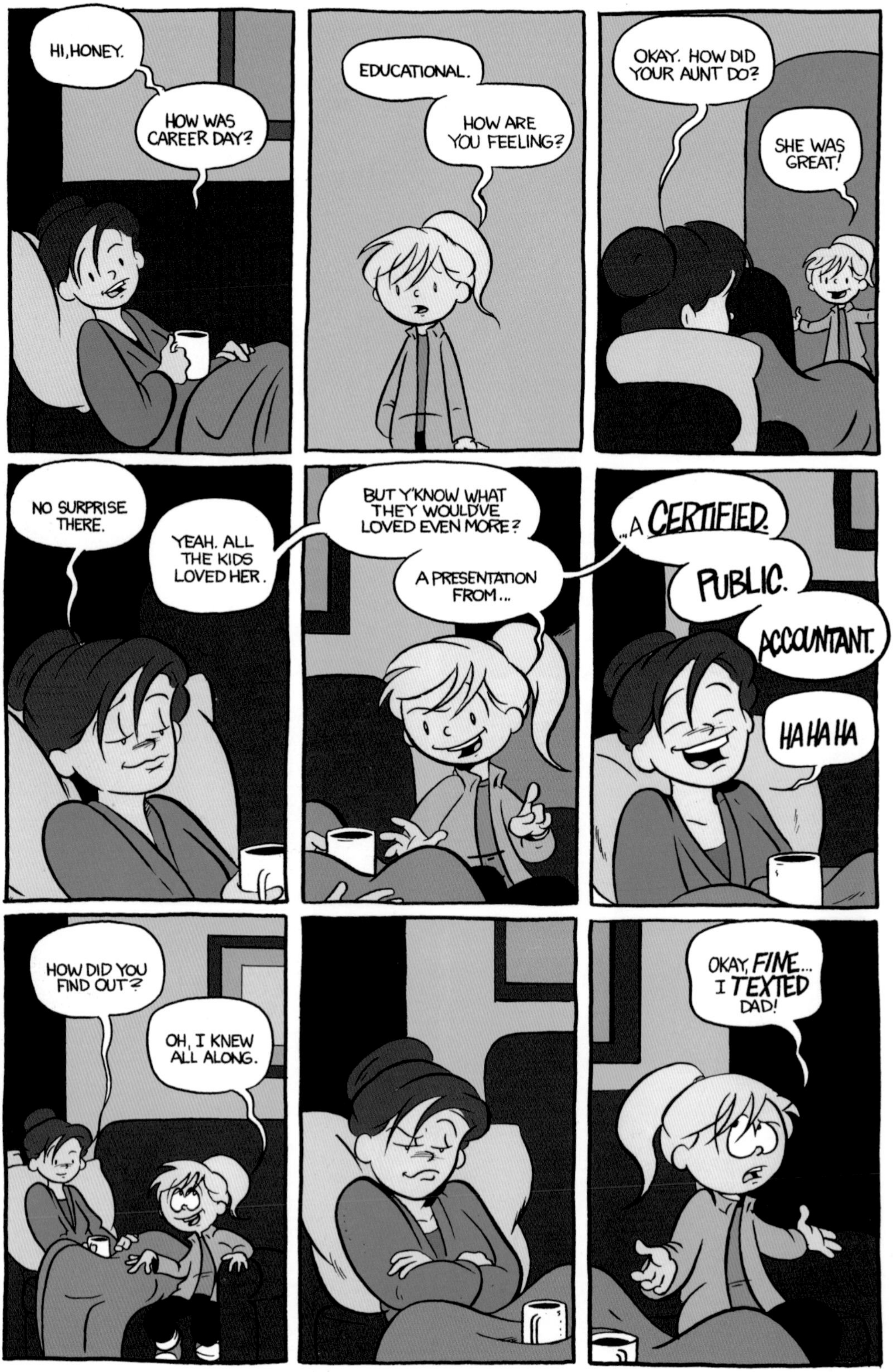
HI, HONEY.
HOW WAS CAREER DAY?
EDUCATIONAL.
HOW ARE YOU FEELING?
OKAY. HOW DID YOUR AUNT DO?
SHE WAS GREAT!
NO SURPRISE THERE.
YEAH. ALL THE KIDS LOVED HER.
BUT Y'KNOW WHAT THEY WOULD'VE LOVED EVEN MORE?
A PRESENTATION FROM...
...A CERTIFIED.
PUBLIC.
ACCOUNTANT.
HA HA HA
HOW DID YOU FIND OUT?
OH, I KNEW ALL ALONG.
OKAY, FINE... I TEXTED DAD!

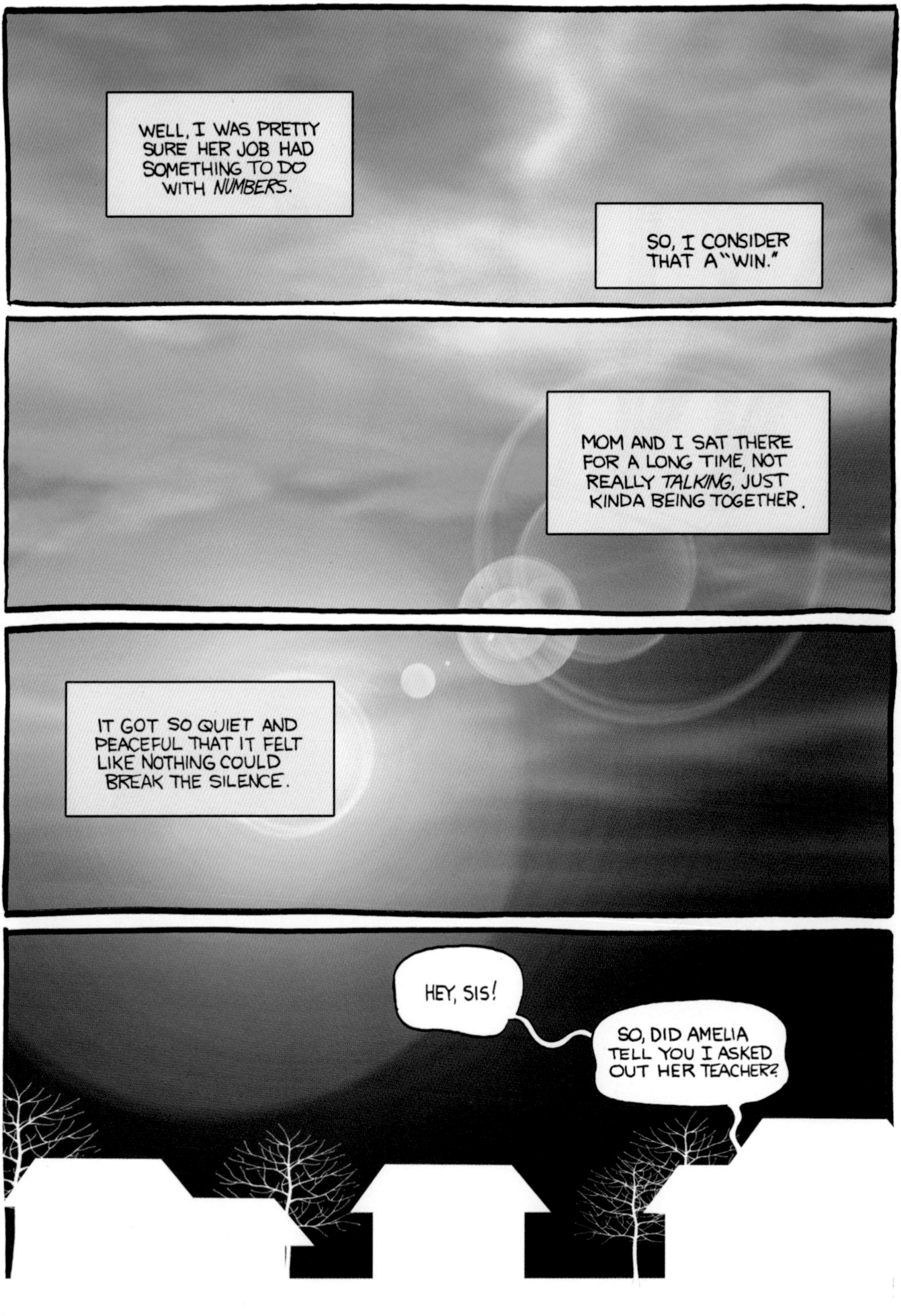
WELL, I WAS PRETTY SURE HER JOB HAD SOMETHING TO DO WITH NUMBERS.
SO, I CONSIDER THAT A "WIN."
MOM AND I SAT THERE FOR A LONG TIME, NOT REALLY TALKING, JUST KINDA BEING TOGETHER.
IT GOT SO QUIET AND PEACEFUL THAT IT FELT LIKE NOTHING COULD BREAK THE SILENCE.
HEY, SIS!
SO, DID AMELIA TELL YOU I ASKED OUT HER TEACHER?

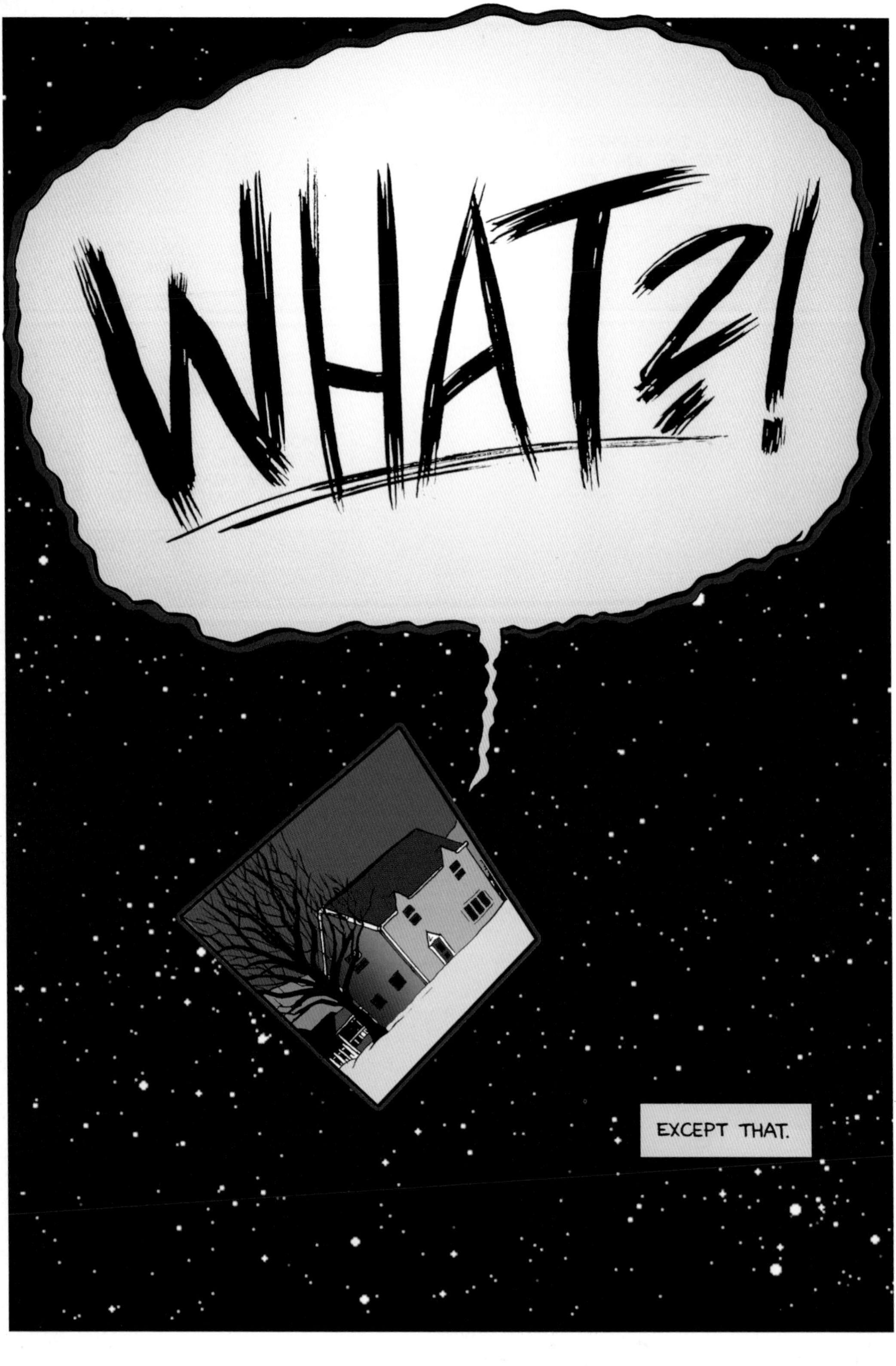
WHAT?!
EXCEPT THAT.

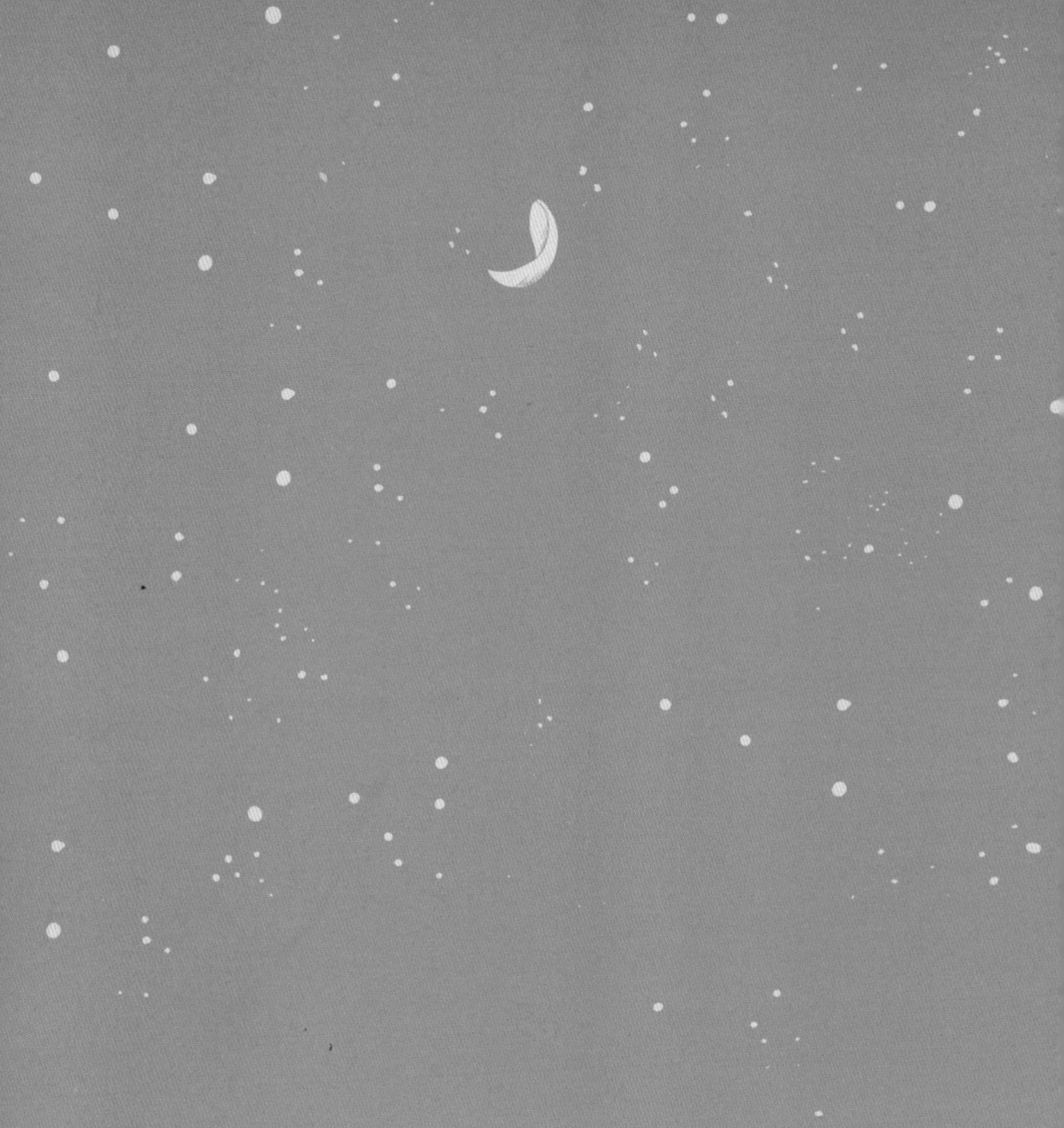

"I think the reason people have kids is so they can pass their own brand of crazy on to a new generation."

-Tanner Clark

in an Interview with Chet McCoy of *Good Morning St. Louis*

BOYFRiENDS

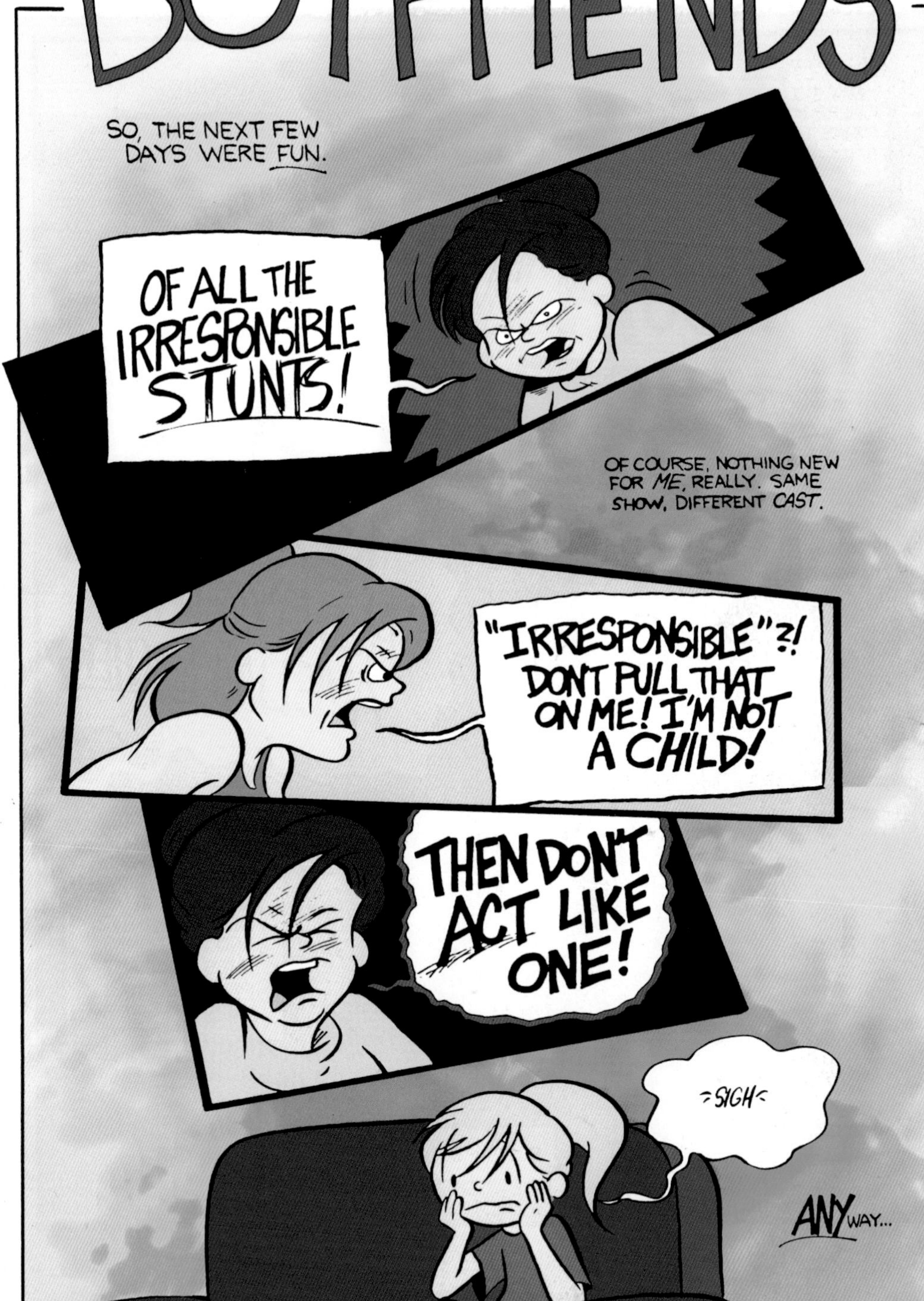
SO, THE NEXT FEW DAYS WERE FUN.
OF ALL THE IRRESPONSIBLE STUNTS!
OF COURSE, NOTHING NEW FOR ME, REALLY. SAME SHOW, DIFFERENT CAST.
"IRRESPONSIBLE"?! DON'T PULL THAT ON ME! I'M NOT A CHILD!
THEN DON'T ACT LIKE ONE!
SIGH
ANYWAY...

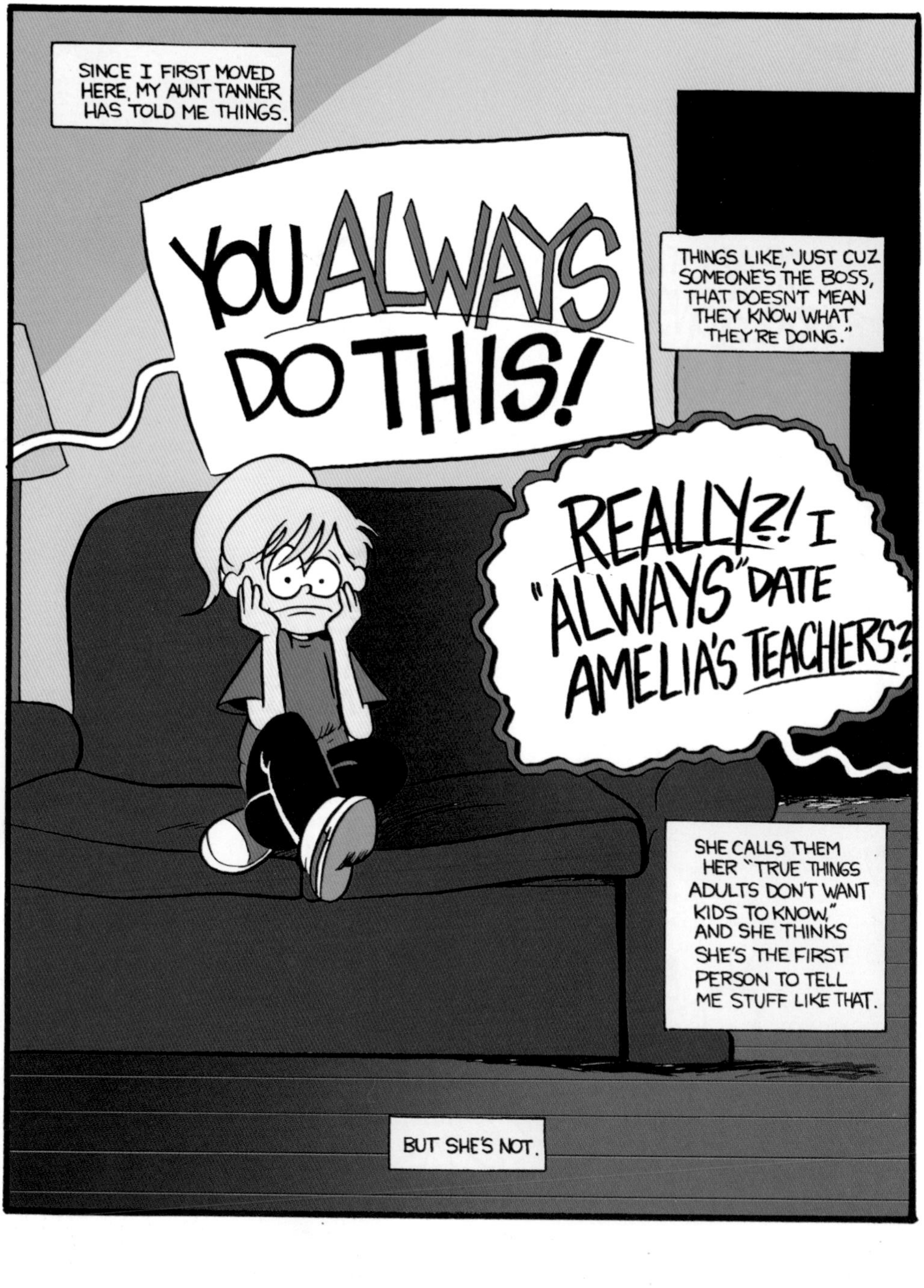
SINCE I FIRST MOVED HERE, MY AUNT TANNER HAS TOLD ME THINGS.
YOU ALWAYS DO THIS!
THINGS LIKE, "JUST CUZ SOMEONE'S THE BOSS, THAT DOESN'T MEAN THEY KNOW WHAT THEY'RE DOING."
REALLY?! I "ALWAYS" DATE AMELIA'S TEACHERS?!
SHE CALLS THEM HER "TRUE THINGS ADULTS DON'T WANT KIDS TO KNOW," AND SHE THINKS SHE'S THE FIRST PERSON TO TELL ME STUFF LIKE THAT.
BUT SHE'S NOT.

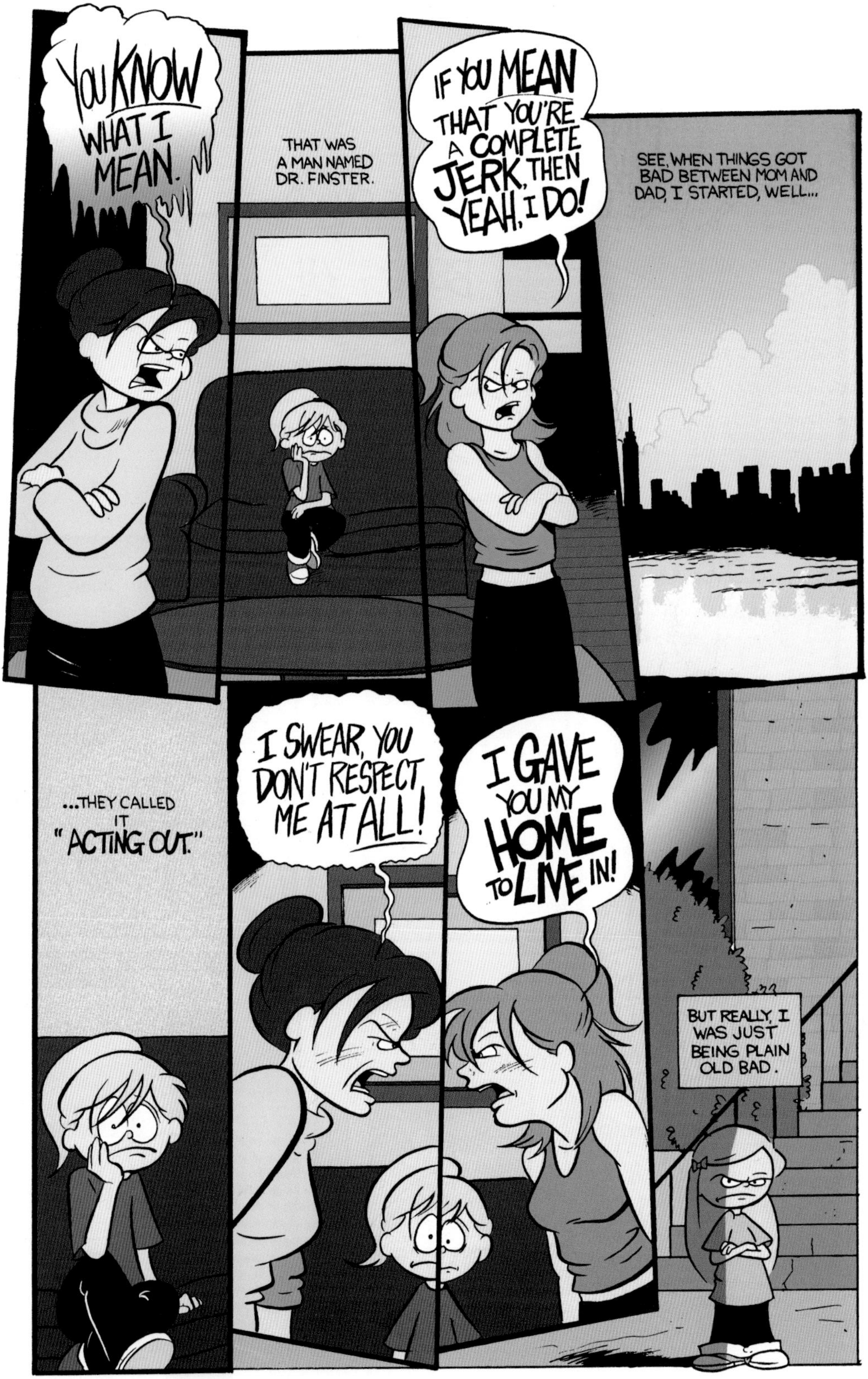
YOU KNOW WHAT I MEAN.
THAT WAS A MAN NAMED DR. FINSTER.
IF YOU MEAN THAT YOU'RE A COMPLETE JERK, THEN YEAH, I DO!
SEE, WHEN THINGS GOT BAD BETWEEN MOM AND DAD, I STARTED, WELL...
...THEY CALLED IT "ACTING OUT."
I SWEAR, YOU DON'T RESPECT ME AT ALL!
I GAVE YOU MY HOME TO LIVE IN!
BUT REALLY, I WAS JUST BEING PLAIN OLD BAD.

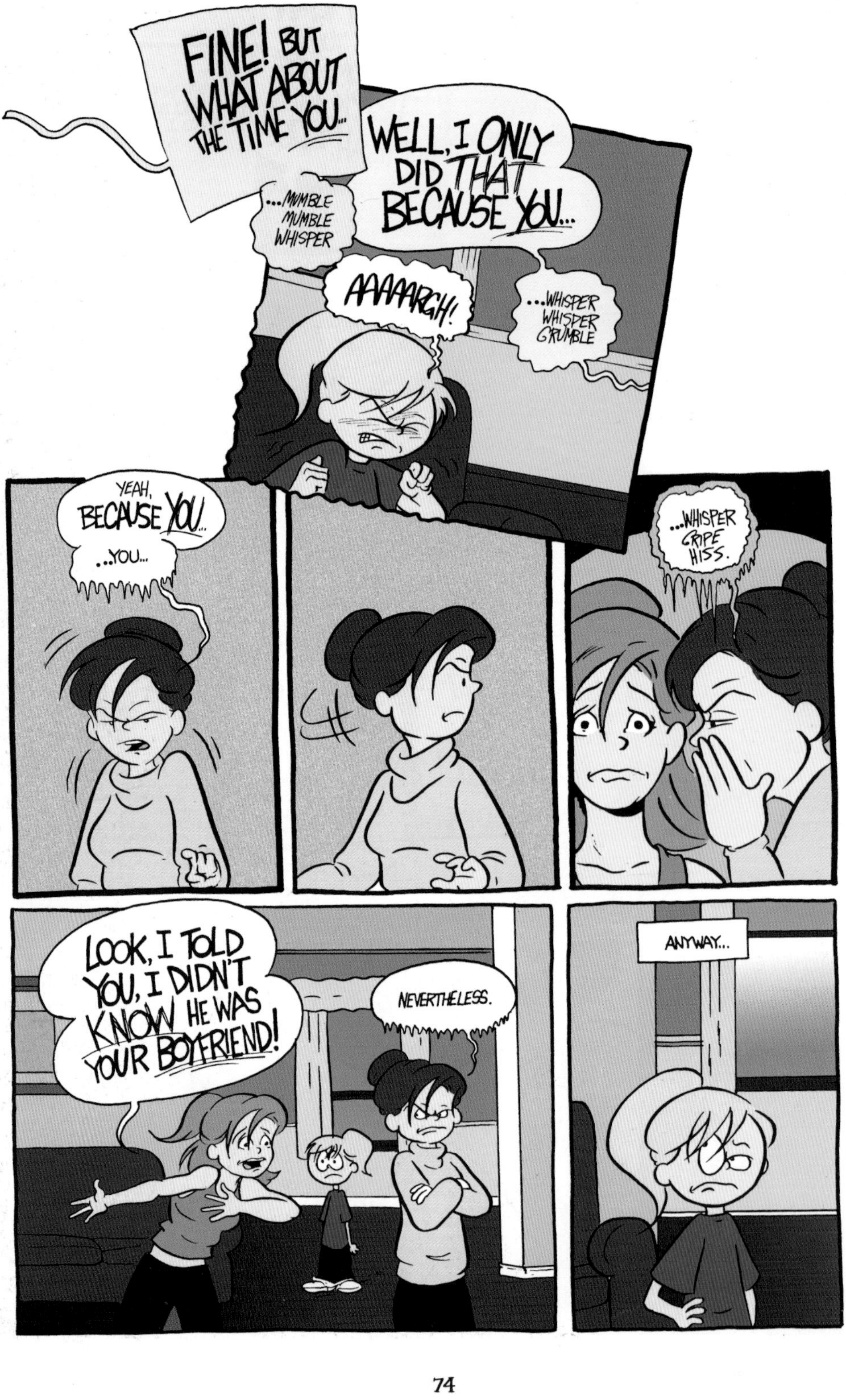
FINE! BUT WHAT ABOUT THE TIME YOU...
WELL, I ONLY DID THAT BECAUSE YOU...
...MUMBLE MUMBLE WHISPER
AAAAARGH!
...WHISPER WHISPER GRUMBLE
YEAH, BECAUSE YOU...
...YOU...
...WHISPER GRIPE HISS.
LOOK, I TOLD YOU, I DIDN'T KNOW HE WAS YOUR BOYFRIEND!
NEVERTHELESS.
ANYWAY...

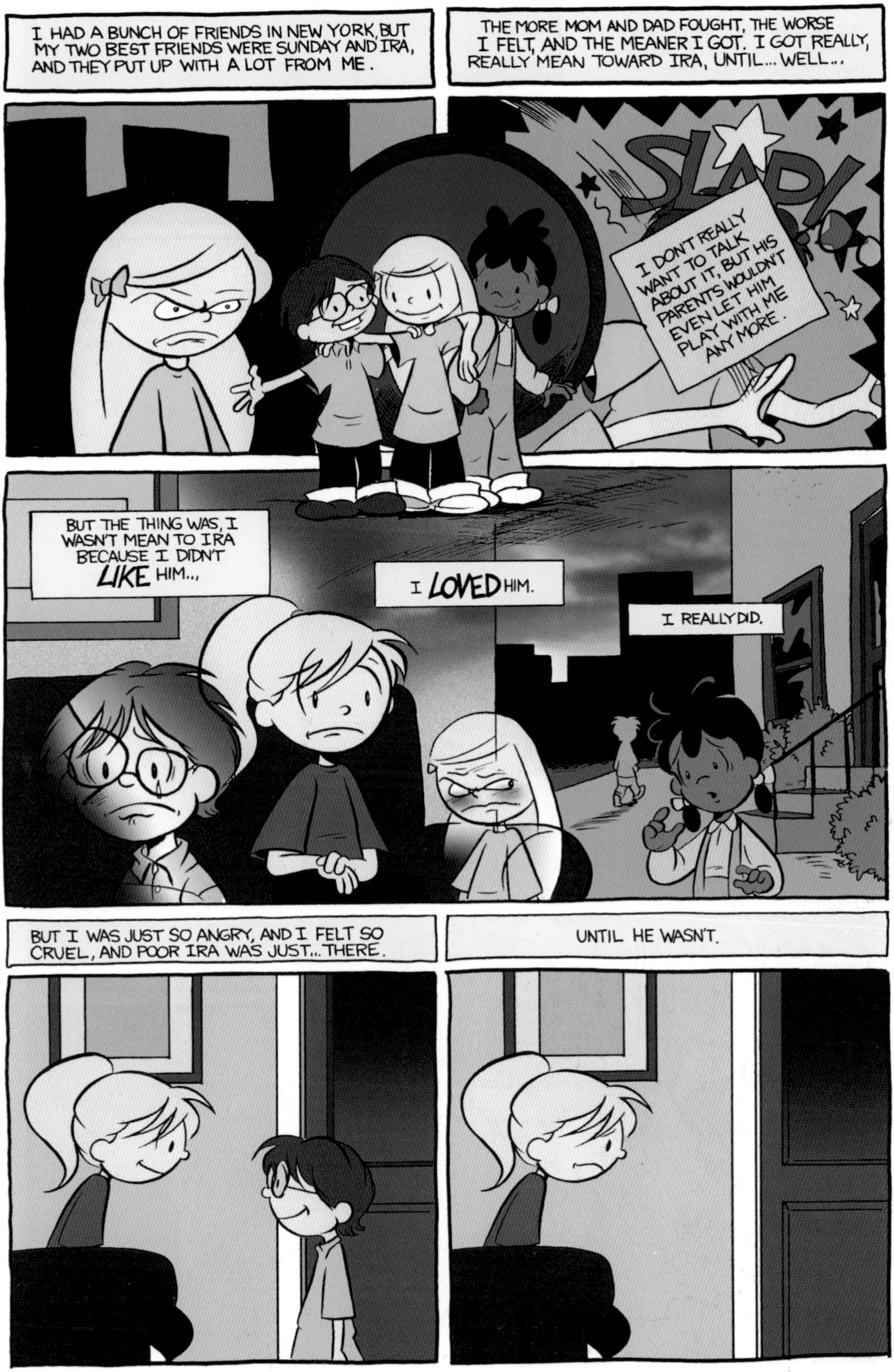
I HAD A BUNCH OF FRIENDS IN NEW YORK, BUT MY TWO BEST FRIENDS WERE SUNDAY AND IRA, AND THEY PUT UP WITH A LOT FROM ME.
THE MORE MOM AND DAD FOUGHT, THE WORSE I FELT, AND THE MEANER I GOT. I GOT REALLY, REALLY MEAN TOWARD IRA, UNTIL... WELL...
SLAP!
I DON'T REALLY WANT TO TALK ABOUT IT, BUT HIS PARENTS WOULDN'T EVEN LET HIM PLAY WITH ME ANY MORE.
BUT THE THING WAS, I WASN'T MEAN TO IRA BECAUSE I DIDN'T LIKE HIM...
I LOVED HIM.
I REALLY DID.
BUT I WAS JUST SO ANGRY, AND I FELT SO CRUEL, AND POOR IRA WAS JUST... THERE.
UNTIL HE WASN'T.

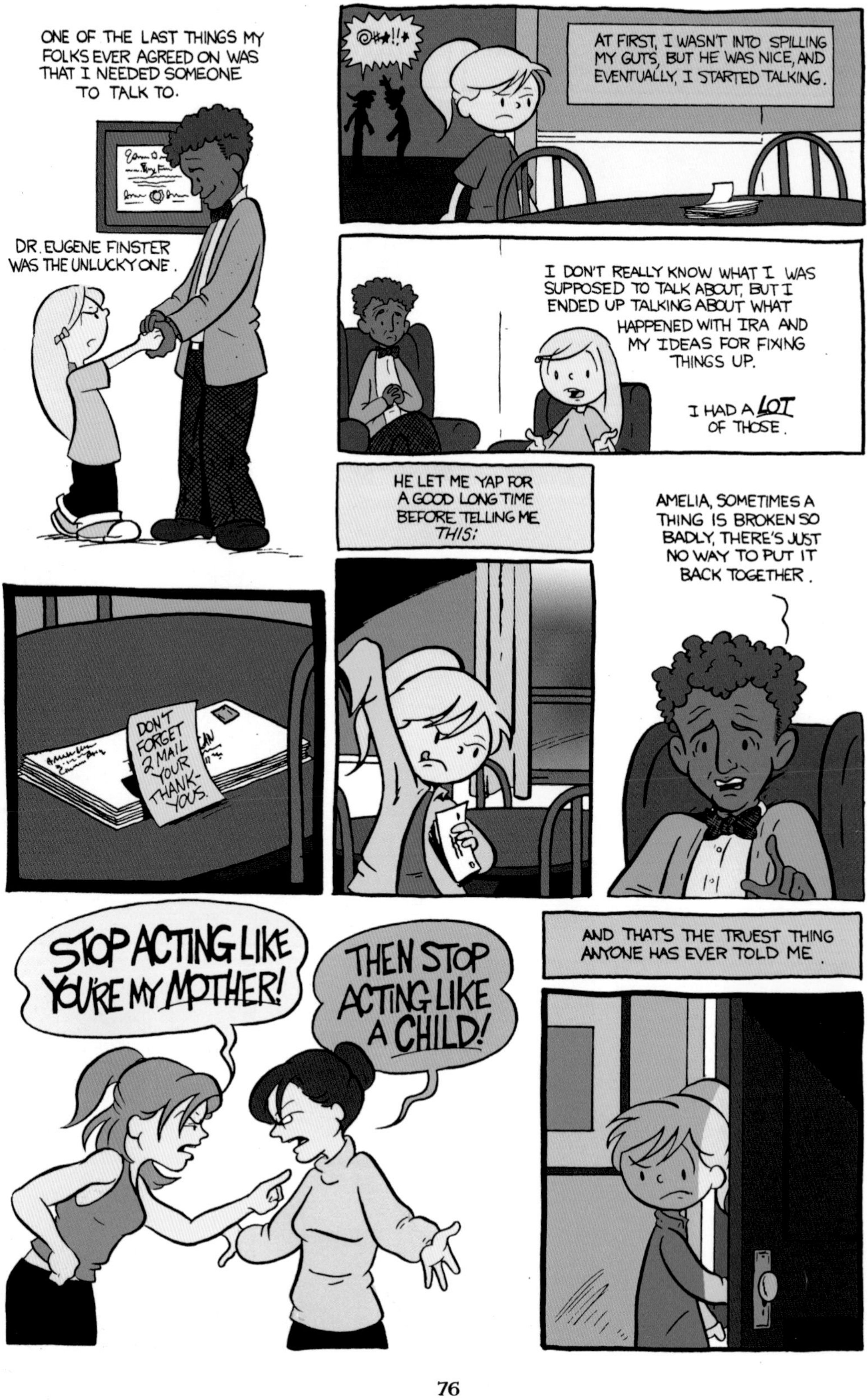
ONE OF THE LAST THINGS MY FOLKS EVER AGREED ON WAS THAT I NEEDED SOMEONE TO TALK TO.
DR. EUGENE FINSTER WAS THE UNLUCKY ONE.
@#*!!*
AT FIRST, I WASN'T INTO SPILLING MY GUTS, BUT HE WAS NICE, AND EVENTUALLY, I STARTED TALKING.
I DON'T REALLY KNOW WHAT I WAS SUPPOSED TO TALK ABOUT, BUT I ENDED UP TALKING ABOUT WHAT HAPPENED WITH IRA AND MY IDEAS FOR FIXING THINGS UP.
I HAD A LOT OF THOSE.
HE LET ME YAP FOR A GOOD LONG TIME BEFORE TELLING ME THIS:
AMELIA, SOMETIMES A THING IS BROKEN SO BADLY, THERE'S JUST NO WAY TO PUT IT BACK TOGETHER.
DON'T FORGET 2 MAIL YOUR THANK-YOUS.
STOP ACTING LIKE YOU'RE MY MOTHER!
THEN STOP ACTING LIKE A CHILD!
AND THAT'S THE TRUEST THING ANYONE HAS EVER TOLD ME.

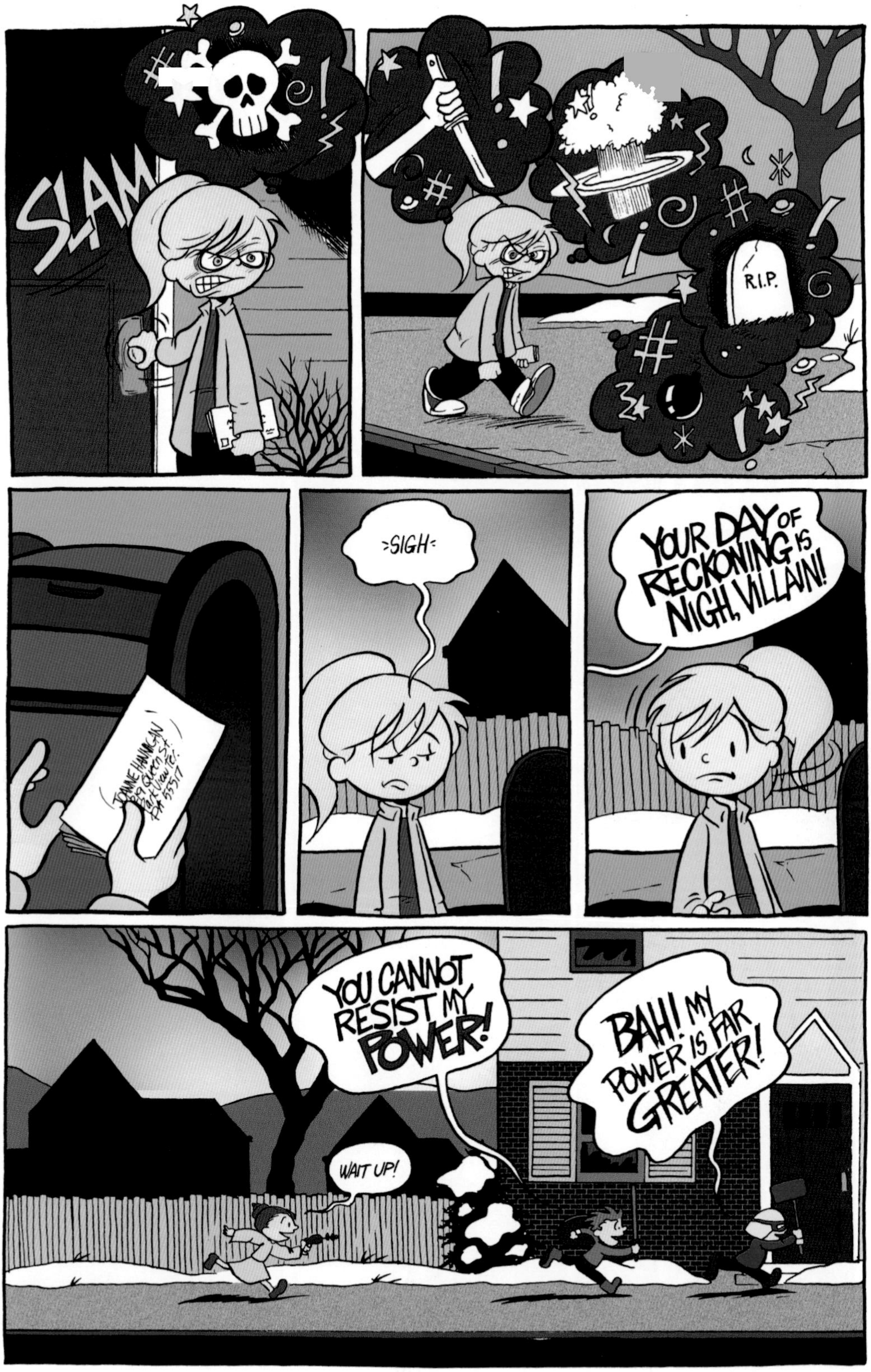
SLAM
R.I.P.
SIGH
YOUR DAY OF RECKONING IS NIGH, VILLAIN!
YOU CANNOT RESIST MY POWER!
BAH! MY POWER IS FAR GREATER!
WAIT UP!

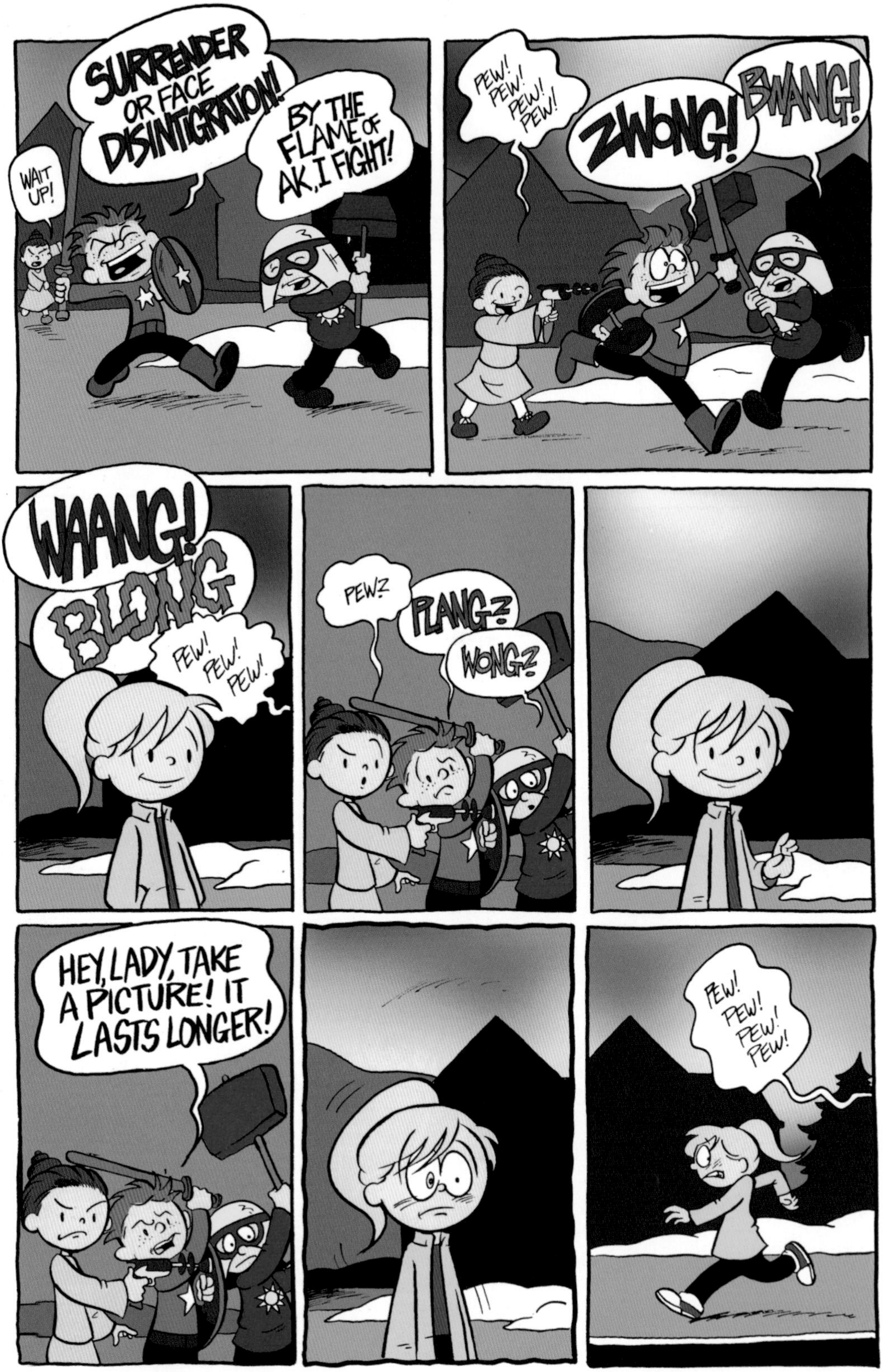
WAIT UP!
SURRENDER OR FACE DISINTIGRATION!
BY THE FLAME OF AK, I FIGHT!
PEW! PEW! PEW! PEW!
ZWONG!
BWANG!
WAANG!
BLONG
PEW! PEW! PEW!
PEW?
PLANG?
WONG?
HEY, LADY, TAKE A PICTURE! IT LASTS LONGER!
PEW! PEW! PEW! PEW!

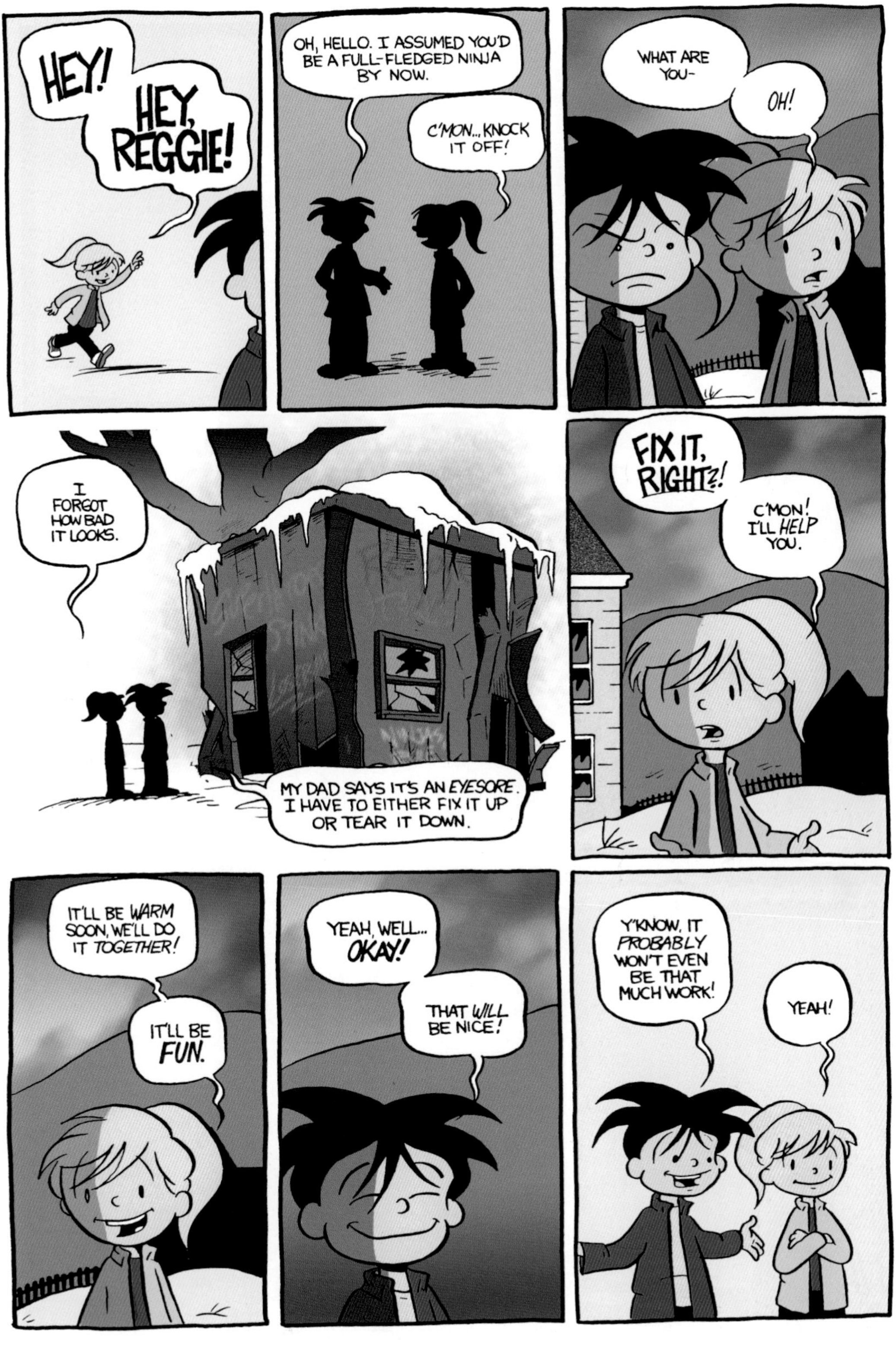
HEY!
HEY, REGGIE!
OH, HELLO. I ASSUMED YOU'D BE A FULL-FLEDGED NINJA BY NOW.
C'MON... KNOCK IT OFF!
WHAT ARE YOU-
OH!
I FORGOT HOW BAD IT LOOKS.
MY DAD SAYS IT'S AN EYESORE. I HAVE TO EITHER FIX IT UP OR TEAR IT DOWN.
FIX IT, RIGHT?!
C'MON! I'LL HELP YOU.
IT'LL BE WARM SOON, WE'LL DO IT TOGETHER!
IT'LL BE FUN.
YEAH, WELL... OKAY!
THAT WILL BE NICE!
Y'KNOW, IT PROBABLY WON'T EVEN BE THAT MUCH WORK!
YEAH!

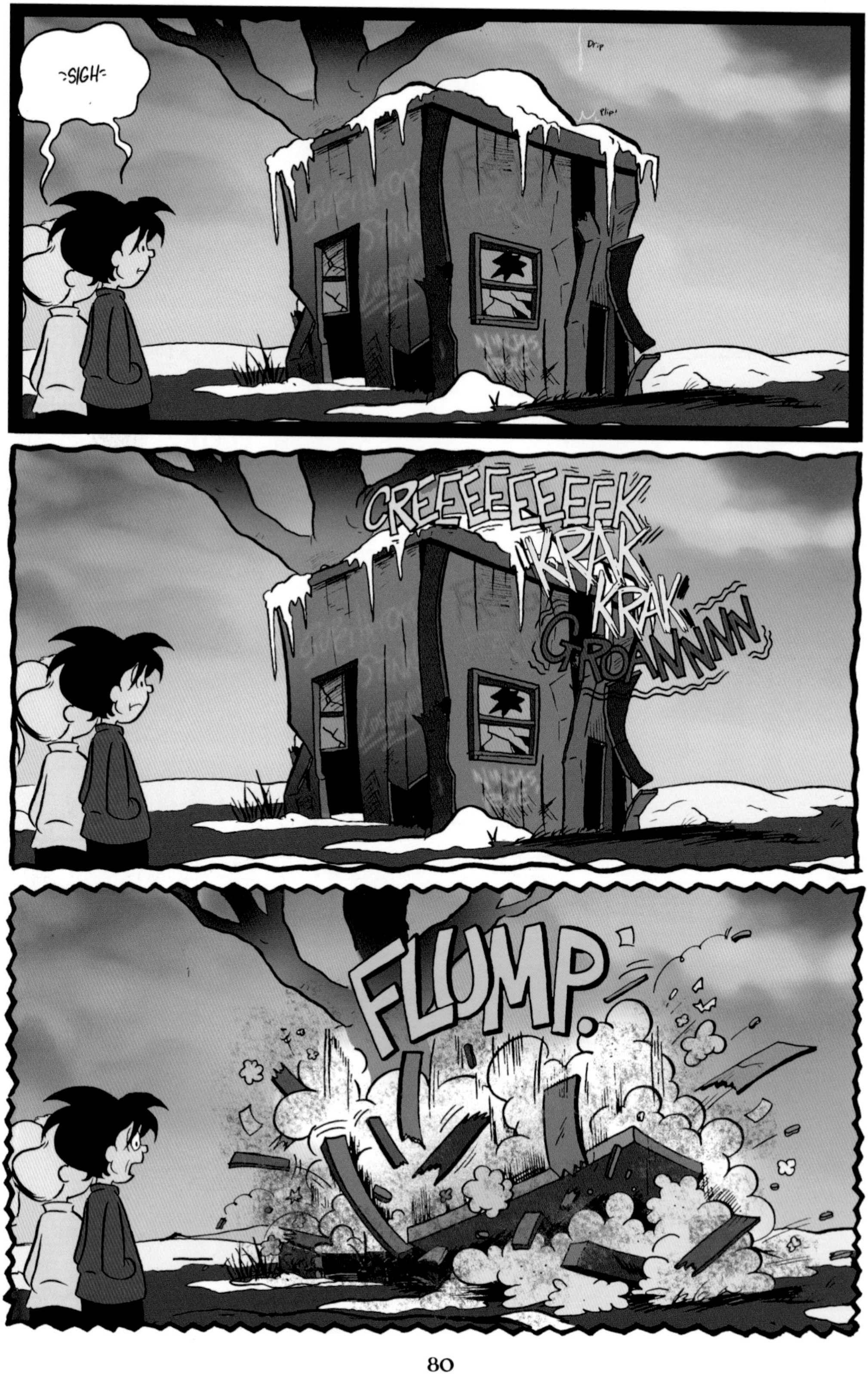
-SIGH-
Drip
Plip!
CREEEEEEEK
KRAK
KRAK
GROANNNNN
FLUMP.

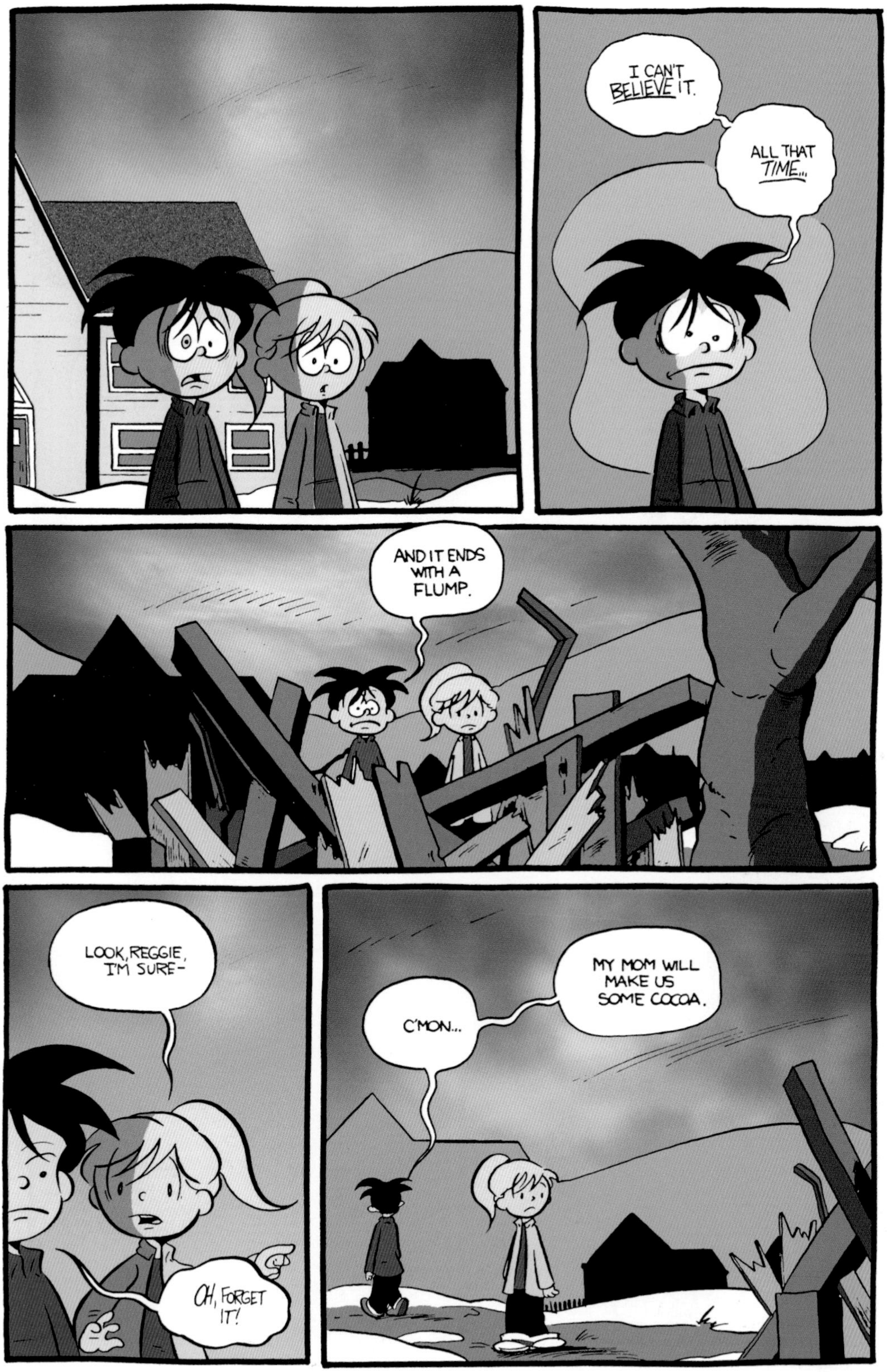
I CAN'T BELIEVE IT.
ALL THAT TIME...
AND IT ENDS WITH A FLUMP.
LOOK, REGGIE, I'M SURE-
OH, FORGET IT!
MY MOM WILL MAKE US SOME COCOA.
C'MON...

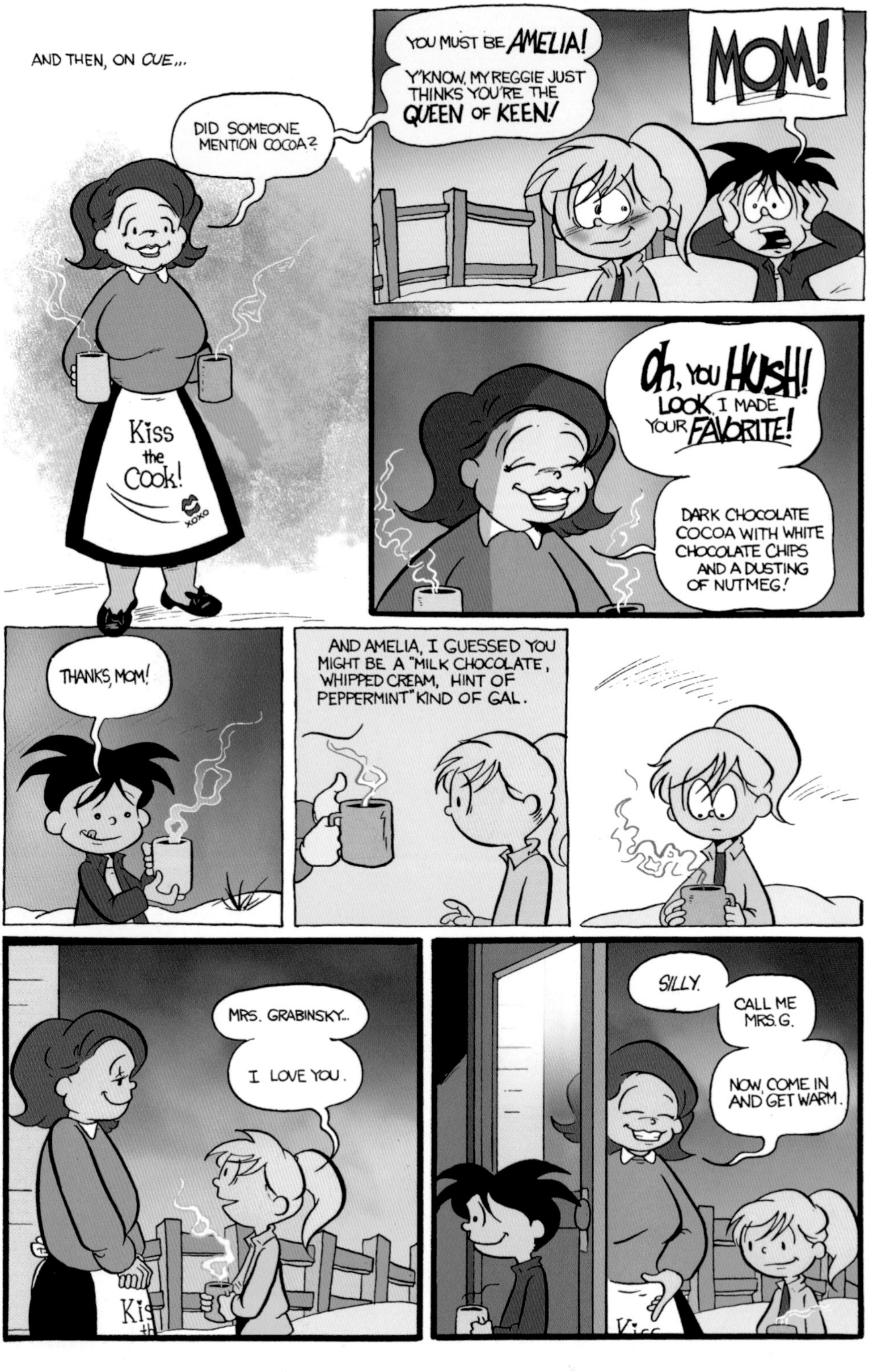
AND THEN, ON CUE...
DID SOMEONE MENTION COCOA?
YOU MUST BE AMELIA!
Y'KNOW, MY REGGIE JUST THINKS YOU'RE THE QUEEN OF KEEN!
MOM!
Kiss the Cook!
XOXO
Oh, YOU HUSH! LOOK, I MADE YOUR FAVORITE!
DARK CHOCOLATE COCOA WITH WHITE CHOCOLATE CHIPS AND A DUSTING OF NUTMEG!
THANKS, MOM!
AND AMELIA, I GUESSED YOU MIGHT BE A "MILK CHOCOLATE, WHIPPED CREAM, HINT OF PEPPERMINT" KIND OF GAL.
MRS. GRABINSKY...
I LOVE YOU.
SILLY.
CALL ME MRS. G.
NOW, COME IN AND GET WARM.

NOW, BETWEEN YOU AND ME, THE FACT THAT REGGIE HAD NEVER INTRODUCED ME TO HIS *PARENTS*...

...WELL...

...IT MADE ME FEAR THE *WORST*, Y'KNOW?

BUT THEY TURNED OUT TO BE *AWESOME!*

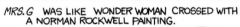

MRS. G WAS LIKE WONDER WOMAN CROSSED WITH A NORMAN ROCKWELL PAINTING.

ZIP!

KICK CLACK

sizzle

Kiss *the* Cook!

HIS DAD WAS A TRIP, TOO.

...WHICH, OF COURSE, IS HOW I DEVELOPED MY LOVE FOR BOTH KABUKI THEATER AND MARSHMALLOW PEEPS.

AND THE WHOLE HOUSE LOOKED LIKE SOME ANTIQUE TOY STORE.

NOW, BEAR IN MIND, THIS WAS BEFORE THE WHOLE UN INCIDENT.

AND THEN IT DAWNED ON ME...

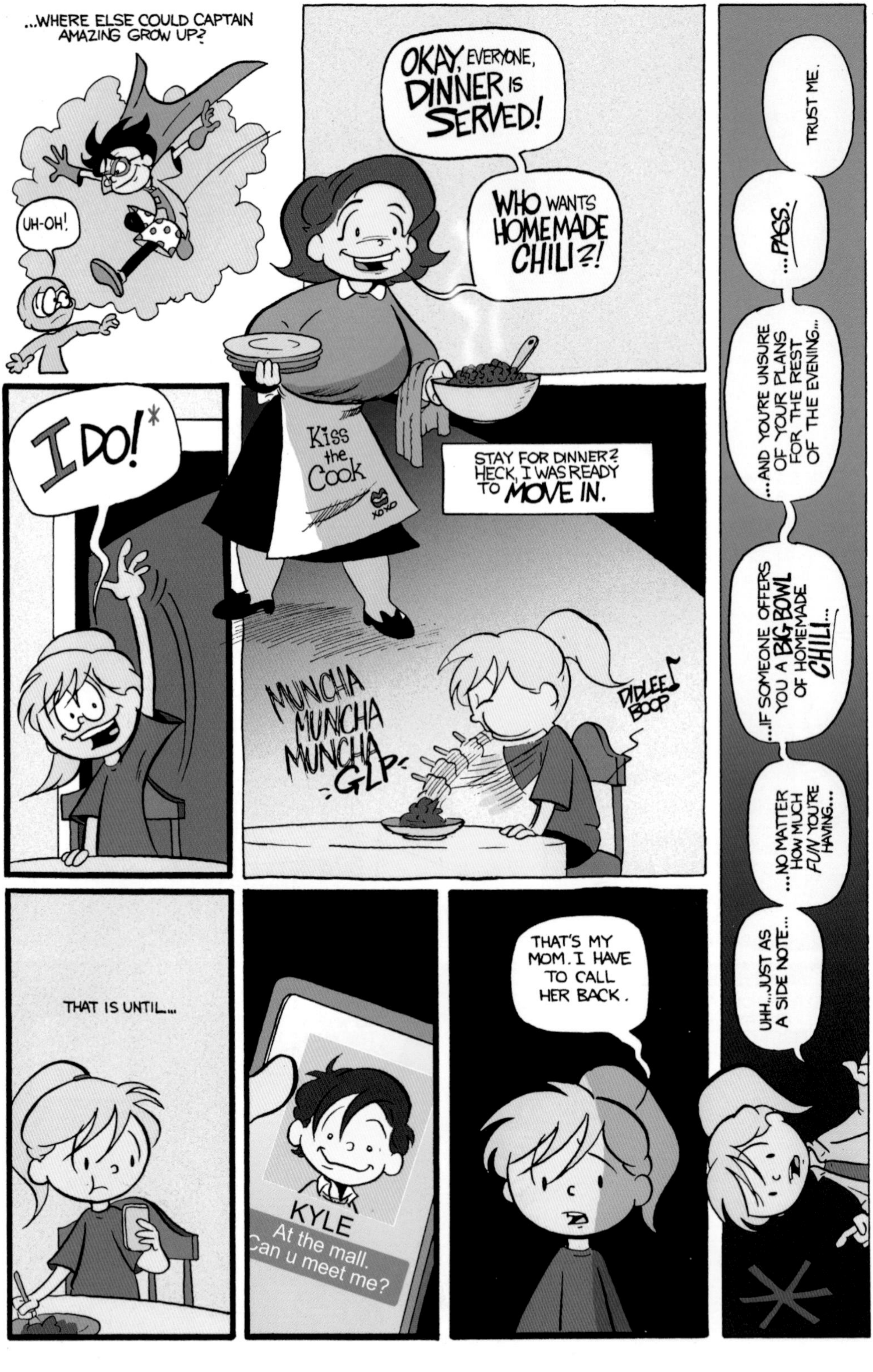
...WHERE ELSE COULD CAPTAIN AMAZING GROW UP?
UH-OH!
OKAY, EVERYONE, DINNER IS SERVED!
WHO WANTS HOMEMADE CHILI?!
I DO!*
Kiss the Cook
XOXO
STAY FOR DINNER? HECK, I WAS READY TO MOVE IN.
MUNCHA MUNCHA MUNCHA GLP
DIDLEE BOOP
UHH...JUST AS A SIDE NOTE...
...NO MATTER HOW MUCH FUN YOU'RE HAVING...
...IF SOMEONE OFFERS YOU A BIG BOWL OF HOMEMADE CHILI...
...AND YOU'RE UNSURE OF YOUR PLANS FOR THE REST OF THE EVENING...
...PASS.
TRUST ME.
THAT IS UNTIL...
KYLE
At the mall. Can u meet me?
THAT'S MY MOM. I HAVE TO CALL HER BACK.

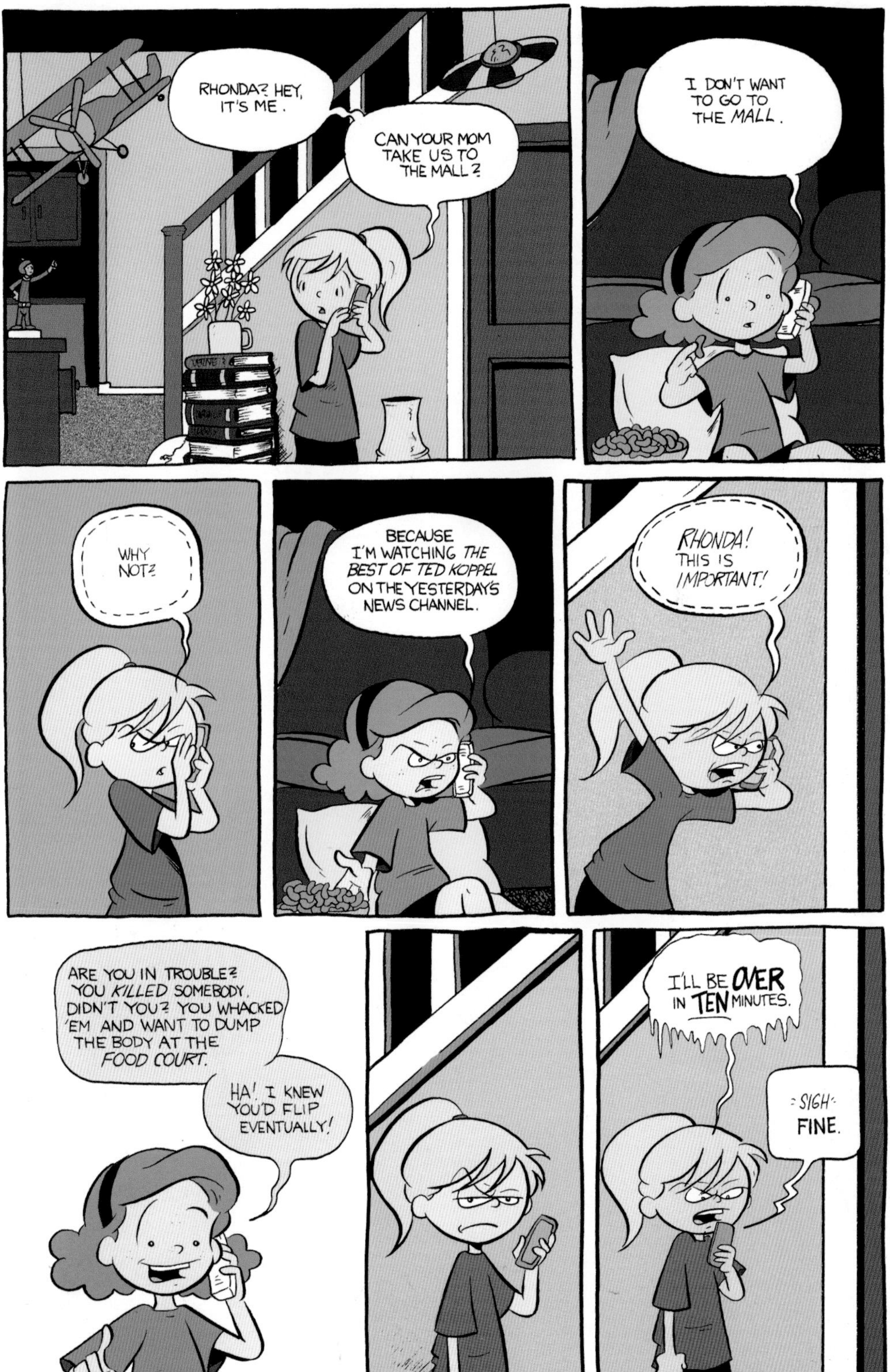
RHONDA? HEY, IT'S ME.
CAN YOUR MOM TAKE US TO THE MALL?
I DON'T WANT TO GO TO THE MALL.
WHY NOT?
BECAUSE I'M WATCHING THE BEST OF TED KOPPEL ON THE YESTERDAY'S NEWS CHANNEL.
RHONDA! THIS IS IMPORTANT!
ARE YOU IN TROUBLE? YOU KILLED SOMEBODY, DIDN'T YOU? YOU WHACKED 'EM AND WANT TO DUMP THE BODY AT THE FOOD COURT.
HA! I KNEW YOU'D FLIP EVENTUALLY!
I'LL BE OVER IN TEN MINUTES.
SIGH
FINE.

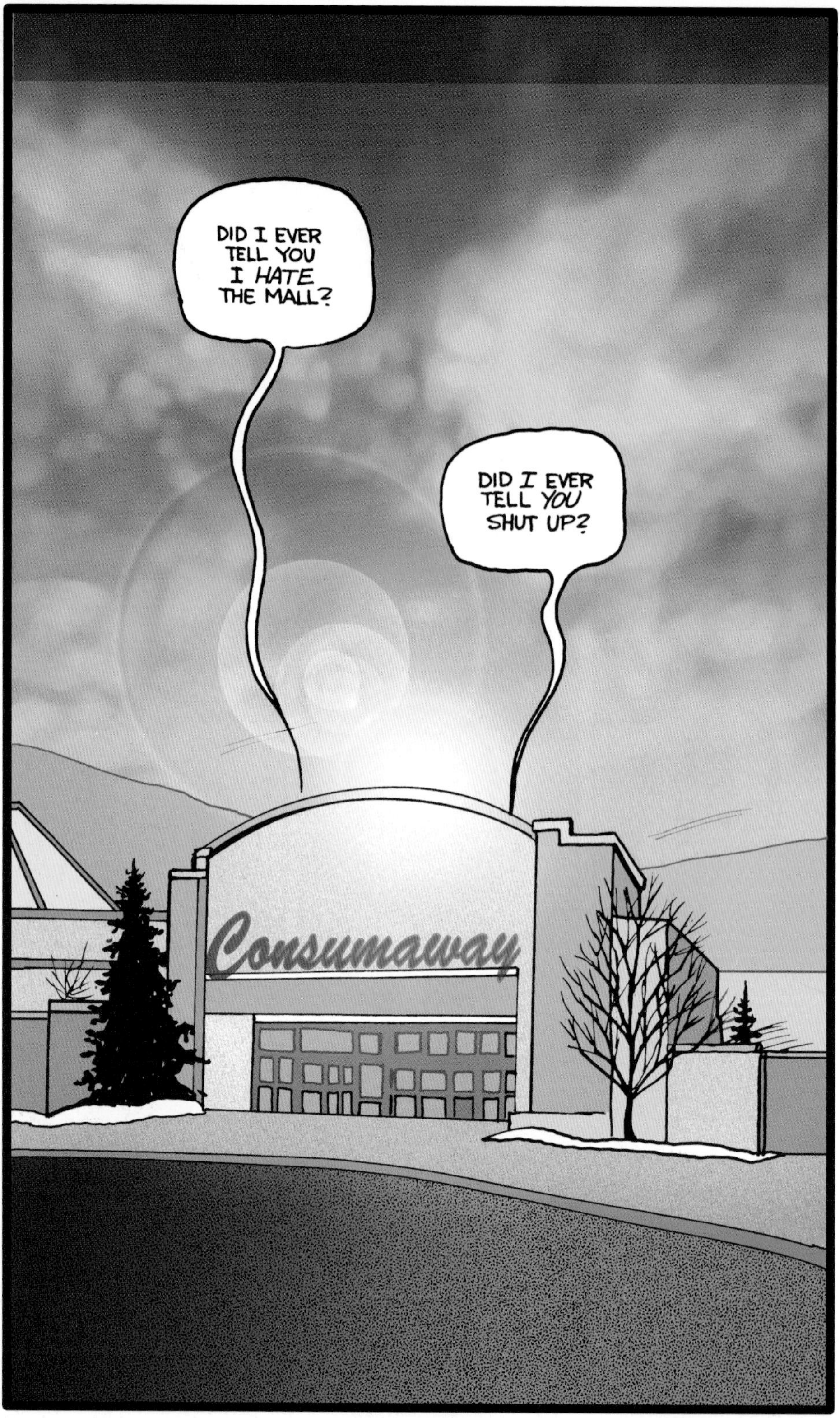
DID I EVER TELL YOU I HATE THE MALL?
DID I EVER TELL YOU SHUT UP?
Consumaway

AMELIA, WE'VE BEEN IN *EVERY* STORE. WHAT ARE WE *LOOKING* FOR ALREADY?

50% OFF!

SALE! MON-FRI

MEN'S

HUH?

WHAT DID YOU *DRAG* US TO THE *MALL* FOR?!

OH!

UHH...

THESE.

NOW!

SAVE MORE!

SLASHING PRICES

BUY ONE GET ON...

ZIP!

?

TIC-TACS? REALLY?

YEAH. WELL, YOU KNOW HOW STRONGLY I FEEL ABOUT BEING...

...MINTY.

$1.50.

MEN'S

OH, WHAT? I HAVE TO *PAY* FOR THEM, TOO?

MY *HALITOSIS* THANKS YOU.

50% OFF!

SALE! MON-FRI

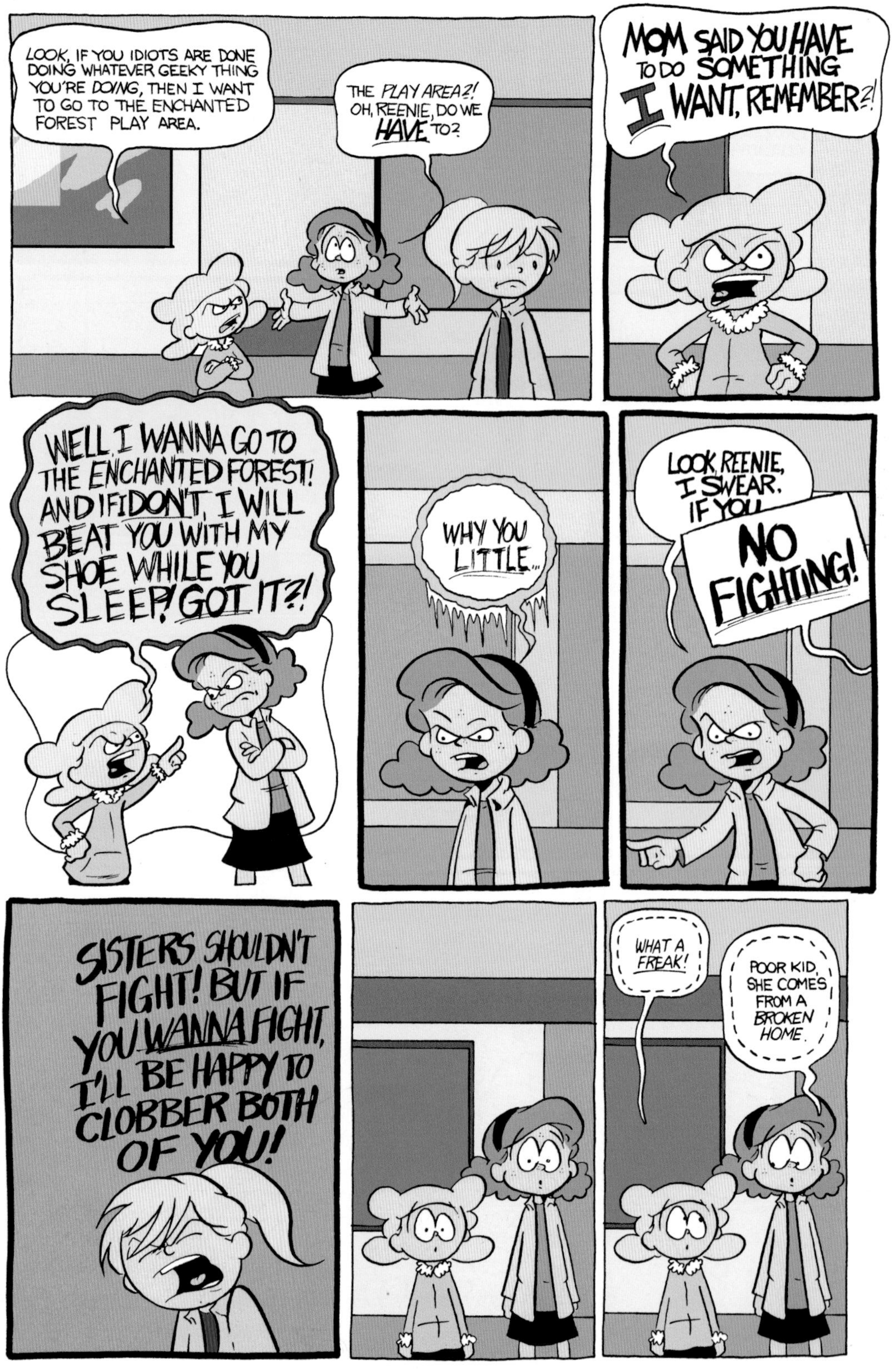
LOOK, IF YOU IDIOTS ARE DONE DOING WHATEVER GEEKY THING YOU'RE DOING, THEN I WANT TO GO TO THE ENCHANTED FOREST PLAY AREA.
THE PLAY AREA?! OH, REENIE, DO WE HAVE TO?
MOM SAID YOU HAVE TO DO SOMETHING I WANT, REMEMBER?!
WELL I WANNA GO TO THE ENCHANTED FOREST! AND IF I DON'T, I WILL BEAT YOU WITH MY SHOE WHILE YOU SLEEP! GOT IT?!
WHY YOU LITTLE...
LOOK, REENIE, I SWEAR, IF YOU
NO FIGHTING!
SISTERS SHOULDN'T FIGHT! BUT IF YOU WANNA FIGHT, I'LL BE HAPPY TO CLOBBER BOTH OF YOU!
WHAT A FREAK!
POOR KID, SHE COMES FROM A BROKEN HOME.

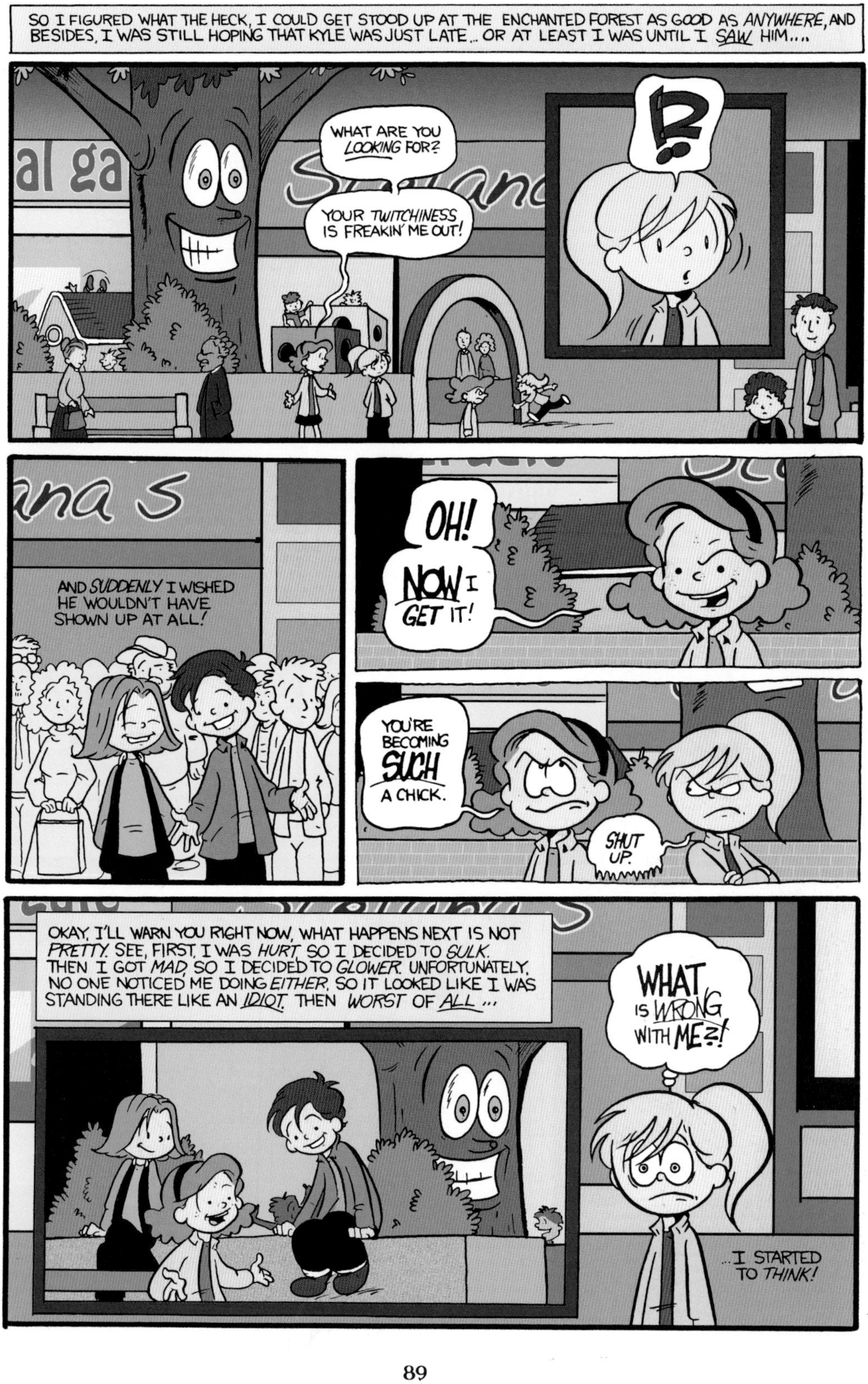
SO I FIGURED WHAT THE HECK, I COULD GET STOOD UP AT THE ENCHANTED FOREST AS GOOD AS *ANYWHERE*, AND BESIDES, I WAS STILL HOPING THAT KYLE WAS JUST LATE... OR AT LEAST I WAS UNTIL I SAW HIM....
WHAT ARE YOU *LOOKING* FOR?
YOUR *TWITCHINESS* IS FREAKIN' ME OUT!
AND *SUDDENLY* I WISHED HE WOULDN'T HAVE SHOWN UP AT ALL!
OH!
NOW I GET IT!
YOU'RE BECOMING SUCH A CHICK.
SHUT UP.
OKAY, I'LL WARN YOU RIGHT NOW, WHAT HAPPENS NEXT IS NOT *PRETTY*. SEE, FIRST, I WAS *HURT*, SO I DECIDED TO *SULK*. THEN I GOT *MAD*, SO I DECIDED TO *GLOWER*. UNFORTUNATELY, NO ONE NOTICED ME DOING *EITHER*, SO IT LOOKED LIKE I WAS STANDING THERE LIKE AN *IDIOT*. THEN *WORST* OF *ALL*...
WHAT IS WRONG WITH ME?!
...I STARTED TO *THINK*!

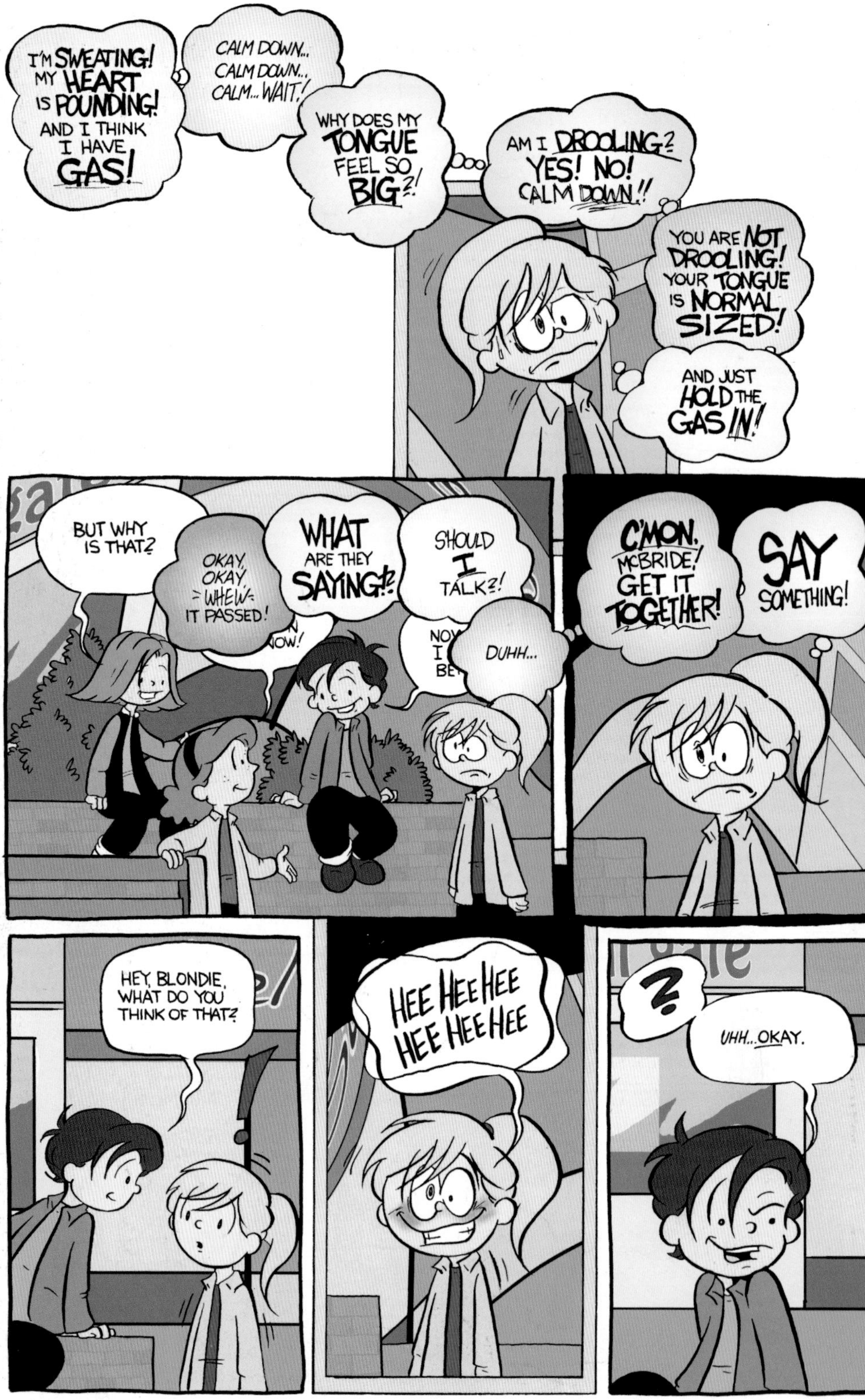
I'M SWEATING! MY HEART IS POUNDING! AND I THINK I HAVE GAS!
CALM DOWN... CALM DOWN... CALM... WAIT!
WHY DOES MY TONGUE FEEL SO BIG?!
AM I DROOLING? YES! NO! CALM DOWN!!
YOU ARE NOT DROOLING! YOUR TONGUE IS NORMAL SIZED!
AND JUST HOLD THE GAS IN!
BUT WHY IS THAT?
OKAY, OKAY, =WHEW= IT PASSED!
WHAT ARE THEY SAYING!?
SHOULD I TALK?!
DUHH...
C'MON, MCBRIDE! GET IT TOGETHER!
SAY SOMETHING!
HEY, BLONDIE, WHAT DO YOU THINK OF THAT?
HEE HEE HEE HEE HEE HEE
?
UHH...OKAY.

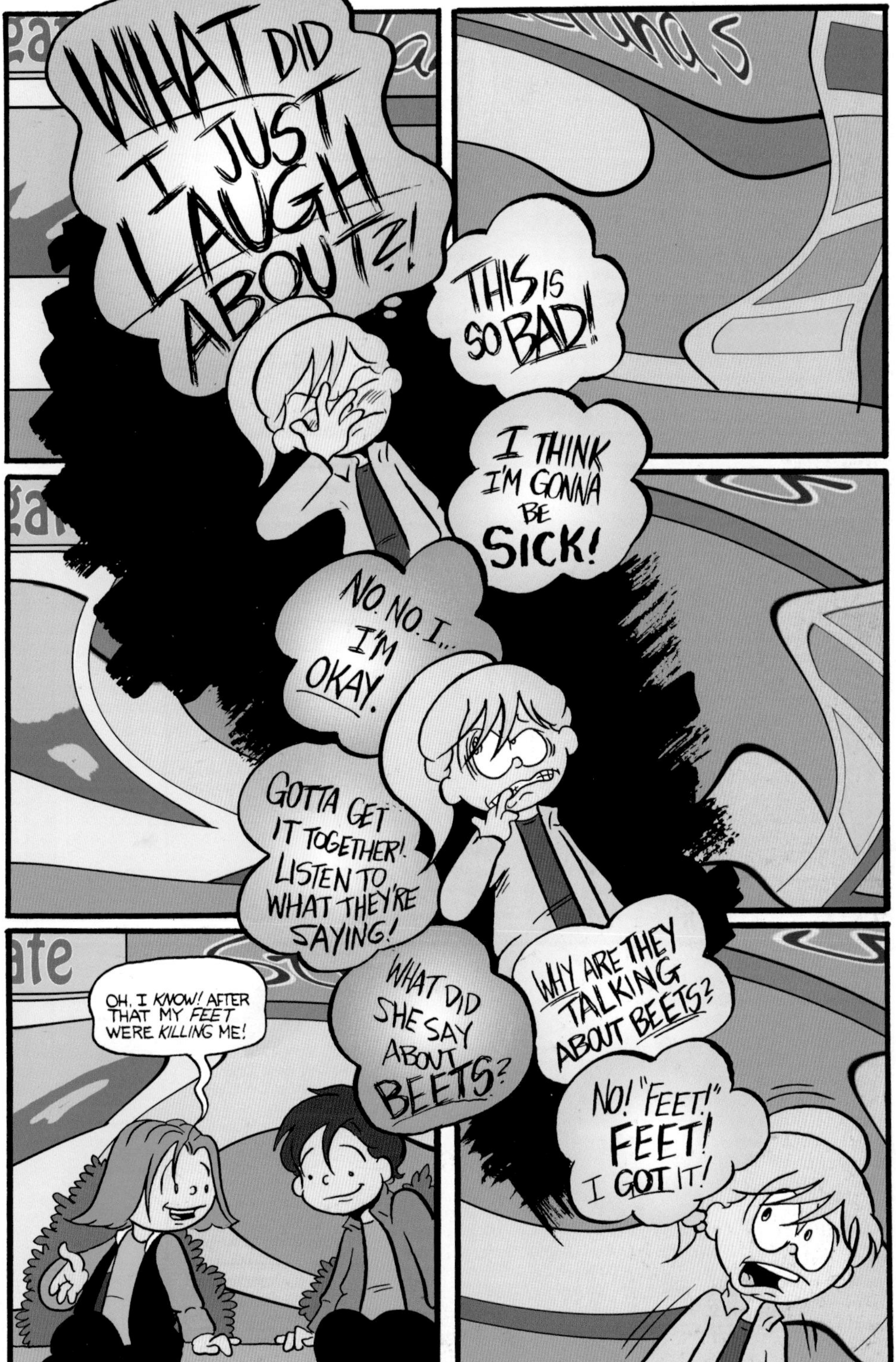
WHAT DID I JUST LAUGH ABOUT?!
THIS IS SO BAD!
I THINK I'M GONNA BE SICK!
NO. NO. I... I'M OKAY.
GOTTA GET IT TOGETHER! LISTEN TO WHAT THEY'RE SAYING!
OH, I KNOW! AFTER THAT MY FEET WERE KILLING ME!
WHAT DID SHE SAY ABOUT BEETS?
WHY ARE THEY TALKING ABOUT BEETS?
NO! "FEET!" FEET! I GOT IT!

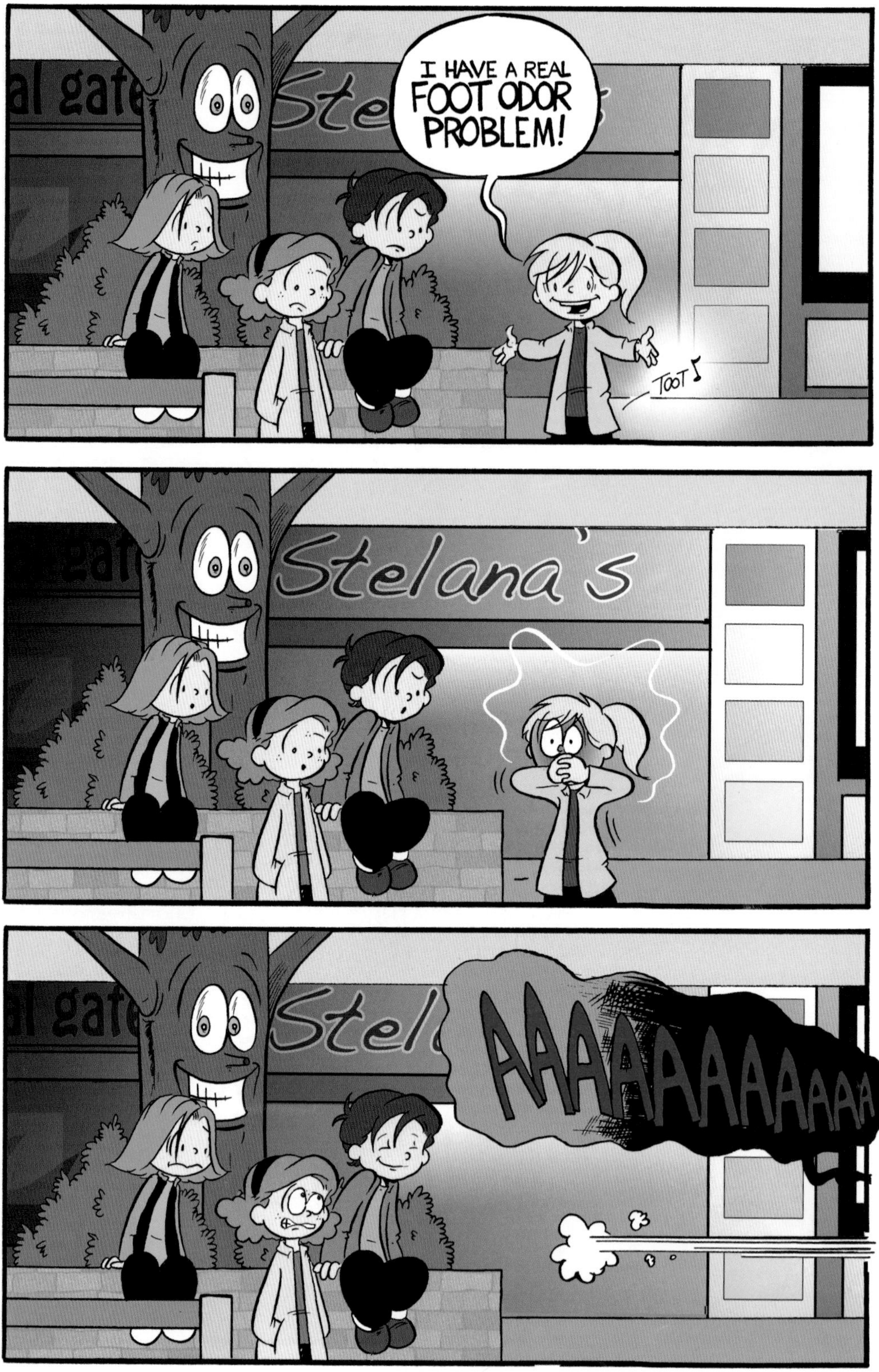
al gafe
I HAVE A REAL FOOT ODOR PROBLEM!
TOOT
Stelana's
AAAAAAAAAAA

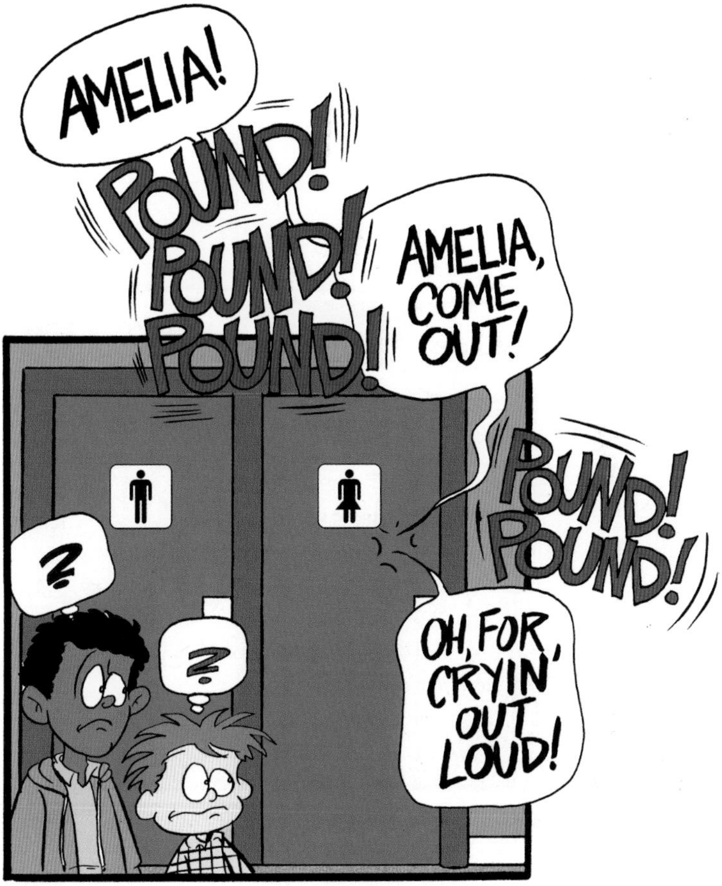
AMELIA!
POUND! POUND! POUND!
AMELIA, COME OUT!
POUND! POUND!
?
?
OH, FOR, CRYIN' OUT LOUD!

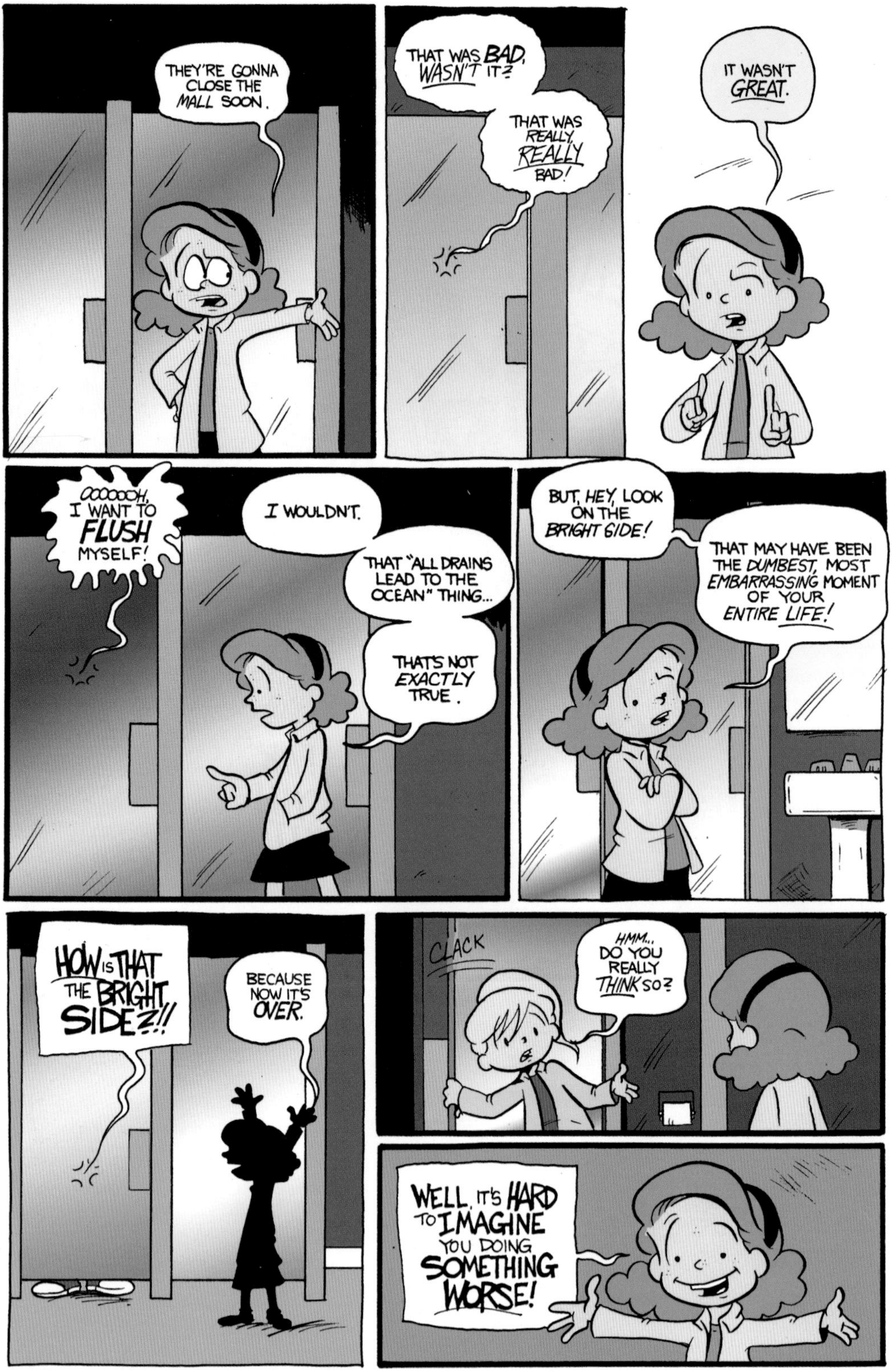
THEY'RE GONNA CLOSE THE MALL SOON.
THAT WAS BAD, WASN'T IT?
THAT WAS REALLY, REALLY BAD!
IT WASN'T GREAT.
OOOOOOH, I WANT TO FLUSH MYSELF!
I WOULDN'T.
THAT "ALL DRAINS LEAD TO THE OCEAN" THING...
THAT'S NOT EXACTLY TRUE.
BUT, HEY, LOOK ON THE BRIGHT SIDE!
THAT MAY HAVE BEEN THE DUMBEST, MOST EMBARRASSING MOMENT OF YOUR ENTIRE LIFE!
HOW IS THAT THE BRIGHT SIDE?!!
BECAUSE NOW IT'S OVER.
CLACK
HMM... DO YOU REALLY THINK SO?
WELL, IT'S HARD TO IMAGINE YOU DOING SOMETHING WORSE!

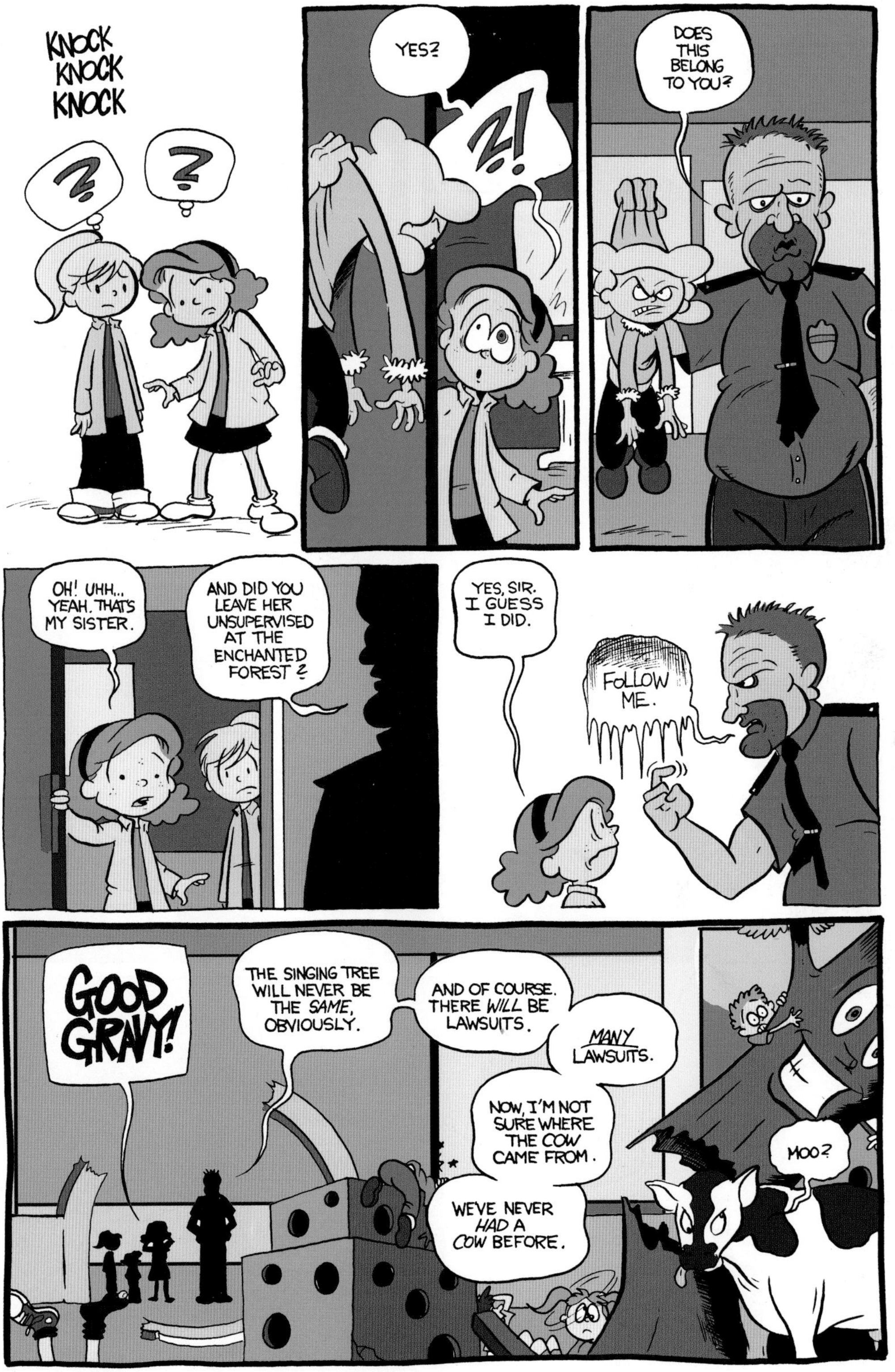
KNOCK KNOCK KNOCK
?
?
YES?
?!
DOES THIS BELONG TO YOU?
OH! UHH... YEAH. THAT'S MY SISTER.
AND DID YOU LEAVE HER UNSUPERVISED AT THE ENCHANTED FOREST?
YES, SIR. I GUESS I DID.
FOLLOW ME.
GOOD GRAVY!
THE SINGING TREE WILL NEVER BE THE *SAME*, OBVIOUSLY.
AND OF COURSE. THERE *WILL* BE LAWSUITS.
MANY LAWSUITS.
NOW, I'M NOT SURE WHERE THE COW CAME FROM.
WE'VE NEVER *HAD* A COW BEFORE.
MOO?

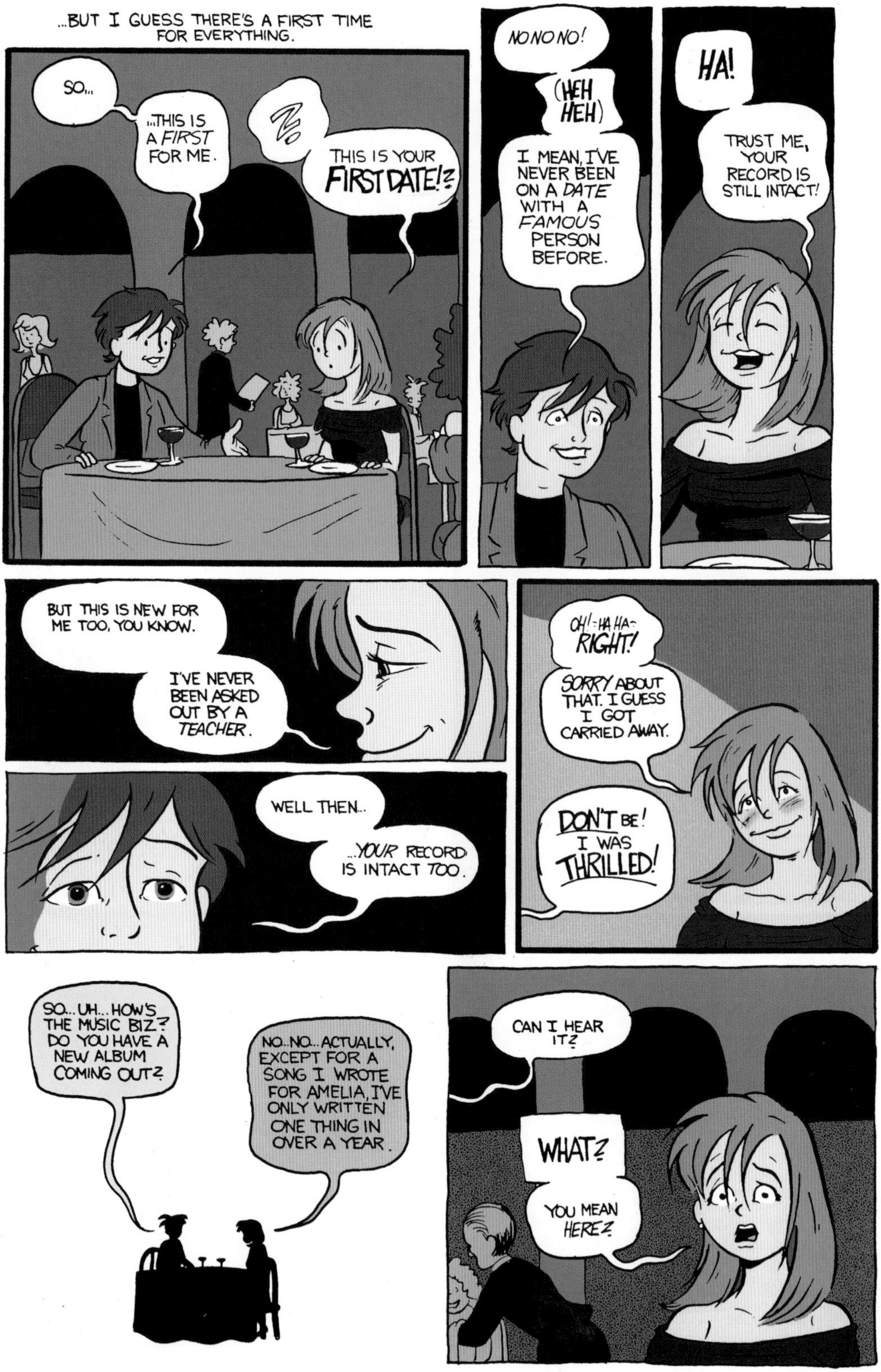
...BUT I GUESS THERE'S A FIRST TIME FOR EVERYTHING.
SO...
...THIS IS A FIRST FOR ME.
THIS IS YOUR FIRST DATE!?
NO NO NO!
(HEH HEH)
I MEAN, I'VE NEVER BEEN ON A DATE WITH A FAMOUS PERSON BEFORE.
HA!
TRUST ME, YOUR RECORD IS STILL INTACT!
BUT THIS IS NEW FOR ME TOO, YOU KNOW.
I'VE NEVER BEEN ASKED OUT BY A TEACHER.
WELL THEN...
...YOUR RECORD IS INTACT TOO.
OH!-HA HA-RIGHT!
SORRY ABOUT THAT. I GUESS I GOT CARRIED AWAY.
DON'T BE! I WAS THRILLED!
SO...UH...HOW'S THE MUSIC BIZ? DO YOU HAVE A NEW ALBUM COMING OUT?
NO...NO...ACTUALLY, EXCEPT FOR A SONG I WROTE FOR AMELIA, I'VE ONLY WRITTEN ONE THING IN OVER A YEAR.
CAN I HEAR IT?
WHAT?
YOU MEAN HERE?

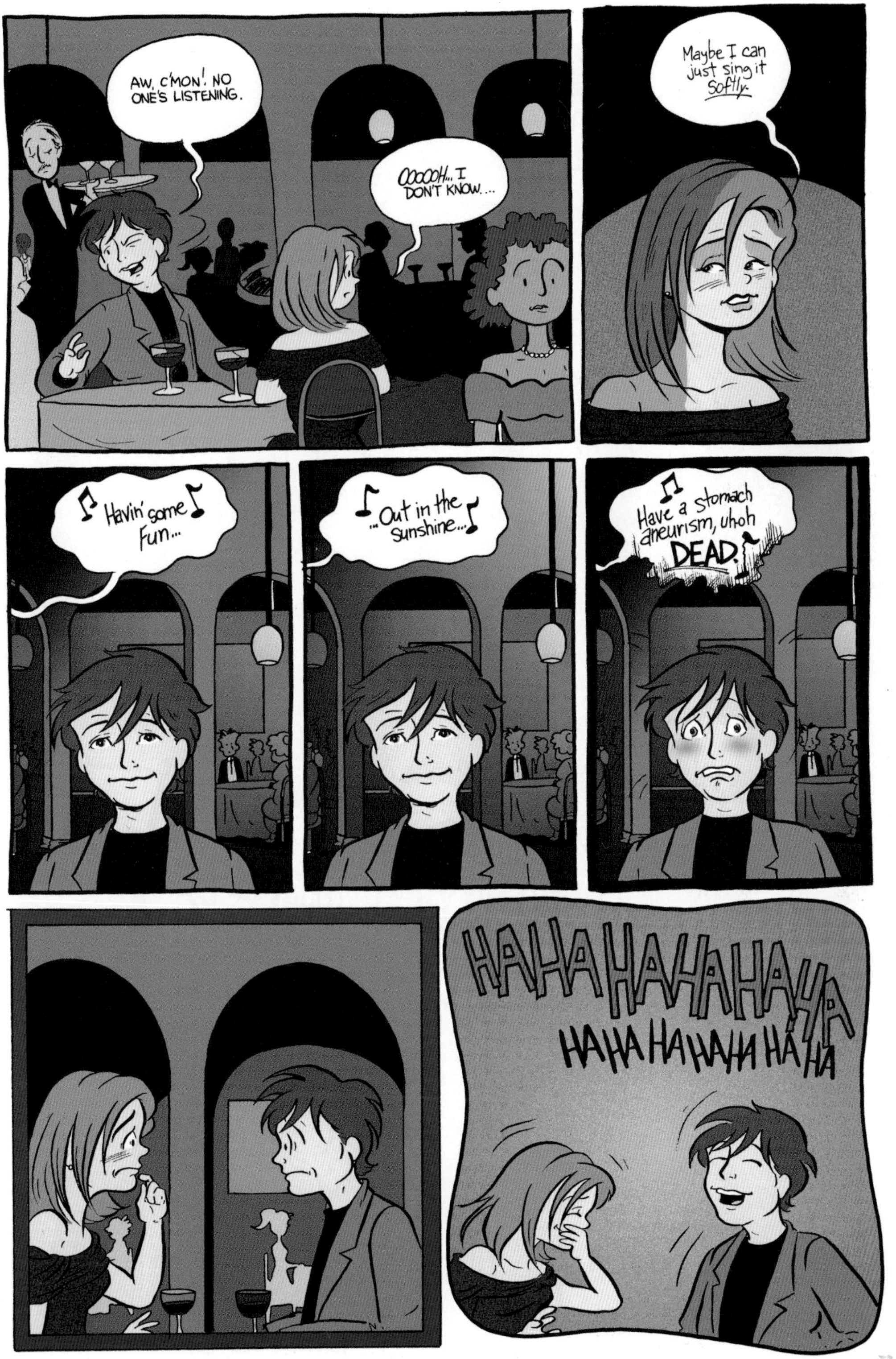
AW, C'MON! NO ONE'S LISTENING.
OOOOOH... I DON'T KNOW....
Maybe I can just sing it softly.
Havin' some Fun...
...Out in the sunshine...
Have a stomach aneurism, uh-oh DEAD.
HAHA HAHAHAHAHAHA
HAHA HA HAHAHA HA HA

SO AFTER A LECTURE FROM THE SECURITY GUARD, THE MALL MANAGER, AND RHONDA'S MOM, I WAS DEFINITELY READY TO GO TO BED.

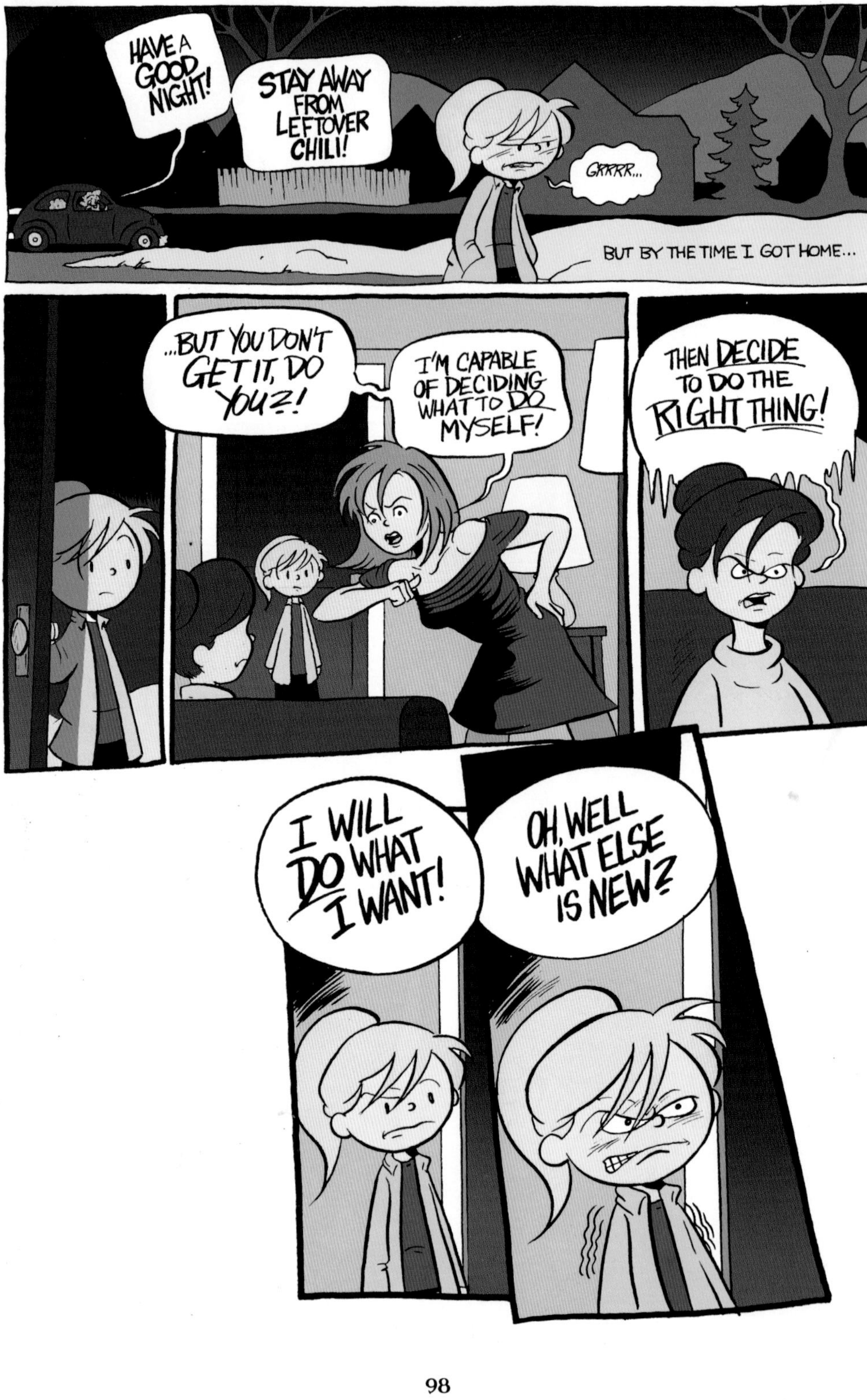
HAVE A GOOD NIGHT!
STAY AWAY FROM LEFTOVER CHILI!
GRRRR...
BUT BY THE TIME I GOT HOME...
...BUT YOU DON'T GET IT, DO YOU?!
I'M CAPABLE OF DECIDING WHAT TO DO MYSELF!
THEN DECIDE TO DO THE RIGHT THING!
I WILL DO WHAT I WANT!
OH, WELL WHAT ELSE IS NEW?

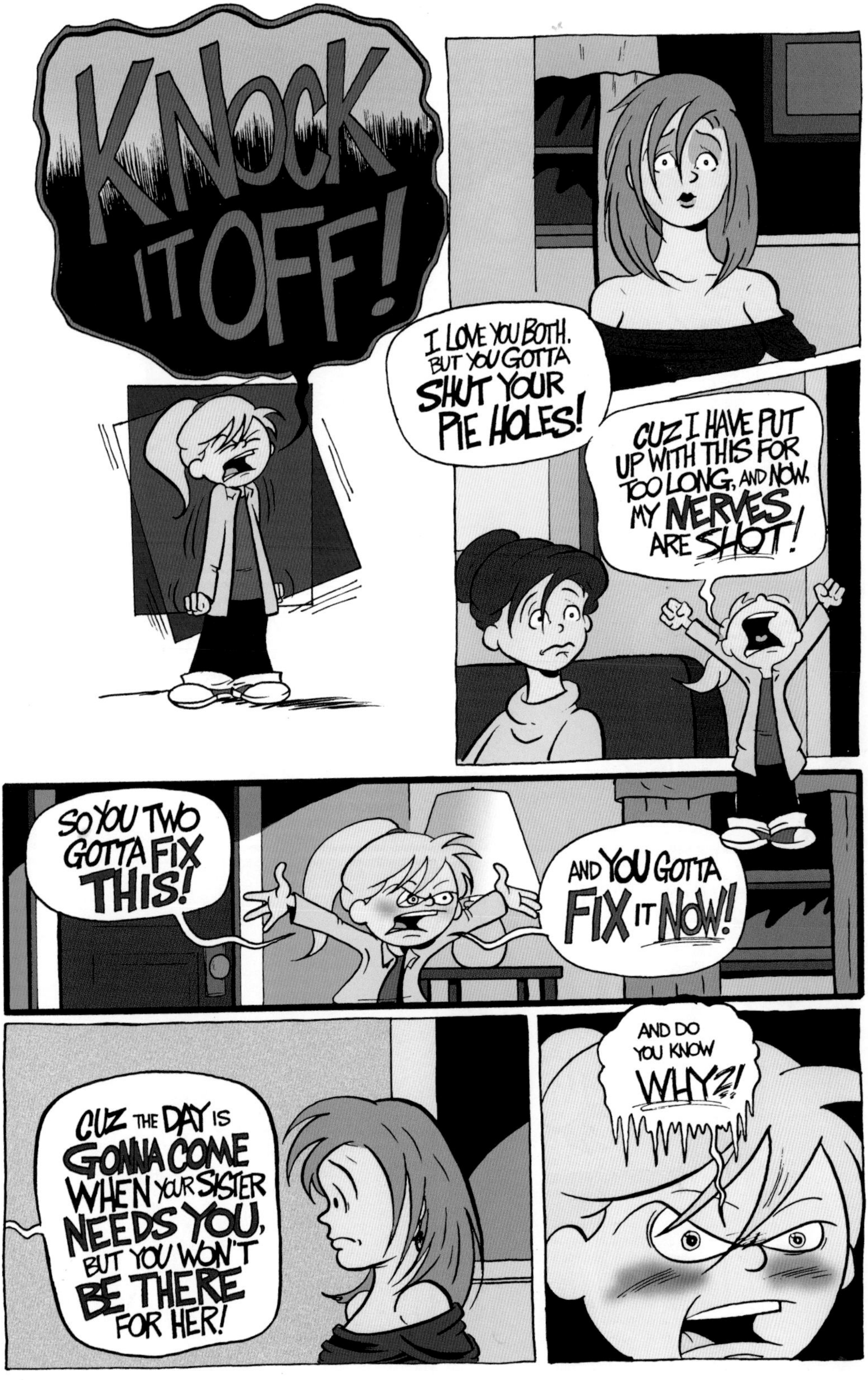
KNOCK IT OFF!
I LOVE YOU BOTH. BUT YOU GOTTA SHUT YOUR PIE HOLES!
CUZ I HAVE PUT UP WITH THIS FOR TOO LONG, AND NOW, MY NERVES ARE SHOT!
SO YOU TWO GOTTA FIX THIS!
AND YOU GOTTA FIX IT NOW!
CUZ THE DAY IS GONNA COME WHEN YOUR SISTER NEEDS YOU, BUT YOU WON'T BE THERE FOR HER!
AND DO YOU KNOW WHY?!

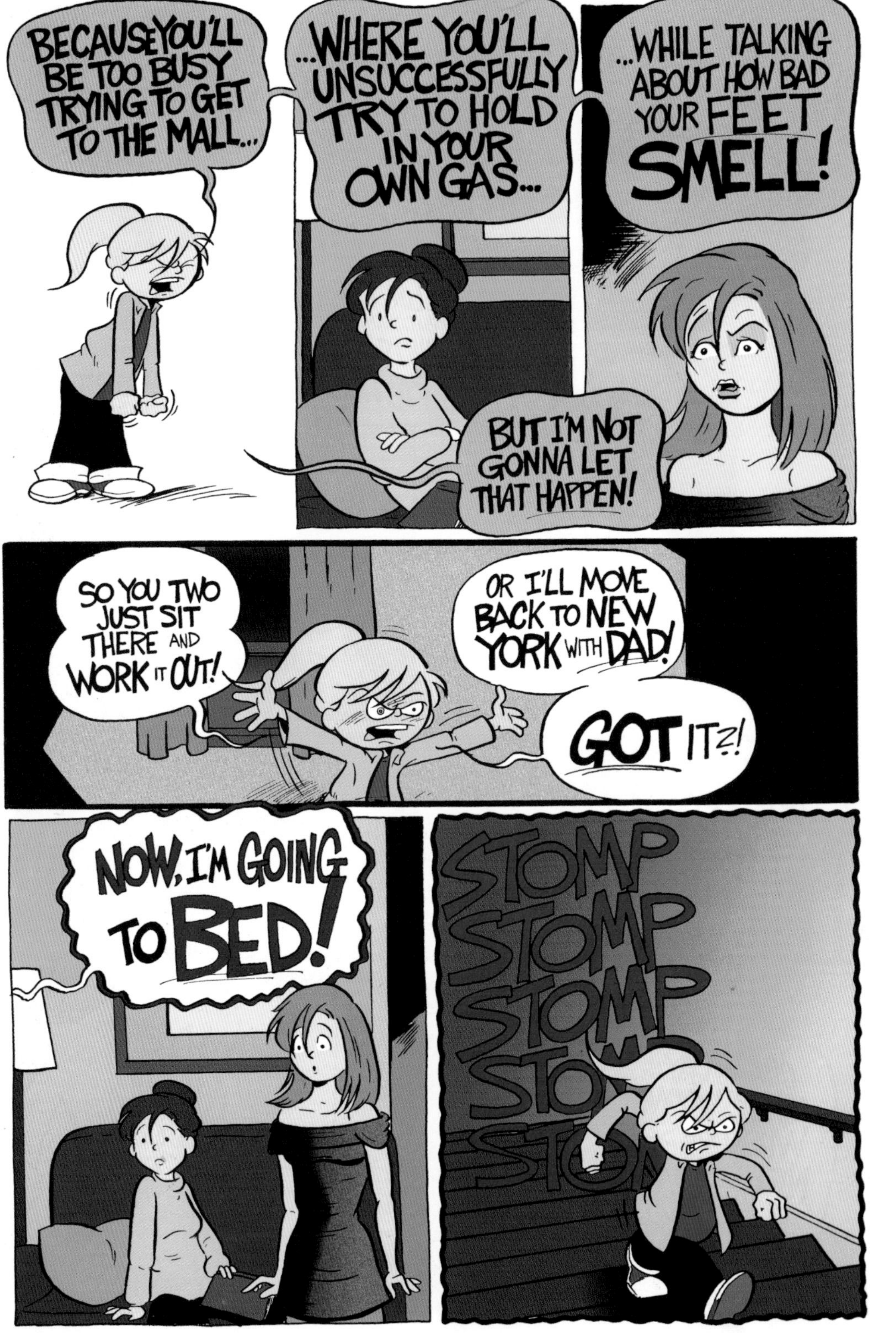
BECAUSE YOU'LL BE TOO BUSY TRYING TO GET TO THE MALL...
...WHERE YOU'LL UNSUCCESSFULLY TRY TO HOLD IN YOUR OWN GAS...
...WHILE TALKING ABOUT HOW BAD YOUR FEET SMELL!
BUT I'M NOT GONNA LET THAT HAPPEN!
SO YOU TWO JUST SIT THERE AND WORK IT OUT!
OR I'LL MOVE BACK TO NEW YORK WITH DAD!
GOT IT?!
NOW, I'M GOING TO BED!
STOMP
STOMP
STOMP

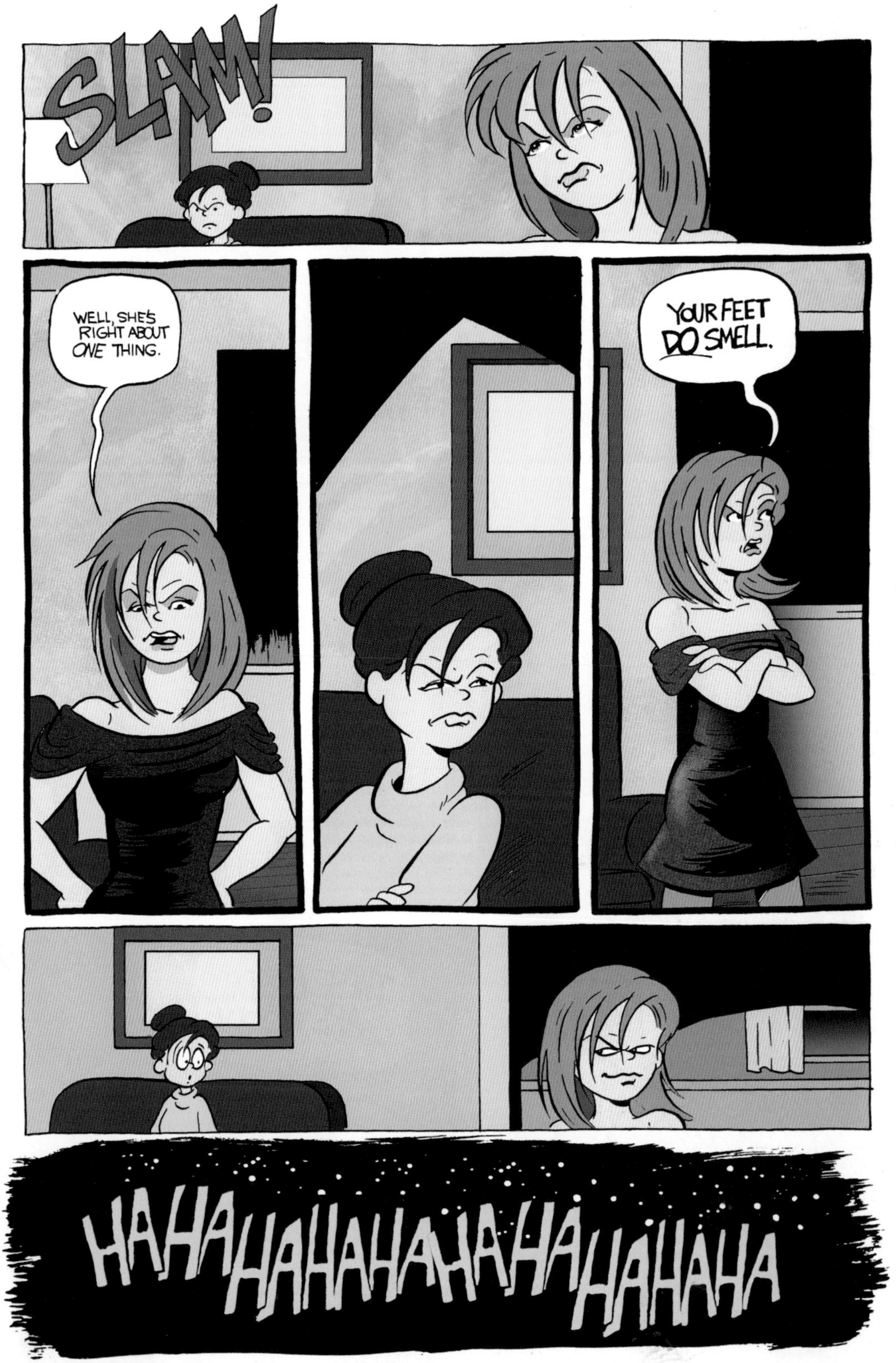
SLAM!
WELL, SHE'S RIGHT ABOUT ONE THING.
YOUR FEET DO SMELL.
HAHAHAHAHAHAHAHAHAHAHAHAHA

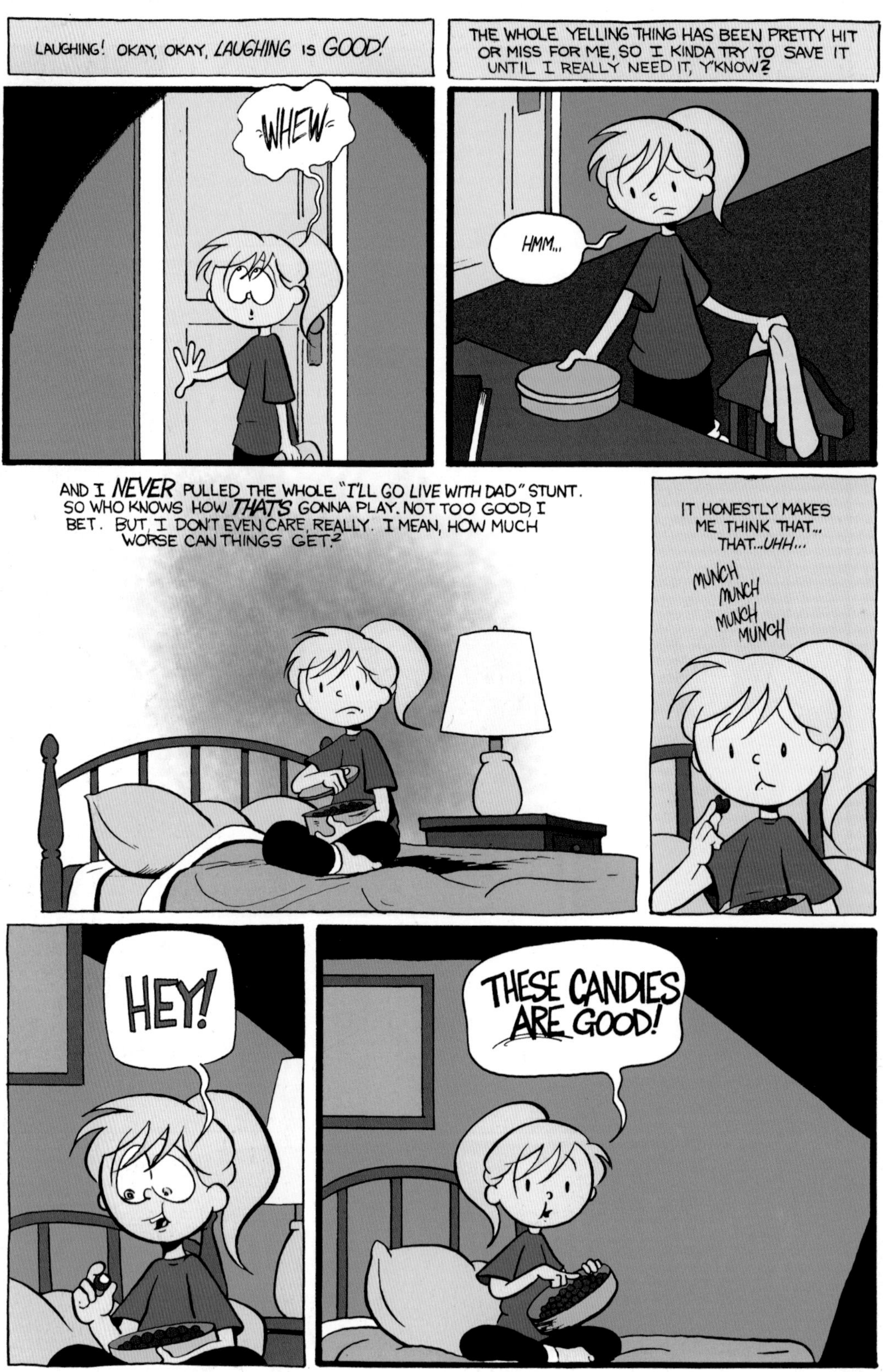
LAUGHING! OKAY, OKAY, LAUGHING IS GOOD!
THE WHOLE YELLING THING HAS BEEN PRETTY HIT OR MISS FOR ME, SO I KINDA TRY TO SAVE IT UNTIL I REALLY NEED IT, Y'KNOW?
WHEW
HMM...
AND I NEVER PULLED THE WHOLE "I'LL GO LIVE WITH DAD" STUNT. SO WHO KNOWS HOW THAT'S GONNA PLAY. NOT TOO GOOD, I BET. BUT, I DON'T EVEN CARE, REALLY. I MEAN, HOW MUCH WORSE CAN THINGS GET?
IT HONESTLY MAKES ME THINK THAT... THAT...UHH...
MUNCH MUNCH MUNCH MUNCH
HEY!
THESE CANDIES ARE GOOD!

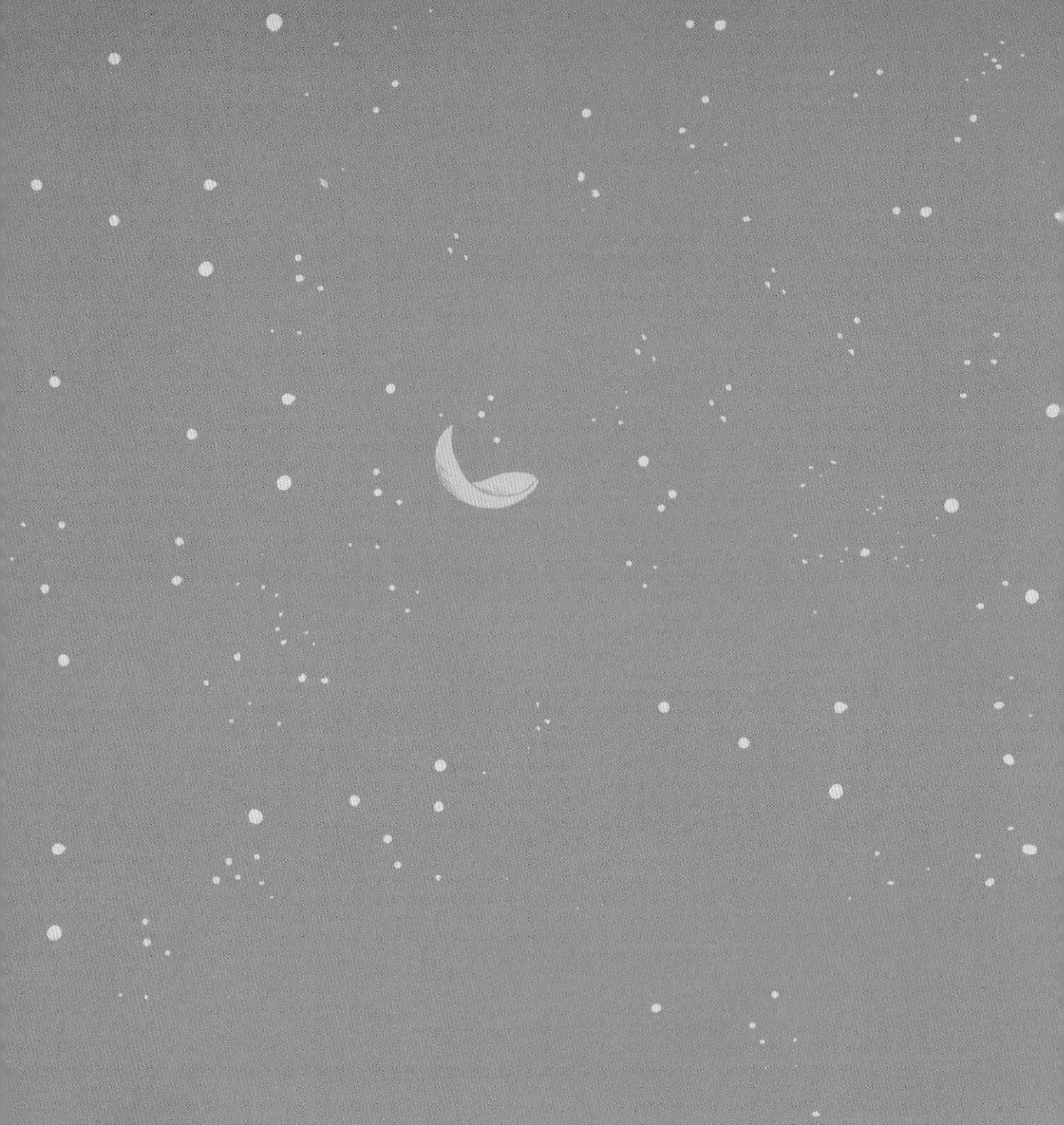

"Art is like a beautiful dream, and the rest of the world is the alarm clock."

-Tanner Clark

from the liner notes of *Broken Record*

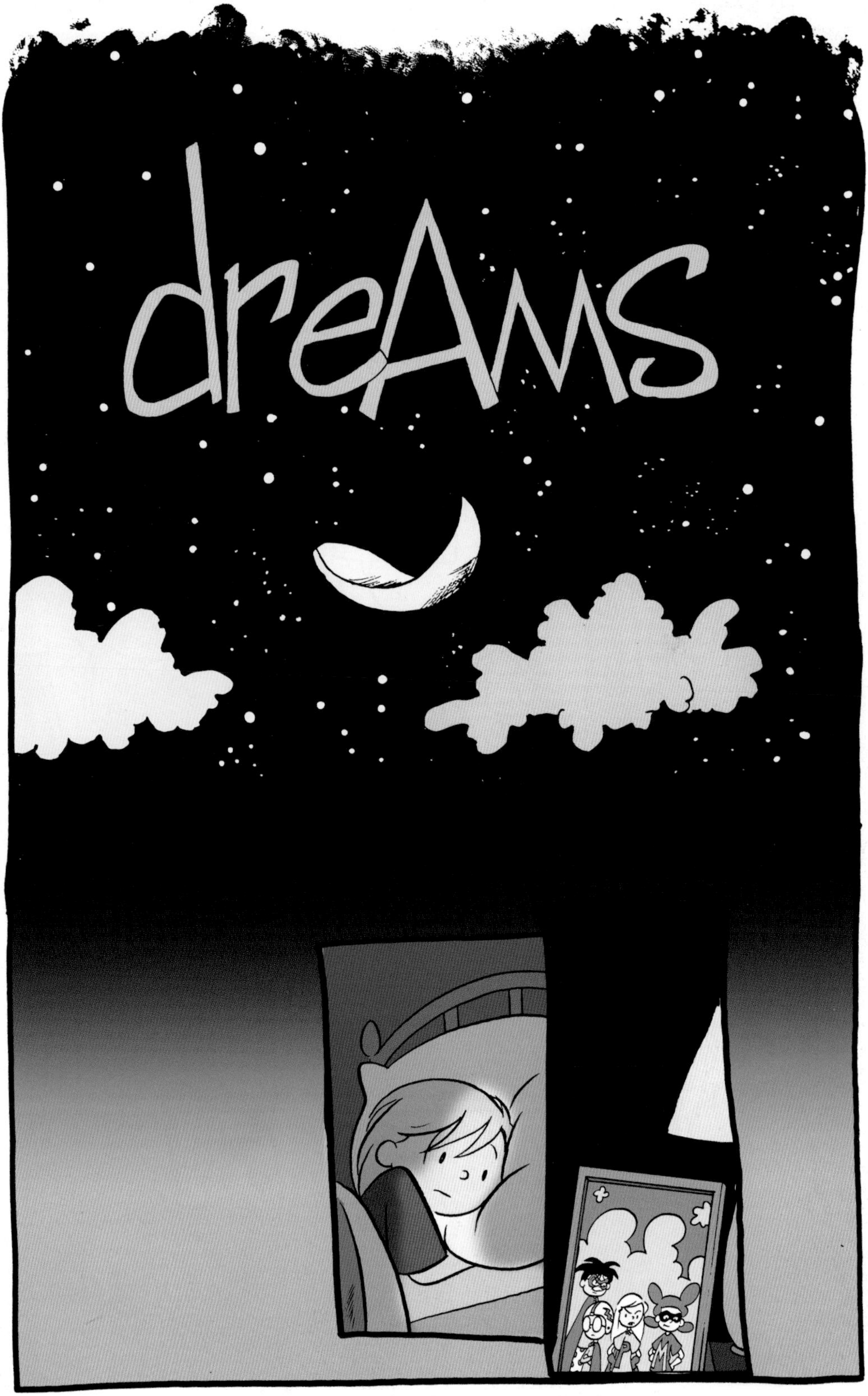
dreAms

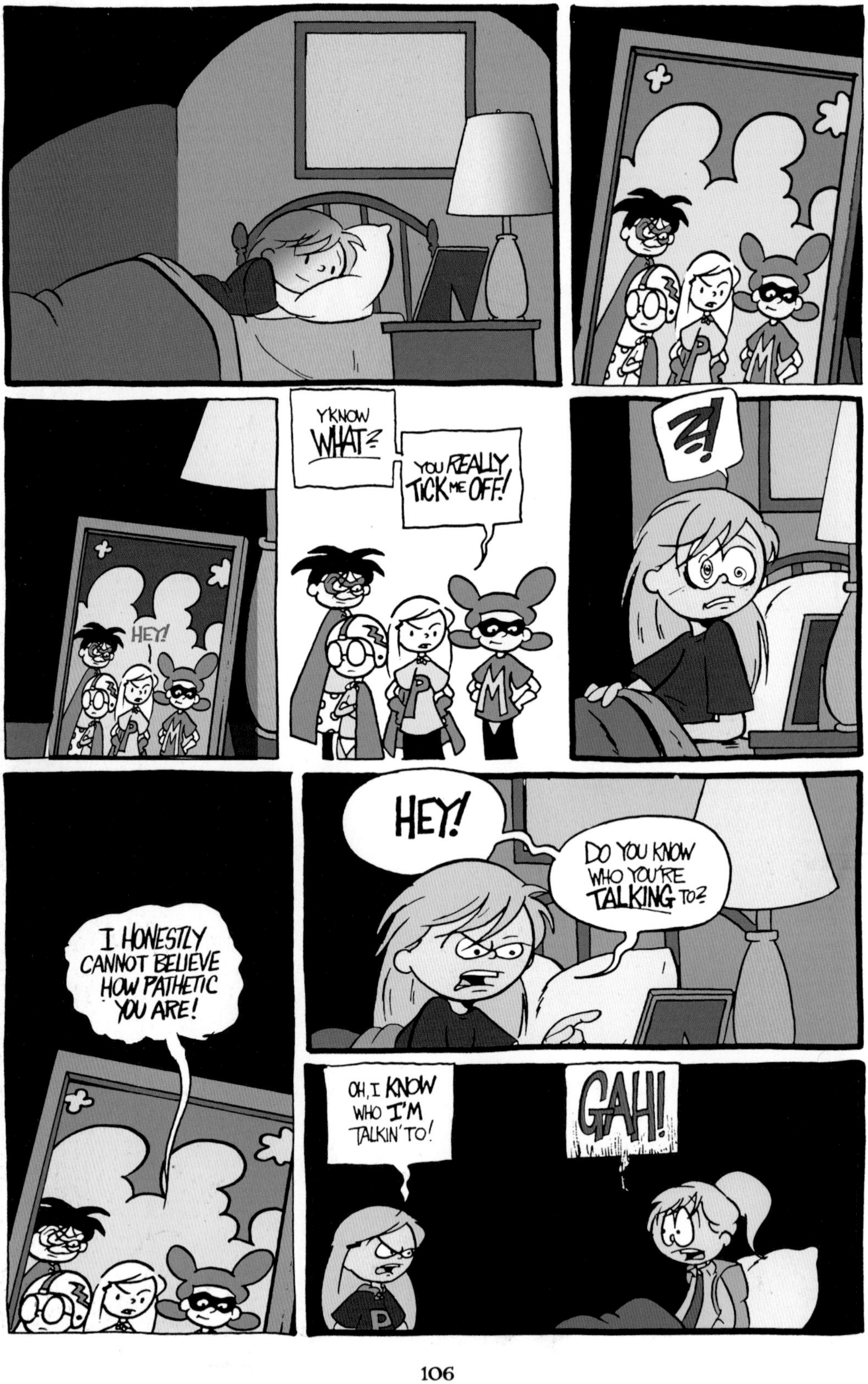
HEY!
Y'KNOW WHAT?
YOU REALLY TICK ME OFF!
?!
I HONESTLY CANNOT BELIEVE HOW PATHETIC YOU ARE!
HEY!
DO YOU KNOW WHO YOU'RE TALKING TO?
OH, I KNOW WHO I'M TALKIN' TO!
GAH!

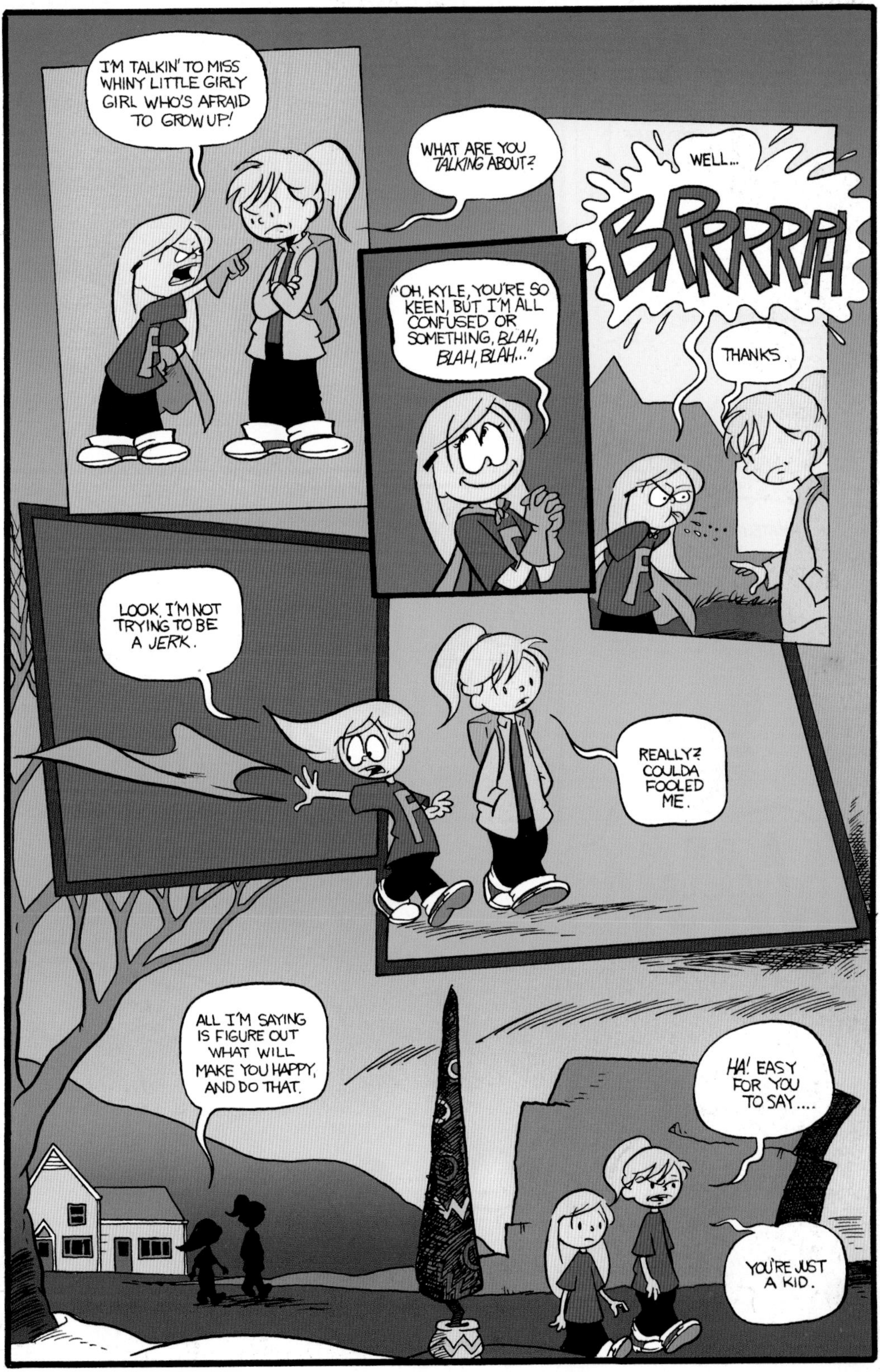
I'M TALKIN' TO MISS WHINY LITTLE GIRLY GIRL WHO'S AFRAID TO GROW UP!
WHAT ARE YOU TALKING ABOUT?
"OH, KYLE, YOU'RE SO KEEN, BUT I'M ALL CONFUSED OR SOMETHING, BLAH, BLAH, BLAH..."
WELL...
BRRRRPH
THANKS.
LOOK, I'M NOT TRYING TO BE A JERK.
REALLY? COULDA FOOLED ME.
ALL I'M SAYING IS FIGURE OUT WHAT WILL MAKE YOU HAPPY, AND DO THAT.
HA! EASY FOR YOU TO SAY....
YOU'RE JUST A KID.

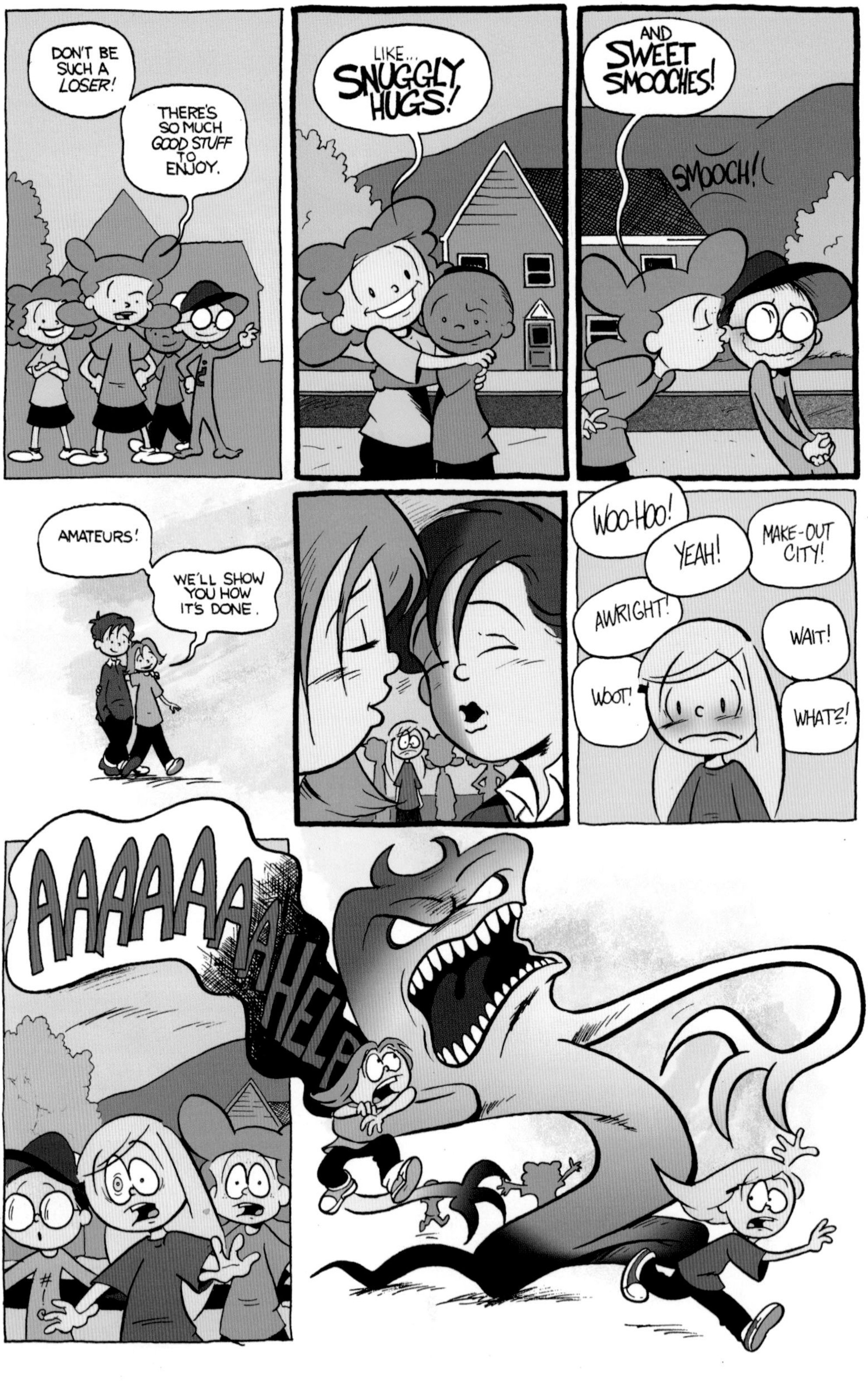
DON'T BE SUCH A LOSER!
THERE'S SO MUCH GOOD STUFF TO ENJOY.
LIKE... SNUGGLY HUGS!
AND SWEET SMOOCHES!
SMOOCH!
AMATEURS!
WE'LL SHOW YOU HOW IT'S DONE.
WOO-HOO!
YEAH!
MAKE-OUT CITY!
AWRIGHT!
WAIT!
WOOT!
WHAT?!
AAAAAAAAHELP

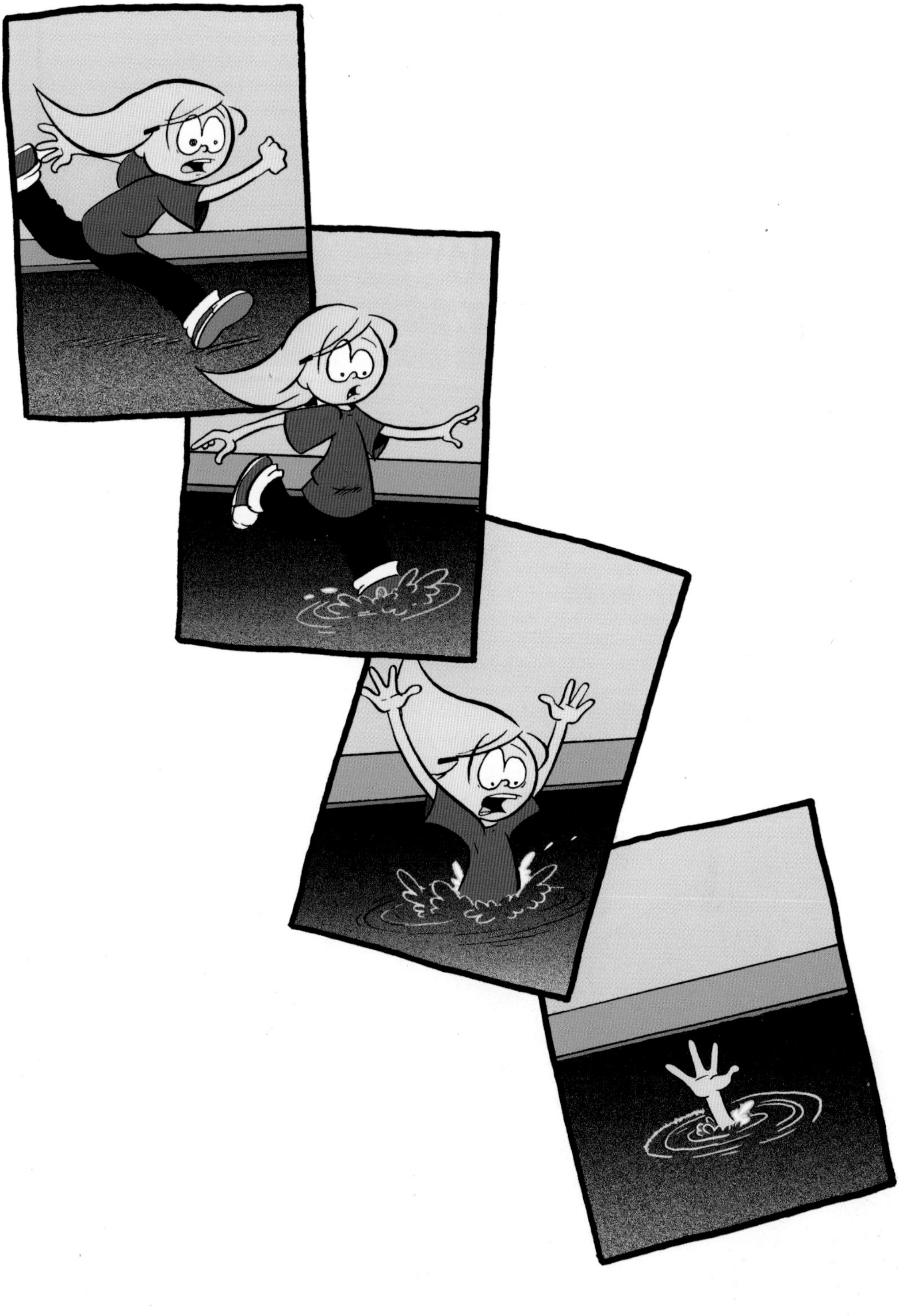

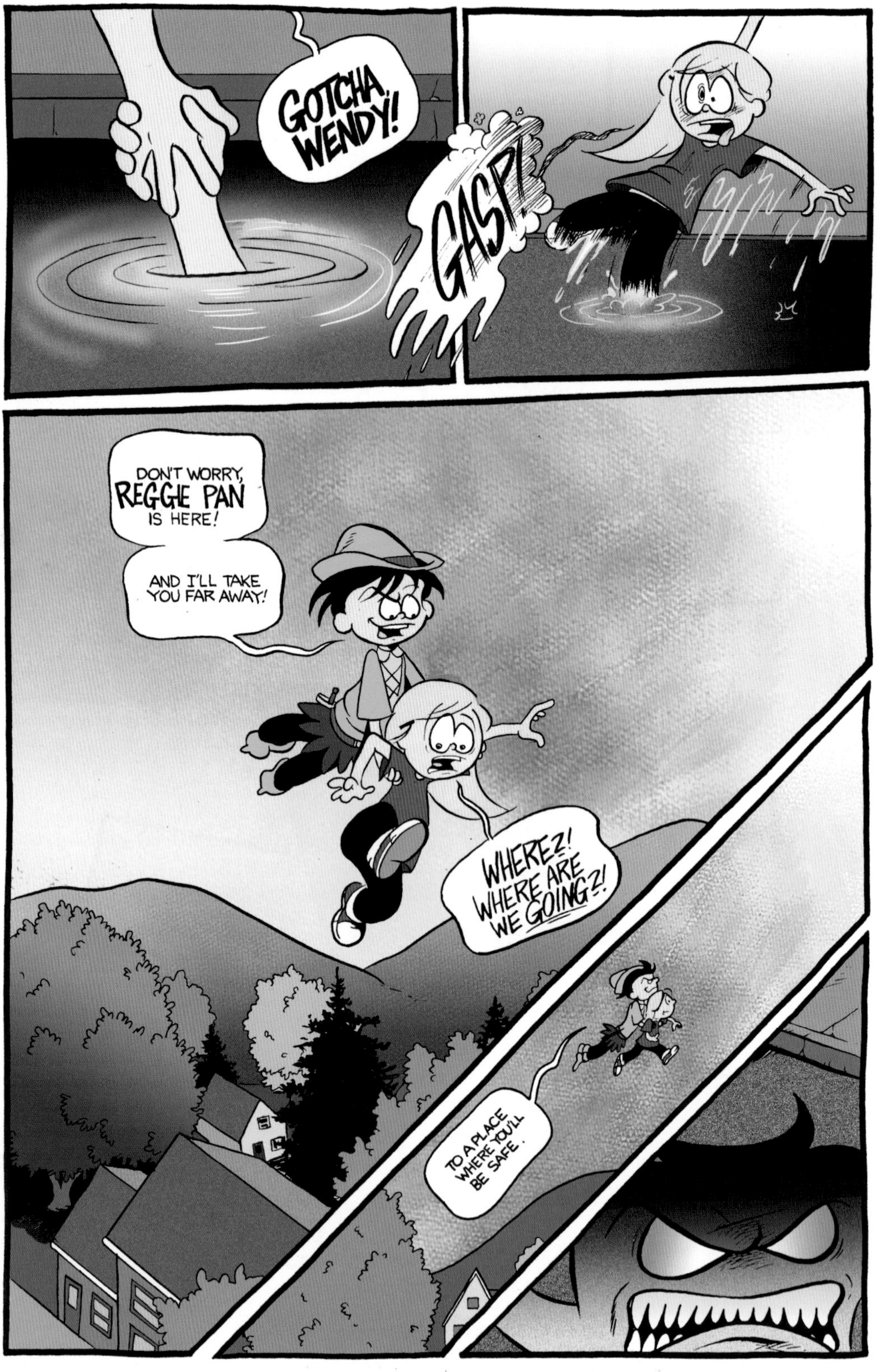
GOTCHA, WENDY!
GASP!
DON'T WORRY, REGGIE PAN IS HERE!
AND I'LL TAKE YOU FAR AWAY!
WHERE?! WHERE ARE WE GOING?!
TO A PLACE WHERE YOU'LL BE SAFE.

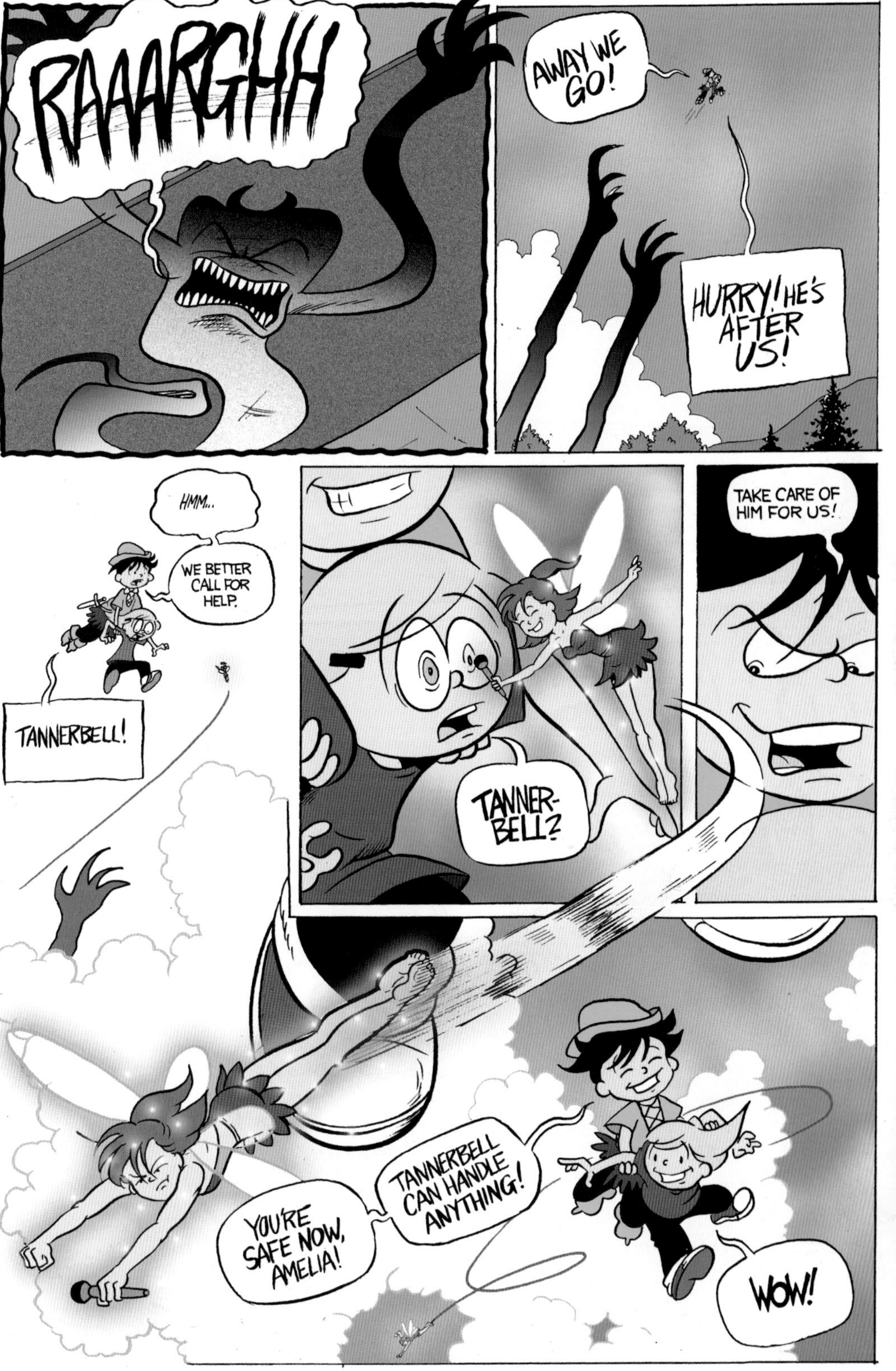
RAAARGHH
AWAY WE GO!
HURRY! HE'S AFTER US!
HMM...
WE BETTER CALL FOR HELP.
TANNERBELL!
TANNER-BELL?
TAKE CARE OF HIM FOR US!
TANNERBELL CAN HANDLE ANYTHING!
YOU'RE SAFE NOW, AMELIA!
WOW!

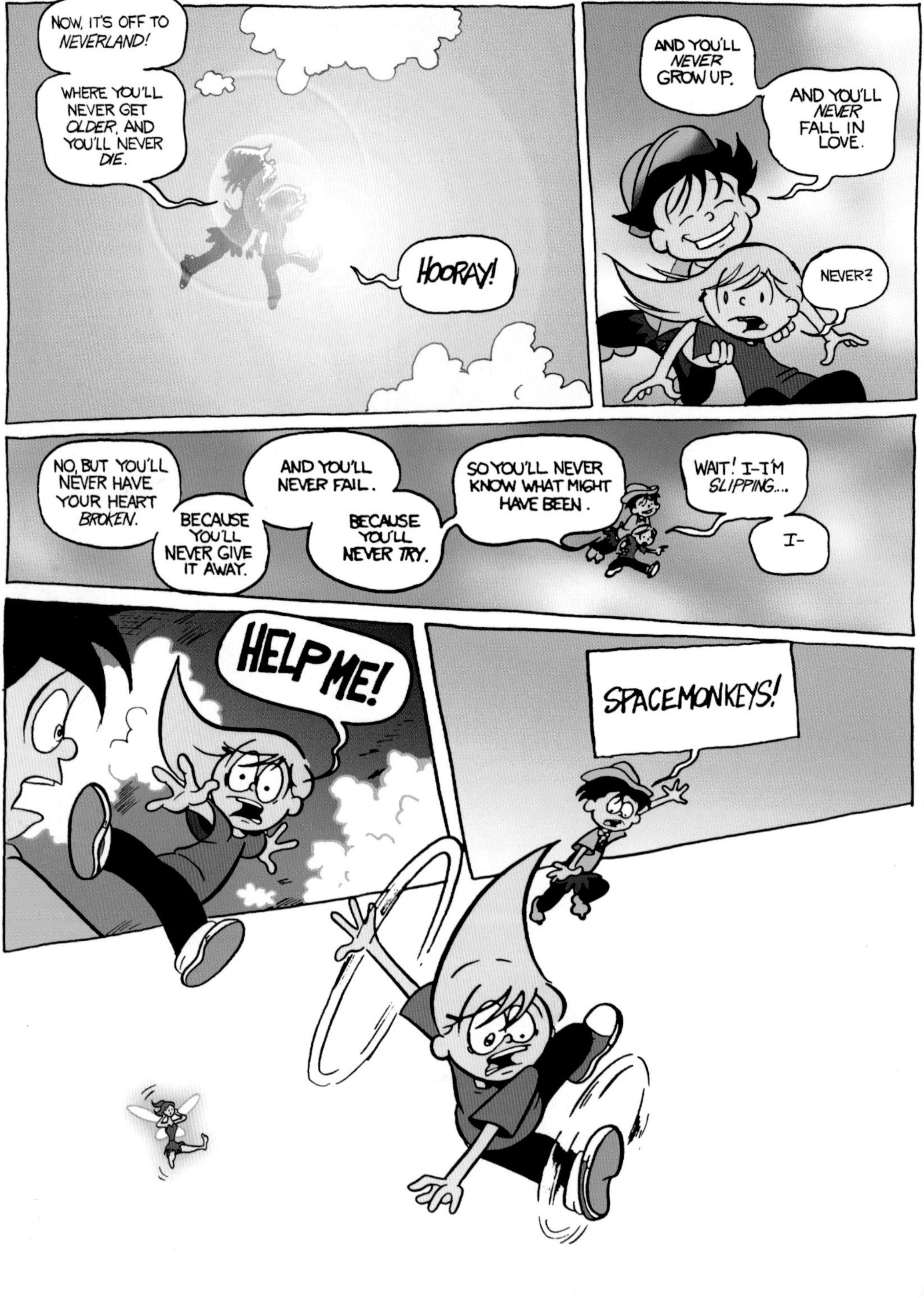
NOW, IT'S OFF TO NEVERLAND!
WHERE YOU'LL NEVER GET OLDER, AND YOU'LL NEVER DIE.
HOORAY!
AND YOU'LL NEVER GROW UP.
AND YOU'LL NEVER FALL IN LOVE.
NEVER?
NO, BUT YOU'LL NEVER HAVE YOUR HEART BROKEN.
BECAUSE YOU'LL NEVER GIVE IT AWAY.
AND YOU'LL NEVER FAIL.
BECAUSE YOU'LL NEVER TRY.
SO YOU'LL NEVER KNOW WHAT MIGHT HAVE BEEN.
WAIT! I-I'M SLIPPING....
I-
HELP ME!
SPACEMONKEYS!

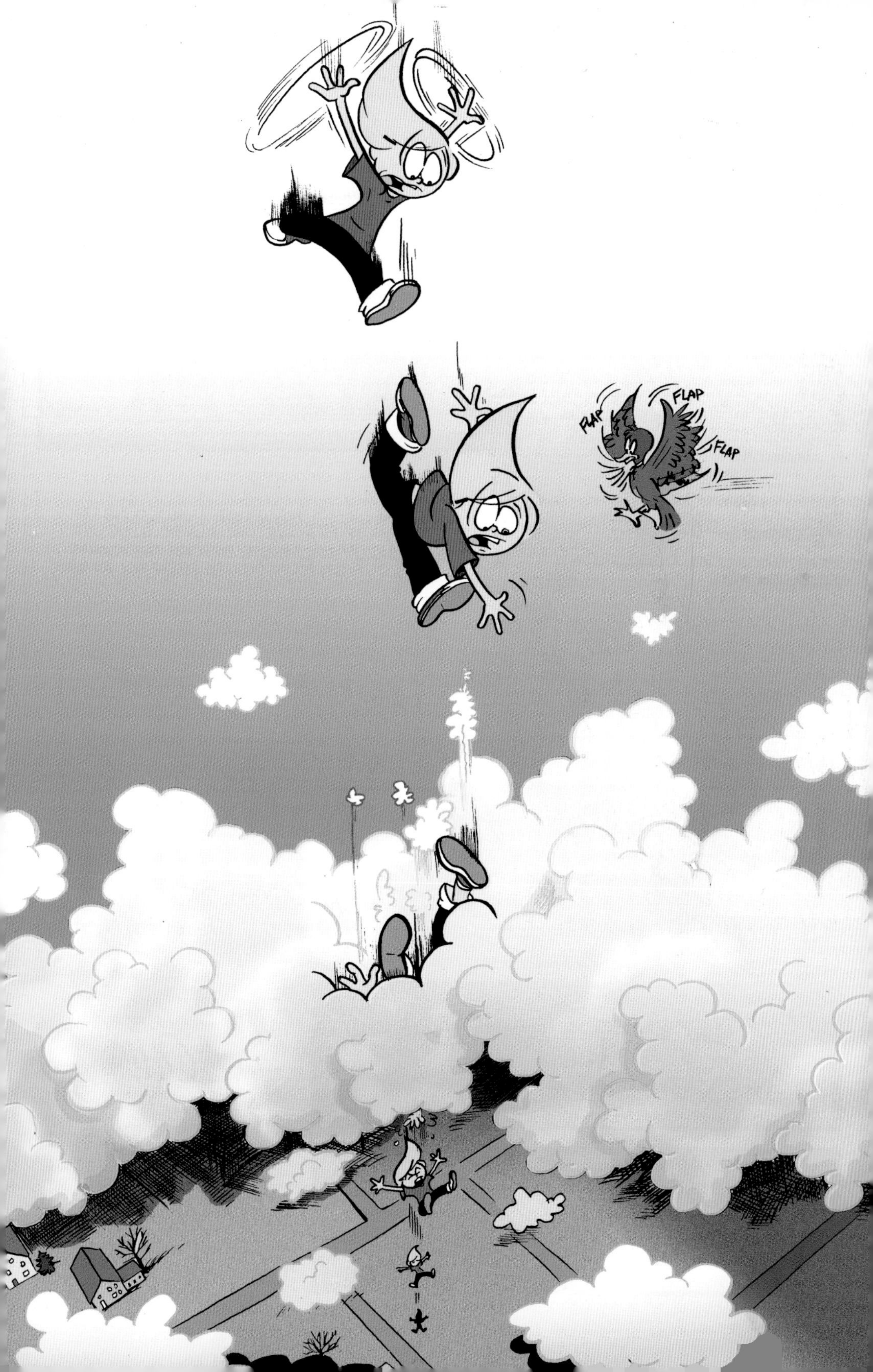
FLAP
FLAP
FLAP

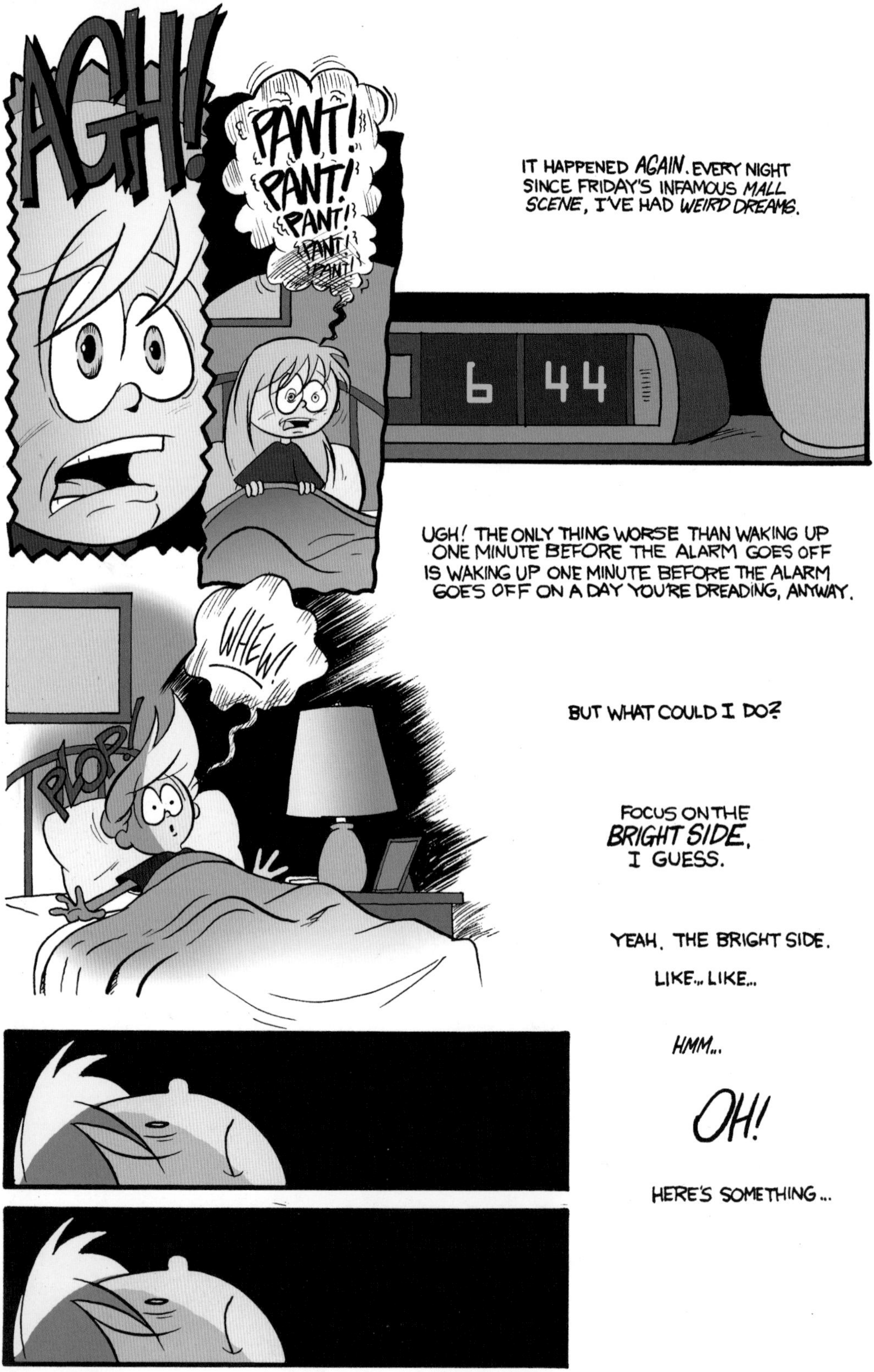
AGH!
PANT! PANT! PANT! PANT! PANT!
IT HAPPENED AGAIN. EVERY NIGHT SINCE FRIDAY'S INFAMOUS MALL SCENE, I'VE HAD WEIRD DREAMS.
6 44
UGH! THE ONLY THING WORSE THAN WAKING UP ONE MINUTE BEFORE THE ALARM GOES OFF IS WAKING UP ONE MINUTE BEFORE THE ALARM GOES OFF ON A DAY YOU'RE DREADING, ANYWAY.
WHEW!
PLOP!
BUT WHAT COULD I DO?
FOCUS ON THE BRIGHT SIDE, I GUESS.
YEAH. THE BRIGHT SIDE.
LIKE... LIKE...
HMM...
OH!
HERE'S SOMETHING...

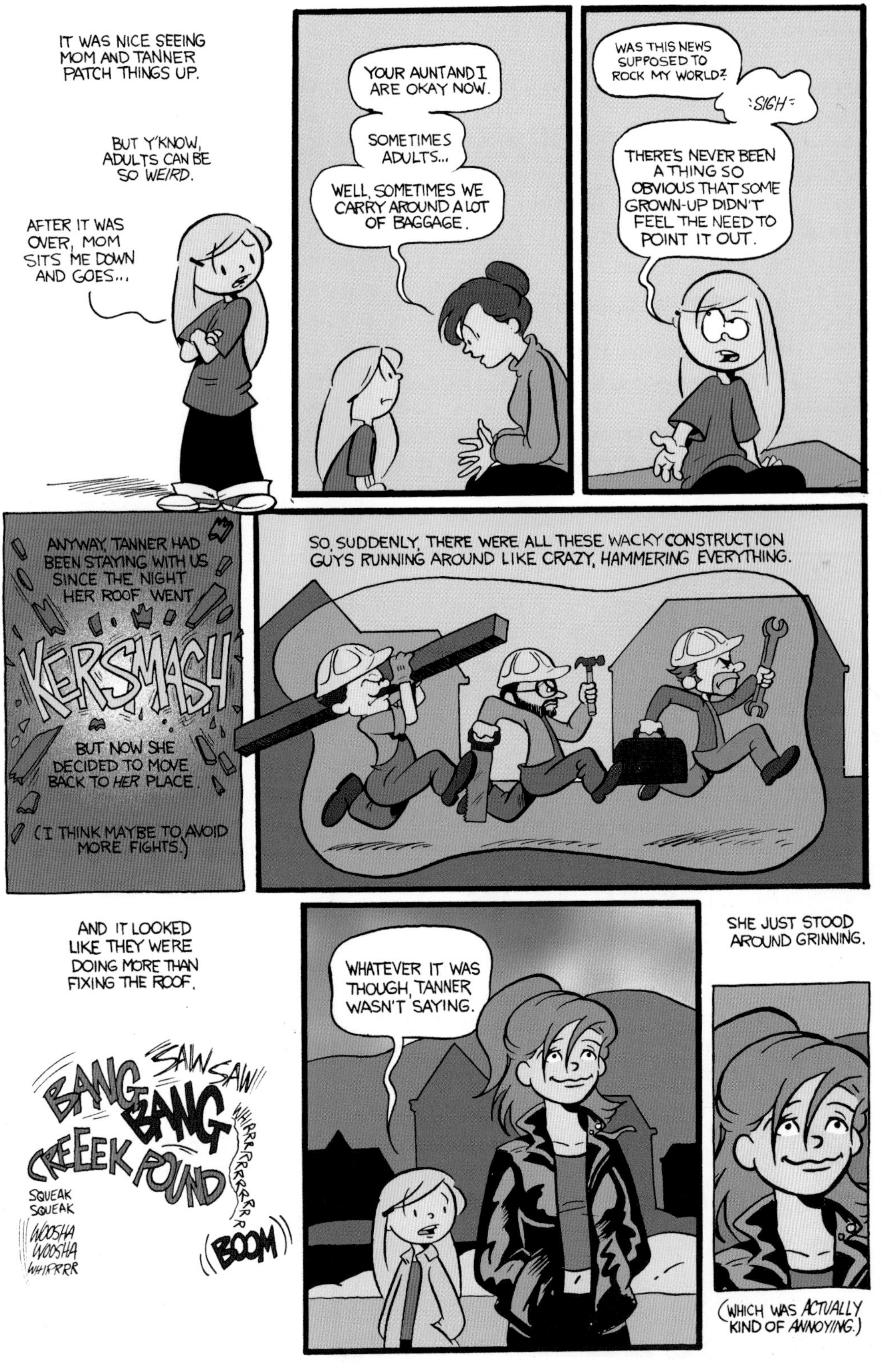

IT WAS NICE SEEING MOM AND TANNER PATCH THINGS UP.
BUT Y'KNOW, ADULTS CAN BE SO *WEIRD*.
AFTER IT WAS OVER, MOM SITS ME DOWN AND GOES...
YOUR AUNT AND I ARE OKAY NOW.
SOMETIMES ADULTS...
WELL, SOMETIMES WE CARRY AROUND A LOT OF BAGGAGE.
WAS THIS NEWS SUPPOSED TO ROCK MY WORLD?
SIGH
THERE'S NEVER BEEN A THING SO OBVIOUS THAT SOME GROWN-UP DIDN'T FEEL THE NEED TO POINT IT OUT.
ANYWAY, TANNER HAD BEEN STAYING WITH US SINCE THE NIGHT HER ROOF WENT
KERSMASH
BUT NOW SHE DECIDED TO MOVE BACK TO *HER* PLACE.
(I THINK MAYBE TO AVOID MORE FIGHTS.)
SO, SUDDENLY, THERE WERE ALL THESE WACKY CONSTRUCTION GUYS RUNNING AROUND LIKE CRAZY, HAMMERING EVERYTHING.
AND IT LOOKED LIKE THEY WERE DOING MORE THAN FIXING THE ROOF.
BANG BANG
SAW SAW
CREEEK POUND
WHIRRRRRRRRR
SQUEAK SQUEAK
WOOSHA WOOSHA WHIRRRR
BOOM
WHATEVER IT WAS THOUGH, TANNER WASN'T SAYING.
SHE JUST STOOD AROUND GRINNING.
(WHICH WAS *ACTUALLY* KIND OF *ANNOYING*.)

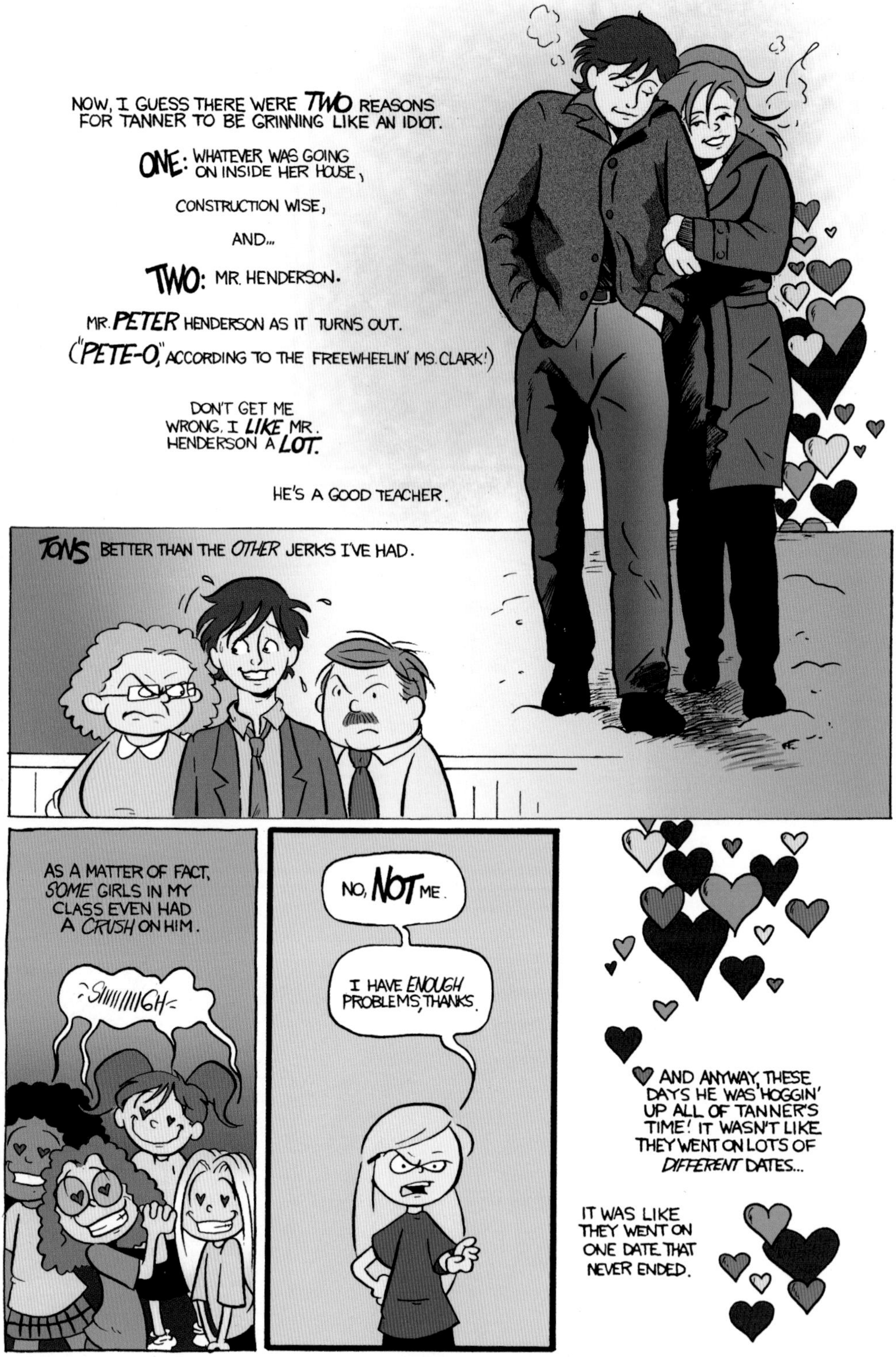
NOW, I GUESS THERE WERE TWO REASONS FOR TANNER TO BE GRINNING LIKE AN IDIOT.
ONE: WHATEVER WAS GOING ON INSIDE HER HOUSE,
CONSTRUCTION WISE,
AND...
TWO: MR. HENDERSON.
MR. PETER HENDERSON AS IT TURNS OUT.
("PETE-O," ACCORDING TO THE FREEWHEELIN' MS. CLARK!)
DON'T GET ME WRONG, I LIKE MR. HENDERSON A LOT.
HE'S A GOOD TEACHER.
TONS BETTER THAN THE OTHER JERKS I'VE HAD.
AS A MATTER OF FACT, SOME GIRLS IN MY CLASS EVEN HAD A CRUSH ON HIM.
SIIIIIIIGH
NO, NOT ME.
I HAVE ENOUGH PROBLEMS, THANKS.
AND ANYWAY, THESE DAYS HE WAS 'HOGGIN' UP ALL OF TANNER'S TIME! IT WASN'T LIKE THEY WENT ON LOTS OF DIFFERENT DATES...
IT WAS LIKE THEY WENT ON ONE DATE THAT NEVER ENDED.

ACTUALLY, THE WHOLE SCENE WAS *ANNOYING!*

BECAUSE, WHILE SHE WAS OFF *WHOOPING* IT UP, I *NEEDED* HER.

TIPTOE THROUGH THE TULIPS!

SKIP   SKIP   SKIP   SKIP   SKIP

I, MEAN, I HAD TO DEAL WITH THE AFTERMATH OF *THIS!*

I HAVE A REAL FOOT ODOR PROBLEM!

TOOT ♪

I *TRIED* TO *FORGET* IT, Y'KNOW?

BUT IT WAS *IMPOSSIBLE!*

IT JUST KEPT *ECHOING* IN MY *MIND!*

IT WAS LIKE EVERY EVENT IN MY LIFE HAD BEEN *ERASED,* AND REPLACED WITH *THIS* ONE.

I REALLY STARTED THINKING THAT *THIS* MIGHT BE MY *PURPOSE.*

LIKE, I COULD BE SAINT AMELIA, PATRON OF THE *HUMILIATED.*

BECAUSE WHATEVER BONEHEADED STUNT SOMEONE MIGHT PULL...

...IT COULD *NEVER* BE AS *EMBARRASSING* AS...

I HAVE A REAL FOOT ODOR PROBLEM!

TOOT ♪

=SIGH=

IT WAS BOUND TO BE ALL OVER SCHOOL BY MONDAY, BUT WHAT COULD I *DO?* I JUST HAD TO GO AND FACE THE *MUSIC.*

TOOT ♪ TOOT ♪ TOOT ♪ TOOT ♪ TOOT ♪ TOOT ♪
TOOT ♪ TOOT ♪ TOOT ♪ TOOT ♪ TOOT ♪ TOOT ♪
TOOT ♪ TOOT ♪ TOOT ♪ TOOT ♪ TOOT ♪ TOOT ♪
TOOT ♪ TOOT ♪ TOOT ♪ TOOT ♪ TOOT ♪ TOOT ♪
TOOT ♪ TOOT ♪ TOOT ♪ TOOT ♪ TOOT ♪ TOOT ♪
TOOT ♪ TOOT ♪ TOOT ♪ TOOT ♪ TOOT ♪ TOOT ♪
TOOT ♪ TOOT ♪ TOOT ♪ TOOT ♪ TOOT ♪ TOOT ♪

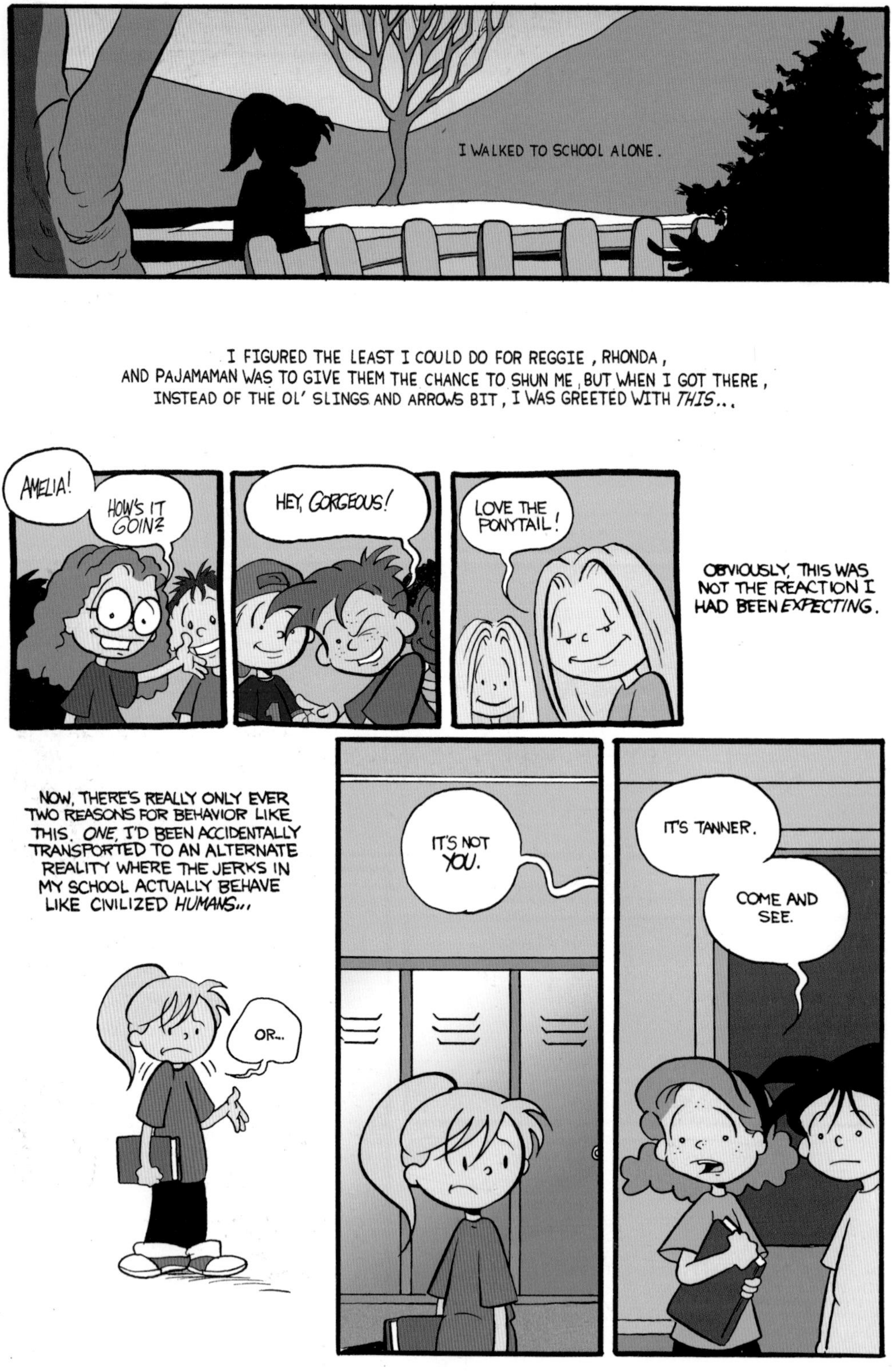
I WALKED TO SCHOOL ALONE.
I FIGURED THE LEAST I COULD DO FOR REGGIE, RHONDA, AND PAJAMAMAN WAS TO GIVE THEM THE CHANCE TO SHUN ME, BUT WHEN I GOT THERE, INSTEAD OF THE OL' SLINGS AND ARROWS BIT, I WAS GREETED WITH *THIS*...
AMELIA!
HOW'S IT GOIN'?
HEY, GORGEOUS!
LOVE THE PONYTAIL!
OBVIOUSLY, THIS WAS NOT THE REACTION I HAD BEEN *EXPECTING*.
NOW, THERE'S REALLY ONLY EVER TWO REASONS FOR BEHAVIOR LIKE THIS. *ONE*, I'D BEEN ACCIDENTALLY TRANSPORTED TO AN ALTERNATE REALITY WHERE THE JERKS IN MY SCHOOL ACTUALLY BEHAVE LIKE CIVILIZED *HUMANS*...
OR...
IT'S NOT *YOU*.
IT'S TANNER.
COME AND SEE.

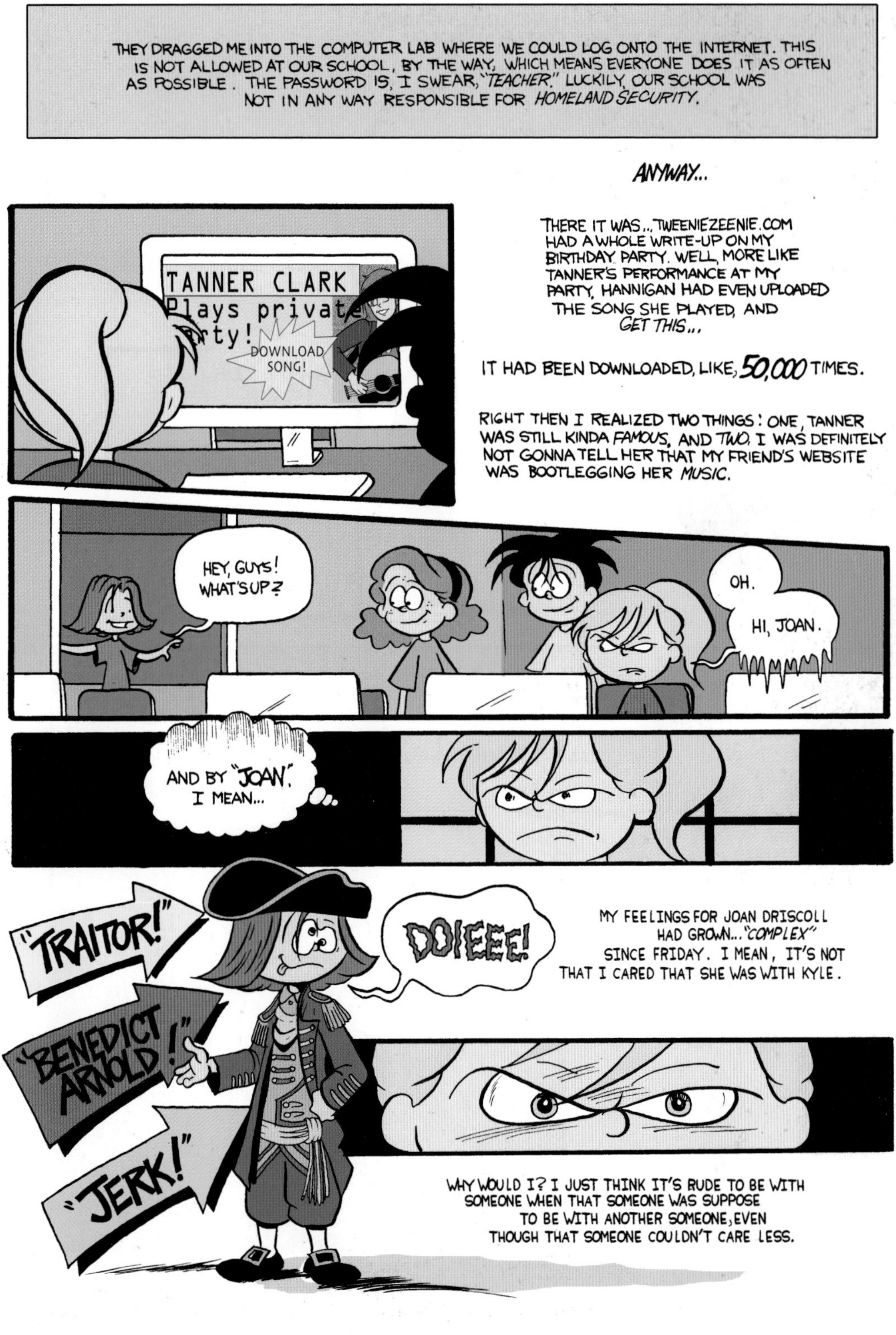
THEY DRAGGED ME INTO THE COMPUTER LAB WHERE WE COULD LOG ONTO THE INTERNET. THIS IS NOT ALLOWED AT OUR SCHOOL, BY THE WAY, WHICH MEANS EVERYONE DOES IT AS OFTEN AS POSSIBLE. THE PASSWORD IS, I SWEAR, "TEACHER." LUCKILY, OUR SCHOOL WAS NOT IN ANY WAY RESPONSIBLE FOR HOMELAND SECURITY.
ANYWAY...
TANNER CLARK
Plays private party!
DOWNLOAD SONG!
THERE IT WAS... TWEENIEZEENIE.COM HAD A WHOLE WRITE-UP ON MY BIRTHDAY PARTY. WELL, MORE LIKE TANNER'S PERFORMANCE AT MY PARTY. HANNIGAN HAD EVEN UPLOADED THE SONG SHE PLAYED, AND GET THIS...
IT HAD BEEN DOWNLOADED, LIKE, 50,000 TIMES.
RIGHT THEN I REALIZED TWO THINGS: ONE, TANNER WAS STILL KINDA FAMOUS, AND TWO, I WAS DEFINITELY NOT GONNA TELL HER THAT MY FRIEND'S WEBSITE WAS BOOTLEGGING HER MUSIC.
HEY, GUYS! WHAT'S UP?
OH.
HI, JOAN.
AND BY "JOAN", I MEAN...
"TRAITOR!"
"BENEDICT ARNOLD!"
"JERK!"
DOIEEE!
MY FEELINGS FOR JOAN DRISCOLL HAD GROWN... "COMPLEX" SINCE FRIDAY. I MEAN, IT'S NOT THAT I CARED THAT SHE WAS WITH KYLE.
WHY WOULD I? I JUST THINK IT'S RUDE TO BE WITH SOMEONE WHEN THAT SOMEONE WAS SUPPOSE TO BE WITH ANOTHER SOMEONE, EVEN THOUGH THAT SOMEONE COULDN'T CARE LESS.

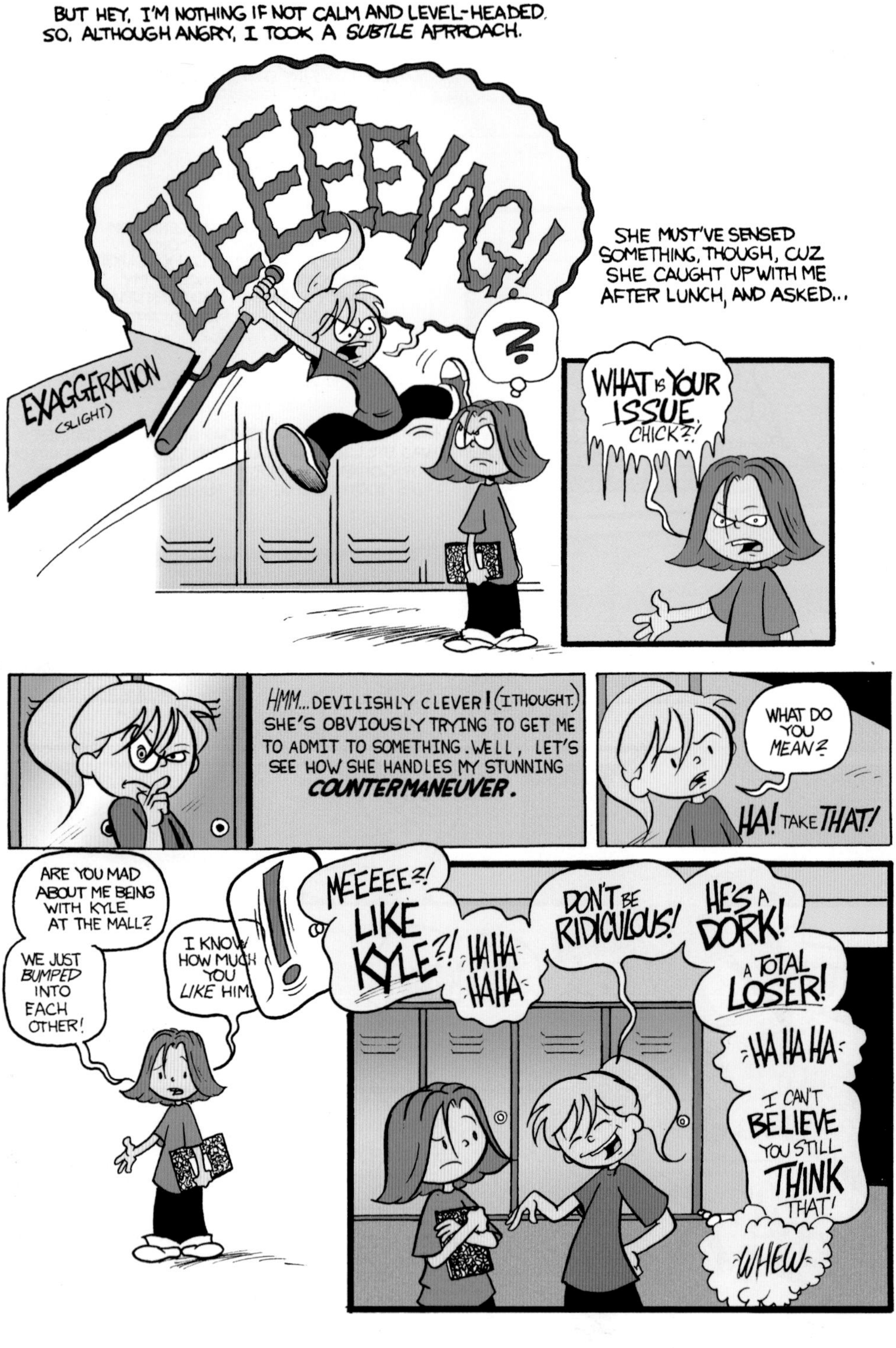

BUT HEY, I'M NOTHING IF NOT CALM AND LEVEL-HEADED. SO, ALTHOUGH ANGRY, I TOOK A SUBTLE APPROACH.
EEEEEYAG!
EXAGGERATION (SLIGHT)
?
SHE MUST'VE SENSED SOMETHING, THOUGH, CUZ SHE CAUGHT UP WITH ME AFTER LUNCH, AND ASKED...
WHAT IS YOUR ISSUE, CHICK?!
HMM... DEVILISHLY CLEVER! (I THOUGHT.) SHE'S OBVIOUSLY TRYING TO GET ME TO ADMIT TO SOMETHING. WELL, LET'S SEE HOW SHE HANDLES MY STUNNING COUNTERMANEUVER.
WHAT DO YOU MEAN?
HA! TAKE THAT!
ARE YOU MAD ABOUT ME BEING WITH KYLE AT THE MALL?
WE JUST BUMPED INTO EACH OTHER!
I KNOW HOW MUCH YOU LIKE HIM!
!
MEEEEE?! LIKE KYLE?!
HA HA HA HA
DON'T BE RIDICULOUS!
HE'S A DORK!
A TOTAL LOSER!
HA HA HA
I CAN'T BELIEVE YOU STILL THINK THAT!
WHEW

OKAY, SO THAT WAS *TWO* THINGS OFF THE OL' *GRAY MATTER*. *ONE*, JOAN WAS NOT INTO *KYLE*! (NOT THAT *I* CARE!)

AND *TWO*, THE SCHOOL WAS NOT AS INTERESTED IN MY *FOOT* AND/OR INTESTINAL ISSUES AS I *THOUGHT* THEY *WOULD* BE!

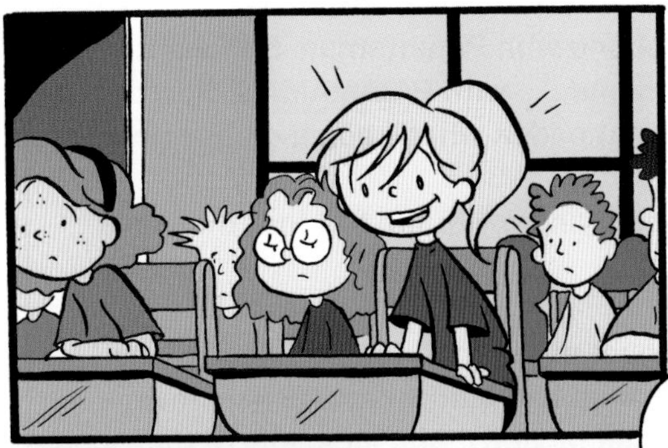

PLUS...

...ON TOP OF THOSE NICE SURPRISES, IN ENGLISH CLASS, WE GOT A NEW ASSIGNMENT... *JOURNAL WRITING.*

HOW COOL IS *THAT*?!

SELF-OBSESSED WHINING AS A WAY TO BOOST A GRADE POINT AVERAGE? *SIGN* ME *UP!*

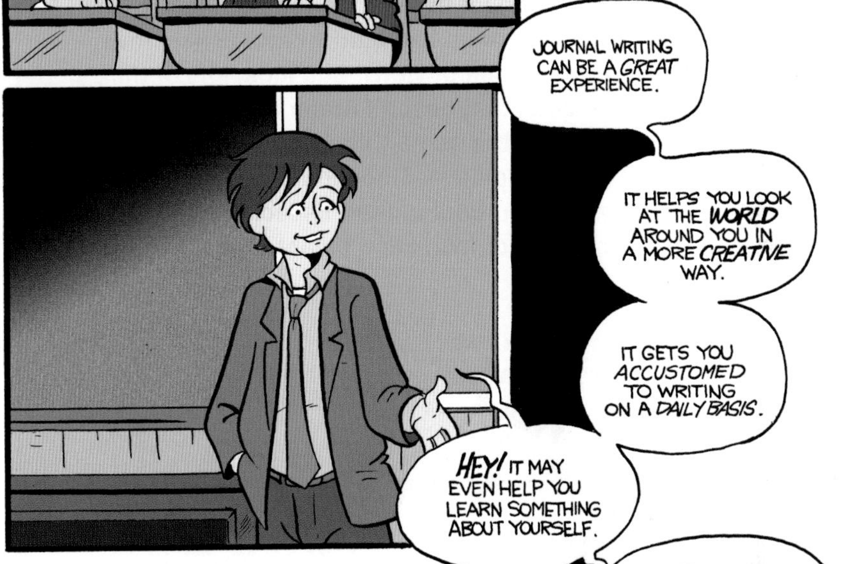

JOURNAL WRITING CAN BE A *GREAT* EXPERIENCE.
IT HELPS YOU LOOK AT THE **WORLD** AROUND YOU IN A MORE *CREATIVE* WAY.
IT GETS YOU *ACCUSTOMED* TO WRITING ON A *DAILY BASIS*.
HEY! IT MAY EVEN HELP YOU LEARN SOMETHING ABOUT YOURSELF.

THIS WAS GOING TO BE A *PIECE* OF *CAKE*!

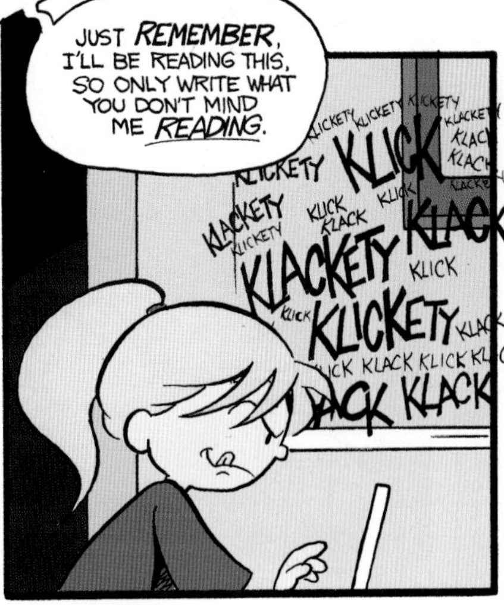

JUST *REMEMBER*, I'LL BE READING THIS, SO ONLY WRITE WHAT YOU DON'T MIND ME *READING*.
KLICKETY KLICK KLACKETY KLACK KLICK KLACKETY KLICKETY KLACK KLICK KLACK KLICK KLACK

I figure if there's one thing I can do, it's express myself. Plus, it's cool that I can actually get school credit for this. I mean, normally when I "express" myself, I just get detention.

And this isn't even all of it. There's much, much more.

Like, Joan was really sorry for the misunderstanding. She swears (SWEARS!) that bumping into Kyle was a coincidence and that she was only at the mall for a few minutes (with her mom) and then went home and spent the night talking on the phone with Pajamaman. Seriously! She says she spends hours on the phone . . . with PAJAMAMAN! How is that possible? I swear, I officially have no idea what's going on anymore.

I think this whole Kyle thing might be frying my brain. Not that there is a Kyle thing.

I mean, yes, he's cute. There's no doubt about that. I really like the way those two little pieces of his hair stick up like bunny ears (or like devil horns, I guess, depending on your point of view). But, look, lots of things are cute. Spider monkeys are cute, that doesn't mean I want to marry a spider monkey, right? Right. So it's the same thing with Kyle. Kyle is just another spider monkey. A spider monkey of looooooove. Agh! Why did I type that?! I don't want my teacher reading that! Especially a teacher that's dating my aunt! As a matter of fact, I don't want ANYONE reading ANY of this.

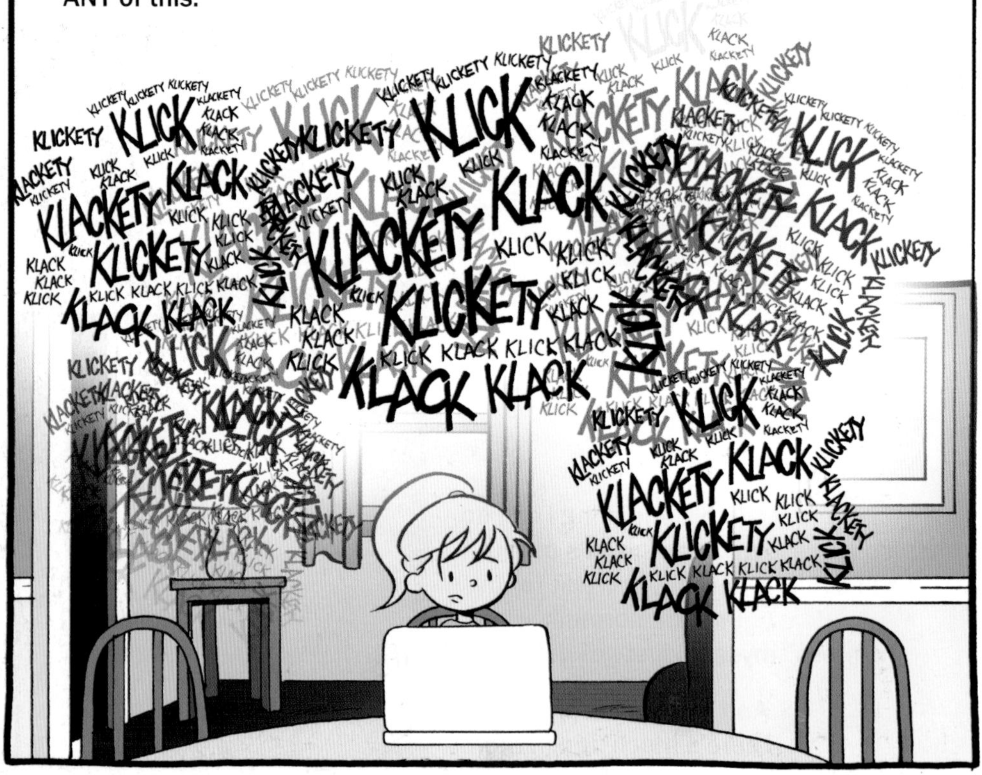

KLICKETY KLICK
KLICKETY KLICK
KLACKETY KLACK
KLICKETY KLACK KLACK
KLACKETY KLACK
KLICKETY KLICK
KLACKETY KLACK
KLICKETY
KLACK KLACK
KLICKETY KLICK
KLACKETY KLACK
KLICKETY
KLACK KLACK

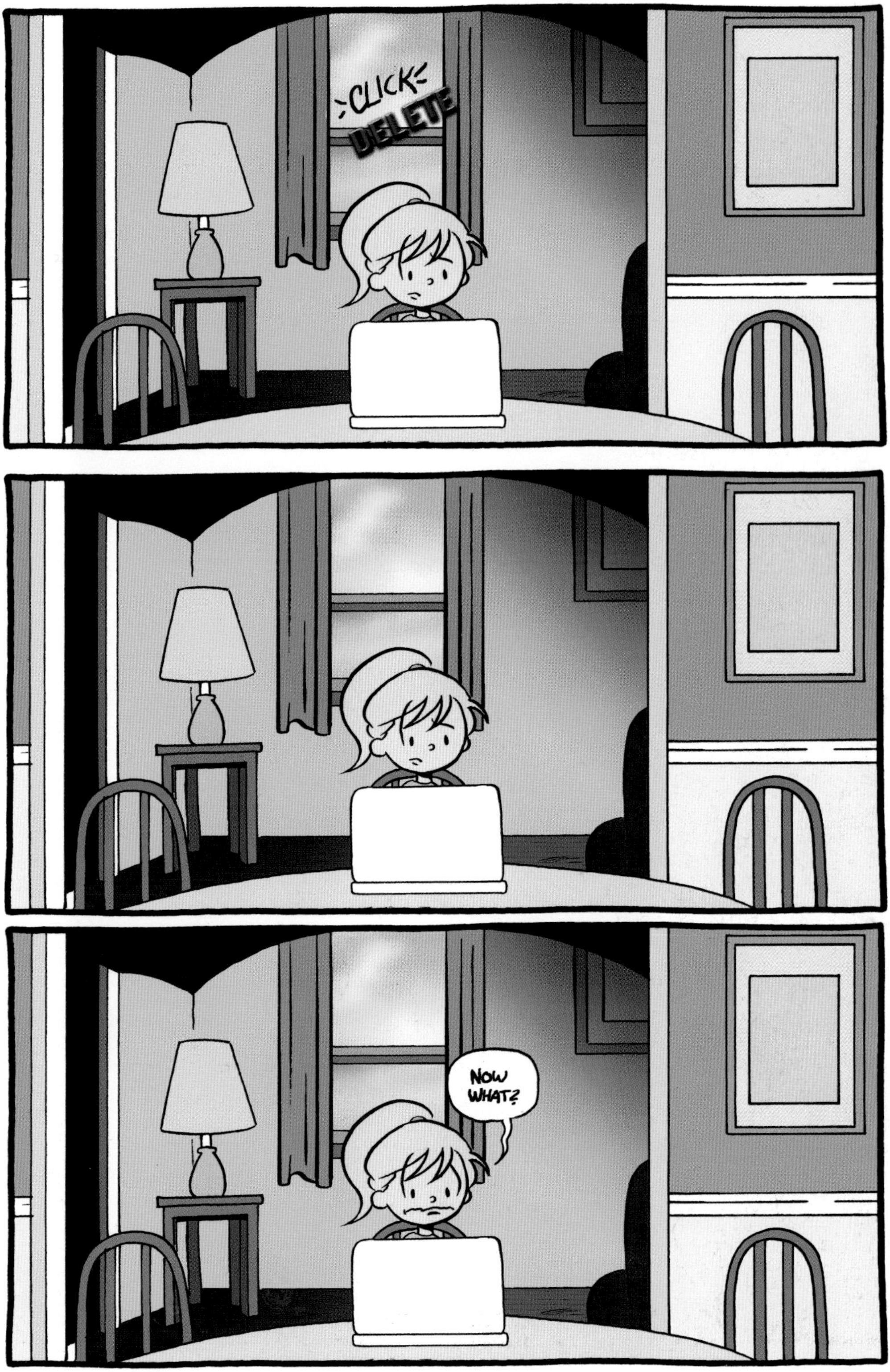
CLICK
DELETE
NOW WHAT?

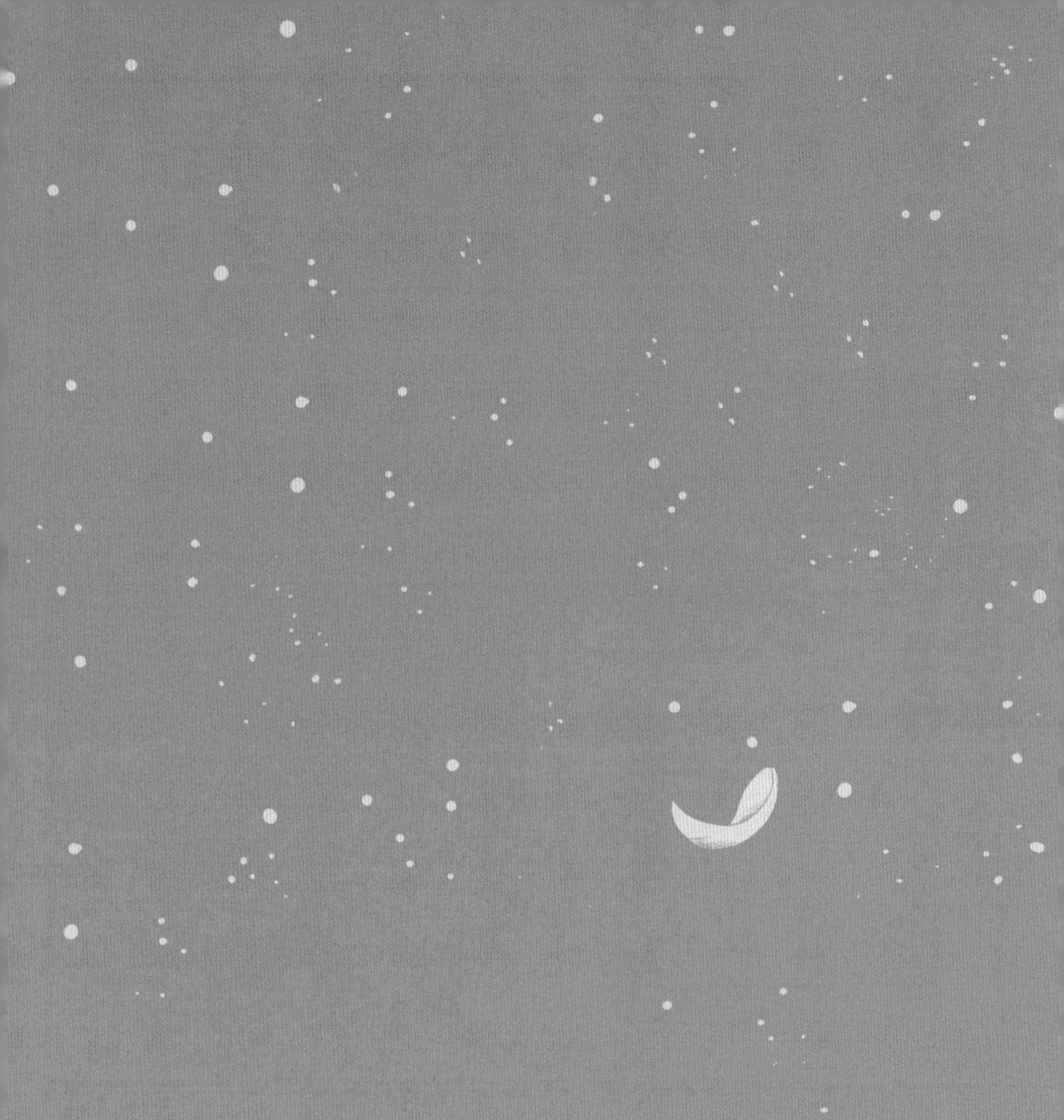

"Growing up is the hardest part of growing up, but what choice do we have?"

-Tanner Clark
in her private journal

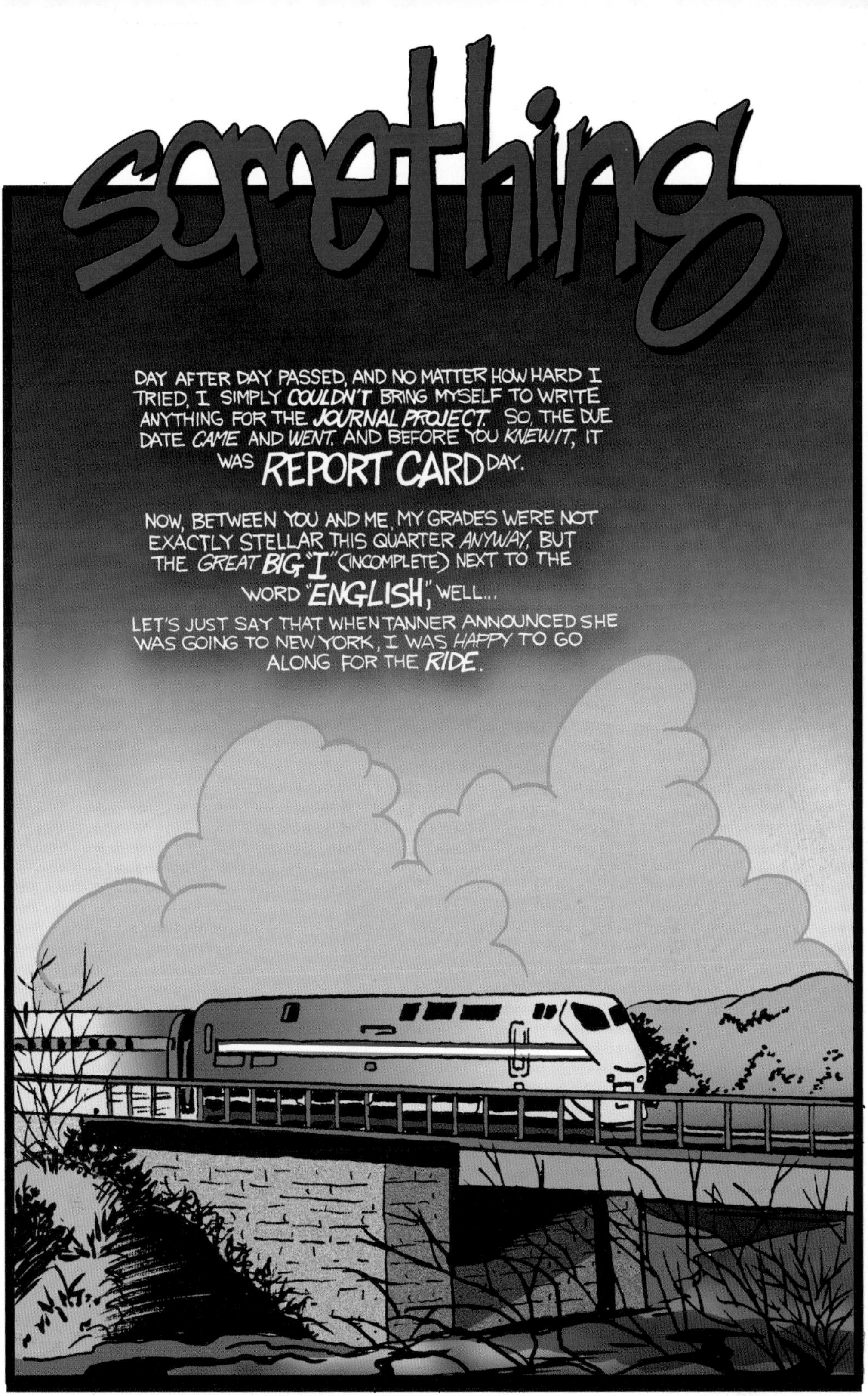
something
DAY AFTER DAY PASSED, AND NO MATTER HOW HARD I TRIED, I SIMPLY COULDN'T BRING MYSELF TO WRITE ANYTHING FOR THE JOURNAL PROJECT. SO, THE DUE DATE CAME AND WENT, AND BEFORE YOU KNEW IT, IT WAS REPORT CARD DAY.
NOW, BETWEEN YOU AND ME, MY GRADES WERE NOT EXACTLY STELLAR THIS QUARTER ANYWAY, BUT THE GREAT BIG "I" (INCOMPLETE) NEXT TO THE WORD "ENGLISH," WELL...
LET'S JUST SAY THAT WHEN TANNER ANNOUNCED SHE WAS GOING TO NEW YORK, I WAS HAPPY TO GO ALONG FOR THE RIDE.

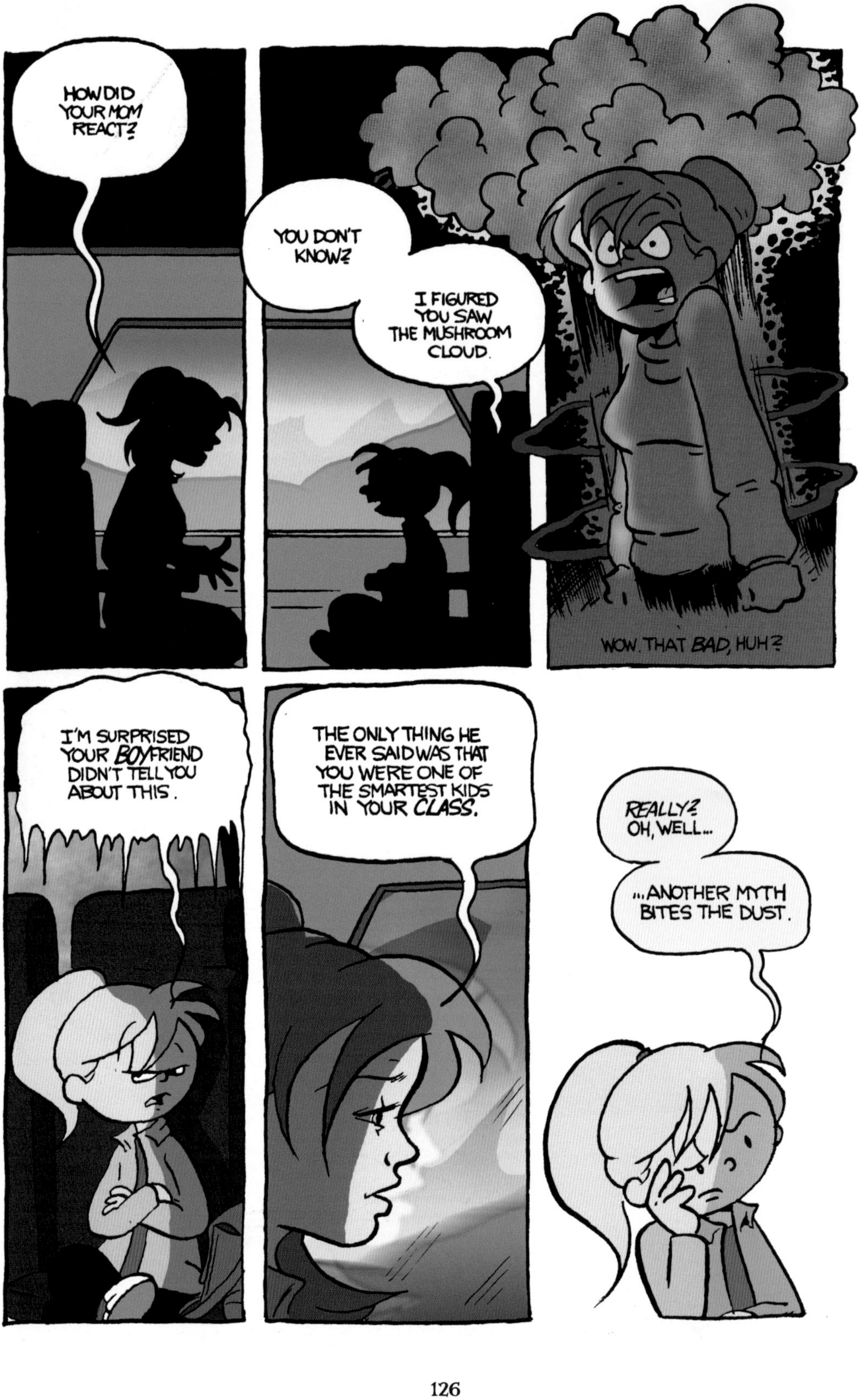
HOW DID YOUR MOM REACT?
YOU DON'T KNOW?
I FIGURED YOU SAW THE MUSHROOM CLOUD.
WOW. THAT BAD, HUH?
I'M SURPRISED YOUR BOYFRIEND DIDN'T TELL YOU ABOUT THIS.
THE ONLY THING HE EVER SAID WAS THAT YOU WERE ONE OF THE SMARTEST KIDS IN YOUR CLASS.
REALLY? OH, WELL...
...ANOTHER MYTH BITES THE DUST.

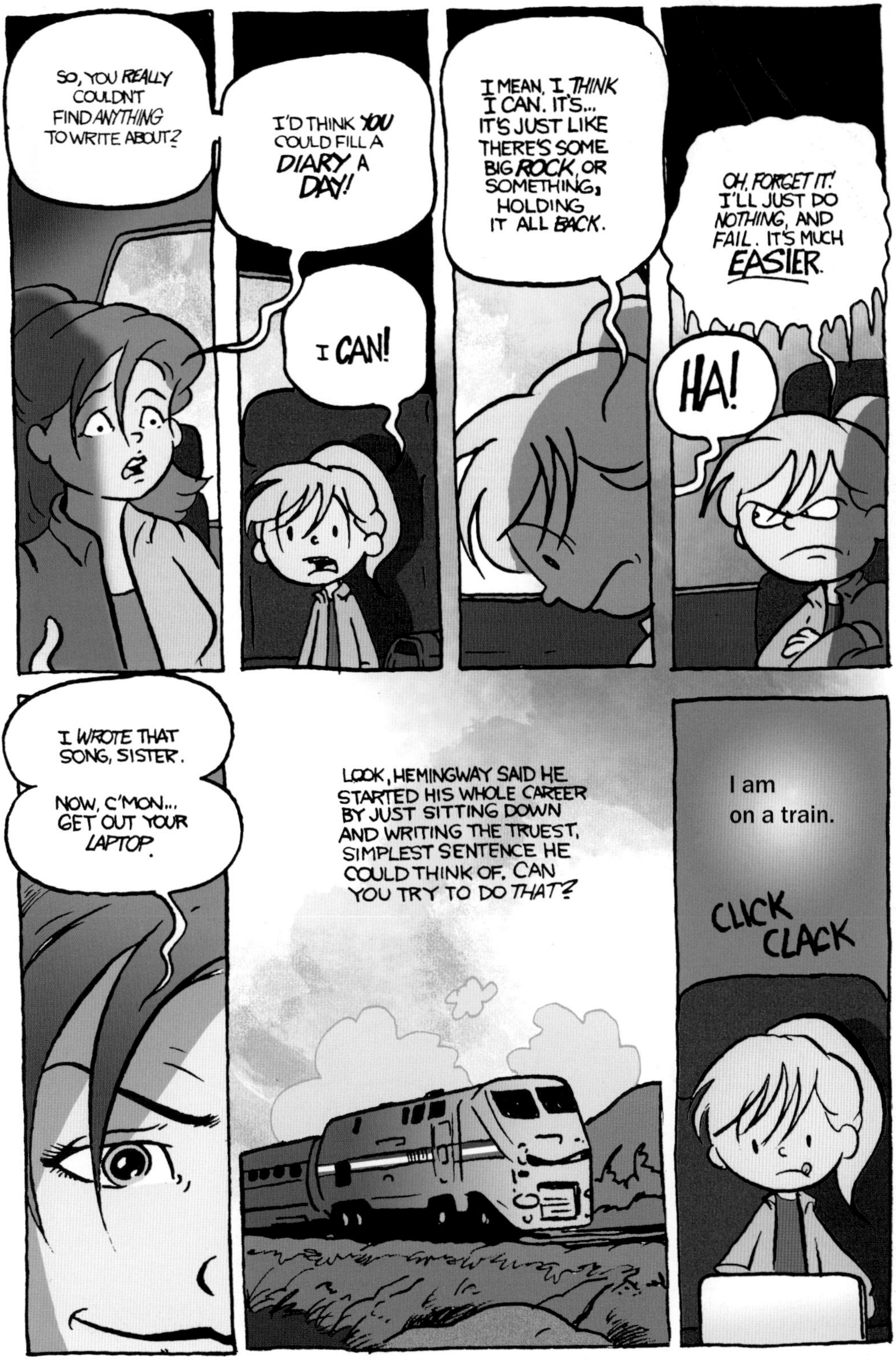
SO, YOU REALLY COULDN'T FIND ANYTHING TO WRITE ABOUT?
I'D THINK YOU COULD FILL A DIARY A DAY!
I CAN!
I MEAN, I THINK I CAN. IT'S... IT'S JUST LIKE THERE'S SOME BIG ROCK, OR SOMETHING, HOLDING IT ALL BACK.
OH, FORGET IT! I'LL JUST DO NOTHING, AND FAIL. IT'S MUCH EASIER.
HA!
I WROTE THAT SONG, SISTER.
NOW, C'MON... GET OUT YOUR LAPTOP.
LOOK, HEMINGWAY SAID HE STARTED HIS WHOLE CAREER BY JUST SITTING DOWN AND WRITING THE TRUEST, SIMPLEST SENTENCE HE COULD THINK OF. CAN YOU TRY TO DO THAT?
I am on a train.
CLICK CLACK

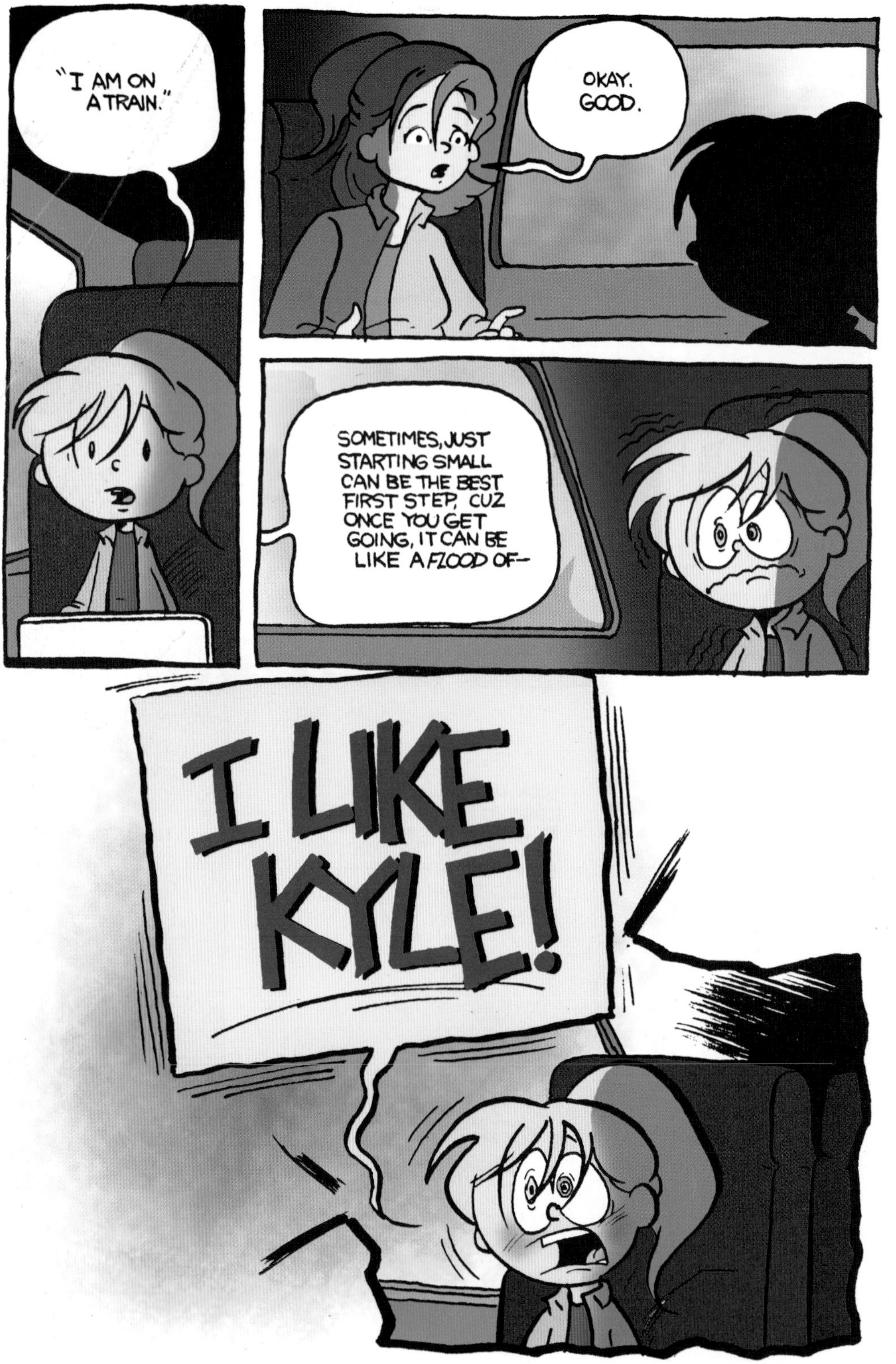
"I AM ON A TRAIN."
OKAY. GOOD.
SOMETIMES, JUST STARTING SMALL CAN BE THE BEST FIRST STEP, CUZ ONCE YOU GET GOING, IT CAN BE LIKE A *FLOOD* OF—
I LIKE KYLE!

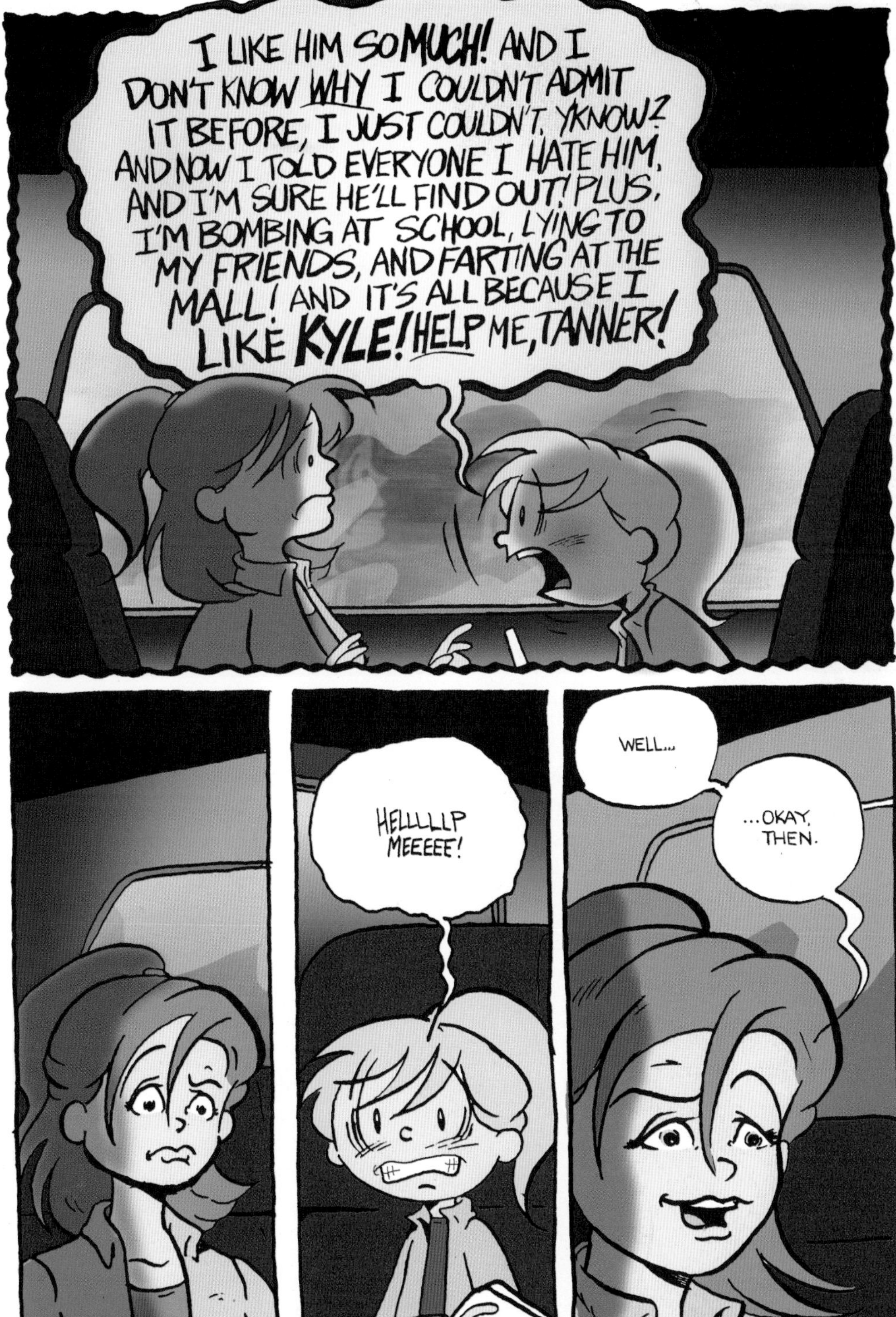
I LIKE HIM SO MUCH! AND I DON'T KNOW WHY I COULDN'T ADMIT IT BEFORE, I JUST COULDN'T, Y'KNOW? AND NOW I TOLD EVERYONE I HATE HIM, AND I'M SURE HE'LL FIND OUT! PLUS, I'M BOMBING AT SCHOOL, LYING TO MY FRIENDS, AND FARTING AT THE MALL! AND IT'S ALL BECAUSE I LIKE KYLE! HELP ME, TANNER!
HELLLLLP MEEEEE!
WELL...
...OKAY. THEN.

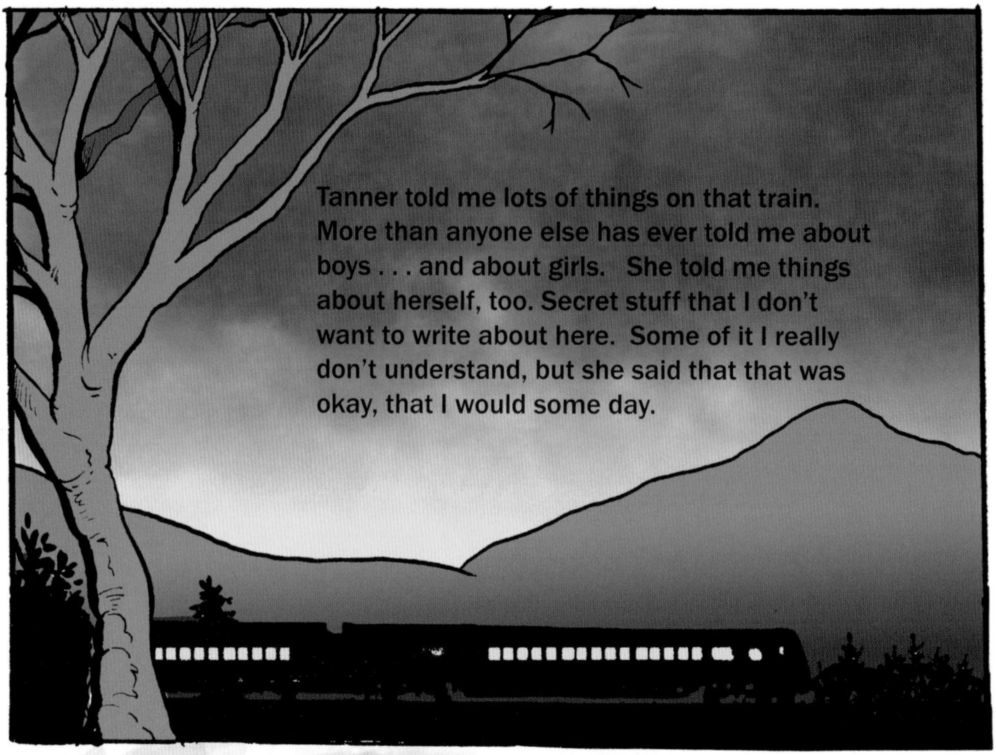
Tanner told me lots of things on that train. More than anyone else has ever told me about boys . . . and about girls. She told me things about herself, too. Secret stuff that I don't want to write about here. Some of it I really don't understand, but she said that that was okay, that I would some day.

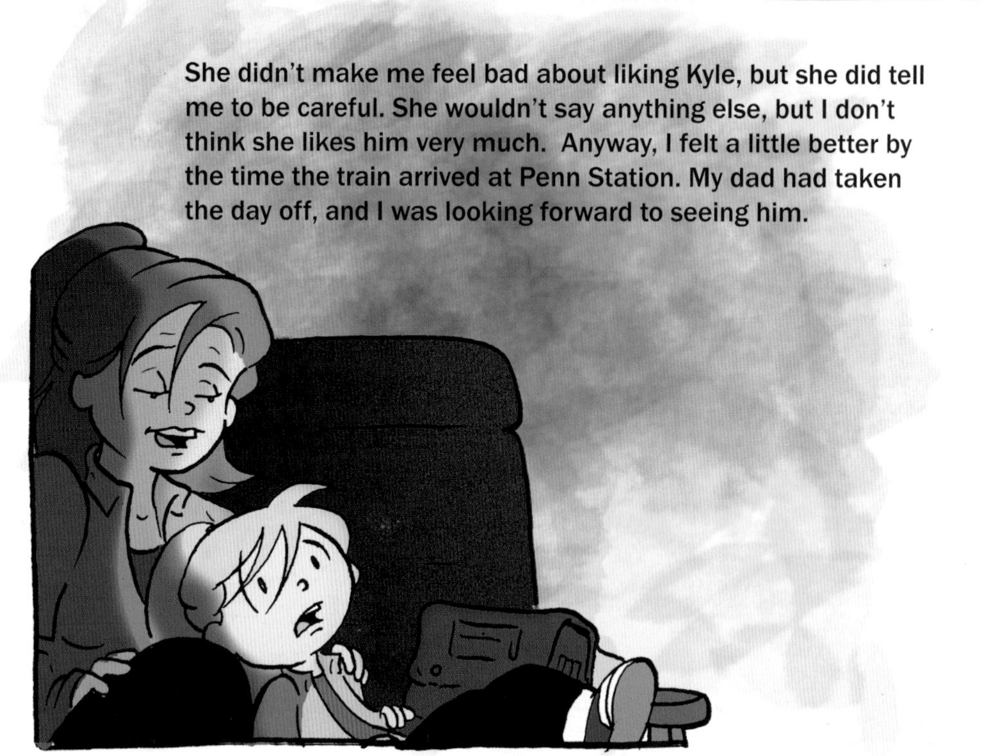
She didn't make me feel bad about liking Kyle, but she did tell me to be careful. She wouldn't say anything else, but I don't think she likes him very much. Anyway, I felt a little better by the time the train arrived at Penn Station. My dad had taken the day off, and I was looking forward to seeing him.

But the only thing worse than the weather in Manhattan that day, was my dad's mood. For the whole first hour of my visit, he was on the phone with his work. Then we were in a cab going TO his work. Then we were in his office, where he and two other guys screamed at each other for 45 minutes. And I mean SCREAMED too. There were only like four words in their whole conversation that I can even write here ("Inflatable," "pie chart," and "Belgium") . The rest were all very NC-17.

Anyway, before you know it we were back in a cab, back in the apartment, and dad was back on the phone. This time, he was screaming at some OTHER guy.

And then, it was time for me to go.

I was so angry, I honestly couldn't see straight. My dad knew it, too. He tried to apologize. He really did. But, I wasn't letting him off that easy.

"I'm sorry," he said. "I hate this job. I hate that we never see each other. I wish I could do something."

"You can," I said. "But you won't."

Dramatic, I know, but I was making a point. This was exactly the kind of thing mom hated, and I guess now I could see why.

We got in a cab, and rode to the train station without saying another word.

Any thoughts I had about complaining to Tanner on the way back died the moment I saw her face.

For the first twenty minutes of the ride home, neither of us spoke. Finally Tanner said, "They didn't want it."

"Want what?" I asked.

"My music." Then she reached into her coat pocket and pulled out an unlabeled CD in a clear plastic case.

"They didn't even listen to it."

I don't really want to write everything that Tanner said, because I think she'd want some of it to be private, but what happened was this:

She wrote a song. My song, the first song she wrote in a long, long time, and it felt good. Then she met a boy. A man, actually. And she liked him. And he encouraged her. So she wrote MORE songs. She didn't have much money, but what she had left, she spent on making a studio for herself. A place where she could write songs, and record them. When she finished five of them, she scheduled a trip to meet with the people who had put out her last record, all those years ago.

It never occurred to her that they wouldn't care.

For the longest time Tanner sat there with her head in her hands. She was crying, but she thought that I couldn't tell. Finally, she looked up and told me not to worry. My mom got her an interview at the place she worked. It was a secretary job. It had nothing to do with music. But it would keep her from losing her house.

"Tanner Clark. Rock-and-roll secretary. Sounds like a musical comedy," she joked.

I laughed. But I didn't feel like laughing.

Eventually, Tanner fell asleep, and I was able to listen to her CD.

It was great.

Of COURSE it was great. It was Tanner.

Since there were only five songs, so I was able to listen to them over and over. Just sitting there, listening, watching her sleep, thinking about everything she has done for me.

I knew what I had to do. I didn't WANT to do it, of course, but I knew I HAD to.

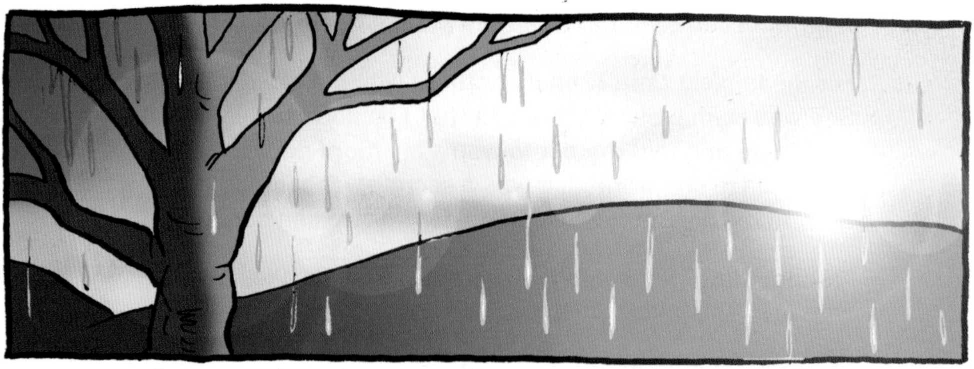

I hadn't been to Joanne Hannigan's house since the day I met her. Back then, the *Tweenie Zeenie* was just a little thing she made on her printer, but now it was a website. Apparently, it was a really, really POPULAR website. Sam still worked with her, but now he was "ART DIRECTOR." That made me laugh. Hannigan couldn't stop bragging. "We have fifty gajillion hits a week. Eleventeen hundred page views per blah, blah, blah."

I asked her how so many people ended up downloading Tanner's song.

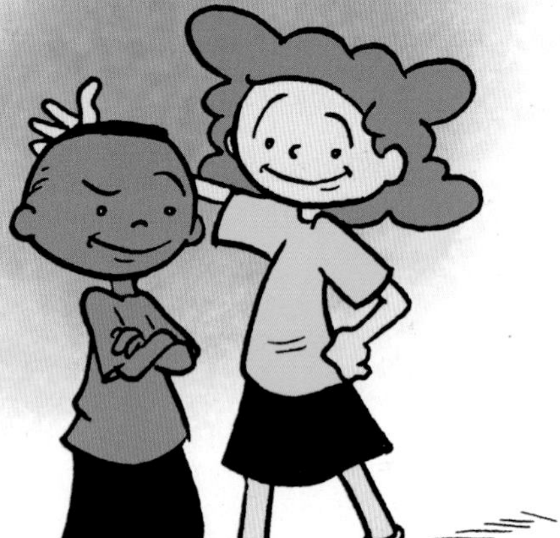

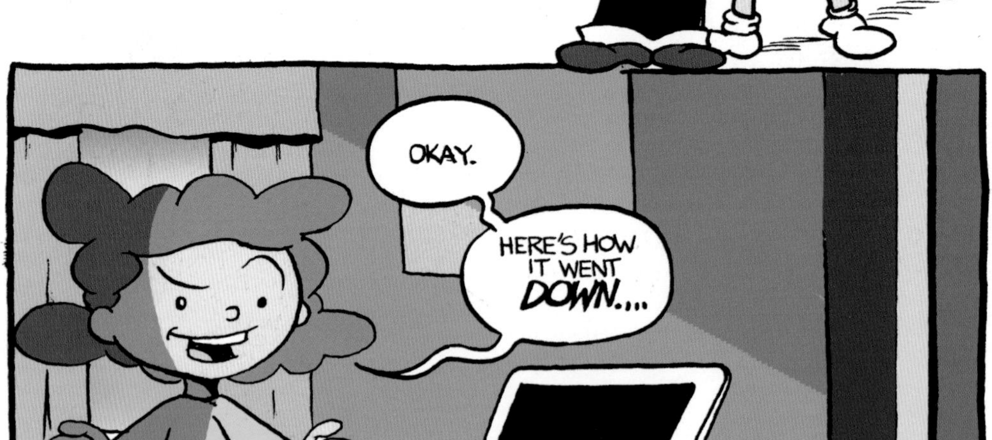
OKAY.
HERE'S HOW IT WENT DOWN....

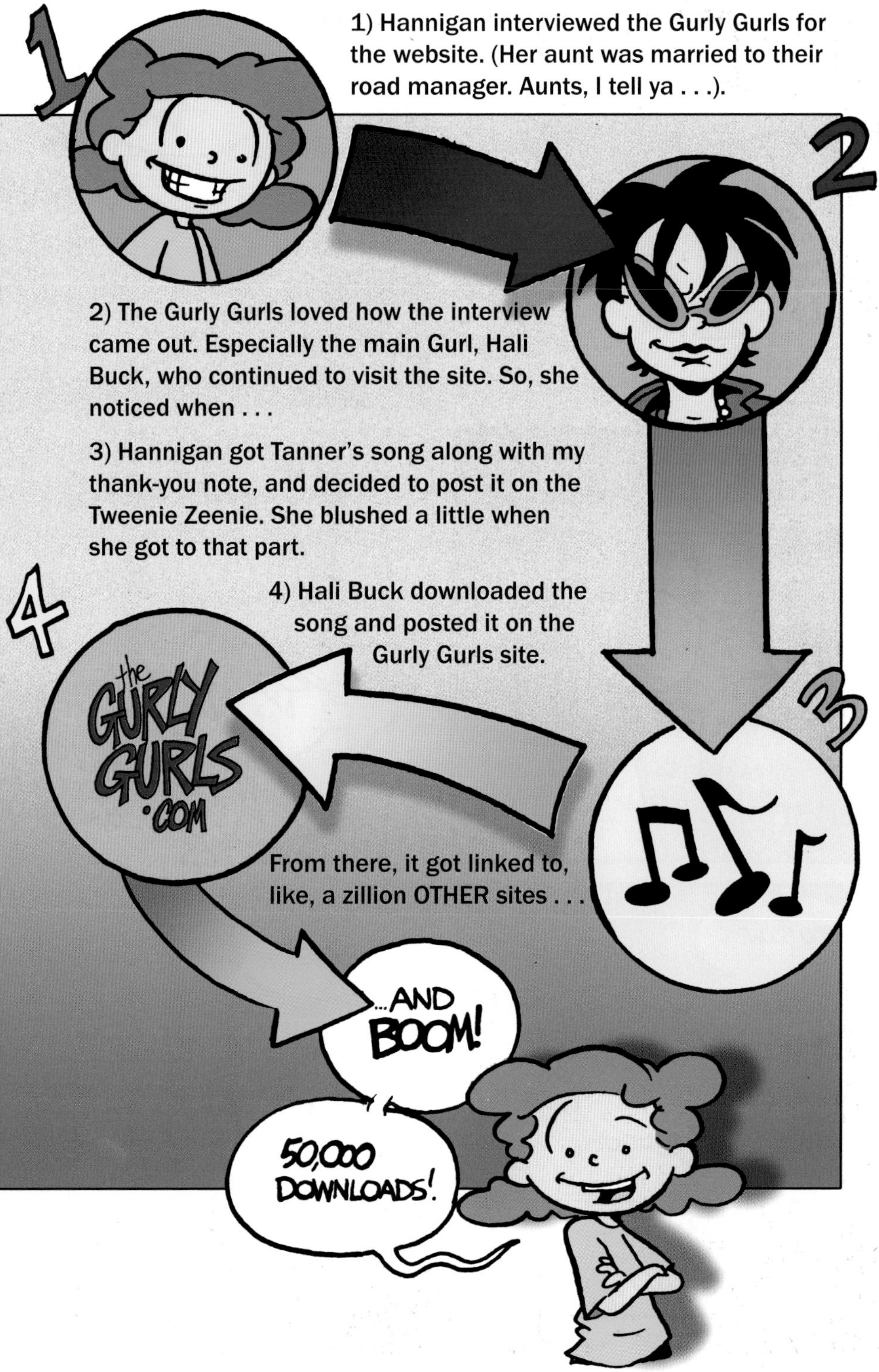
1) Hannigan interviewed the Gurly Gurls for the website. (Her aunt was married to their road manager. Aunts, I tell ya . . .).
2) The Gurly Gurls loved how the interview came out. Especially the main Gurl, Hali Buck, who continued to visit the site. So, she noticed when . . .
3) Hannigan got Tanner's song along with my thank-you note, and decided to post it on the Tweenie Zeenie. She blushed a little when she got to that part.
4) Hali Buck downloaded the song and posted it on the Gurly Gurls site.
the GURLY GURLS .COM
From there, it got linked to, like, a zillion OTHER sites . . .
...AND BOOM!
50,000 DOWNLOADS!

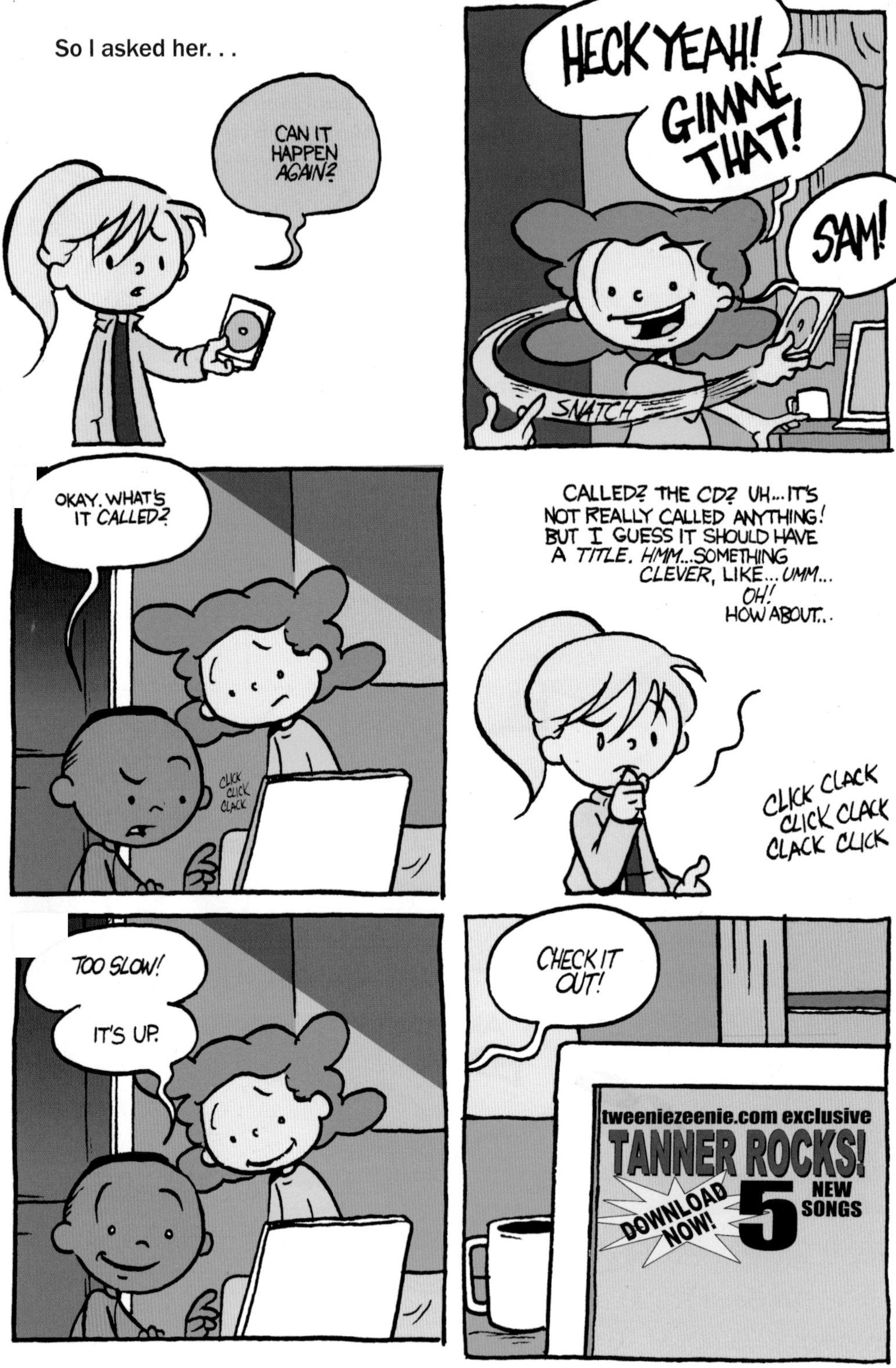
So I asked her. . .
CAN IT HAPPEN AGAIN?
HECK YEAH! GIMME THAT!
SAM!
SNATCH
OKAY. WHAT'S IT CALLED?
CLICK CLICK CLACK
CALLED? THE CD? UH... IT'S NOT REALLY CALLED ANYTHING! BUT I GUESS IT SHOULD HAVE A TITLE. HMM...SOMETHING CLEVER, LIKE... UMM... OH! HOW ABOUT...
CLICK CLACK CLICK CLACK CLACK CLICK
TOO SLOW!
IT'S UP.
CHECK IT OUT!
tweeniezeenie.com exclusive
TANNER ROCKS!
DOWNLOAD NOW!
5 NEW SONGS

Before you knew it, the album was everywhere. Tons of sites were linking to it, people were sharing it, blogging about it, reviewing it. It was crazy.

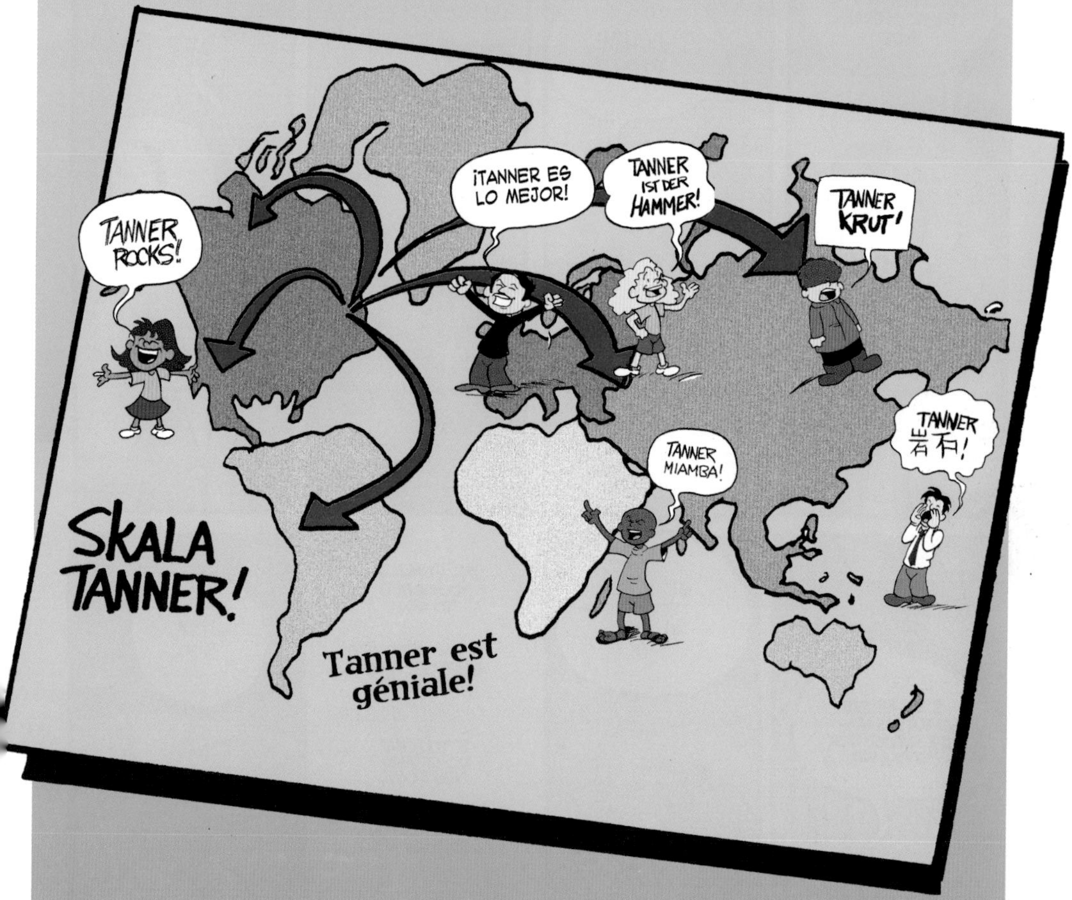

TANNER ROCKS!
¡TANNER ES LO MEJOR!
TANNER IST DER HAMMER!
TANNER KRUT!
TANNER 岩石!
TANNER MIAMBA!
SKALA TANNER!
Tanner est géniale!

And the whole time, I kept trying to figure out how to tell Tanner that I, let's say, "distributed" her album for her. I didn't want to say anything at first, because I figured she'd be mad. But one day, she came over and said she'd been getting tons of e-mails about her new music. She must've known I was the one who posted it, but she never said a word.

I think she was just happy that people liked the songs. It seemed like that might've been enough.

But a few days later the big bombshell arrived.

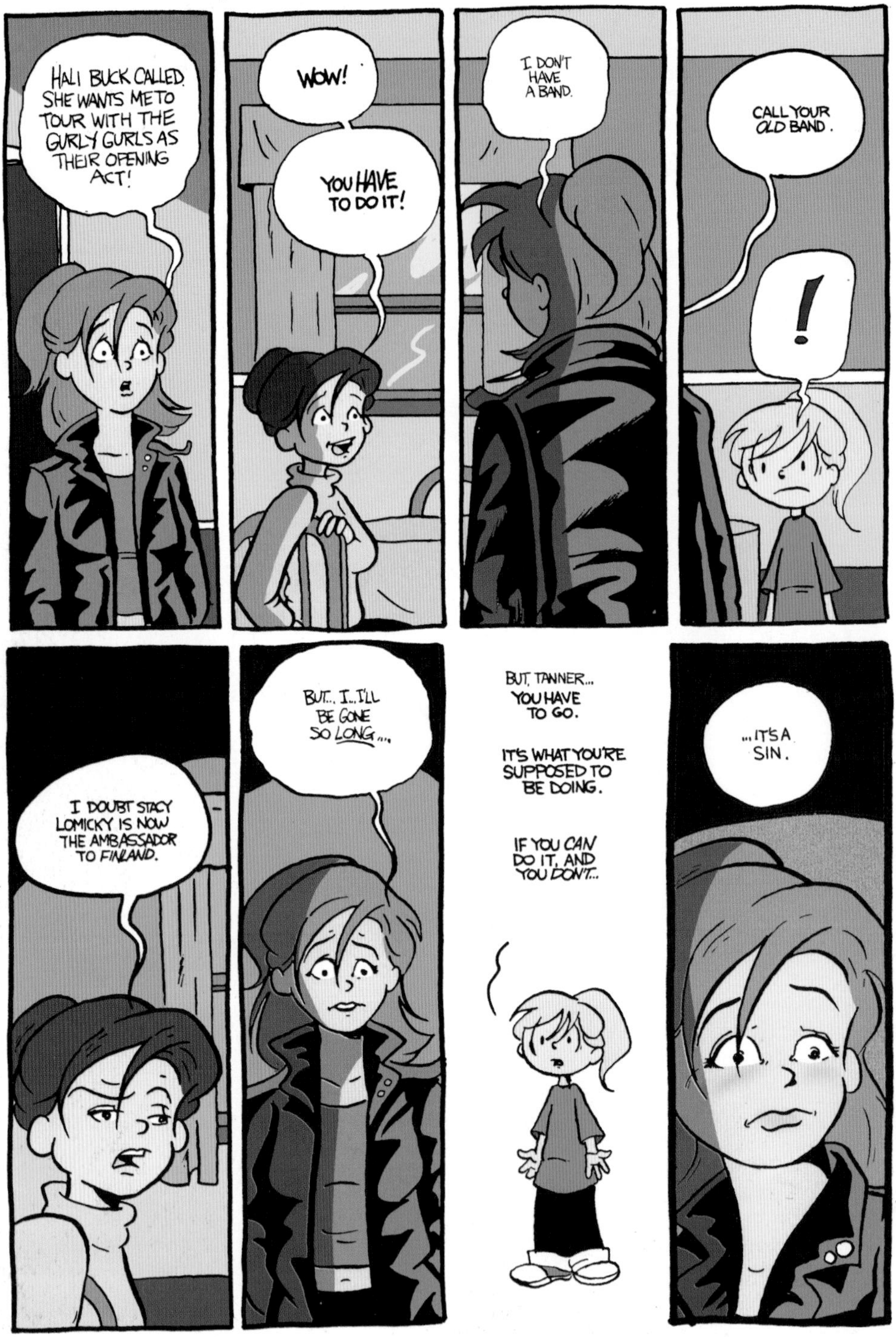
HALI BUCK CALLED. SHE WANTS ME TO TOUR WITH THE GURLY GURLS AS THEIR OPENING ACT!
WOW!
YOU HAVE TO DO IT!
I DON'T HAVE A BAND.
CALL YOUR OLD BAND.
!
I DOUBT STACY LOMICKY IS NOW THE AMBASSADOR TO FINLAND.
BUT... I... I'LL BE GONE SO LONG....
BUT, TANNER... YOU HAVE TO GO.
IT'S WHAT YOU'RE SUPPOSED TO BE DOING.
IF YOU CAN DO IT, AND YOU DON'T...
...IT'S A SIN.

The last thing I wanted to do was to tell Tanner to leave, but what could I do? She's always ready to help me, how could I not help her?

It was announced that before the tour kicked off, there would be a bon voyage performance, Tanner AND the Gurly Gurls. So I put the fact that Tanner would be leaving out of my mind by working on one of my other problems. I put on my nice dress (my OTHER nice dress) and went over to Kyle's house.

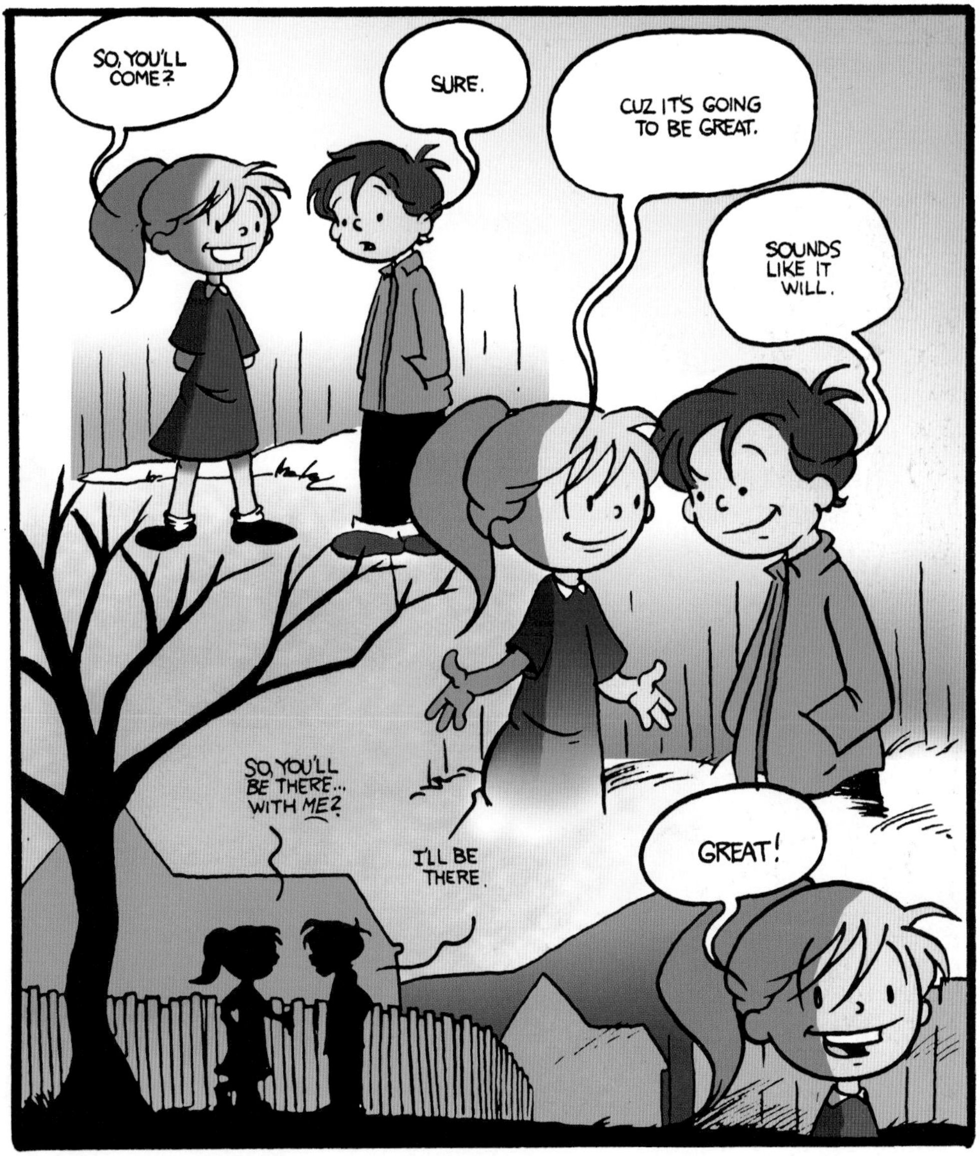

SO, YOU'LL COME?
SURE.
CUZ IT'S GOING TO BE GREAT.
SOUNDS LIKE IT WILL.
SO, YOU'LL BE THERE... WITH ME?
I'LL BE THERE.
GREAT!

Over the next week, I didn't see Tanner much at all. She was either with the Gurly Gurls, rehearsing, or with Mr. Henderson.

I made sure all my friends got to go to the show, and I made doubly sure they were in the front row. I got to be backstage, which was AWESOME. From there, I was able watch as the people started filtering in, and eavesdrop as they told one another stories about Tanner's music, and what it meant to them.

I wasn't really surprised when Mom told me Dad couldn't make it. Apparently, he had something more important to do. I *was* surprised by all the signs. So many people showed up with these signs, and banners, and they all had Tanner quotes or lyrics on them.

I guess I wasn't the only one Tanner had been telling true things to over the years.

About ten minutes before showtime, I positioned myself by the entrance. I was starting to get worried that Kyle wasn't coming or that he'd miss me or that somehow security wouldn't let him in.

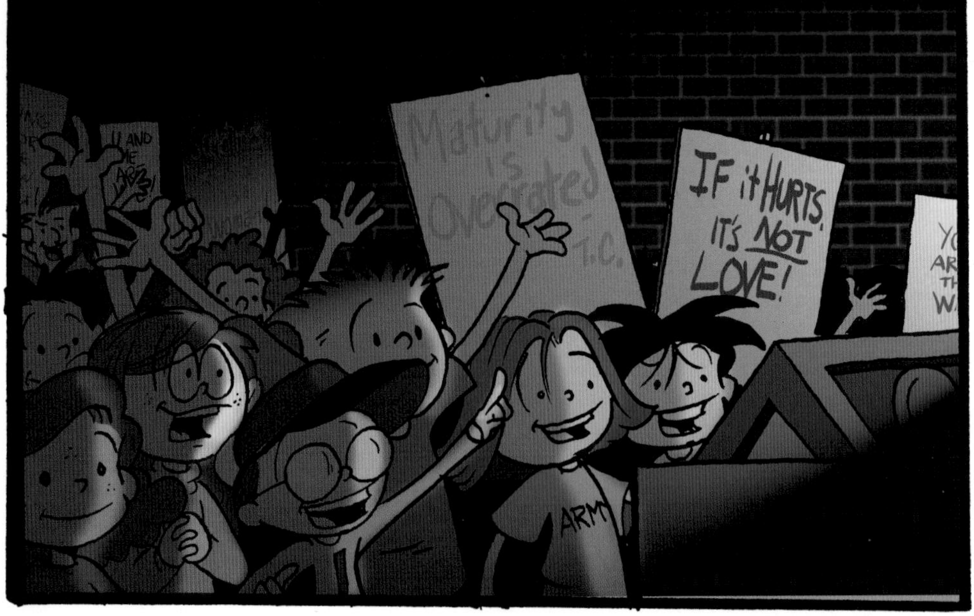
Maturity is Overrated - T.C.
IF it HURTS, IT'S NOT LOVE!

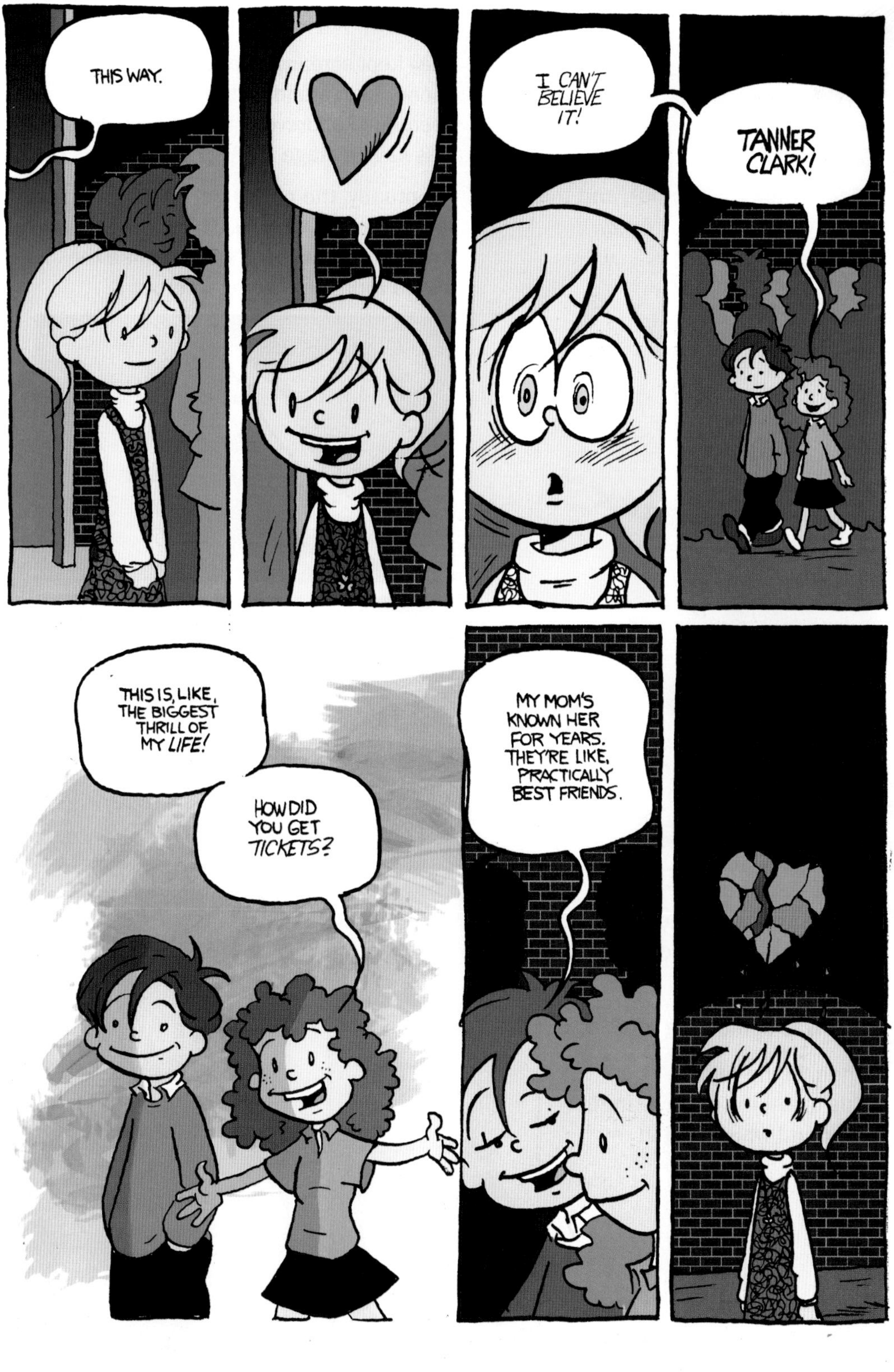
THIS WAY.
I *CAN'T* BELIEVE IT!
TANNER CLARK!
THIS IS, LIKE, THE BIGGEST THRILL OF MY *LIFE!*
HOW DID YOU GET *TICKETS?*
MY MOM'S KNOWN HER FOR YEARS. THEY'RE LIKE, PRACTICALLY BEST FRIENDS.

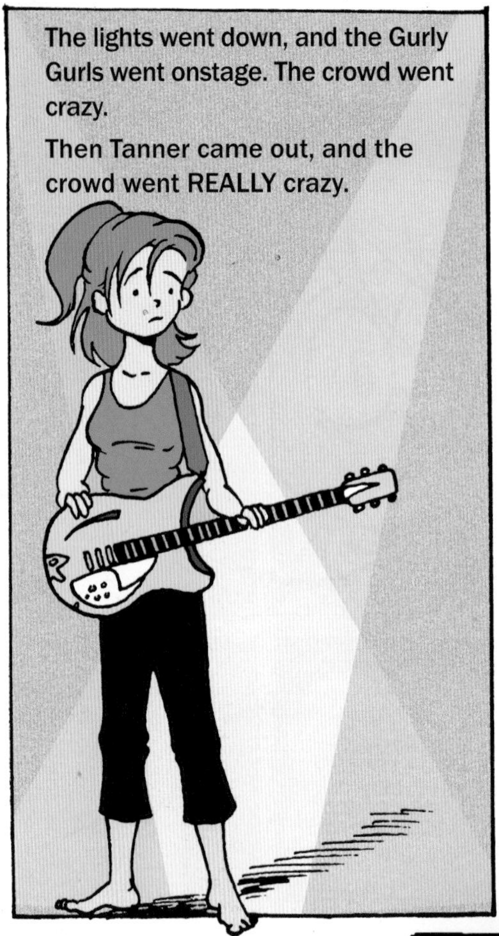
The lights went down, and the Gurly Gurls went onstage. The crowd went crazy.
Then Tanner came out, and the crowd went REALLY crazy.

They kept screaming and yelling, and Tanner kept standing there for what seemed like forever. I thought maybe she was having stage fright or something.

Eventually, the crowd got so loud, I could feel the room vibrate. And then, at just the moment when it seemed like the whole room was going to erupt . . .

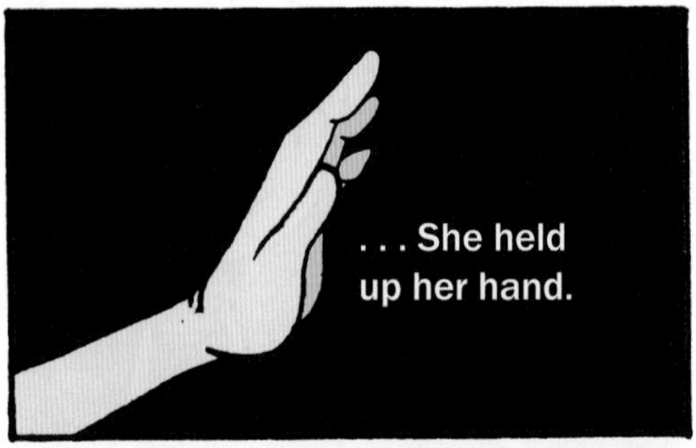
. . . She held up her hand.

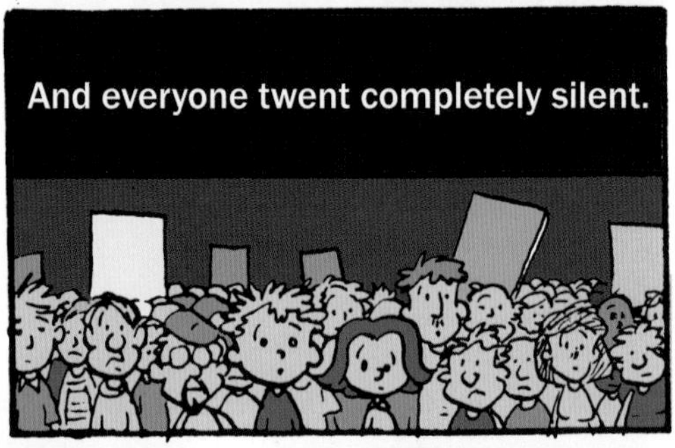
And everyone twent completely silent.

The woman onstage didn't even look like Tanner, anymore.

She was something else.

Then, in the middle of all this quiet, my mom leaned over and whispered in my ear . . .

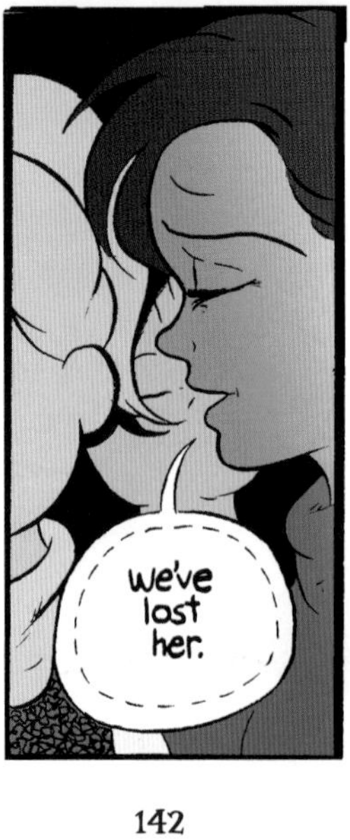
we've lost her.

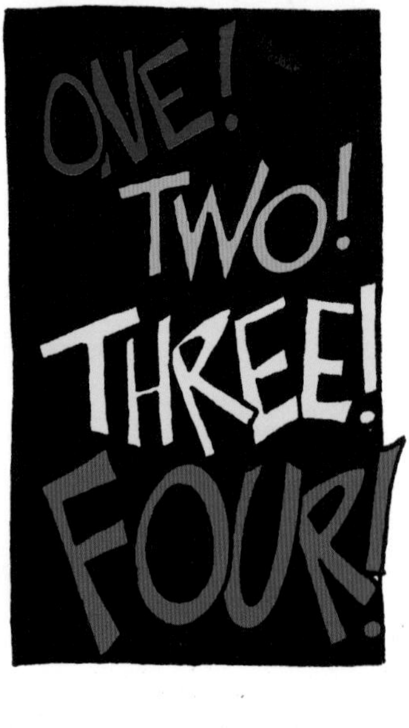
ONE!
TWO!
THREE!
FOUR!

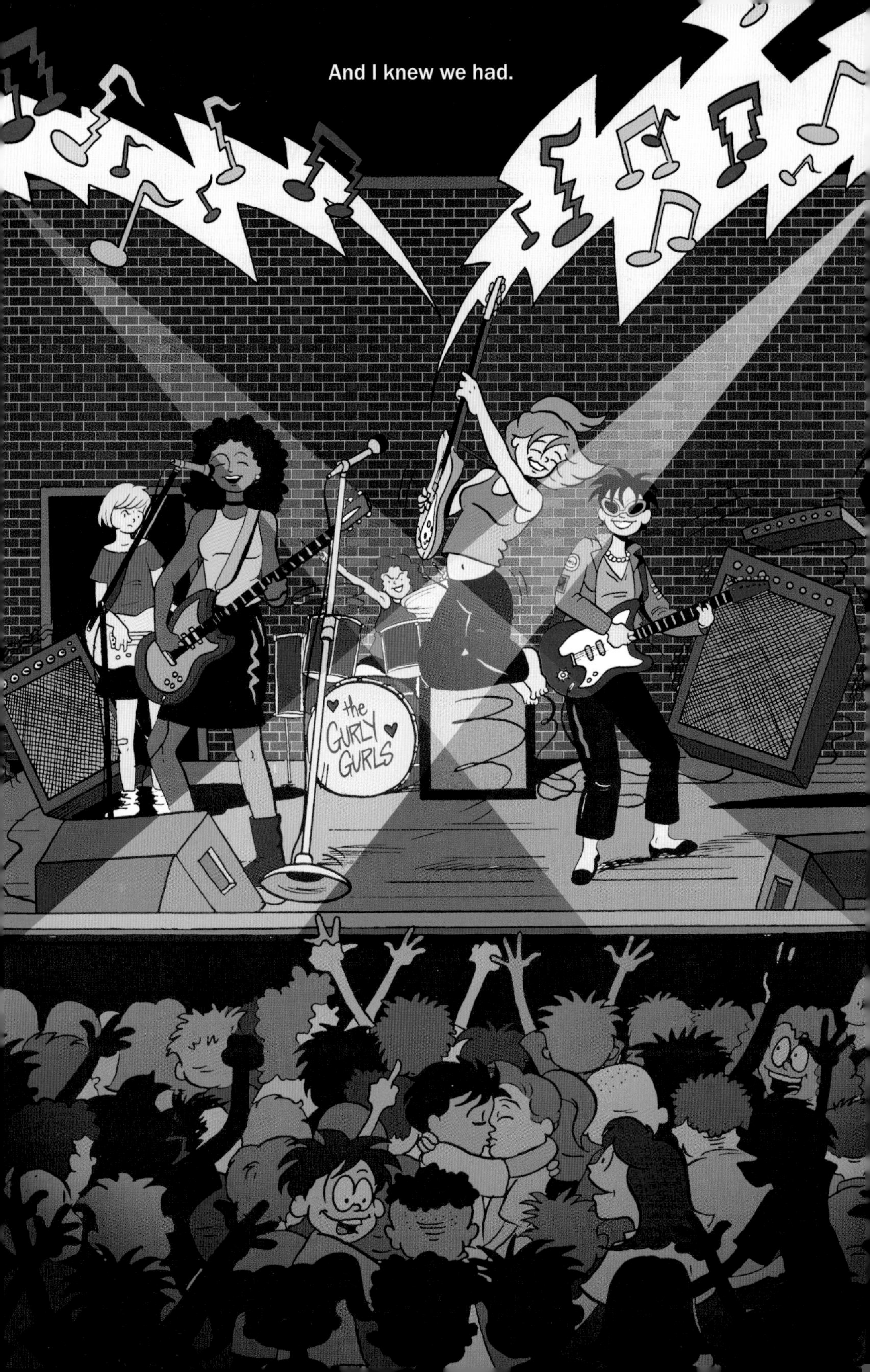
And I knew we had.
the GURLY GURLS

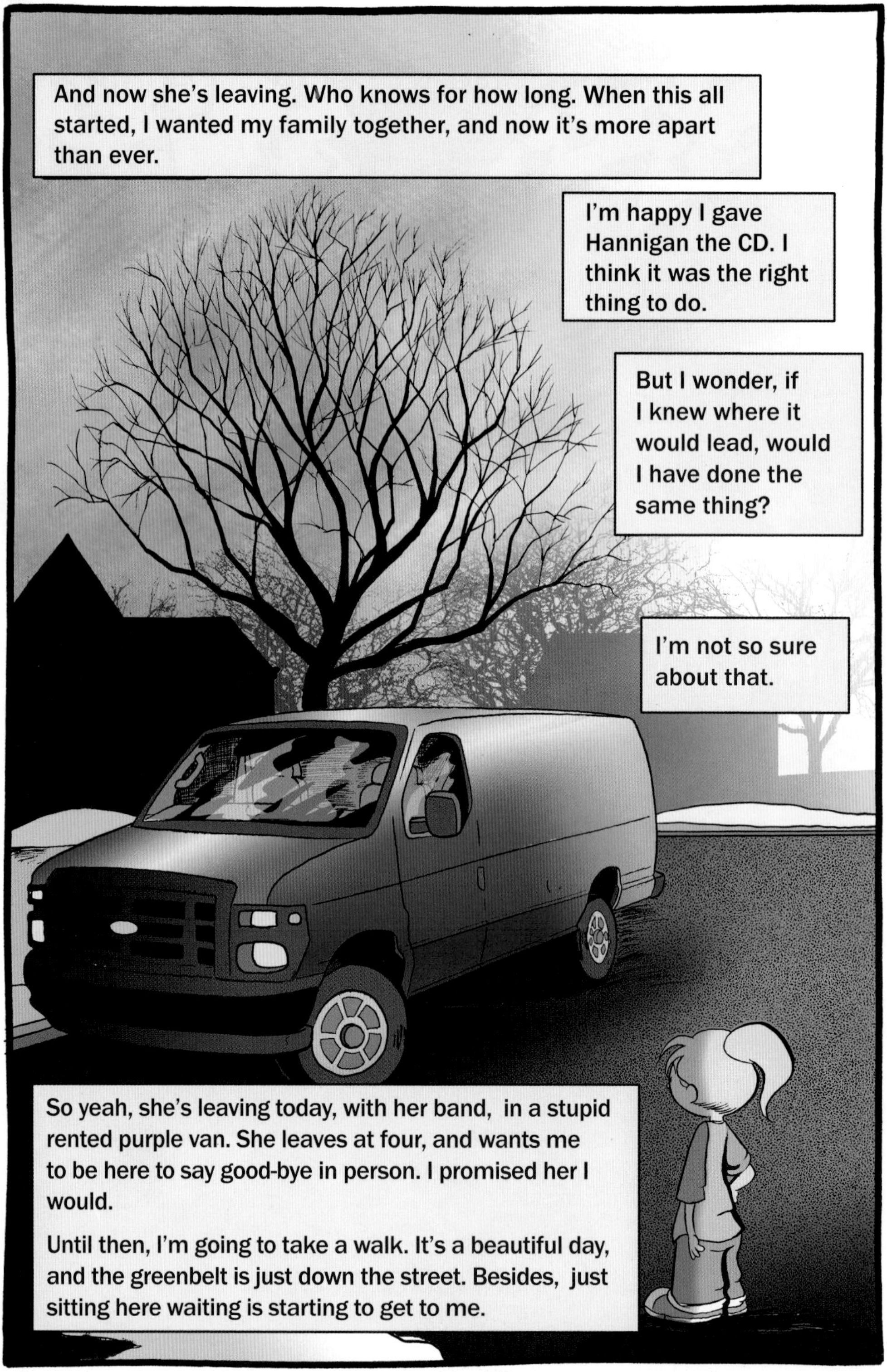

And now she's leaving. Who knows for how long. When this all started, I wanted my family together, and now it's more apart than ever.
I'm happy I gave Hannigan the CD. I think it was the right thing to do.
But I wonder, if I knew where it would lead, would I have done the same thing?
I'm not so sure about that.
So yeah, she's leaving today, with her band, in a stupid rented purple van. She leaves at four, and wants me to be here to say good-bye in person. I promised her I would.
Until then, I'm going to take a walk. It's a beautiful day, and the greenbelt is just down the street. Besides, just sitting here waiting is starting to get to me.

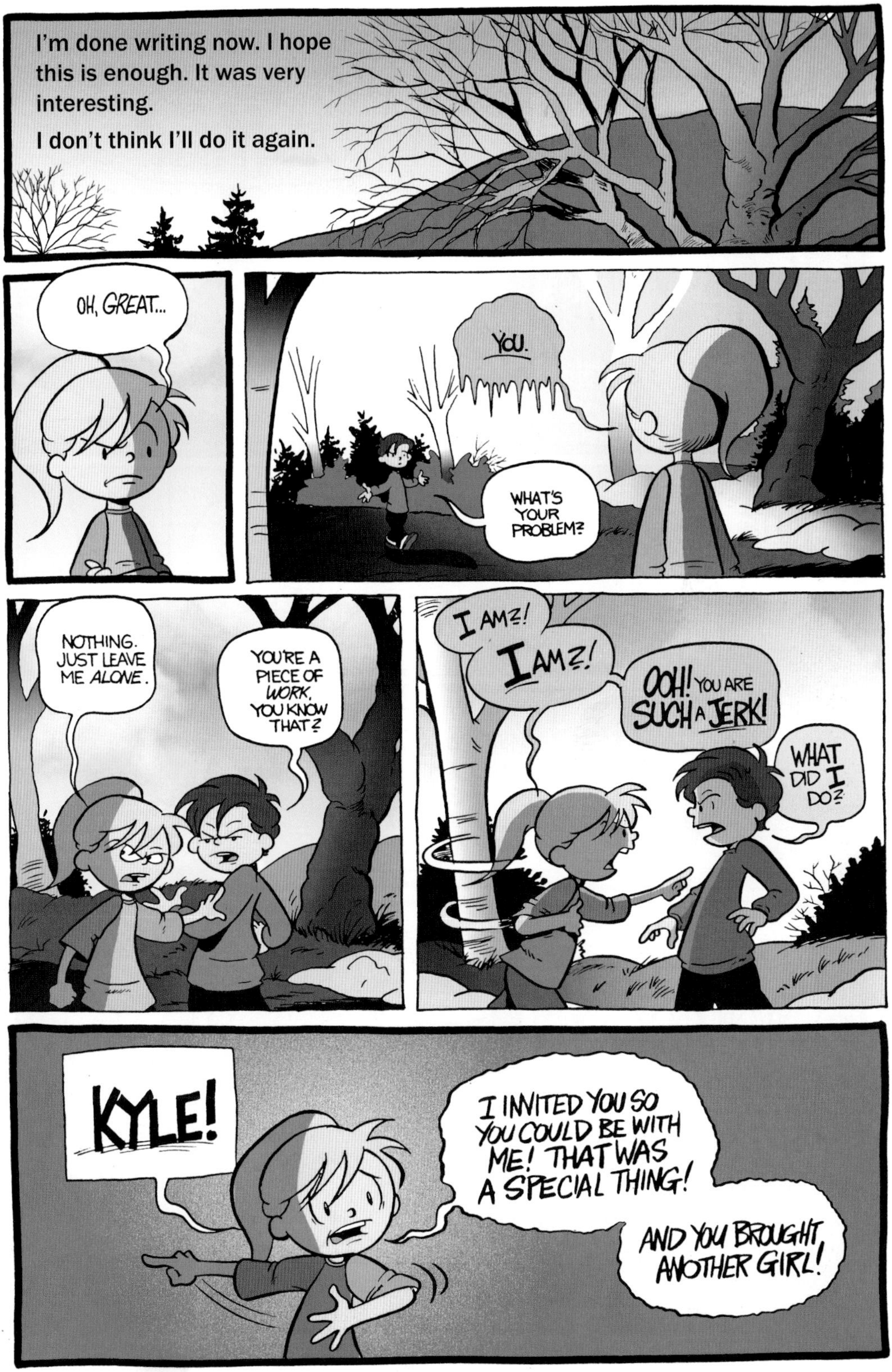
I'm done writing now. I hope this is enough. It was very interesting.
I don't think I'll do it again.
OH, GREAT...
YOU.
WHAT'S YOUR PROBLEM?
NOTHING. JUST LEAVE ME ALONE.
YOU'RE A PIECE OF WORK, YOU KNOW THAT?
I AM?!
I AM?!
OOH! YOU ARE SUCH A JERK!
WHAT DID I DO?
KYLE!
I INVITED YOU SO YOU COULD BE WITH ME! THAT WAS A SPECIAL THING!
AND YOU BROUGHT ANOTHER GIRL!

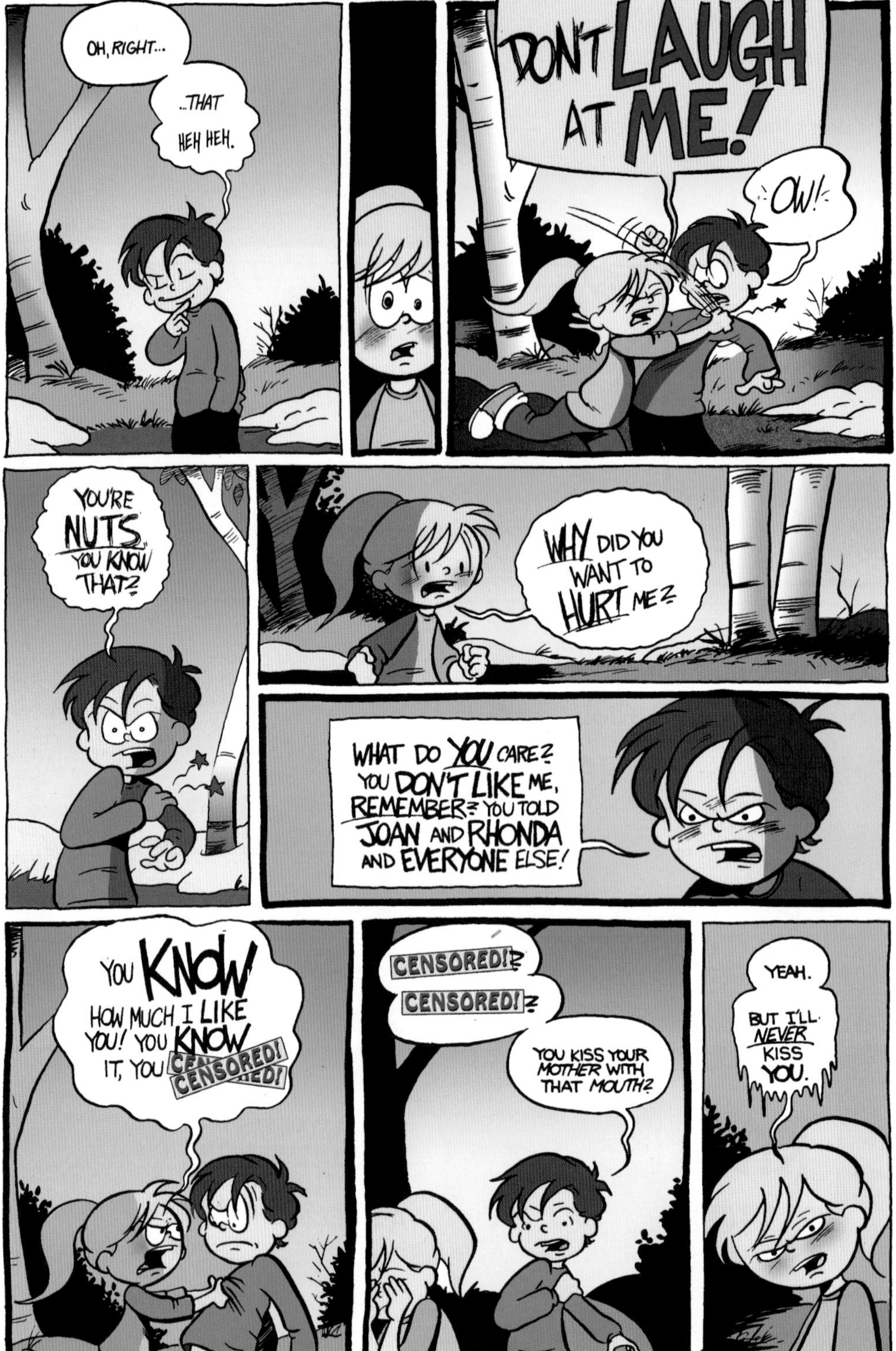
OH, RIGHT...
...THAT
HEH HEH.
DON'T LAUGH AT ME!
OW!
YOU'RE NUTS, YOU KNOW THAT?
WHY DID YOU WANT TO HURT ME?
WHAT DO YOU CARE? YOU DON'T LIKE ME, REMEMBER? YOU TOLD JOAN AND RHONDA AND EVERYONE ELSE!
YOU KNOW HOW MUCH I LIKE YOU! YOU KNOW IT, YOU CENSORED! CENSORED!
CENSORED!?
CENSORED!?
YOU KISS YOUR MOTHER WITH THAT MOUTH?
YEAH.
BUT I'LL NEVER KISS YOU.

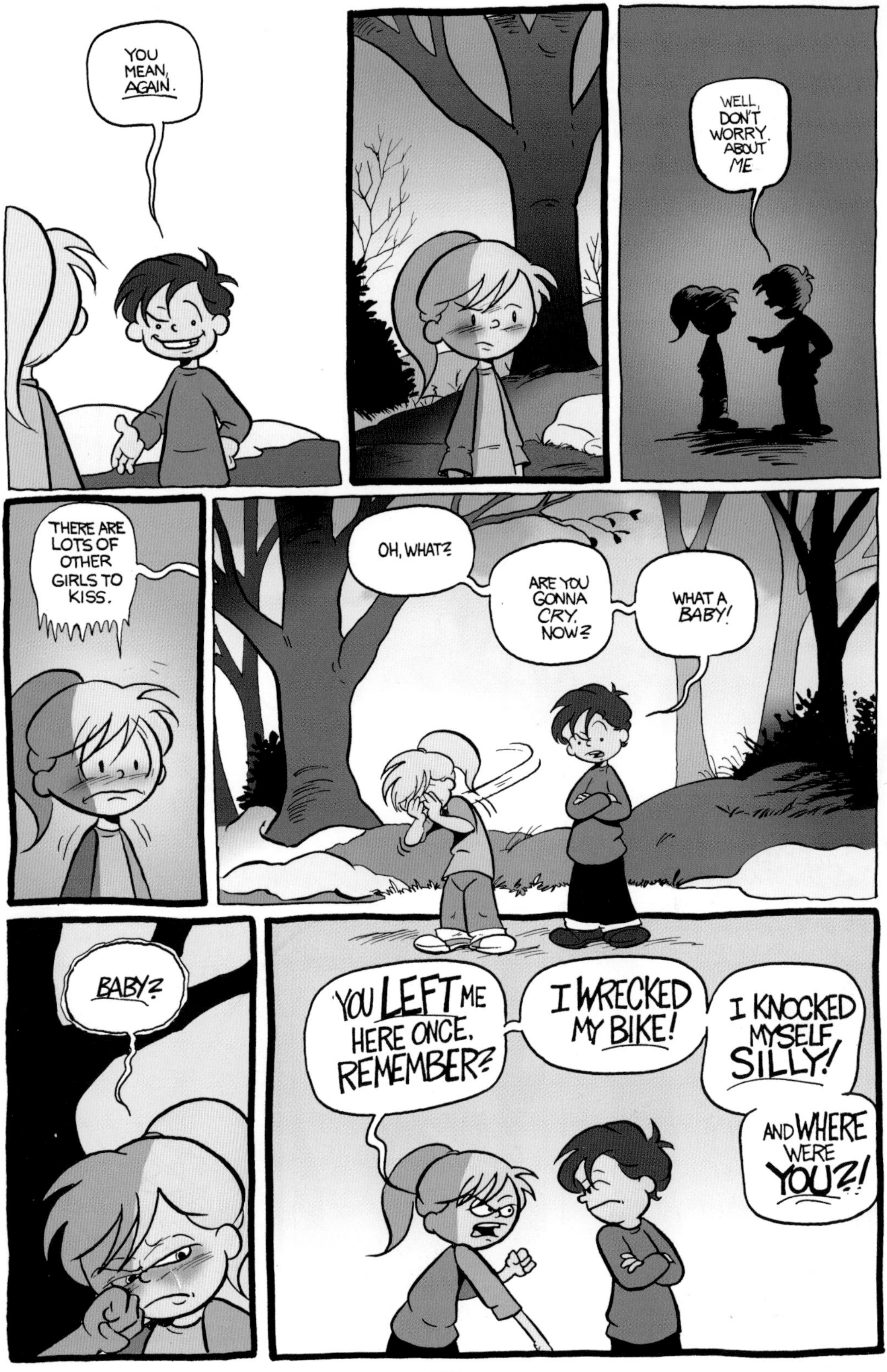
YOU MEAN, AGAIN.
WELL, DON'T WORRY. ABOUT ME
THERE ARE LOTS OF OTHER GIRLS TO KISS.
OH, WHAT?
ARE YOU GONNA CRY, NOW?
WHAT A BABY!
BABY?
YOU LEFT ME HERE ONCE, REMEMBER?
I WRECKED MY BIKE!
I KNOCKED MYSELF SILLY!
AND WHERE WERE YOU?!

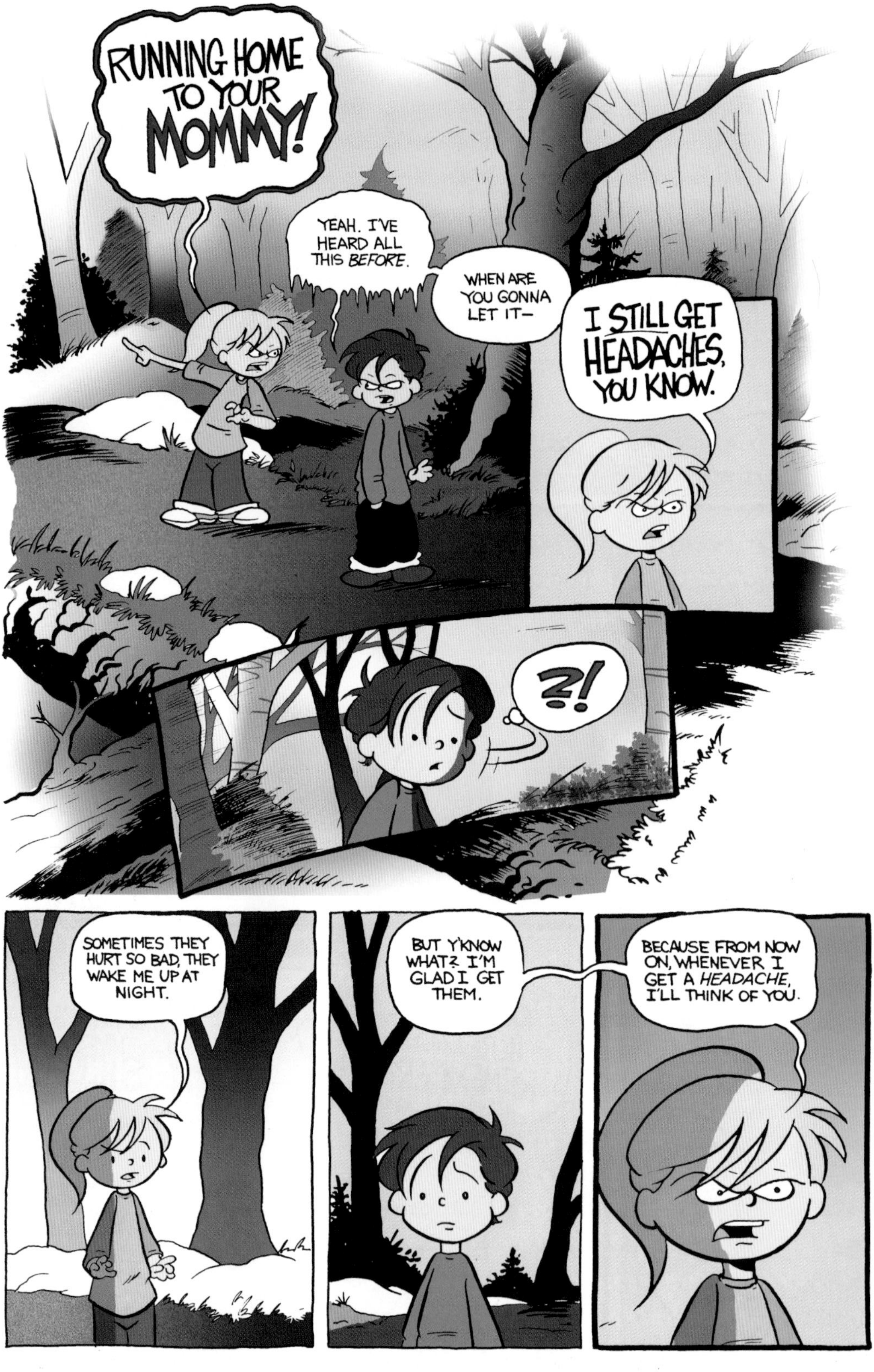
RUNNING HOME TO YOUR MOMMY!
YEAH. I'VE HEARD ALL THIS BEFORE.
WHEN ARE YOU GONNA LET IT—
I STILL GET HEADACHES, YOU KNOW.
?!
SOMETIMES THEY HURT SO BAD, THEY WAKE ME UP AT NIGHT.
BUT Y'KNOW WHAT? I'M GLAD I GET THEM.
BECAUSE FROM NOW ON, WHENEVER I GET A HEADACHE, I'LL THINK OF YOU.

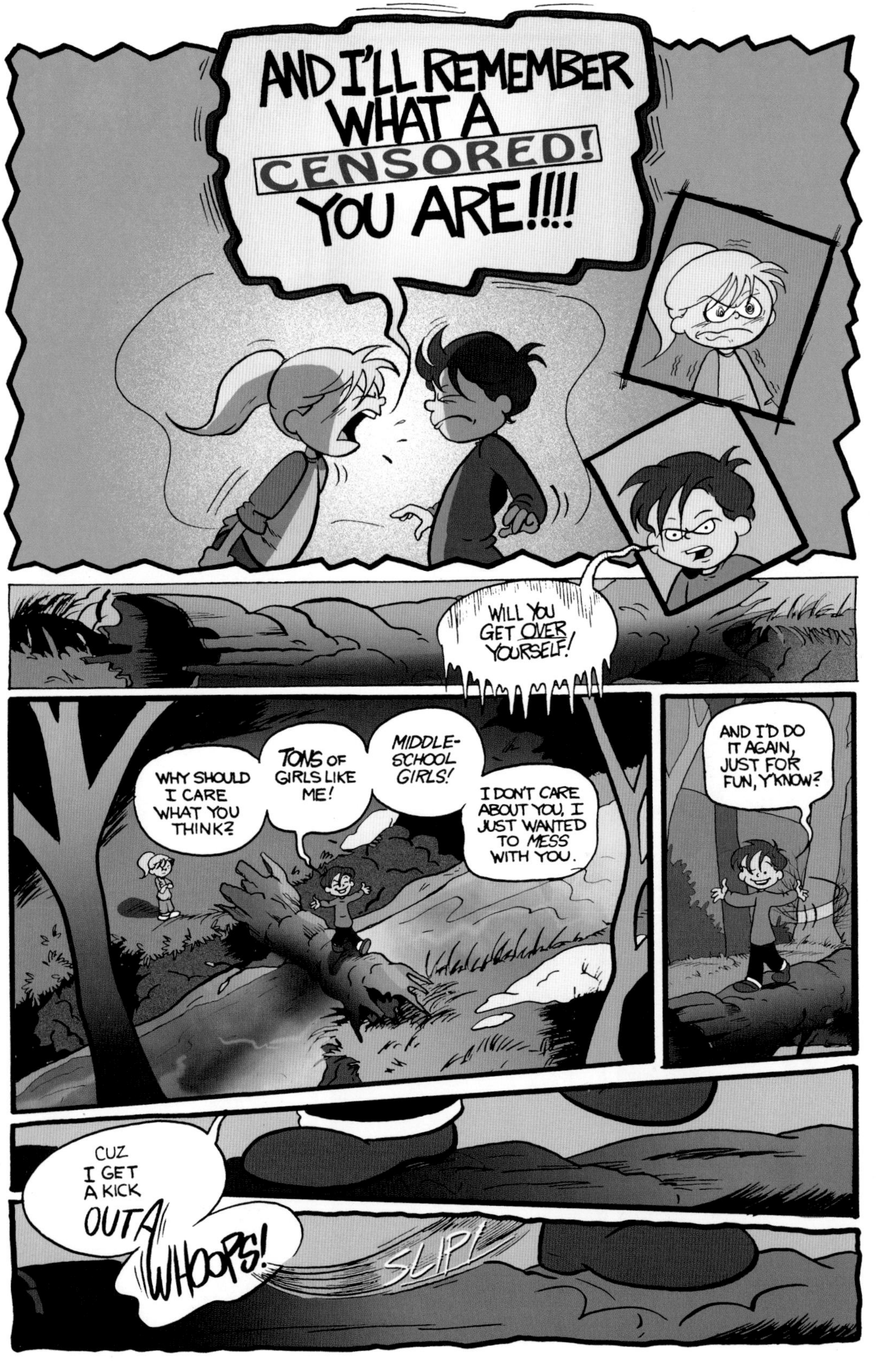
AND I'LL REMEMBER WHAT A CENSORED! YOU ARE!!!!
WILL YOU GET OVER YOURSELF!
WHY SHOULD I CARE WHAT YOU THINK?
TONS OF GIRLS LIKE ME!
MIDDLE-SCHOOL GIRLS!
I DON'T CARE ABOUT YOU, I JUST WANTED TO MESS WITH YOU.
AND I'D DO IT AGAIN, JUST FOR FUN, Y'KNOW?
CUZ I GET A KICK OUTA
WHOOPS!
SLIP!

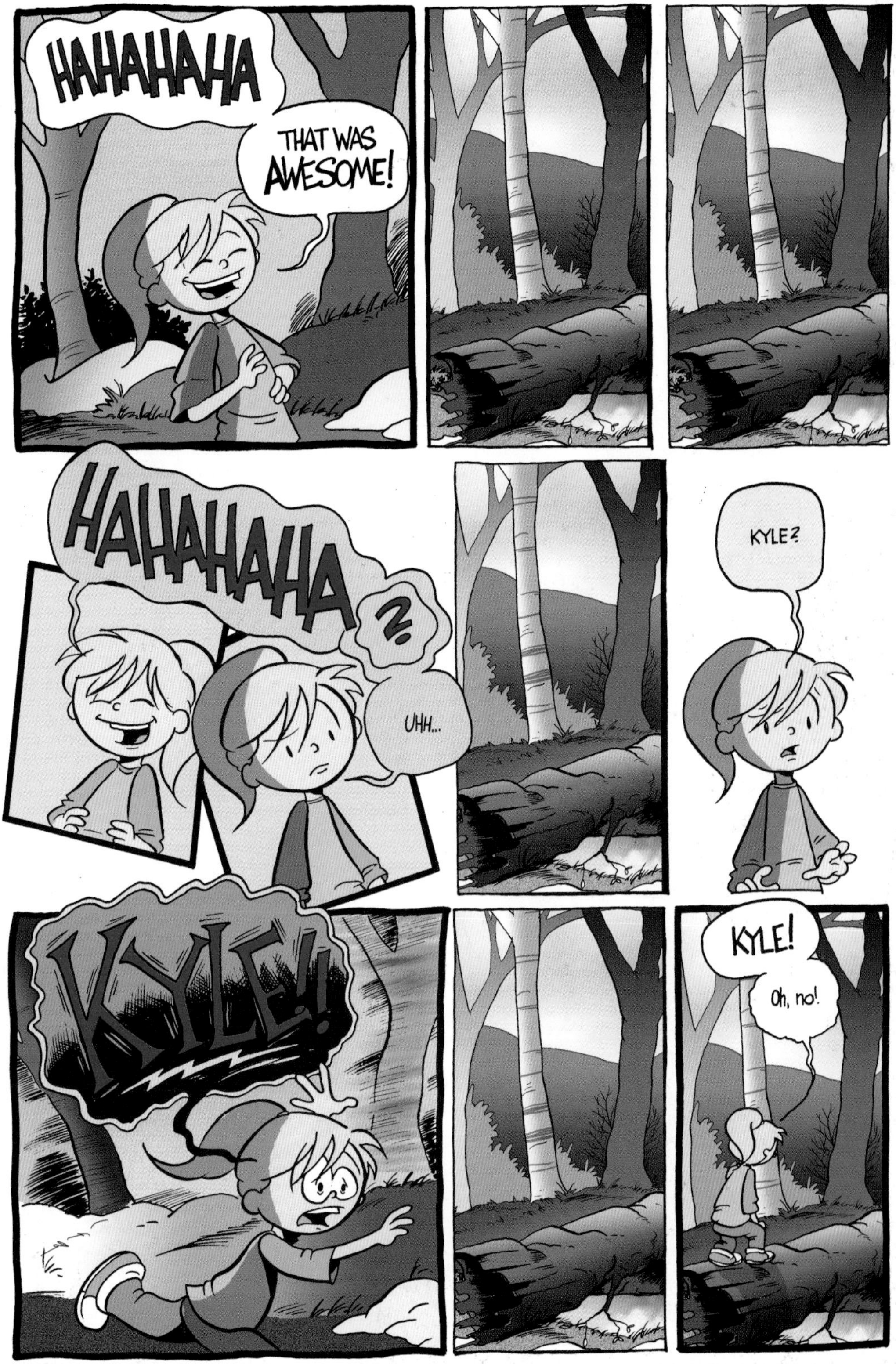
HAHAHAHA
THAT WAS AWESOME!
HAHAHAHA
?
UHH...
KYLE?
KYLE!
KYLE!
Oh, no!

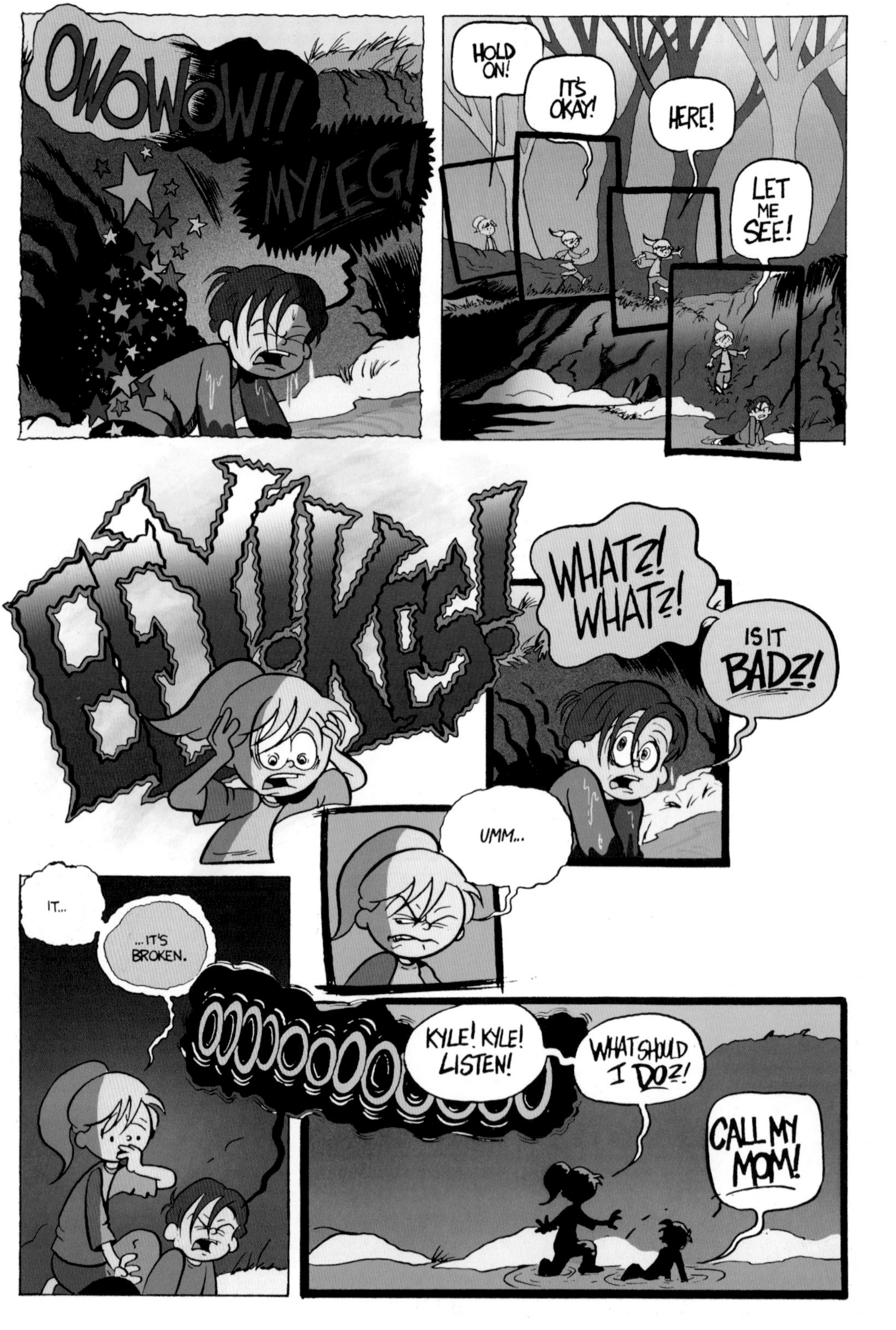

OWOWOW!!
MY LEG!
HOLD ON!
IT'S OKAY!
HERE!
LET ME SEE!
WHAT?! WHAT?!
IS IT BAD?!
UMM...
IT...
...IT'S BROKEN.
OOOOOOOOOOOOOOO
KYLE! KYLE! LISTEN!
WHAT SHOULD I DO?!
CALL MY MOM!

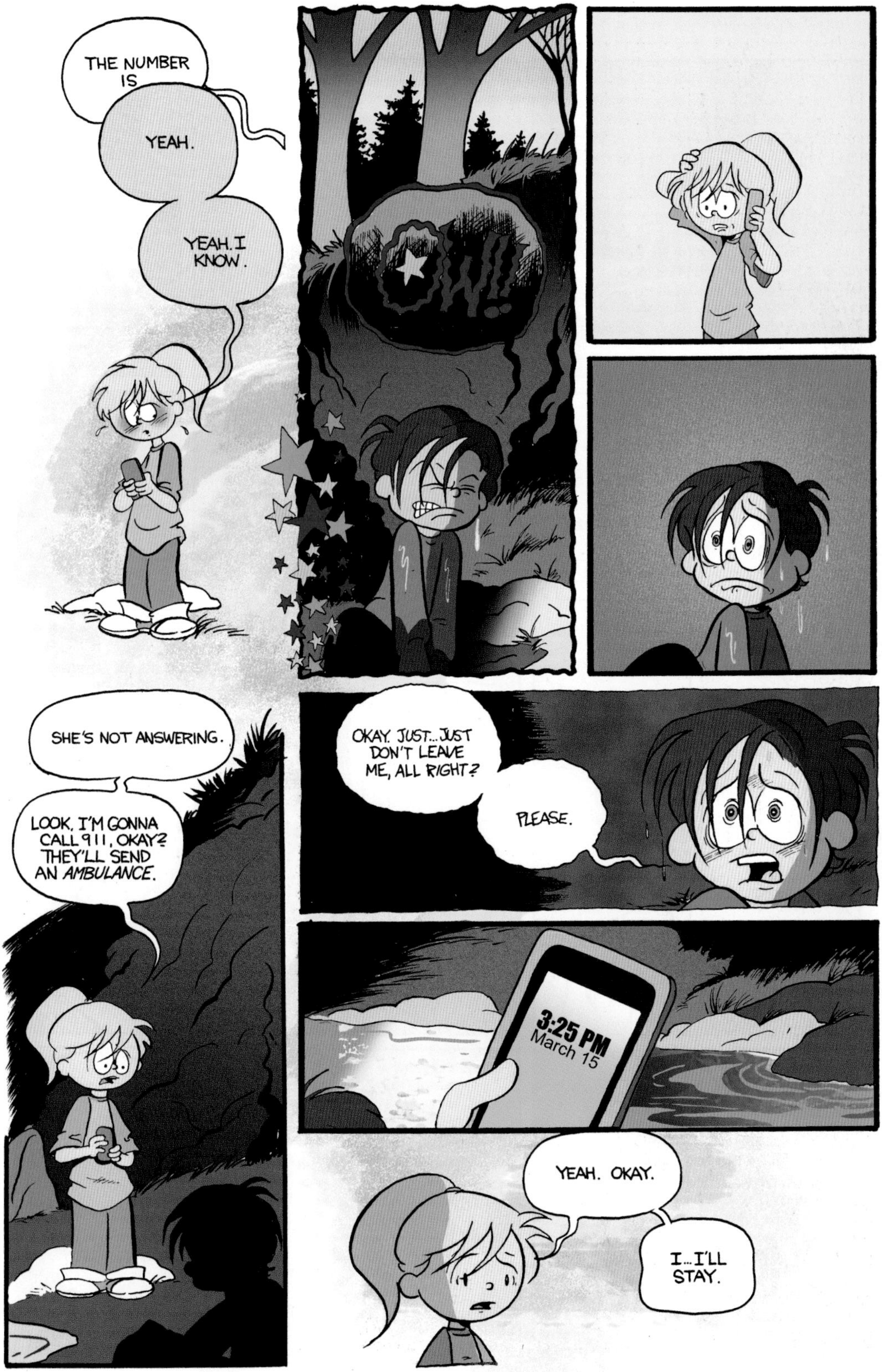
THE NUMBER IS
YEAH.
YEAH. I KNOW.
OW!!
SHE'S NOT ANSWERING.
LOOK, I'M GONNA CALL 911, OKAY? THEY'LL SEND AN *AMBULANCE*.
OKAY. JUST... JUST DON'T LEAVE ME, ALL RIGHT?
PLEASE.
3:25 PM
March 15
YEAH. OKAY.
I... I'LL STAY.

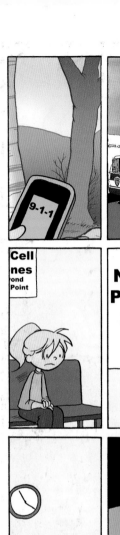

No Cell Phones
Beyond
this Point

Cell
nes
ond
Point

HE WANTS
TO SEE
YOU.

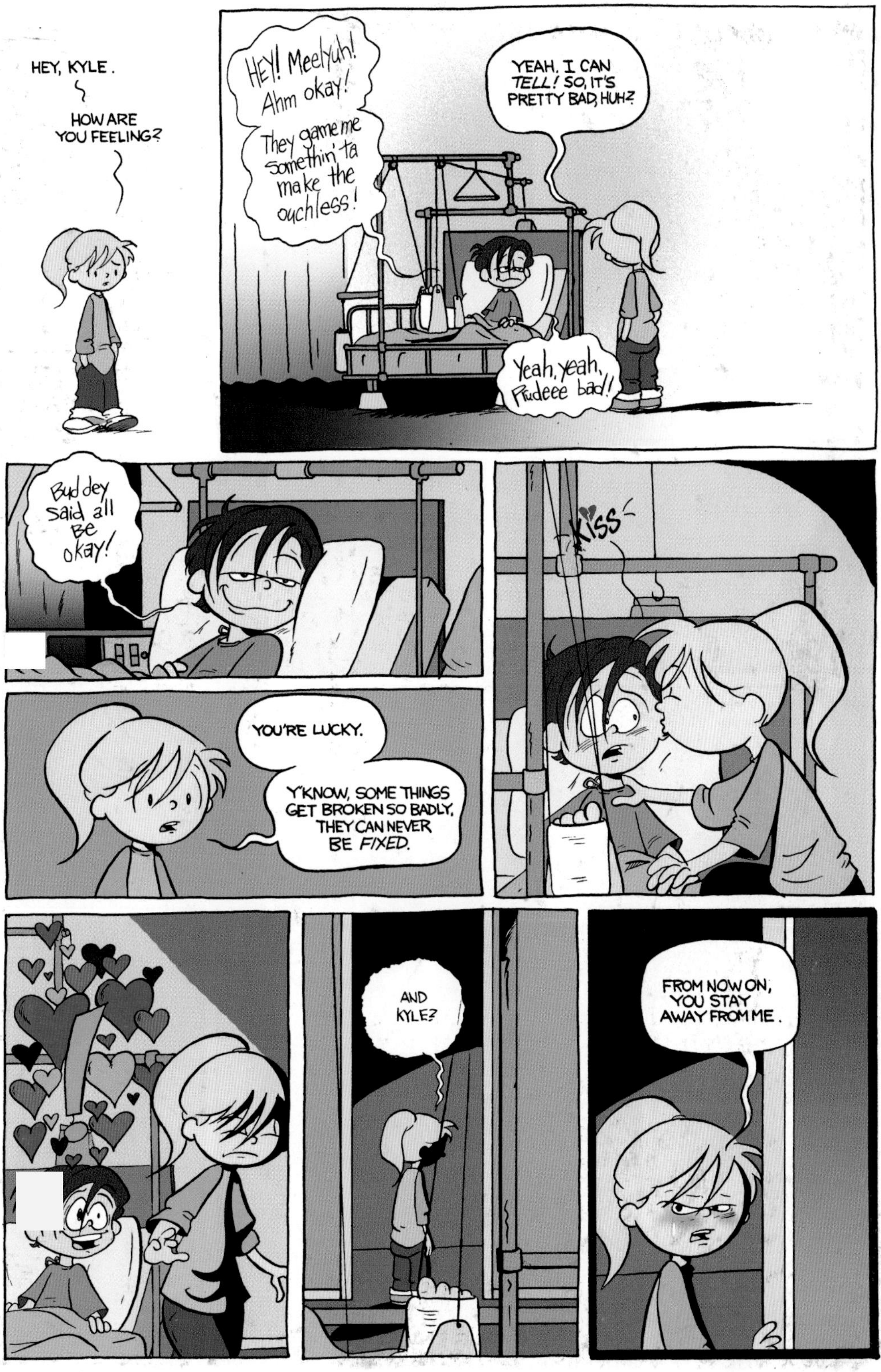
HEY, KYLE.
HOW ARE YOU FEELING?
HEY! Meelyuh! Ahm okay!
They game me somethin' ta make the ouchless!
YEAH. I CAN TELL! SO, IT'S PRETTY BAD, HUH?
Yeah, yeah, Prudeee bad!
Buddey said all Be okay!
KISS
YOU'RE LUCKY.
Y'KNOW, SOME THINGS GET BROKEN SO BADLY, THEY CAN NEVER BE FIXED.
AND KYLE?
FROM NOW ON, YOU STAY AWAY FROM ME.

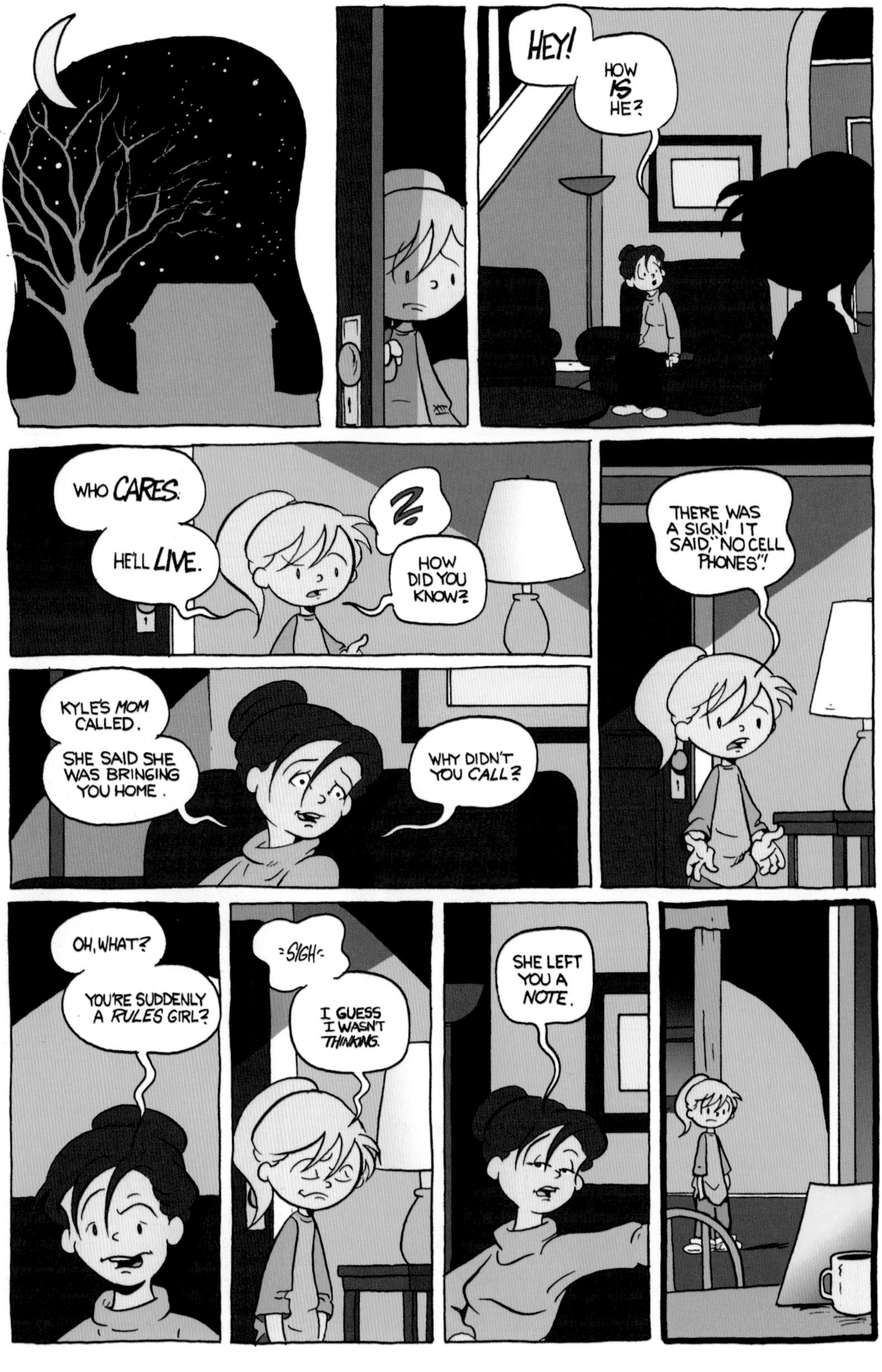
HEY!
HOW IS HE?
WHO CARES.
HE'LL LIVE.
?
HOW DID YOU KNOW?
KYLE'S MOM CALLED.
SHE SAID SHE WAS BRINGING YOU HOME.
WHY DIDN'T YOU CALL?
THERE WAS A SIGN! IT SAID, "NO CELL PHONES"!
OH, WHAT?
YOU'RE SUDDENLY A RULES GIRL?
SIGH
I GUESS I WASN'T THINKING.
SHE LEFT YOU A NOTE.

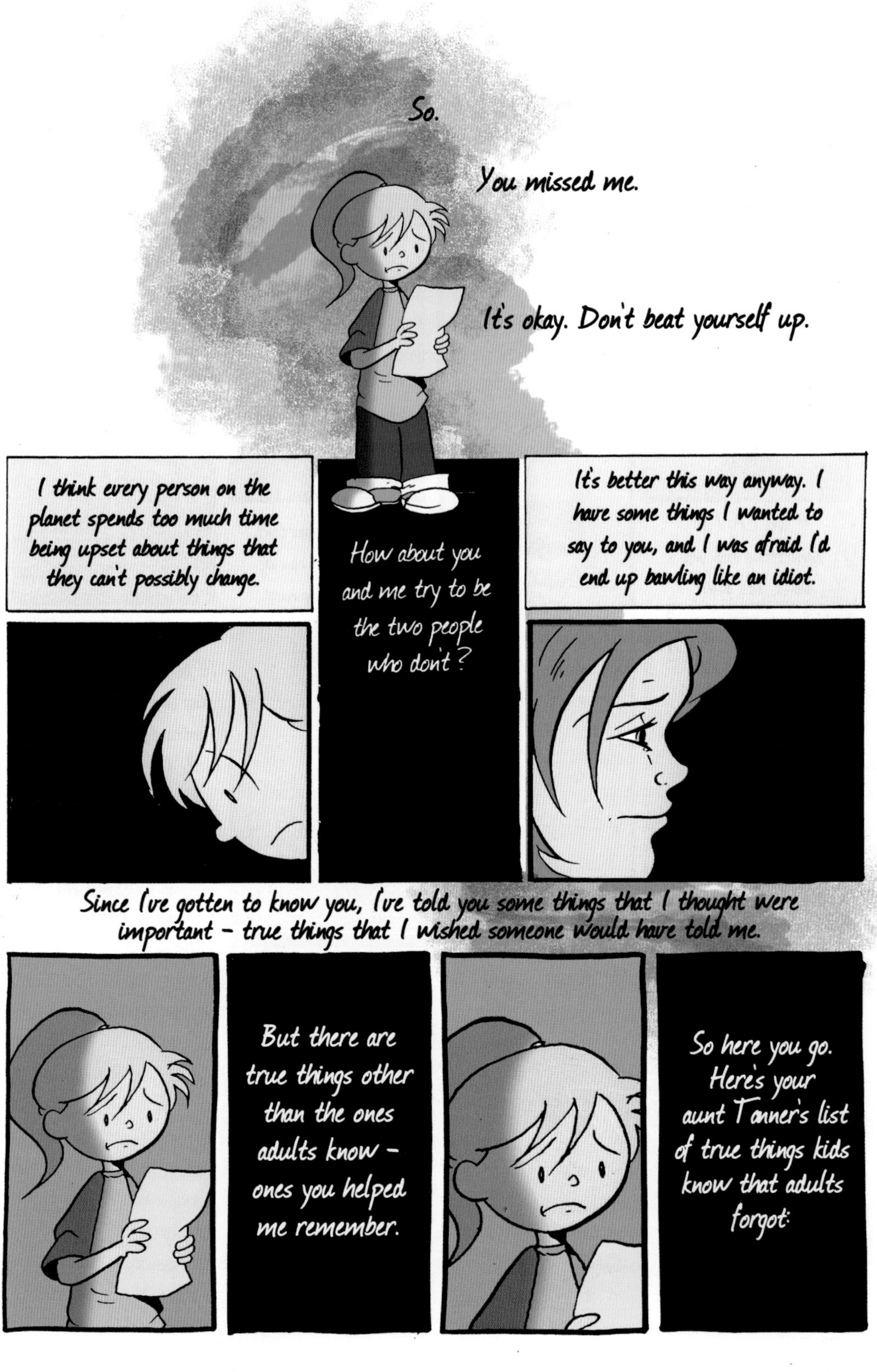
So.
You missed me.
It's okay. Don't beat yourself up.
I think every person on the planet spends too much time being upset about things that they can't possibly change.
How about you and me try to be the two people who don't?
It's better this way anyway. I have some things I wanted to say to you, and I was afraid I'd end up bawling like an idiot.
Since I've gotten to know you, I've told you some things that I thought were important – true things that I wished someone would have told me.
But there are true things other than the ones adults know – ones you helped me remember.
So here you go. Here's your aunt Tanner's list of true things kids know that adults forgot:

The little things are important, because that's how all the big things start.

If you CAN do something and you don't, it's a sin.

ROOM
OR ME,
I
BOUT
ING ON.

>SIGH<

"I USED TO BE DISGUSTED... NOW I TRY TO BE AMUSED."

N'T
AVE

TH

YOU'LL LIKE IT. IT'S GOT LYRICS YOURE TOO YOUNG TO HEAR.

No matter how you look at it, somehow, some way, Santa Claus is real.

And most important, growing up can be really, really hard.

Just because you're not old enough to deal with something, doesn't mean you won't have to deal with it anyway.

I'll be back, okay? I won't stay away forever. But I gotta do this, y'know? Well, I know you know. If it weren't for you, I...

I love you, Amelia. You're an awesome kid, and my best friend.

I'm proud to know you. Love, Tanner

PS: Go to my house tomorrow at 1pm, for one last surprise.

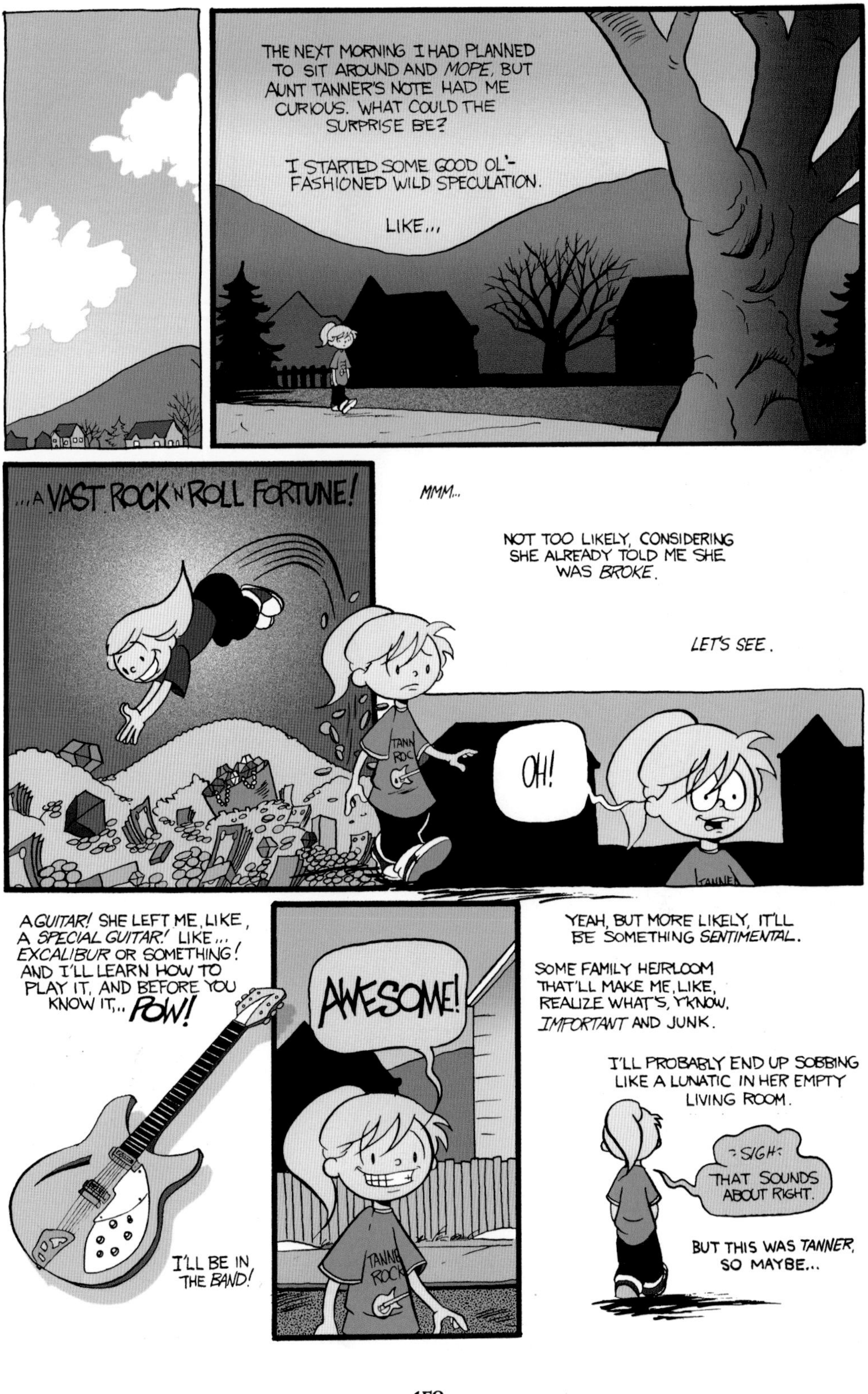

THE NEXT MORNING I HAD PLANNED TO SIT AROUND AND *MOPE*, BUT AUNT TANNER'S NOTE HAD ME CURIOUS. WHAT COULD THE SURPRISE BE?
I STARTED SOME GOOD OL'-FASHIONED WILD SPECULATION.
LIKE...
...A VAST ROCK 'N' ROLL FORTUNE!
MMM...
NOT TOO LIKELY, CONSIDERING SHE ALREADY TOLD ME SHE WAS *BROKE*.
LET'S SEE.
OH!
A *GUITAR!* SHE LEFT ME, LIKE, A *SPECIAL GUITAR!* LIKE... *EXCALIBUR* OR SOMETHING! AND I'LL LEARN HOW TO PLAY IT, AND BEFORE YOU KNOW IT... *POW!*
I'LL BE IN THE *BAND!*
AWESOME!
YEAH, BUT MORE LIKELY, IT'LL BE SOMETHING *SENTIMENTAL*.
SOME FAMILY HEIRLOOM THAT'LL MAKE ME, LIKE, REALIZE WHAT'S, Y'KNOW, *IMPORTANT* AND JUNK.
I'LL PROBABLY END UP SOBBING LIKE A LUNATIC IN HER EMPTY LIVING ROOM.
:SIGH: THAT SOUNDS ABOUT RIGHT.
BUT THIS WAS *TANNER*, SO MAYBE...

...IT WOULD BE SOMETHING *PERFECT*.

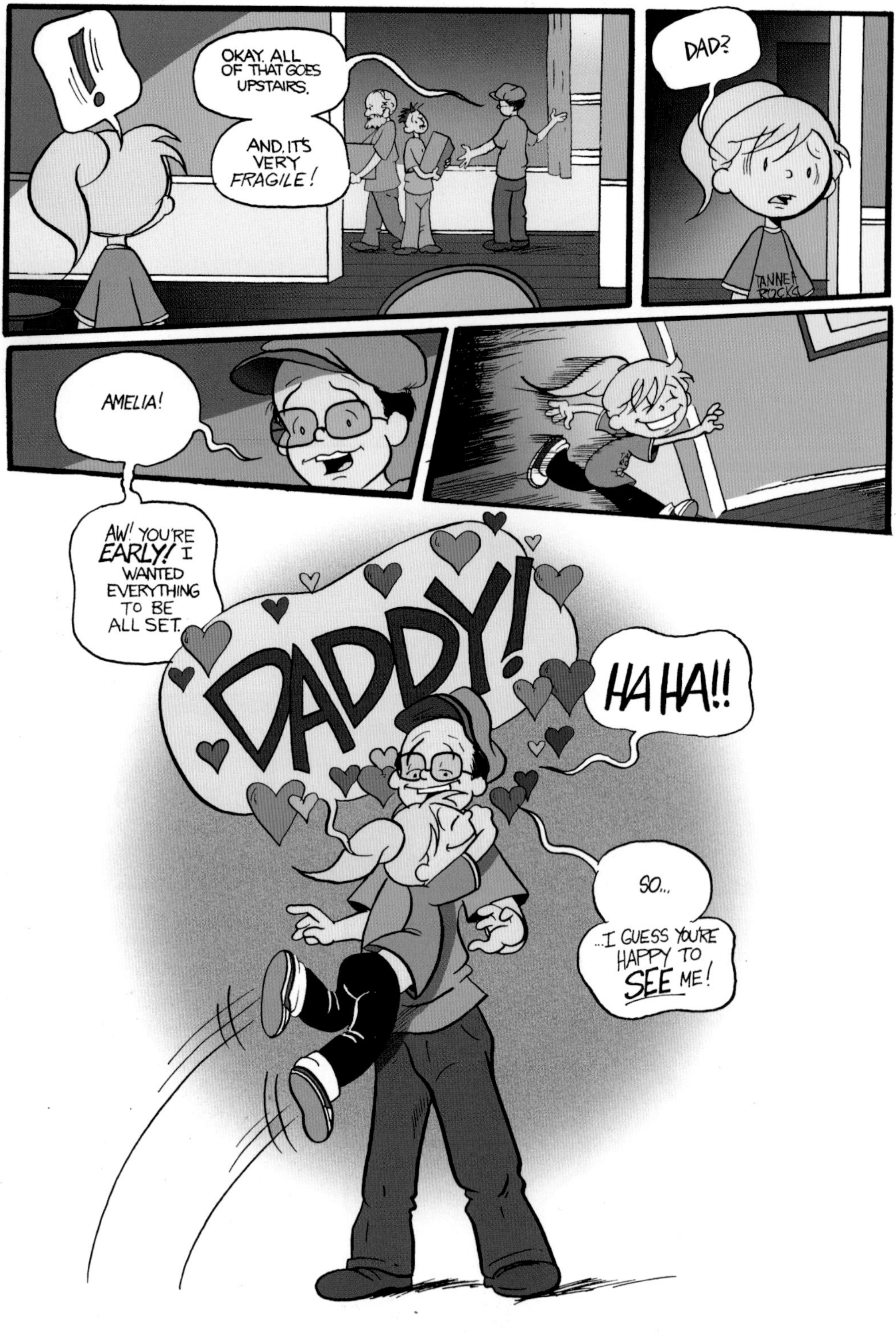

!
OKAY. ALL OF THAT GOES UPSTAIRS.
AND, IT'S VERY FRAGILE!
DAD?
AMELIA!
AW! YOU'RE EARLY! I WANTED EVERYTHING TO BE ALL SET.
DADDY!
HA HA!!
SO...
...I GUESS YOU'RE HAPPY TO SEE ME!

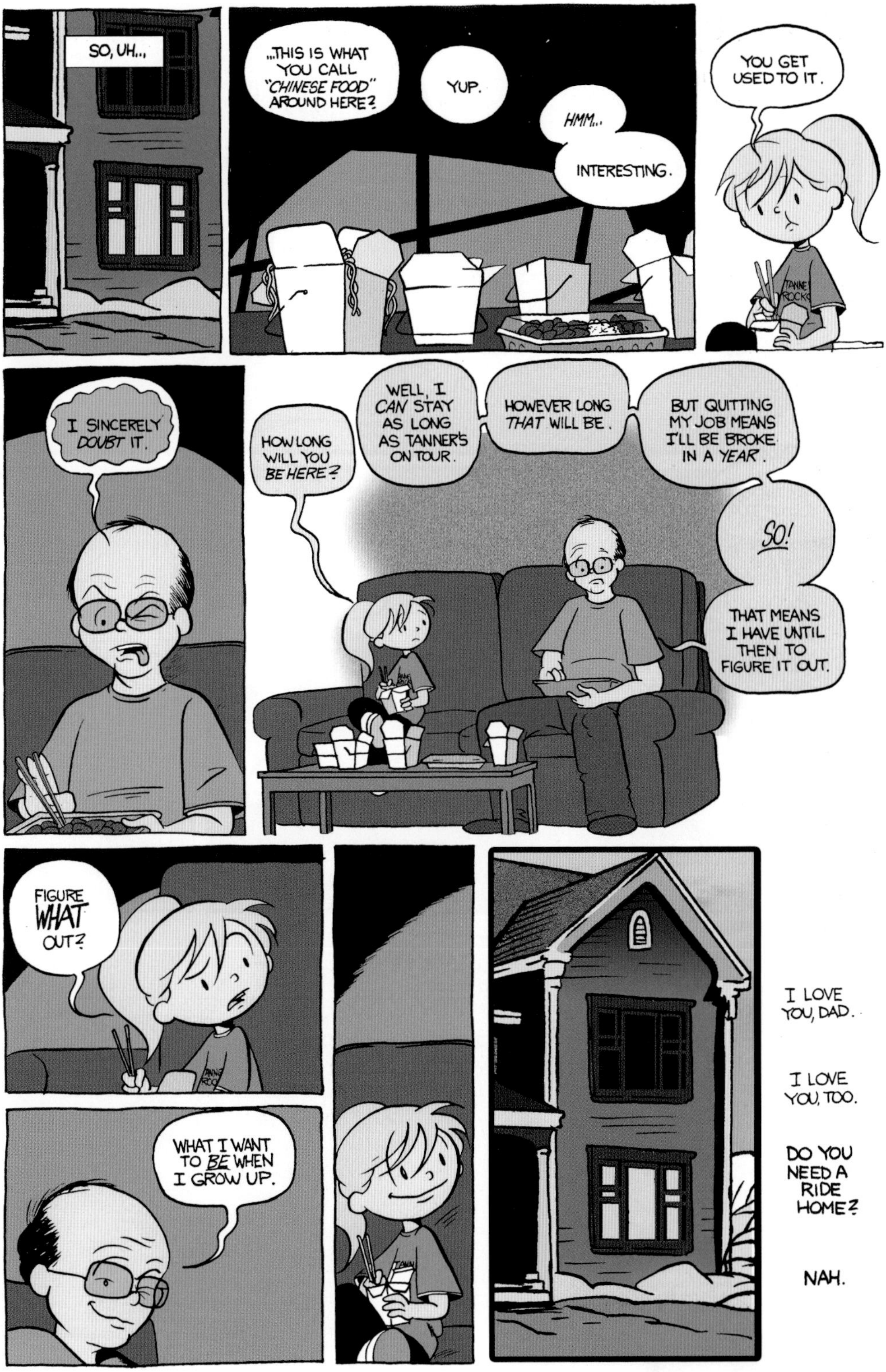
SO, UH...,
...THIS IS WHAT YOU CALL "CHINESE FOOD" AROUND HERE?
YUP.
HMM...
INTERESTING.
YOU GET USED TO IT.
TANNER ROCKS
I SINCERELY DOUBT IT.
HOW LONG WILL YOU BE HERE?
WELL, I CAN STAY AS LONG AS TANNER'S ON TOUR.
HOWEVER LONG THAT WILL BE.
BUT QUITTING MY JOB MEANS I'LL BE BROKE IN A YEAR.
SO!
THAT MEANS I HAVE UNTIL THEN TO FIGURE IT OUT.
FIGURE WHAT OUT?
WHAT I WANT TO BE WHEN I GROW UP.
I LOVE YOU, DAD.
I LOVE YOU, TOO.
DO YOU NEED A RIDE HOME?
NAH.

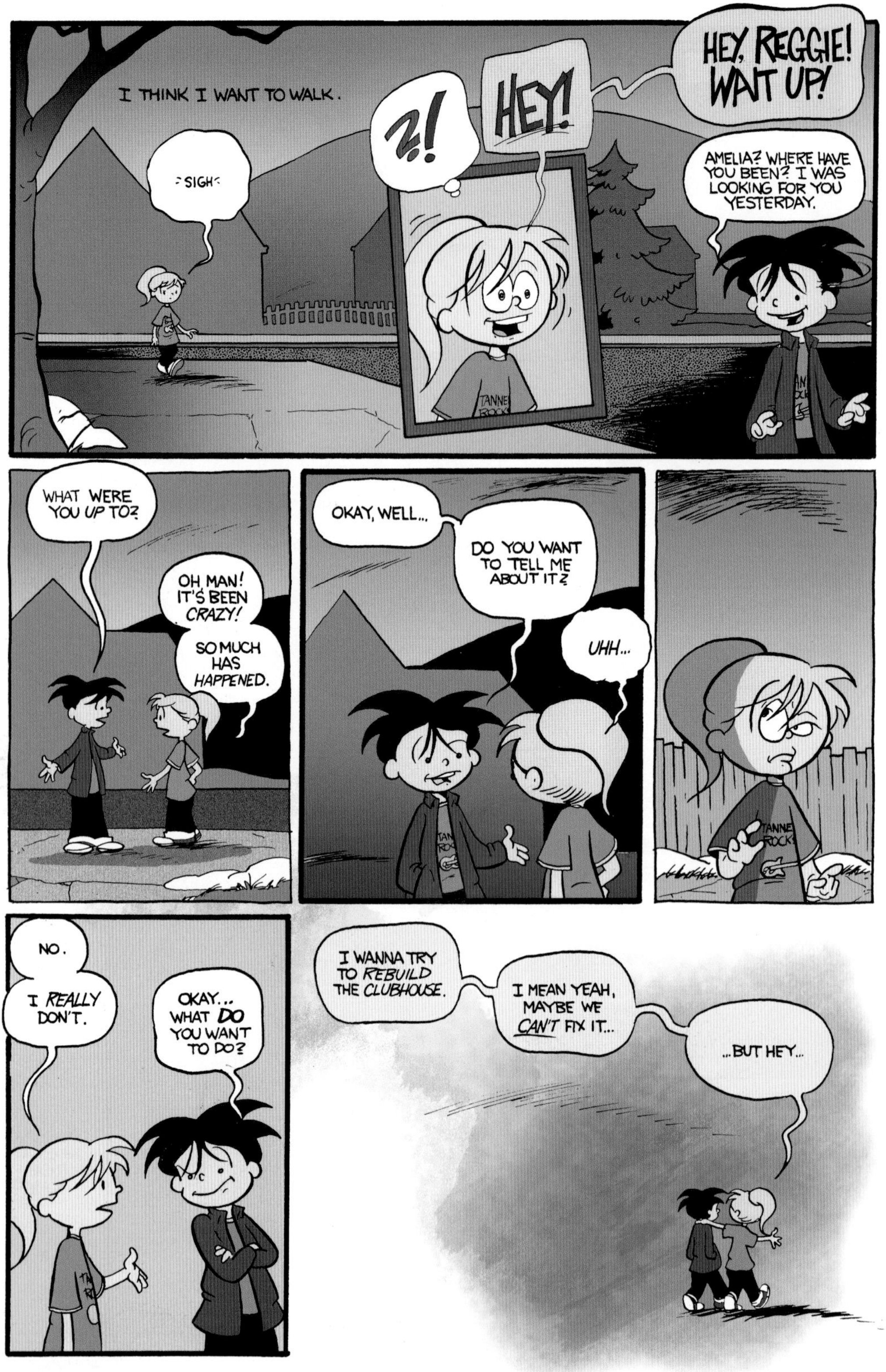
I THINK I WANT TO WALK.
SIGH
?!
HEY!
HEY, REGGIE! WAIT UP!
AMELIA? WHERE HAVE YOU BEEN? I WAS LOOKING FOR YOU YESTERDAY.
TANNER ROCKS
WHAT WERE YOU UP TO?
OH MAN! IT'S BEEN CRAZY!
SO MUCH HAS HAPPENED.
OKAY, WELL...
DO YOU WANT TO TELL ME ABOUT IT?
UHH...
NO.
I REALLY DON'T.
OKAY... WHAT DO YOU WANT TO DO?
I WANNA TRY TO REBUILD THE CLUBHOUSE.
I MEAN YEAH, MAYBE WE CAN'T FIX IT...
...BUT HEY...

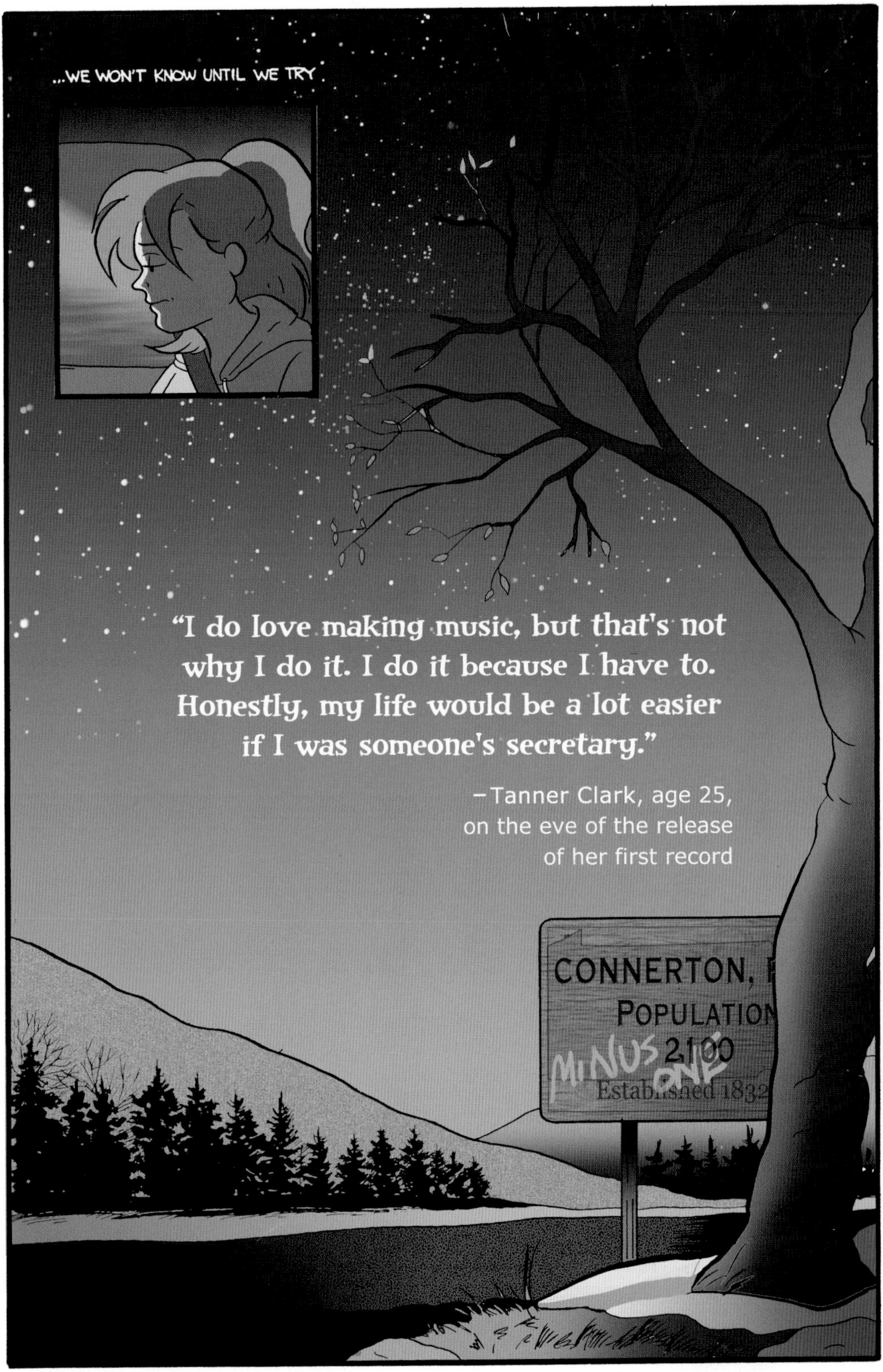
...WE WON'T KNOW UNTIL WE TRY.
"I do love making music, but that's not why I do it. I do it because I have to. Honestly, my life would be a lot easier if I was someone's secretary."
–Tanner Clark, age 25, on the eve of the release of her first record
CONNERTON,
POPULATION
2,100
MINUS ONE
Established 1832

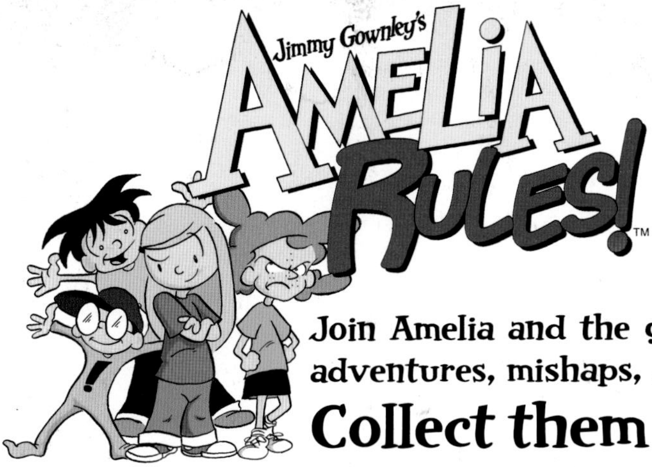
Jimmy Gownley's
AMELIA
RULES!
TM

Join Amelia and the gang for adventures, mishaps, and homework.

Collect them all!

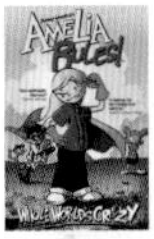

☐ *The Whole World's Crazy*
ISBN: 978-1-4169-8604-1

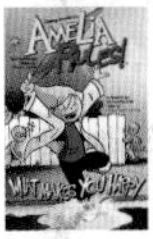

☐ *What Makes You Happy*
ISBN: 978-1-4169-8605-8

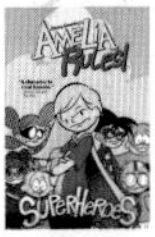

☐ *Superheroes*
ISBN: 978-1-4169-8606-5

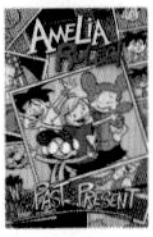

☐ *When the Past Is a Present*
ISBN: 978-1-4169-8607-2

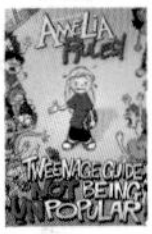

☐ *The Tweenage Guide to Not Being Unpopular*
ISBN: 978-1-4169-8610-2 (hc)
ISBN: 978-1-4169-8608-9 (pbk)

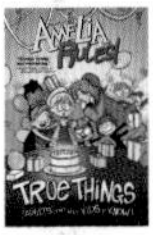

☐ *True Things (Adults Don't Want Kids to Know)*
ISBN: 978-1-4169-8611-9 (hc)
ISBN: 978-1-4169-8609-6 (pbk)

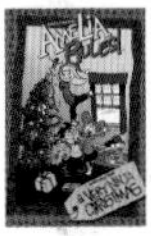

☐ *A Very Ninja Christmas*
ISBN: 978-1-4169-8959-2